TIMOTHY HALLINAN lives in Los Angeles. This
is the first of his three Simeon Grist detective
novels, the second of which, *Everything But the
Squeal*, is available in an NAL Books edition.
He lives in Los Angeles and on the island of Koh
Samui, Thailand.

THE FOUR LAST THINGS

A SIMEON GRIST SUSPENSE NOVEL

TIMOTHY HALLINAN

A SIGNET BOOK

NEW AMERICAN LIBRARY

A DIVISION OF PENGUIN BOOKS USA INC., NEW YORK

SIGNET
Published by the Penguin Group
Penguin Books USA Inc., 375 Hudson Street,
New York, New York, 10014, U.S.A.
Penguin Books Ltd, 27 Wrights Lane,
London W8 5TZ, England
Penguin Books Australia Ltd, Ringwood,
Victoria, Australia
Penguin Books Canada Ltd, 2801 John Street,
Markham, Ontario, Canada L3R 1B4
Penguin Books (N.Z.) Ltd, 182-190 Wairau Road,
Auckland 10, New Zealand

Penguin Books Ltd, Registered Offices:
Harmondsworth, Middlesex, England

The Four Last Things previously appeared in an NAL Books edition.

First Signet Printing, July, 1990
10 9 8 7 6 5 4 3 2

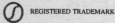 REGISTERED TRADEMARK—MARCA REGISTRADA

Printed in Canada

PUBLISHER'S NOTE
This is a work of fiction. Names, characters, places, and incidents either are the
product of the author's imagination or are used fictitiously, and any resemblance to
actual persons, living or dead, events, or locales is entirely coincidental.

This one is for my
mother, who read it,
and my father, who
said he did,
and for
Munyin.

Your past is your enemy.
—Attributed to
L. Ron Hubbard

The Four Last Things: In Roman Catholic
theology, the final events in human existence:
Death, Judgment, Heaven, and Hell.
—*Encyclopedia of Religion*

I

Death

1

I was just beginning to like her when she got killed.

One of the interesting things about surveillance—make that the only interesting thing about surveillance—is the relationship between watcher and watched. Study the outside of anybody's life long enough and you'll develop some sort of emotional reaction. Sometimes you feel like an entomologist looking at a particularly loathsome new insect; you wish you could do it from farther away. Sometimes you fall in love.

I wasn't in love with Sally Oldfield yet, but I knew I'd like to get closer than across the street.

Sarah Marie Theresa Oldfield, *née* Murphy, thirty-two years old, married. Light brown hair, gray eyes, tiny hands and feet, skin with a natural golden cast to it. Big thick horn-rimmed glasses that she wore on top of her head when driving. Farsighted. The cleanest automobile I'd ever broken into. You could have performed brain surgery on the front seat. Ms. Oldfield also had a quick, broad smile, sturdy runner's calves, and an utterly guileless demeanor.

A thief and a spy, according to the man who had hired me. A dangerous drain on the precious capital of Monument Records. He obviously expected me to break out in a cold sweat when he uttered those accusations. I didn't, but I worked up a sympathetic shiver when it became apparent that the man was willing to pay about twice my usual fee.

I don't like surveillance. I didn't like him, either. Nevertheless, I picked her up at lunchtime on the first day right where he said I would, just outside the Monument Records building on Gower.

Even in Hollywood, which has the same relationship to architecture that the radioactive bug movies of the fifties have to biology, the Monument Records building is a standout. To the best of my knowledge it's the only structure ever built intentionally to look like a stack of records. With a stylus on top. It was built to suggest forty-fives back before the era of the LP; now that forty-fives are no-tech, they're talking about chrome-plating it and rededicating it to CD's.

One-ten on a glum, gray November afternoon. I was stopped in a no-stopping zone and trying to blend in with all the other illegally parked cars when the first few raindrops took the big jump and splattered on Alice's dusty windshield. The dust was Alice's camouflage: she's a dumped, vintage Buick painted horsefly metallic blue. I'd removed the furry dice that had dangled from the rearview mirror the night I won her at a game of poker in a garage somewhere in Pacoima, but otherwise she was still Jaime's dream of heaven on wheels. Jaime was the guy I won her from. I'd never seen him again, but I had Alice to remember him by.

Rain always catches Californians by surprise, even when it's been gray for days. There was the usual sidewalk scurrying in anticipation of Noah's flood. People looked at the sky disbelievingly. The weatherman had said it might rain, so everyone was sure it wouldn't. In L.A., where the weather is the same three hundred and fifty-five days a year, the weatherman is right about fifteen percent of the time, roughly the same average as the handicappers at Santa Anita, astrologers, and the guys who predict lower gasoline prices. Faith in the U.S. Meteorological Service does not run high in Los Angeles. Astrologers, on the other hand, do a boom business.

In all the hubbub, I almost missed her. A bunch of people rushed into the stucco entrance to Monument Records as another bunch of people rushed out. In the day of the forty-minute lunch hour and the fifty-minute psychiatrist's hour, the hungry and the disturbed do not dawdle. There was some milling around and a few collisions, and Neil

Diamond managed to escape from Alice's radio. I looked down to change the station. When I looked back up, Sally Oldfield was crossing the street.

She walked fast. She was wearing a bright print dress and as the rain increased she glanced up and laughed. Everybody was standing in doorways looking like bums, except for the real bums, who were using the shower to get clean. She bounced down the sidewalk alone, happy, and wet.

When she turned the corner onto Fountain, I pulled Alice out into traffic and followed. The light at Gower and Fountain was red. It's always red, no matter which street you're on. I sat there muttering at it, and she darted across Fountain and jumped into a white late-model Corvette with a man in it. The car pulled away from the curb, fishtailed on the wet asphalt, and sped down the block. I looked both ways carefully, like they tell you to do in driving school, and ran the light.

She surprised me twice the first day. Surprise number one was the little white car's destination: a run-down hot-bed motel on one of the worst blocks of Sunset, and Sunset has a lot of bad blocks. At least four colors and three sexes of wet hookers squinted into the rain, trying to catch a glimmer of interest behind the busy windshield wipers. Nobody was buying.

The white sports car was already parked when I hit the first speed bump in the motel parking lot. Sarah Marie Theresa Oldfield was halfway up the stairs, followed by a slender, well-dressed man with blow-dried blond hair. No check-in for them; they already had a key.

After the door closed behind them I went upstairs and checked the room number: 207. Getting progressively wetter and feeling progressively sillier, I went back downstairs to note the number of the sports car's license plate and take a look inside. Nothing of interest but the fullest ashtray this side of Philip Morris corporate headquarters. Then I dodged wet traffic to get to a phone booth on the north side of Sunset and called the number I'd been given.

"Harker," Ambrose Harker said. The guy didn't waste a lot of energy on charm.

"And a good afternoon to you too," I said. "It's raining. The old dog is snoring."

"I don't know what you mean," he said. He said that a lot, I'd noticed.

"It's code," I said. "If you had your one-time pad with you, you'd know that it means she's in the Sleepy Bear Motel, 1589 Sunset, in room 207, with a light-haired guy who drives a white eighty-six Corvette, license number 1LBS004. Why do you suppose they don't start license plates with zero? It'd give them another twenty-six trillion numbers to play with."

He didn't say anything.

"I've got a lot of interesting questions," I said. "Would you like to hear some more?"

"No. What does the man look like?"

"He has a very good haircut on the back of his head."

"That's amusing," Harker said in the tone of voice of a man who hadn't laughed since the day the hogs ate grandma. "Is that your entire description?"

"Until he turns around. I could tell you that he moves with an easy, athletic grace or that he has a port-wine birthmark covering the left side of his face, or that his knuckles scrape the ground, but none of it would be true."

"When will he turn around?" Harker said patiently.

"Most likely when he comes down the stairs. Graceful or not, he'll probably come down facing front."

"Call when he does," Harker said.

"When they split up, who do you want me to follow?"

"Who were you hired to follow?" Harker asked. Then he hung up.

I was debating whether to call him back and blow the whole thing off when I saw the bum. He was standing outside the door, waiting to get into the booth and away from the rain. I hung up the phone, fingered the coin return out of habit, and came up with a quarter. I gave it to the bum as I came out. He looked at it as if it were a button.

"Get a cup of coffee," I said.

"You can't get a cup with a quarter," he said sullenly through all four of his teeth.

"Then get a saucer."

He mumbled something unpleasant and I reached out and took the quarter back. Slowly he looked down at his dirty, empty hand and then back up to me.

"Have a nice day," I said.

I'd taken the job, in spite of my dislike for surveillance in general and Harker in particular, first, because I couldn't afford not to, and second, because I wasn't working on anything else except the Case of Mrs. Yount's Cat. Mrs. Yount had a pendulous lower lip, a mountainous bosom, and a European buffer-state accent that was as Balkan as Polish sausage but not as identifiable. She also had the house I lived in, such as it was. Mrs. Yount was my landlady. She loathed me. I wasn't crazy about her either, but it had seemed politic to say I'd look for her cat. She'd named it, in a burst of inspiration that must have left her limp, Fluffy.

I thought briefly about calling her to report my total lack of progress, looking back at the phone booth while the bum mumbled mutinously over my shoulder, and decided I wasn't up to it. I waded back across Sunset to the car.

The rain stopped while I sat in Alice, looking up at room 207. Across the street the bum huddled in the phone booth and looked at me. I was checking the street to see if anybody was looking at the bum when the door to room 207 opened and the man came out. He came down the stairs alone, gave me an incurious glance, and climbed into his car. He was in his middle thirties, Germanic-looking, with sharp features and a long needle nose that looked like it ran a lot. He wiped it once on his elegant coat sleeve, smoothed his hair in the mirror, and scooted the little car out into traffic.

Five minutes later a Courtesy Cab pulled into the parking lot and honked twice. Sally Oldfield came down the stairs, looking buoyant, and hopped in the back. She'd been inside thirty-eight minutes. I took it on faith that they'd be going back to Monument Records, but I followed anyway. Faith carried the day, as it so infrequently does. I called Harker, gave him a riveting description of Sally's boyfriend, and settled in to wait for quitting time.

I got my second surprise at six-twenty-three that evening,

after I followed Sally Oldfield home. When her electric garage door opened, there wasn't another car there, just stacks of boxes that looked like they were filled with papers of some sort, a bicycle, and some dumpy-looking furniture. I drove casually past as she pulled into the garage, and then I tore around the block and parked a few houses down.

Maybe her husband didn't drive, I thought. There must be someone in L.A. who doesn't drive. Maybe he parked on the street. Except that the lights in the house were out. She'd stopped at a Ralphs' supermarket to pick up dinner or something, so she had to unload the car before she went to the door, and the house was darker than Monaco's Olympic hopes when she finally got up to the door. She flipped on the porch light, fumbled around with her keys, brushed a wisp of hair away from her face, and pushed the door open with her foot. One of the grocery bags slipped from her grasp and hit the porch. She looked down at it for a few seconds and then laughed and left it there. I watched lights come on as she made her way to the kitchen to stash the groceries. A few minutes later she retrieved the bag she'd dropped and went back inside. Then the living-room light came on.

Maybe Mr. Oldfield got home late. I'd been told to watch until nine, but I sat there sacrificing my eardrums to L.A. radio until ten-forty, when the house went dark. There was a new disc jockey at the top of my lengthy list of most-hated disc jockeys, but there was no Mr. Oldfield. So it wasn't an earth-shaking point. Maybe the man traveled. All I knew was that I'd have been home if I'd been Mr. Oldfield, even if Mrs. Oldfield did have a boyfriend.

I was already beginning to like her.

2

On the evening two days before I started to fall in love with Sally Oldfield, a young lady named Roxanne and I had indulged in a foolish amount of red wine, unleavened by a loaf of bread but accompanied by plenty of thou. We had reached the delicate point at which our relationship was about to change gears when the phone rang. That was the first time I'd ever talked to Ambrose Harker. In my eagerness to get back to the clutch, I'd made a few perfunctory notes and promised to meet him in a Hollywood restaurant the next day.

The headache that accompanied me into Peppernell's at about one the following day was not improved by the sight of several of L.A.'s best-known disc jockeys sucking up the suds on their break from the radio station next door. There was one man who, I knew from one of his ex-girlfriends, was a permanently vitalized speed-freak whose idea of a black-tie evening was drinking fourteen quarts of beer and then urinating on her in the bathtub. Another one, a guy whose hair looked like something you'd pay, but not much, to gawk at on the grounds of Lion Country Safari, was on my D.J. hate-list without the benefit of personal details: he dropped G's like they weighed three pounds each to make him sound folksy and emitted wolf howls at calculated intervals. Just a regular, everyday, white loafered werewolf to whom some misguided radio executive had given a microphone and a forty-thousand-watt signal. In Hollywood he made ninety thousand a year. In my neighborhood he'd have been wearing his tongue for a necktie.

"Mr. Ambrose," I'd said to the sour-looking man who flipped fastidiously through the reservation book. Upon receiving a stare of well-paid incomprehension, I'd given the memory an energetic toss or two and come up with another name. "Mr. Harker. Twelve-thirty. Table for two, or something."

The maître d' gave me a reproving look. "He's been here for quite a while," he said. It was only twelve-fifty.

"Lucky him," I said. "All this atmosphere. You want to take me to the table, or do you want me to wander around with my hand out?"

He looked at my clothes. Up to then, I'd felt well-dressed. Then the schmuck snapped his fingers. A waiter materialized at his side. "Table twelve," the schmuck said.

"Are you sure you weren't a disc jockey in a former life?" I asked him as I followed the waiter.

"Don' worry, sir," the waiter said in the best uptown Spanglish. "Him, he's like that wi' everyone."

"God, I'm glad," I said. "I thought it was my breath."

"You breath is okay," he said graciously, giving me another reason to be thankful for Hispanics. "His breath, is—it's . . . like the message from the grave, you know? *El día de los muertos.*"

"*Es verdad. Como se llama usted?*"

"Roberto. You' Spanish is very good."

"Hangover Spanish," I said. "And this must be Mr. Ambrose."

"Harker," he said, without getting up. "And you're late."

"That's already been brought home to me in two languages," I said. "Whatever happened to L.A. time? It was such a comfortable convention."

He toyed with the glass in front of him. He'd made a number of rings on the table with it already, linking some of them into watery Olympic symbols. "Los Angeles time is an excuse for imprecise behavior."

"I'd love to sit down," I said. "Thanks for asking. *Muchas gracias*, Roberto."

"*De nada, señor.*" He went back toward the door.

"Greasers," Ambrose Harker said, pulling a complicated Swiss Army knife out of his jacket pocket and paring his nails with it. "You want to know what's wrong with this city? Greasers."

"It's been a terrific lunch," I said, getting up again. "I'll send you a bill for the mileage."

"Sit down," Harker said, still working on his nails.

I stood above him. "I didn't like' you on the phone," I said. "I don't like you in person. Why on God's green earth would I want to eat lunch with you?"

"Money," Harker said, dangling the Swiss Army knife back and forth like a hypnotist. "Money, money, money."

I didn't sit down, but I didn't leave either. One of the reasons I was pretending to look for Mrs. Yount's cat was that I was uncomfortably short on the rent. "How much money?"

"Enough to overcome your scruples."

"Scruple you," I said. "It's going to be a nice sunset if the clouds clear."

"They won't. You've driven all the way from Topadoa or wherever the hell it is. It's going to rain on you going back. You've got a hangover. Wouldn't you like a beer?"

I took a breath. "Well," I said, sliding back into the booth, "since you put it that way."

Harker rubbed a hand across his chin and I heard whiskers bristle. He gestured for a waiter and I ordered a Beck's; they didn't have Singha. While we waited for my medication, I looked at him.

He looked like a cop: in fact, more than anything else in my fractured frame of reference he conjured up William Burroughs' Thought Police. Thirty-five to thirty-eight, spare and snaky thin, a taut, high-boned face, skin drawn tighter than a snare drum, clear blue eyes, and a jutting chin. He had a bony, possibly broken nose, an angular Adam's apple, a flat-top, and thin, muscular wrists that stuck out from cuffs that were half an inch too short. He seemed big somehow, although I had the feeling that he was shorter than I was. For a man who looked as though his nails might usually be dirty, he sure put a lot of effort into them. He'd started on his left hand.

A burst of disc-jockey laughter, hearty, abandoned, and insincere, greeted a disc-jockey joke at the bar as Roberto put a cold bottle of Beck's in front of me. I waved away the glass, asked for another beer in three minutes, and upended the green bottle into my mouth. Harker watched with something that would have passed for envy in a less abstemious man, put the red knife down, and sipped at his half-empty club soda. It had a crushed wedge of lime floating on top of it.

"I wonder what they used to do with all those limes," I said after I'd knocked back half the beer. "It's like mesquite."

"I don't understand," he said. "What's like mesquite?"

"Before people stopped drinking. Now everybody has a lime in his bubble water. Look around. Half the poor souls in this room are kicking the DT's with lime and carbonation." He took a gulp from his. "What did they do with all those limes before?"

"What's that got to do with mesquite? Mesquite's a wood, isn't it?"

"It's *the* wood," I said. "Try to get a piece of fish that hasn't been cooked over mesquite. Thank you, Roberto," I said, as Roberto plunked another Beck's in front of me. *"Momentito."* I drained the first and handed it to him. "If half the mesquite-grilled food we eat in L.A. is really cooked on mesquite, there must be acres of mesquite, forests of mesquite, hundreds of thousands of square miles of mesquite somewhere. Have you ever been in a mesquite forest?"

"No," he said shortly.

"Neither have I. Neither, I'd be willing to bet, has anyone else in this appalling room. So where's it all come from?"

He took a disapproving sip of his club soda. "Do you really think this is interesting?" he said.

"It'll do until you say something that is."

He smiled wolfishly and I could hear spit bubbles popping in his mouth. He reached into a pocket and his clothes rustled. That was why he seemed big: all his sounds were amplified. He tossed a photo on the tabletop and it made a plopping sound. His blue eyes bored into mine.

"Sally Oldfield," he said. "I want you to follow her."

I picked up the photograph. "Nice face. A fine, inviting overbite. What's she done? And have you got any identification?"

Crisp rustling this time, as he reached into his breast pocket and pulled out a card. He dropped it, with predictably ear-splitting results, next to my bottle. AMBROSE HARKER, it read. CHIEF OF SECURITY. MONUMENT RECORDS. Then some phone numbers.

"She's stealing money," he said. "And she's leaking our release schedule to the competition. We also believe she's helping other labels get in touch with our talent."

"Why would they want to do that?"

"To steal them. To sign them, to take them away from us. Do you know what I mean?"

The phrase had sharpened my headache and refreshed my memory. It had run through our phone conversation like an operatic recitative.

"You ask that more often than anyone I've ever met. I'll bet you make the waitress show you her order pad before she goes to the kitchen."

"Understanding is important," he said, as though he were reciting dogma. Dogma silences me: what can you say to someone who's just told you that, in essence, he's signed away his free will? Fortunately, I was spared the necessity of thinking of anything to say by the sight of Roberto, standing above us with pad in hand. Harker ordered first with the air of someone who usually orders first. He said, very slowly and clearly, and more loudly than was strictly necessary, that he wanted a chef's salad, making absolutely sure that Roberto understood he didn't want any ham, and I ordered a burger.

"Onions, *sí* or no?" Roberto said.

"Sí, and then *sí* again," I said.

"You mean two onions?" Harker said.

"Let it rest," I said. "And another beer."

"On the way," Roberto said cheerfully, already heading for the kitchen.

"You're going to get two slices of onion," Harker predicted gloomily. "You just watch."

"I've faced more compelling crises. If I do get two, I'll give you one."

"You certainly take a careless approach to life."

"Mr. Harker," I said, "it's my life. I'll be careful with yours, okay?"

"Just don't be careless with Sally Oldfield."

My beer looked very good all of a sudden and I drained it. Harker passed a hand over the back of his neck. His hair crackled. "You have to stay with her," he said. "I don't tolerate slip-ups."

"Yipes," I said. There was a long pause. "Why don't you fill me in?"

"She's in A&R," he said.

"Here's your big chance. I don't understand."

"Artists and repertoire. The people at a label whose job it is to look for talent. She was hired because she had a good background in underground music," he said distastefully. "The kind of bands that play in the little clubs."

"Head-banging," I said. "Heavy metal, mohawks, chain saws, and G-strings."

He didn't ask me what I meant this time. "Exactly," he said. "It's important in music to be, um, current. If bands that play heads of cabbage are what sells, you look for bands that play heads of cabbage." Roberto or somebody put another beer on the table and I picked it up.

"You drink too much," he said.

"But my heart is pure. So what's she doing wrong?"

He eyed the beer and hefted his own glass. It was empty. No one scurried to refresh it. He put it down again and sipped a bit dolefully from a glass of water. "A lot of money, cash money, flows through A&R," he said. "These kids in these shit bands, they've never seen a buck. Let's say someone from Monument shows up at one of these places and hands them a thousand bucks not to sign with anyone else. They don't. Or maybe they do."

"And if they do, the money sets up housekeeping in the debit column."

"There's virtually no way to recover it. These musicians, they're using drugs and, um, drinking. If you confront them they say they've never seen anyone from Monument, and who can prove the contrary?"

"Who indeed? How much money do you think?"

"More than thirty-one thousand dollars of Monument's

operating capital." He lifted his arm, and a moment later Roberto slapped another beer on the table.

"For *me*," Harker said, turning a shade of red that would have interested a cardiologist. He picked up the Swiss Army knife and slammed it onto the table. "Perrier for me, okay? Do you understand?"

"Comin' up," Roberto said, and disappeared forever.

"What about the rest of it? Release schedules and all that?" I shoved my water across the table at him as a pacifier.

"Schedules are everything," he said, taking a dour sip. "You can sell two million copies of an album by putting it on the market at the right time, or half a million by doing it wrong. Let's say you've got an album by a middle-selling band, someone like, oh, who knows, the Dranos. Put it out in a week when nobody else is releasing, and you'll do okay, maybe a few million units. Put the Dranos out against Michael Jackson, you're looking at returns. And the label behind Michael Jackson picks up most of the few million units you were counting on."

"Big bucks," I said.

"Five or six million dollars. As you would say, big bucks."

A waiter we'd never seen before put some food down in front of us. Harker waved his glass ineffectually at the waiter's retreating back and then glanced down at my plate. "See?" he said, by way of revenge, "no onion at all. You have to be more precise."

"Who gave you my name?" I asked.

The blue eyes came up to meet mine. "What's the difference?" he said.

"I like to know who my friends are. Or my acquaintances, at any rate. Why? Is that a hard question?"

"Sally Oldfield, that's your only business." His eyes wrestled mine to the mat, won, and came up for more.

"Not until I say it is," I said without looking away. "And while we're at it, why don't you go to low beams?"

"I beg your pardon?"

"It's considered polite to dim your headlights when approaching an oncoming vehicle. Anyway, if you want me to remember anything you're saying, you've got to stop trying to outstare me. It makes me feel like I'm arm-wrestling."

The waiter reappeared with a plate covered by a silver dome. He put it down on my right and whisked the dome off to reveal about seventy-five slices of onion.

"Hah," Harker said in a vindicated voice.

The waiter winked at me and ignored Harker's waving hand.

"You," Harker said. "You. Waiter. Goddammit, I'm trying to get another Perrier. Perrier, don't you understand English? Perrier, Perrier, Perrier," he said three times in French. He hit the table with the knife every time he said it, three amplified whacks. It even cut through the disc jockeys' egos; some of them actually looked at us.

The waiter looked down at my beer and then at me. I nodded and he headed for the bar.

"You sure know how to handle help," I said.

"Nobody speaks English anymore. This goddamned city is full of immigrants."

"America is full of immigrants," I said. "I'm an immigrant. You're an immigrant. Now, why don't you tell me who recommended me?"

"Skippy Miller," he said sulkily, taking a browser's bite of his salad.

"Why is that such a big deal?"

"You're for hire, right? That's what you do. Hire yourself out. Why should you care who gave me your name?"

"Listen. You may have two last names to my one, but that doesn't mean I'm going to go all buttery just because you offer me a job. I like to know what I'm doing, why I'm doing it, and who I'm doing it for. What did Skippy tell you about me?"

"He said that you'd helped him out when his series was in its first year and one of the scandal papers had gotten something on him that could have ruined everything. He didn't tell me what it was."

"He wouldn't," I said. Skippy was a big, fat, middle-aged actor with an extremely sloppy private life. Not a bad guy, but a messy one. "What else did he say?"

"That you were bright."

"How dangerous is this going to be?"

"Dangerous? She's a girl."

"So are black widows."

He was looking around the room, trying to catch the waiter's eye. He snapped his fingers and gestured impatiently at the table. "She's not a spider," he said.

I sighed and palmed his card. "Enjoy your salad, but try not to get too festive," I said, sliding across the seat of the booth. "People might think you're a disc jockey."

"Where are you going?"

"I'd say I want to wash my hands, but you might misunderstand. I have to go to the john, okay? You can catch up on your nails while I'm gone."

The telephone was in the men's room. I wanted to make sure that Harker was really Harker. First I called Skippy and got a woman on his service who knew me. Skippy, she said, was on a one-week retreat someplace near Big Sur and wouldn't be back for six days. Then I called the private number Harker had given me. No one else ever answered it, he said. It rang eleven times before I hung up and called the main number of Monument Records, which he'd said I was never to call.

I asked for Ambrose Harker's office and was put through. Mr. Harker, I was told, was at lunch.

"This is Clyde Barrows," I said, trying for a drawl. "I'm Mrs. Harker's brother. Do you know where he's eating?"

"Does Mr. Harker know you're in town, Mr. Barrows?"

"Ackshully, me and Bonnie, that's the little woman, just got in from Oklahoma. We're going to Singapore on a four-o'clock plane. So we'll either say hi at lunch or not at all. Be a shame to miss old Ambrose."

"I've never heard anyone call him old Ambrose," she said in a pleased voice.

"Hell, honey, we all call him that. Man was thirty-nine when he was born."

"If he was born," she said. "Don't tell him I said that."

"Your lips to God's ears."

"Thanks. The reservation was for twelve-thirty at Nickodell's on Melrose. Do you know where that is?"

"Honey, even the French, may they all go to heaven and

never throughout all eternity meet anyone who isn't French, know where Melrose is. Think there'd be room for us at the table?"

"I don't know," she said thoughtfully. "The reservation was for two."

"Well, we'll just pull up some chairs and squat for a while. If you can't eat squattin', the food ain't no good, as Bonnie always says." I had a feeling I'd gone too far.

I was wrong. "Order the chicken salad," she said. "And have a nice squat."

I hung up and went back into the restaurant. Even from fifteen feet away, Ambrose Harker looked mad. On the table in front of him were three full glasses of Perrier. With lime.

3

On the second day of my surveillance, I burglarized her car.

It couldn't have been much easier. The security guard watching over Monument Records' underground parking lot was a dozing fat man. Sleepy eyelids flicked in my direction as I walked by, and for a moment I thought he was going to establish a personal best by getting up three times in a single day. I jingled my keys over my head and grinned at him, and he settled back into a torpor that would have made a giant sloth look like Ralph Nader.

I already knew what the car looked like, an Oldsmobile Cutlass in an institutional shade of gray, not at all what I would have expected after her rainbow wardrobe. It opened as gratefully as a Catholic at her final confession.

The car was as spotless as a martyr's conscience: the Immaculate Conception by General Motors. For the first time, I got suspicious of Sarah Marie Theresa Oldfield. In L.A., most people's cars are full of junk: wads of used Kleenex, bills they haven't paid yet, McDonald's coupons, the detritus of a life spent largely on wheels. If this Oldsmobile had been a time capsule, archaeologists would have concluded that no one lived there. It was a cipher.

The rain was threatening a return engagement, so I went back to Alice and endured the radio. People told me I could consolidate my bills with a quick and easy loan and I laughed. Other people invited me to stash my parents in various rest homes; elderly parents are an awkward intrusion into the Southern California life-style. I thought about dragging my profane and politically radical parents, kicking, screaming, and cursing me inventively, into a rest home, and laughed again. About the only thing that wasn't funny, if you didn't count the disc jockeys, was the music. It had all the verve and variety of a sheet of stamps.

Sally came out at precisely one-twenty. The rain had given up on L.A. and gone east to give the desert a hard time. Traffic was flowing. I managed to muscle my way into it in time to watch the light at Gower and Fountain turn red just as she jumped once again into the white Corvette.

I looked left. I looked right. Then I stopped looking at anything but the stoplight. An LAPD black-and-white cruised in a stately manner through the intersection, heading east on Fountain. The hell with it. I knew where Oldfield and friend were going anyway.

The Sleepy Bear Motel was doing its usual landmark business in midday quickies. Mr. Needle-nose's Corvette was in its usual parking space. It wasn't raining, so the usual bum wasn't in his usual phone booth. I grabbed my usual space and settled into my usual wait. My eyelids sagged into their usual half-mast position. God, surveillance was exciting.

Someone rapped on the window. I looked up to see a tired-looking Chicana peering in at me. She was wearing a red dress that somehow managed to be both low-cut and high-cut.

"Hi, handson," she said. "You wan' a date?"

I lifted my arm and checked my watch, a complicated electronic affair given me for my birthday by my ex-girlfriend, Eleanor. It told me the time, the date, the day of the week—everything but the humidity. "I've already got one," I said. "November eleven."

She took an apprehensive look at the sky. It might rain yet. "You know wha' I mean," she said. "Half-hour, fifty bucks. We can do it here." She thumbed over her shoulder in the direction of the Sleepy Bear. Then she looked down and said, "No, Dulcita, no' yet. Down."

"*You* can do it here," I said. "Keep me out of it." I leaned sideways to look out the window. A white toy poodle sat at her feet, looking up at her. It had a neat little red bow tied to its collar.

"What's with her?"

"She goes wi' me. They don' mind. She's always real good." The poodle sensed she was being talked about and wagged her tail wildly. "Aren' you, sweetie?" the girl said. *"Querida mía."* Then she looked back up at me. "Fifty bucks, no big deal. I promise you have a good time."

"No, thanks," I said.

"So why you parkin' here?"

"I'm out of gas," I said. "Just waiting for the Auto Club." I looked up at room 207 and suddenly thought about how much I disliked Ambrose Harker. I pulled a wad of his money out of my pocket. "How about I just give you the fifty?" I said.

"For what?" She unsnapped her little white handbag and looked into it, as if the answer to how low she would go was inside, next to her face powder.

"For going away. For hitting the next block." I peeled off five tens and waved them at her. The little dog sat up on its rear legs, front paws in the air.

"Honey," she said, "you don' want nothin'?"

I passed the money to her. "Darling, we're both too pretty to die. Haven't you heard about AIDS?"

She looked at the bills and then back up at me. "You for real? This is jus' for me?"

"This is for just taking care of yourself. Be careful, okay?"

Her eyes narrowed. "Gimme a hunred," she said.

"For what?"

"So my man don' hit me."

"What about tomorrow?"

"Tomorrow is tomorrow. I already did fi' hunred today. Si' hunred is enough, Dulcita and me can go to bed."

I gave her another fifty. "Go to bed," I said. "But if I see you on Sunset again today, I'll take the money back and call the cops. Got it?"

"Don' be funny. I been working since three A.M. All I wan' is dreamlan', you know?"

The door to room 207 opened.

"Lean inside the car," I said.

She did. "What do you want?" she asked a little apprehensively. Up close, I realized she was no more than eighteen or nineteen. A little gold crucifix dangled at her throat.

"Your perfume," I said.

She looked alarmed. "You wan' my perfume?"

Needle-nose came down the stairs and walked past us on his way to the Corvette. If he registered Alice it didn't show, and he couldn't get much of a shot at me with Dulcita's mistress filling the driver's window.

"I don't want your perfume," I said, watching him in the rearview mirror. "I like it. I want to know what it is."

"You got some nose," she said. "Is flea shampoo, for Dulcita. I washed her this mornin' in the dark. Ho, perfume, says the guy. Like I say, you got some nose." She laughed and suddenly looked a lot prettier.

The Corvette caught and pulled out. Needle-nose didn't look back.

"Well, it smells good on you," I said.

Her face was about a foot from mine. She *did* smell good. "You know," she said, "you' pretty cute."

"You're not exactly chopped liver yourself. Why don't you get a job?"

"Don' start with me, okay? I do the bes' I can."

"Go home, then," I said. "Go to bed, like you said."

"Ri' after I feed Dulcita. Listen, thanks. He be aroun' pretty quick now, so I gotta be on the sidewalk. He see me yakkin', he gets upset, you know? Like he starts to play with his knife, shinin' up the blade and stuff. Thanks for the hunred."

She headed for the sidewalk, a little brown girl in a red dress on a gray day, with a white dog at her heels. She took up an alert stance at the curb and combed the oncoming traffic for her pimp. Dulcita sat at her feet and gave herself a professional-looking scratch behind the ear. A car honked twice.

It was Sally Oldfield's Courtesy Cab, a different number this time but the same company. After a moment the door to 207 was thrown open and Sally hurried out and down the steps. She threw the driver a radiant smile and got in back. She sure in hell was happy about something. She'd been in the room thirty-eight minutes, same as yesterday.

As the cab door closed, I saw a flash of red on the sidewalk. The Mexican girl had picked up Dulcita and tucked her under a slender brown arm, and now she was wading out into the traffic. Pulled into the curb across the street was a white Cadillac convertible with gold wire wheels and a spare mounted behind the trunk. Very fancy. The driver's window slid down and I saw a skinny, sharp-featured white guy with hair so blond he looked albino. He was, presumably, the hooker's man.

Sally Oldfield's cab made a right onto Sunset and headed back toward Monument Records, where another five hours of listening to the radio awaited me. I hadn't brought a book. I sighed and snapped on my turn indicator.

The Mexican girl was standing on the passenger side of the Cadillac. She was saying something, trying the door handle. It wouldn't open. She looked very unhappy.

I let an opening in the traffic go by and watched the white car. The passenger window went down about eight inches and the man at the wheel stuck out his hand. The girl looked even more unhappy, shook her head, and tried the handle again. No go. It was locked.

She slipped an arm over the top of the open window and tried to unlock the door inside. The driver hit the button, and the window went up and clamped onto her arm. He let the car roll forward at about five miles an hour.

The girl stumbled on her high heels and fought her way to her feet again. She slipped off the curb and cracked her head on the roof of the car. Dulcita trotted anxiously along at her heels, barking.

After half a block the driver of the Cadillac hit the brakes. The girl straightened up, crying, as he put the window down and extended a waiting hand. She rubbed the arm that had been caught in the window, then reached into her purse and handed him a wad of money. He rolled the window back up, put on a pair of mirrored shades, and took off into traffic.

The girl stood at the curb, looking at nothing. She was still crying. Dulcita sat down at her feet.

I'd really had enough surveillance for one day. Nothing was going to happen anyway; Sally Oldfield was back at

Monument now and she'd stay there until quitting time,
when I'd trail her home again. And if I was wrong, and
something did happen, maybe Harker would fire me. Maybe
I'd quit even if he didn't fire me. I could always start
looking for Mrs. Yount's cat.

The next thing I knew, I was two cars behind the white
Cadillac, heading east on Sunset. The pimp made a right
onto Cahuenga. So did I. Then we both made a left on
Franklin and headed for the hills.

The second girl was an emaciated blond in a thin blue
dress who looked like she was freezing to death on the
corner of Franklin and Highland. No argument this time, just
more money passed in through the passenger's window.
Then the blond boyo at the wheel slid on up Franklin and
turned right on Outpost, into a residential area of tree-hung
streets, big fenced yards, and lots of privacy.

If he'd looked back he would have spotted me easily, but
he was busy. He needed all this privacy in order to deliver a
to-go order to his nose, and that plus the demands of navi-
gating the curves kept him fully occupied.

I reached over and popped open Alice's copious glove
compartment. First I took out a pair of tortoiseshell glasses
I'd found in a parking lot. They were mended over the
bridge of the nose with white surgical adhesive. My ex-
girlfriend, Eleanor Chan, said they made me look like Jerry
Lewis. I slipped them on, refocused through the distortion
of the lenses, and then reached deep into the glove compartment to pull out a small flat-black automatic with a big, very
black hole at the end of its barrel. I dropped it into the
pocket of my windbreaker and waited for the right curve to
come along.

We hit it as we went back downhill. On either side of the
street were high walls, protecting the folks behind them
from exposure to all us drive-by riffraff. Pepper trees trailed
their tendrils at car-top level, further reducing the visibility.
As the white Caddy went into the curve I punched Alice's
accelerator to the floor and rear-ended the pimp's car at
about thirty miles an hour.

The whore's man was a terrible driver. He did everything
wrong, hitting the brakes and crimping the wheel in the

opposite direction. The car skewed around, out of control, and the front-left wheel jumped the curb. One second later, the Cadillac was half in the road and half on the sidewalk, and I was already out and running toward it, pushing my voice up into an unthreatening music-hall tenor.

"Oh, my golly, I'm so sorry, oh, Jesus, this is terrible, are you hurt? I don't know what happened, the car just seemed to jump, and all of a sudden there we were, *colliding* like that. . . ."

The glasses had slipped partway down the bridge of my nose. I shoved them back up and kept coming. He'd opened the driver's door by now, and I saw the knife gleam in his hand.

"You fuckin' jackoff," he said. "That's my fucking spare wire wheel back there." He put the knife hand behind him and started to climb out.

"Oh, I know it," I said, "don't look, it's terrible, that's the trouble with gold automobiles; they're so *soft*." He had one leg out now, still holding the knife behind him, and I reached out my left hand to help him.

"But what's important," I babbled, "is no loss of life and limb. Are your limbs all right?" He looked at my extended left hand as though he was going to spit on it, and I pulled my right from my jacket pocket and touched the gun to a spot midway between his eyes. "Say anything at all," I said, "and I'll put a picture window in the back of your head. Now, take your right hand out from behind you very slowly, and it had better be empty."

He was cross-eyed looking at the gun. He licked his skinny little lips and started to say something. I poked him between the eyebrows with the gun barrel, hard, and he thought better of it. When the hand came up it came up open. There was nothing in it.

"Good boy," I said. "All it would take for me to kill you would be the wrong syllable. Since you don't know what the right syllable is, just don't say anything. Now, put your right hand on top of the steering wheel and keep it there until I tell you to move it."

He did as he was told. His eyes kept flicking from the gun

to me and back again. A car went by without slowing, obeying the First Urban Commandment: Don't Get Involved.

"Okay," I said. "I want all the money, and I mean every last cent. Use your left hand, keep the right on the wheel, don't even twitch it. I saw where you put it, so just reach very, *very* carefully into your upper-left-hand pocket and pull it out."

His mouth knotted into a hard, ugly little line and the knuckles of the hand on the steering wheel were bone-white and bloodless, but he did as he was told, twisting his left hand awkwardly to reach the wad.

"Big man," I said. My throat felt like it was paved with gravel. "Big man who likes to turn the little girls out, put them on the street so you can drive your big white car and fill up your big white nose. Does it bother you that the little girls are going to die? Does anything bother you?"

His lips parted. I prodded him with the gun again. His pale, mean little eyes watered. "Ah-ah," I said. "Careful. Now, hand me the money."

There was a lot of it. I wedged it down into the pocket of my windbreaker and then looked up and down the street. Nobody was coming. "Okay," I said cheerfully, "close your eyes and open your mouth."

He was so surprised he forgot he wasn't supposed to say anything. "Huh?" he said.

"You heard me. Didn't you ever play this when you were a little kid? Close your eyes and open your mouth."

He looked at me like I was deranged, but he did it. Uncontrollably, one eye flickered open and then shut again.

"Now, now, no peeking. And come on, you can open your mouth wider than that."

His eyes were clamped shut and his mouth gaped open, revealing broken yellow teeth. He looked like a bottle-opener. "Now say 'Aaaaahhh,' " I said.

"Aaaaahhhhh," he said.

"That's the wrong syllable," I said. I slammed him full in the face with the gun butt. Blood spurted from his nose and his eyes popped open, rolling crazily. "Nobody said life was fair," I told him, cracking him dead-center in the forehead. He slapped both hands over his face and I shoved violently at his near shoulder, toppling him sideways onto the seat. He was making a high-pitched, wavering sound.

"Big man," I said, picking up the knife. "You stay right there and bleed on your upholstery. If I see your head above the back of the seat before I leave, I'll put a permanent dimple in it. Got it?"

He kept keening, face in hands. The big man had wet himself.

I closed the door and went to the back of the car. He kept the knife sharp for the little girls; it only took me about thirty seconds to slash both his rear tires. I left the Caddy sagging despondently, its tailpipe touching the asphalt, and pointed Alice downhill. Before I reached Franklin, I'd tossed the automatic and the knife into the glove compartment and snapped it shut. I drove very safely; the LAPD is touchy about guns and knives.

She was where I'd left her, but now she was sitting on the curb. She had one arm around her knees and the other on Dulcita's head. When I stopped the car she didn't even look up.

I got out and touched her shoulder. "Thirty-three hundred bucks," I said. "Buy some perfume." I held the money out to her.

For a moment she didn't recognize me. I'd forgotten about the glasses. I took them off and put them into my jacket pocket, and her eyes traveled from my face to the money. Her face turned ashen.

"You din't," she said.

"I sure did."

"Oh, my gosh. He always searches me when he picks me up. He'll kill me."

"He'll kill you a number of times. I also broke his face and slashed his tires. He's not going to be in a good mood."

"What am I s'posed to do?" There was an edge of panic in her voice, and she looked up and down the street as if she expected him to appear, tires squealing and knife in hand, to julienne us both right there on the sidewalk.

"Here's what you're supposed to do. You're supposed to take a cab to the bus station and buy a ticket for someplace nice, like San Antonio. He'll find you anyplace you go in

L.A. Get a job in a dry cleaner's or something. Send some money to your mom. Say thirty novenas. Do anything you like, but get out of the Life and get out of here."

"Sure," she said hopelessly, looking up at me. She hadn't reached out for the money.

"Sugar," I said, "he's got wet pants, a broken nose, and two flat tires, but he's going to show up sooner or later. If I were you, I'd be heading east in something fast when he does. Anyway, you need a little fresh air."

She reached up lifelessly and I put the money in her hand. As I did it I saw the scars, some of them old, some new and still scabbed, on the inside of her arm. The sun went behind a cloud. Now we both knew she wasn't going anyplace.

I squatted down next to her. Dulcita gave me a tentative growl. "Okay," I said. I was the oldest man in the world. "I left him on the street just west of Outpost, about five blocks above Franklin. Take the money back to him and be a hero. Tell him I'm a creep who saw him drag you down the street and decided to act like Superman. He'll be there for a while."

She fumbled with her purse and stuffed the money into it. "Leave me alone," she said. "I'll get a cab."

"You can still go to San Antonio. I've known people who kicked dope. If they did it, you can."

"*Cabrón,*" she said. "Do me a favor, okay? Don' help me anymore."

"Sorry," I said. I went to the car, feeling like a Don Quixote who had just learned that windmills bleed. As I opened the door, she called out something from behind me. I turned and looked at her inquiringly.

"Has he got the knife?" she asked again.

"Not if he only had one," I said.

"Tha's somethin'," she said. "Now go away."

I went. In the rearview mirror I saw her standing at the curb, looking at the phone booth. The little dog with the bow on its collar stared up at her, wondering what came next. That dog sure loved her.

Sally Oldfield surprised me for the next-to-last time that day at three-fifty-two. She came out of the entrance to Monument Records with a young woman, a dark-haired, chubby person in dieter's clothes: a too-tight short skirt and a bright pink blouse with enough ruffles on its front to decorate a Laura Ashley boutique. Sally slipped her arm unself-consciously around her friend's waist and the two of them headed down Gower to what had to be the friend's car. I jotted down the plate number as the two of them climbed in and I then followed them to a bridal shop on Sunset that was called, a little anxiously, I thought, I Do, I Do. One more "I Do" would have been a dead giveaway. Fifteen minutes later they came out. The chubby one was carrying a big white box with a satin bow on it. They were talking a mile a minute in the excited, intimate way that men never manage. The friend laid the box lovingly in the trunk and then they headed back to Monument. I parked in the no-parking zone and settled in for a long winter's nap.

No matter how boring a stakeout is, you should never make assumptions. I'd made one, that she wouldn't come out until quitting time, and that she'd come out in her car when she did. It almost cost me the whole mile. It was quitting time but she was on foot. She was most of the way to Fountain before I realized who she was.

Same as before: the white Corvette parked out of sight around the corner. The same delighted hop into the car, the same quick trip to the Sleepy Bear, the same tandem climb up the stairs, the man holding her hand this time. It started to sprinkle.

The rain had begun in earnest when Needle-nose came out, right on schedule, thirty-three minutes after they went in. Four minutes later I turned on the windshield wipers and started looking for her cab.

At six-twenty the neon came on above me with a sudden snap of pink light and an electric buzz. A fuchsia bear holding a candle in its right paw trotted blissfully toward the sack. Neon being what it is, he was going to walk all night.

The evening bloomed damp and unpromising before me. I reproached myself for not having the courage to complain to Mrs. Yount about the leak in my living room ceiling and hoped briefly that Ambrose Harker's roof was leaking directly above his bed. Resignedly I turned on the radio and fiddled with the knobs. Sally Oldfield's cab was obviously sitting in rush-hour traffic somewhere, its driver swearing at the rain.

At six-forty-five I began to get nervous. The doors of the Sleepy Bear had been slapping open and closed at the bidding of cheerful adulterers like the stage set in a French bedroom farce, but the door to room 207 remained shut. She hadn't even lifted the curtain on the front window to look for her cab.

Then the pink light became redder and the cops arrived. They went straight to room 207. There were a lot of them.

Discretion is almost always the better part of valor. I locked Alice and went across the street to my phone booth. There was no bum in it, but it stank of urine and the floor was littered with crumpled balls that had been ripped from the Yellow Pages to meet needs more elemental than finding the nearest interior decorator. I was still standing there, breathing in Hollywood's heady perfume, an hour and a half later when two uniformed patrolmen wheeled Sally Oldfield out feetfirst. A white sheet covered her face.

4

There was no answer.

That made nine times, five from various phone booths and four from my living room, where water was dripping from the leak in the ceiling and the wood-burning stove was consuming oak and cedar at a rate guaranteed to chase away the chill about half an hour after I climbed shivering into a clammy bed. Right after I fell asleep the bedroom would warm up. By the time I woke up again it would have been cold for an hour.

Sarah Marie Theresa Oldfield had been cold for more than four hours. I hung up.

"It's a work number," Roxanne said from the couch. She was wearing the only bathrobe I had. It looked warm. "He wouldn't be at work now. You said so yourself."

"I'm no authority," I said. "The last time I was right about anything, Wendell Willkie was president."

She squinted at the red wine in her glass and fluffed through her memory for anything that made sense. "Wendell Willkie was never president."

"Right," I said. "But isn't it a great name?"

"Millard Fillmore," she said, draining her glass and holding it out to me. "*That's* a great name. Sounds like a cross between a duck and a dance hall."

"I'm going to try Information," I said.

"Real detectives, which is to say the detectives in books, never use Information. They use intuition, they use connections downtown, they use informants in corner pool parlors. But they never use Information."

A minute later we both knew why. "He's not listed," I said.

"Nobody in L.A. is listed. I'm not listed, you're not listed."

"Yes, I am."

"But your address isn't. S. Grist, it says. Address nowhere. Your first name could be Susan. You live wherever the phone rings. Not very helpful to a girl in a hurry."

"She's dead," I said. "She's not in a hurry."

"I'm alive," she said, "and I'd like some more wine. If I hold this glass out any longer I'll get pins and needles."

I poured without saying anything. I was remembering Sally Oldfield, holding the man's hand in hers as she hurried upstairs to the room he planned to kill her in. I was remembering the Chicana hooker, the tracks on her arms. I was counting my options, comparing them with theirs, and coming up sorry. It must have showed.

"Hey," Roxanne said. "She's not going to care if you drink. You can't bring her back to life by joining the Temperance League, if there's still such a thing. There's a big woolly bathrobe over here and I've already warmed it up."

The world spun once or twice and then steadied itself, and she was right. Roxanne was on the couch, all milky and smooth, holding the bathrobe open so I could crawl in. She had four beautiful little moles, a sort of dermatological Little Dipper, just above her navel. Rain spattered singlemindedly on the roof. Sally Oldfield was on a slab somewhere, offering her secrets to the forensic team. The Chicana was probably shivering at an intersection, selling her secrets to make the money the body shop would charge for the Cadillac. Outside was there and inside was here. That was the reason people went inside.

"Roxanne," I said, "the world is something you scrape off your shoe."

"That's why there's religion," she said. "To teach you the difference between your sole and your soul."

I lifted the bottle and drank from it. The wine had the good, dusty taste of sunshine and Italian dirt. I held it out to her and she shook her head, hair falling around her face. Her glass was on the table in front of her.

"Come to mama," Roxanne said. The robe was still open.

An hour later we were asleep, curled into a tight, chaste knot against the damp. Twice during the night I woke up, thinking the phone was ringing. It wasn't.

Roxanne was gone when I woke up. Adding to her already overwhelming total of karmic points, she'd made a pot of coffee. Clutching a cup for dear life, I went outside. The root garden, the sparse little plot where I grow my radishes, onions, garlic, and potatoes, was thriving. This time of year neither of us needed water. Not that I ever did.

Eight-thirty. The music business lurches foggily into gear sometime in the digestive interval between brunch and lunch. I tried Harker's number anyway; maybe corporate cops got in early so they could snoop through the secretaries' desks, looking for evidence of embezzlement or back issues of *Playgirl*. I got the same old lonely ring, the sound of a telephone in an empty room.

Well, no one could say I hadn't tried. I'd thought that the death of the subject might be of interest to the man who'd hired me to trail her, and I'd spent many of Monument Records' nickels to report it. It wasn't my fault that the creep who was paying me was a nine-to-five bureaucrat addicted to an eight-hour workday. Although God only knew what a joyless slug like Harker did with the time he didn't spend at work. Probably combed through back issues of *Popular Mechanics* in search of new insights into human psychology.

I tried the number again anyway. Zero. Harker was off practicing his eyelock in a bathroom mirror or working up expressions that would persuade the fired help to quit without severance. With a third cup of Roxanne's coffee in hand, I climbed out onto the deck to look at the world.

All was right with it. The clouds were lifting to reveal a hard line of silver above the mountains that God put there to keep me from wasting my days staring at the Pacific, and things smelled wet and clean, with that sharp, new odor that rain always leaves as a consolation prize for slick roads and leaky roofs. A mockingbird, drunk on clean air, let rip with a confused jigsaw puzzle of other birds' songs. Mozart would have envied it. It was a morning Sally Oldfield would have enjoyed. She would have looked at it and laughed. She was the only woman I'd ever seen who laughed at a dropped bag of groceries.

And that made me mad enough to try the sacrosanct corporate number, the one he'd told me never to use. I stood there chewing on the grounds in the bottom of the cup while the Monument Records switchboard did its clumsy imitation of the human nervous system, ultimately directing my call to the waiting ear of Harker's secretary.

"Mr. Harker's office," she said in the voice of a woman who'd said it too often. She was the same one I'd talked to in my prior incarnation as Clyde Barrows.

No, he wasn't in. He usually got in about ten or ten-thirty, but if it was urgent she promised to have him call me the moment he lifted his oversize shoes across the threshold. I left my name, number, and the assurance that the call was urgent, and looked at a couple of empty hours.

There was the computer to kill time with. I'd recently bought a spreadsheet program that snickered at my finances every time I booted it. I didn't feel up to it. There was always Flight Simulator, but recently I'd felt less assured that my career path would ever lead me to the point where I'd be trying to land my private plane at Burbank Airport. That left the phone, so I used it.

"Henry, city desk," said my ex-student. He'd overcome a lot of obstacles, including the course in Precursors of Shakespeare that I'd taught at UCLA and the fact that his given name was Patrick, to land a job as a reporter at the L.A. *Times*.

"Pat," I said. "Simeon. What's yellow journalism paying these days?"

"Green," he said. "How much of it do you need?"

"It runs into seven figures. As in a license plate. Have the cops run a make yet on the car in that motel murder last night?"

"Motel murder where?"

"Jesus, Pat, how many were there?"

"Three."

I wondered whether Norman Bates was in town. "This was on Sunset, in Hollywood."

"Jane Doe," he said.

I digested that.

"White woman," Pat said. "Early thirties, right?"

"No identification?" I said.

"Clean as a whistle. Just like it said in the paper," He paused for a second. "Do you know anything I don't know?"

"I probably know lots of things you don't know."

"Anyway," he said, "what makes you think there was a car involved?"

"It was a motel. Motelo take license numbers. Checks bounce but license plates don't."

"This one did," he said. "As you'd know if you read the *Times* or anything more current than Homer. The car was stolen."

"From whom?" I said.

"Why?" he said.

"I'm a concerned citizen. You know how concerned I am. Remember how concerned I was when you bought your term paper from that Iranian?"

"There was nothing wrong with that paper," he said defensively. It was an old argument.

"No. It would have been perfect if it hadn't implicated Allah as the deity responsible for the deus ex machina in the last act of an Elizabethan play. That's one of the things I know that you don't know, that Elizabethans didn't know Allah from Colonel Sanders."

"You didn't flunk me," he said.

"No, I didn't. So who was the car stolen from?"

There was a pause. "I don't know. I should, but I don't."

"If you find out, call me, okay?"

"Tell me why."

"Tell me about that term paper."

"Oh, shit. I'll call you. But when there's something we can print, you tell me first, right?"

"Make a deal?"

"Let's hear it."

"Here's another license plate. Check it for me and I promise that I'll call you first if there's ever anything."

"Cross your heart and swear to God?"

"Come on, Pat. You know I can't do two things at the

same time." I gave him the license number of Sally Oldfield's chubby girlfriend.

"I'm going to have to talk to the cops, you know."

"Tell them it has to do with the Girl Scout Cookie scam."

"The *what* scam?"

"Read the *Herald Examiner*," I said. I hung up.

An hour later Harker still hadn't called, although Mrs. Yount had. Twice. I'd let her talk to the answering machine while I did two hundred sit-ups as part of the installment plan on a flat stomach I was purchasing with sweat and boredom, and I'd fed a little lettuce to my one surviving parakeet, Gretel. Someone had twisted Hansel's head off by way of saying hello a few months earlier. That time I'd been lucky; Hansel was the only one I'd cared about who'd been killed.

Thirty minutes and half a new pot of coffee after that, my patience had given out. This time Harker's secretary told me that he was in a meeting and couldn't be disturbed.

"I'm *very* disturbed," I said. "Tell him it's Simeon Grist and tell him that I'm calling the cops if he does't talk to me."

"Geez, the cops?" she said. "Will he know what it's about?"

"Tell him Sally Oldfield."

"He knows Miss Olfield. What about her?"

"You have a lovely voice," I said. "Will you put me on hold and give him the message?"

"Gee, thanks, I mean, I don't know. He's like a grizzly bear when he gets interrupted."

"Interrupt him. Tell him I'm going to the cops if he won't talk to me."

"Jeez," she said again. "Hang on a minute."

I held on. One of Monument Records' nominal stars crooned something about love on the run. It sounded uncomfortable.

"He got all grizzly," she said. "But he held up twelve fingers, I mean first ten and then two—even he doesn't have twelve fingers—and I think that means he'll see you at noon. Do you know where we are?"

"Everyone in the world knows where that building is. See you at noon."

We both hung up, the one form of climax that people frequently attain simultaneously. I pulled on some running clothes and headed for the beach.

I ran five miles in the softest sand I could find and then headed uphill toward Santa Monica. By the time I got back down to Alice, I knew what I wanted to say to Ambrose Harker. I had a lot of general questions about the surveillance, and a lot of specific questions about Sally Oldfield. It was pretty clear that most of what I'd been told was goop, pure and simple, and I thought the police would be interested in it. Enjoying the prospect of ruining Harker's day, I jumped into a cold wave and washed the sweat off before driving to UCLA for a long sauna.

All of what Eleanor calls the toxins had been sweated out of my system by the time I gave my name to the guard at Monument Records. He checked the list and directed me to Harker's office on the eighth floor, higher than the hoi polloi but well below the upper-executive stratosphere.

The secretary with the lovely voice weighed two hundred chocolate-ridden pounds. The terrible thing was that her face was so beautiful and that her smile could have illuminated Century City. A wedding ring cut deeply into her finger. Maybe it was the man's fault. For lack of anything better to do, I sat on the couch and picked up a copy of *Record World*.

A buzzer on her desk did its thing. "He'll be right out," she said, with her incandescent smile.

Ambrose Harker strode out of his office door looking grim and businesslike. He didn't extend his hand.

"Okay," he said. "What's all this crap about the cops?"

I knew I was supposed to say something, but I couldn't, because my mouth was hanging wide open. I'd never seen Ambrose Harker in my life.

5

Big Sur is a long way from anywhere, and that's where it should be. If it were any closer it would look like the rest of the world.

As it is, it looks like Big Sur: cliffs overhanging the grayest Pacific on earth, Monterey cypresses perched on fragile spits of land, defying gravity to dangle their gray-green needles over the eternal churn of the sea. It's so perfect that a Hollywood boy like me expects a credit roll scrolling above the horizon. Scenic designer: God. Special effects: the Apostles, and so forth.

Only two kinds of people lived there, rich straights and poor crazies. As I steered a rented car out of Carmel airport at five P.M., I had no idea which kind I was going to see.

I'd made an embarrassed exit from Ambrose Harker's office, thinking about calling the cops, but to give them what? They already had Needle-nose's description from the motel, they already had the license number of his stolen car, they already had the number of times he and Sally had been there. What I had was a client who didn't exist and a burning sense of having been suckered.

They didn't have Sally's name, but they'd get that quickly enough. And if they didn't, I might be able to use it as a bargaining chip for a fact or two.

I also had the fact that Skippy Miller had recommmended me for the job. And that was all I had. A poor thing, but mine own.

Cypress Grove was a conference center located in the center square of God's country. On a map of paradise, it

would have been C-3. I hiked down the hill from the parking
lot through a stiff November sea breeze, to Reception.

WELCOME, the banner read. THE CHURCH OF THE ETERNAL
MOMENT IS HERE AND NOW. Beneath the banner was a long
Formica table at which were seated two identically gray-
costumed individuals wearing Chinese cadre jackets that
Mao wouldn't have sneered at. The nameplates in front of
them read LISTENER DOOLEY and LISTENER SIMPSON. Listener
Dooley was a red-faced Irishman with the kind of highly
weathered nose that, when it occurs in fur-bearing species,
causes taxidermists to look for new materials; Listener Simpson was about twenty-four and very pretty. Listener Dooley
was snoring gently, which made it easier to follow my in-
stincts and choose Listener Simpson.

"Welcome to the present," Listener Simpson said. Her
eyes were a disconcerting shade of ice-blue. Behind her
hung a beautifully lit color photograph of a woman and a
little girl of eleven or twelve. The little girl's blond hair
cascaded down over the shoulders of her immaculate white
dress.

"It's kind of hard to escape from the present," I said.
"People spend millions trying to do it. Looks like Listener
Dooley's managed."

Listener Simpson's cool blue eyes flicked down to a pho-
tocopied sheet in front of her and her voice cooled a couple
of degrees. "Are you expected?" she asked.

"Anything can happen in the present. 'Expected' is sort
of future tense, don't you think?"

"I think that you don't understand the present," she said
without looking up. "Everything is here and everything is
now. Could I have your name, please?"

"Grist," I said. "But you won't find it there. I'm looking
for Skippy Miller."

"Mr. Miller is here."

"And now. Can someone tell him I'm also here? Now?"

Her eyes engaged mine and held them. "That depends,"
she said, "on what you want, and on whether he'll want to
see you."

"He'll see me whether he wants to or not." She didn't

look away, and neither did I. "He owes me a few. A six-pack, at least."

"He's in Listening," she said. She was still staring straight into my eyes. "He won't be free until seven-fifteen, just before the Revealing."

"That's about an hour."

"As you say." It was one of the most noncommittal responses I'd ever provoked. "Whom shall I say wants to see him?"

"Whom? Simeon Grist."

She turned a pad of paper toward me. It said PUBLIC CHURCH BUSINESS at the top. "Could you please print that?" she said.

"Hell," I said, "I could probably even write it."

"We'd prefer printing." She gave me a tiny public-relations smile. "For the sake of clarity."

"Ah, clarity," I said, doing as I was told, "we worship at thy shrine."

Listener Simpson pushed a button at her right hand and the door behind her opened to admit a clear-eyed fifteen-year-old girl wearing tight black jeans, a blouse of Chinese-checker red, and a pair of seventy-dollar Reeboks. She surreptitiously shifted a wad of chewing gum to her cheek as she approached the table. Simpson scrawled something on the bottom of the page I'd printed my name on, glanced at her watch, and noted the time in the lower-right-hand corner. "This is for Mr. Miller," she said. "He'll come out of Listening in 12A in forty-six minutes. He's to choose whether he wishes to come here or not."

"Yes, Listener," the girl said around her gum. "Should I make a copy before I deliver it?"

"Of course," Listener Simpson said a little peevishly. "If it's not in the files it doesn't exist," she added with the air of one repeating a well-worn dictum. The girl didn't look particularly grateful for the advice. She let out a world-weary sigh and left the room as though she were happy to be out of it, cracking her gum as the door closed behind her.

"Kids," Listener Simpson said to herself. Listener Dooley emitted a sympathetic snore.

"You were probably like that once," I said. "All energy and no direction."

She gave me a grave look and then shook her head. "I was worse," she said. "I don't know why nobody killed me."

"Children seem to be important to the church. Kids as couriers, the little girl on the poster behind you."

"Children are important to every Church. Like them or not, they're the messengers to the future. 'Suffer the little children to come unto me.' Jesus was only one of the religious leaders who realized that children were essential."

"A high-priority demographic group."

She weighed it for a second. "A little bald, but accurate. It's probably better than sentimentalizing them."

"Tell me about the Church."

"I'm not qualified. I can only tell you a few things, and those are more what we're not than they are what we are. Does that make sense?"

"It's not one of clarity's better moments, but I followed it."

"What do you want to know?"

"Well, to start with, who are the people on the poster?"

"Mary Claire and Angel Ellspeth. Angel is the Church's Speaker. Mary Claire is her mother."

"I know what a mother is. What's a Speaker?"

"That's a little complicated, and it sounds like mumbo-jumbo unless you've heard a Revealing. We're encouraged not to answer that question, but to ask you to attend a Revealing instead. Like the one at seven-fifteen this evening."

"Is the Church Christian?"

"Some of us are Christian. I am. Some of us are Jews, some of us are Buddhists, some don't believe in God at all. It's not important. The Church teaches us to address the Spirit in ourselves. Do you believe in God?"

"No."

"You don't even have to think about it?"

"I've already thought about it. Boy, have I thought about it."

"Don't you believe you have a spirit of some kind?"

"It's not something I consider every morning right after I

get up. I believe in right and wrong. I guess that must mean I think people are more than just ambulatory mixtures of chemicals. Who cares what happens to a chemical? Is it right to use zinc to make corrugated roofing and wrong to put it on your nose to keep from getting sunburned?"

"Zinc's a metal," she said, "but I understand your example. Moral principles don't make sense in a purely physical world."

"That's what I said."

"Of course it was." Her smile was friendlier now, and her eyes seemed to be looking into mine rather than challenging me. She really was very pretty. I would have asked her what time she got off, but I had a feeling she didn't.

"What's the Eternal Moment?" I asked instead.

"Now," she said in italics. "You already knew the answer to that."

"I guess I did. What's a Listener?"

"That comes later. Don't look for a contradiction, there isn't one. You just don't understand Now."

"Take pity on a poor pilgrim."

"Well," she said with a smile, "I'm listening to you now, aren't I?"

Listener Dooley shifted on his hard wooden chair, mumbled something, and opened his eyes. He looked at me once, incuriously, and let his lids droop again. Nevertheless, I had a sense that Listener Simpson wasn't the only one whose ears were working.

"I guess you are. Do you get paid for it?"

"The laborer is worthy of his hire."

The door behind the Listeners opened and a dark, extremely handsome man came in. He had blue-black hair and plenty of it, startlingly pure blue eyes, and the kind of beard that actors and politicians shave twice a day. His deep tan was set off by a coral polo shirt, complete with an amphibian of some kind over the left nipple. He'd tucked the shirt meticulously into pleated blue slacks to show off the fact that he'd inherited Fred Astaire's waistline. I disliked him on sight.

"Well," he said, "so you're here to see Mr. Miller." He

smiled, revealing white, slightly pointed teeth. "I'm Dick Merryman."

Dick Merryman held out a hand and I shook it. It was warm and hard, with short curly black hairs on the backs of the fingers.

"I'd say I'm Simeon Grist," I said, "but you already know it."

He must have thought that was funny because he laughed. "Has Listener Simpson been helpful?"

"She's been a delight. I was about to tell her my entire life story."

He laughed again and tossed a mean little glance at Listener Simpson, who blushed scarlet to the roots of her hair. "He's just kidding, Dr. Merryman," she said.

"Doctor?" I said. "What kind of doctor? Ph.D.? L.L.D.? Chiropractic?"

"M.D.," he said. "An internist, actually, Simeon. Why?"

" 'Doctor' is such a loose term, isn't it, Dick? The Germans call everybody 'doctor,' and Americans are only slightly more selective. So what's an internist doing at a gathering of the Church of the Eternal Moment?"

"We're not Christian Scientists," he said in an agreeable tone that sounded like it took a little work. "People get sick, you know."

"Then you're not a member of the Church?"

"Of course I am. The Church has a lot of professional men—doctors, lawyers—and blue-collar workers, housewives, what-have-you. Everybody's welcome. Are you a friend of Mr. Miller's?"

"I've known him a long time. I've done him some favors."

"Don't think we're security-happy," Merryman said, reading my mind. "It's just that Mr. Miller is a celebrity, and we've learned to be careful with people who say they want to see one of our celebrities."

"One of your celebrities?"

"We have many people whom the world thinks of as celebrities. There are eight or nine here right now."

"Eight? Or nine?"

"Eight, actually," he said, giving me the teeth again. What do you do, Simeon?"

"Good question, Dick. You could say I'm self-employed."
We smiled at one another.

"And you say 'doctor' is a loose term." He chuckled. I
chuckled back at him. Then we both stopped chuckling and
he waited for me to say something.

When the silence had gotten awkward and Listener Simpson had cleared her throat twice, he rubbed his hands together. "Well," he said, "Mr. Miller will be getting your
message soon, and he'll probably come out to see you. Even
if he doesn't, I hope you'll stay for the Revealing. You've
come all this way, after all."

"All this way from where?" I hadn't told Listener Simpson where I'd come from.

Merryman's smile broadened. "No one really lives in Big
Sur, Simeon. Just take a seat. Have you brought anything to
read?"

"That's okay. I'll meditate on the present."

"You do that. Even without training, it can't do any
harm. Listener Simpson, I think it's time for your next
session."

Listener Simpson looked faintly fuddled. "Of course it is,
Dr. Merryman. I was just, um, waiting to be relieved."

"Listener Dooley can handle it."

Listener Dooley snapped out of his coma and looked
alert. "Sure I can, Dr. Merryman." He had a whiskey voice
to match his nose.

"Nice to have met you, Simeon," Merryman said. "See
you at the Revealing." He took Listener Simpson's elbow
and guided her out of the room. He had the posture of a
professional ballroom dancer, but his fingers cut into the
flesh of her arm.

"What an interesting guy," I said to Listener Dooley as
the door swung shut behind them. "I always think doctors
should be unattractive."

"You do, huh? I think everybody should look like what
they want to look like."

I calculated the odds against Listener Dooley having chosen his face and came up with the kind of number astronomers are always trying to explain to the rest of us. Conversation with Dooley held no mysteries that I cared to penetrate so I went to a chair and meditated on the present.

Quite a lot of it had flowed seamlessly past when the door opened once again and Skippy Miller jiggled through it. He looked genuinely happy to see me, happier than anyone I'd run into in a long time.

"Simeon, this is great, this is terrific," he boomed in his actor's voice. He looked, as always, like his mother had dressed him in the dark. Skippy wasn't heavy or husky or any of the current euphemisms: Skippy was fat, with the dedicated fat man's fastidious touches—a scarf around the neck, trousers darker than his shirt, shirt loose to conceal the blossoms of flesh inside. Except that, on Skippy, the touches always went awry. The scarf around his neck was too tight, emphasizing the rolls of fat below his chin. The trousers had bulging safari-style pouches that made him look like a man with an extra set of hands in his pockets. But his face was genuinely open and obviously pleased.

"It is? I mean, I'm happy to see you too, Skippy, but why is this such a crowd-pleaser?"

"Well, because you're here. You have to give me credit, Simeon, I never preached to you, but that doesn't mean I'm not happy to see you here."

Listener Dooley was sitting straight up now, or as straight as his paunch would let him, taking it all in.

"Skippy," I said, "you're going a little fast for me. Is there someplace we can talk?"

Listener Dooley looked vaguely affronted and then remembered that he wasn't supposed to be Listening.

Skippy cast a guileless glance around the room. "There's nobody here," he said.

"Think again. How about the parking lot?"

He gazed through the windows. "It's dark out there."

"Darkness is an illusion. If you could see through it, it'd be light."

"Simeon," he said, his face falling, "you mean the only reason you're here is to see me?"

"Well, I didn't fly four hundred miles to be told it's dark outside."

"Aw, hell," he said. "I thought . . ."

"Maybe later. I've been invited to the Revealing."

He lit up again. "You're going to go, aren't you?"

I took his arm. "We'll see," I said, steering him through the door. "Let's talk first."

In the parking lot, Skippy shivered as if he somehow lacked the fat man's natural insulation. "You really should come to the Revealing," he said a trifle sulkily. "It'd be good for you."

"Skippy, the plane home doesn't leave until ten. Tell me what I want to know and I'll sit through a Maria Montez movie."

"You'll love it. Honestly, you've never seen anything like it. This little girl, except it's not her really, of course, but whoever it is, it's something."

"I'm sure it is."

"So you'll stay?"

"First things first. Do you know anyone who calls himself Ambrose Harker?"

"I think I might have known a Harker a long time ago. I don't think I've ever met anyone named Ambrose."

"Who was the Harker, then?"

"Her name was Alice. Jesus, this is when I was in high school. A little pale girl with terrible skin. A physics brain, remember physics brains? I sat behind her in math so I could cheat off her tests."

"What about her brothers?" I knew I was getting nowhere, but the only way you learn the answer to a question is by asking it.

"Alice Harker? If she'd had brothers they wouldn't have admitted it."

"So who *have* you talked to me about?"

He rubbed his chin and then transferred his attention lower down, tugging at his loose shirt where the fat bulged through. "Nobody," he said at last. "Why?"

"Nobody came to you and asked for a recommendation?"

"Simeon," he said, "I haven't told anybody about what you did for me." He finished with his shirt. "How could I, you know?"

"Sensitive."

"Dynamite. Especially for a fat middle-aged actor who's

earning a decent paycheck for the first time since he stopped selling real estate."

"So not a soul?"

He opened his mouth and then closed it again. "Nobody at all."

"Okay. Do you know a guy in his late thirties, bony and unpleasant, with a flat-top? Got a tailor who should be a vivisectionist, makes a lot of spit noises when he talks?"

"I certainly hope not."

"Big Adam's apple? Blue eyes?"

"Uh-uh."

"Insists on perfect understanding all the time?"

Something flickered in Skippy's eyes. "Like how?" he said.

"Like asking 'Do you understand?' after every declarative sentence. Like grilling waiters on whether they've got his order straight."

"No," Skippy said shortly. He looked nervous. "Why?"

"Somebody's jerking me around. Somebody who said you sent him."

"Simeon, I didn't send anybody."

"Somebody who maybe set somebody up to get killed."

Skippy's eyes widened. Then a peal of bells rang out, a secular angelus floating through the mists of Big Sur.

"That's it," he said. "Come with me?"

"You don't know anything about it."

"Zip," he said, "nothing. I'm sorry. Come on, I want a decent seat."

"For what?"

"The Revealing."

6

"I t's the best thing that's happened to me since my second divorce," Skippy said earnestly as he steered us between buildings toward a large lighted structure. He was making an obvious effort to keep his fervor in check, but his hammy hand clutched my arm as if he were afraid I'd try to make a break for it.

The paths were full of people, young, old, and in between, mostly white, mostly prosperous-looking, clearly eager to answer the summons of the bell. Ever the gentleman, Skippy stopped to allow an old lady in a walker to make a wobbly right from a tributary path onto the main drag. Listener Simpson was helping her, to the old lady's obvious irritation, and she flashed us a harried smile. Once they'd set off in front of us, Skippy hit his pedestrian's overdrive and dragged me past them.

"So why is it so great? Are your arteries any better? Is your blood pressure down?"

"No and yes, in order. Even with all this blubber, my blood pressure is lower than it's ever been. And without medication, too," he added triumphantly.

This was a revelation. Back when I'd known him, Skippy's medicine cabinet had been bigger than my living room. "Your druggist must be furious," I said.

We were slowing now as the faithful converged into a couple of well-behaved lines in order to pass through the single open door. The light flooding through the door was brilliant. We'd walked a quarter of a mile, and despite the coolness of the night, Skippy's face was filmed with an enthusiast's sweat.

"Calm down," I said. "Bliss can kill. Orgasms claim many lives each year."

"That's another thing," he said, heedless of all the ears around us. "I feel much less compelled to womanize." One of Skippy's problems was that he didn't have a subconscious. Like a character in a Dostoyevsky novel, he said everything, and usually to the wrong person.

We were toddling slowly along in the line now. Skippy's eyes shone and he licked his lips hungrily. I felt as if I were boarding an airplane for Akron or Duluth, someplace I'd never been and didn't want to go.

"It's changed my life," he said. "The Church has changed my life. And at my age, too."

He was so eager for me to ask him about it that I almost didn't have the heart not to. But I managed.

"Look at me, Simeon," he finally said. "Do I look like a success?"

"Do you want me to say no? You're doing okay. Take away most successes' Piaget watches and they look like shoe salesmen. Dress a bum in Armani and spritz him with cologne, and he looks like the CEO of Gulf and Western."

"Yeah, yeah, turn it into a joke. But do I look like a Hollywood success?"

"Somebody has to play people who look like you."

"That's what I did for years. Walked by in the background wearing a plaid shirt and carrying a bottle in a bag. Bumped into featured players in elevators. I had a three-year stretch where my longest line was 'Oops.' Now I'm a star. So what's the difference?"

"I give." I hate guessing.

"The Church."

"The Church made you a star?"

"Sure it did. Of course it did. I'm only a TV star, I know that, but, Jesus, Simeon, do you know how much money I made last year?"

"Skippy," I said, disappointing the people nearest to us, "there are a few secrets a man should keep."

He clapped a hand guiltily over his mouth. "You're right," he said from behind it.

"But it's the Church that made the difference," I said by way of a prompt.

"Didn't I say so?"

"Can we be specific, or is that against the rules?"

"There aren't really any rules. It just gave me access to what I already had. I had the skills, I had the experience, the voice, I had all the resources it took to be successful. But I didn't know how to get to them. It was like I was living in a diamond mine but I didn't know what a diamond looked like."

"At the risk of prolonging the metaphor, diamonds look like gray pebbles until they're cut."

"Yeah, and I kept picking up the wrong pebbles. Except there aren't really any wrong pebbles, it all depends on what you want to do with them. If you're going to throw one at a dog, it doesn't have to be a diamond. It all depends on what the moment demands."

"The moment." We were close to the door now, and the hard white light bathed Skippy's face like a second-rate special effect in an Old Testament movie. He looked like a tax collector about to be born again, bad casting for Saul of Tarsus.

"Do you have any idea how terrified I used to be in auditions?"

"No," I said, "but I would be too."

"I couldn't look anybody in the eye. I couldn't use my voice, I'd just mumble at the floor. I couldn't find the experiences that would have brought the part to life. I was picking up all the wrong pebbles."

"Good evening, Mr. Miller," said a woman at the door whom I'd never seen before. "Good evening, Mr. Grist. Welcome to your first Revealing."

Skippy beamed and we filed past. "Christ," I said, "even Japan isn't that efficient."

"So the thing is," Skippy continued as we went through the brilliant light, courtesy of half a dozen thousand-watt spots, and through a second door into the auditorium proper, "the thing is that I didn't realize that everybody—all those casting directors and producers and directors—was in the moment with me and that the moment was in perfect harmony. And I had all my memories and all my experiences with me too."

We were sloping down an aisle in a large hall that was already mostly full. Looking around, I realized that we hadn't had to hurry; here, as in Orwell, some were more equal than others, although Skippy had missed it. A gray-suited Listener, or something, beckoned us to two seats down front. The stage had more flowers on it than the average gardener sees during the month of May. Bells tintinnabulated over the loudspeakers.

"The thing is," Skippy said again, "that there's no reason to be frightened by any situation if you know the moment is in harmony, and especially not if the other people *don't* know it." He counted on his fingers to make sure he had his verbs straight and then nodded. "All you have to do is key into the moment, surf it like a wave. It's all going in one direction. If you try to fight it, like I used to do, you drown. If you paddle too hard, then you get ahead of it, like I also used to do, and you get slammed into the sand. Just sense it and you can glide down its surface, like the surfer and the wave."

We were sitting, surrounded by people. The bells inspissated in the air. They sounded vaguely Tibetan.

"Swell," I said. "What happens if it gets choppy?"

"What's choppy? Everything's choppy. Nobody's ironed time for us to make it all smooth and starchy. A storm is just a succession of moments, and even that's an illusion. There's only one moment, now, and it and the storm are one. Nothing from the past should weigh you down. Nothing in the future should surprise you. It's all one everlasting moment, and you're already in balance with it. Do you think the ocean is surprised by the waves on its surface? All you have to do is let it carry you."

Skippy laughed just as the lights dimmed. "You just ride on in,' he said. A couple of people shushed him. When they recognized Skippy, they stopped shushing.

The lights on the stage were tremendous enough to make me wonder what the Church of the Eternal Moment's electrical bills might be. A sober-looking individual in a dark suit welcomed us from behind a bleached pine podium. When he'd finished, a curtain behind him rose soundlessly and a sextet—guitar, piano, and four vocalists—went to work.

Their specialty was rewriting the hits. They started with "It Only Takes a Moment" and then segued into the Beatles' "Yesterday," with some minor reworking of the lyrics. Next to be butchered was the Stones' "Time Is on My Side," followed by a version of "By the Time I Get to Phoenix" that I couldn't follow at all. The general theme, though, was clearly time.

Skippy leaned over to me. "I've talked to them about the music," he whispered. "This isn't the good part."

"I hope to Christ not. I've heard better in an elevator."

"Just wait," Skippy said.

After the music ground to a merciful end and the curtain came down again, consigning the sextet to whatever richly deserved purgatory awaited them, the lights refocused to reveal the dark-suited individual at his place behind the podium. Two ordinary folding chairs had been placed stage center.

"Please compose yourselves," said the man at the podium as if he were trying to quell an irresistible mob impulse to dance in the aisles. "Make yourselves ready for the revealing."

All around me I had the sense of people taking a deep breath and holding it. From stage left a slender woman in her late thirties came out. She was followed by a golden-haired girl with long Alice in Wonderland locks falling around her shoulders. Cradled in the little girl's arms was a tiny gold kitten that matched her hair. The woman went to the podium and adjusted the microphone downward; she was much shorter than the man in the dark suit. The girl went straight to one of the chairs and sat down, facing out, with the kitten in her lap. She twisted one ankle behind the other nervously.

Applause rippled across the now-darkened auditorium.

The woman at the podium raised a hand. "Hello," she said into the darkness.

"Hello, Mary Claire," Skippy said. Skippy and about a thousand other people.

"Angel has an upset stomach tonight," the woman said into the microphone. "What can I say? She's a little girl."

There was a wave of sympathetic laughter. Mary Claire waved it away cheerfully.

"So anyway, nothing may happen. For those of you who have seen Revealings before, and I guess that's most of you, that should be no big deal. You know it doesn't happen every time. For the others, well, we're sorry. This isn't a fast-food restaurant. You can't always get a Big Mac here."

A few people clapped manfully, but it had a disappointed sound to it.

The little girl clutched the kitten and looked at her mother out of bewildered eyes and then gazed out at the audience. More than anything else she reminded me of a puppy who'd done something wrong but didn't know what it was.

"Poor baby," I said to Skippy.

"It's rough on her sometimes," Skippy said, "but it's worth it."

"It's worth it to you. What about her?"

"I'd trade places with her in a minute," he said.

"If I'd had my way," Mary Claire was saying in her amplified voice, "we wouldn't have come onto the stage tonight. I'd have put my baby to bed. But she wouldn't let me. There are a lot of people here, she said. Maybe something will happen. Didn't you, Angel?"

Angel looked at her mother and nodded distantly. She seemed to be receding, growing smaller and more distant, like Alice after the second "Drink me." Her dress was immaculate white, a blinding white that seemed somehow to make her hair even blonder. She was wearing white socks above flat black patent leather shoes. In all, she was a truly beautiful child.

"Isn't she gorgeous?" Skippy said. It was the second time my mind had been read that evening. I felt like a library book; anybody could check me out.

"Even if nothing happens," Mary Claire said, "we'll meet you in the other room afterward. Or I will, anyway. Angel may not feel up to it. Are you okay, Angel?"

Angel was staring at her mother. Slowly she shook her head in the negative. Her jaw was hanging open.

Mary Claire looked at her watch. "We've been up here four minutes," she said a little nervously. "If Angel doesn't Speak in a minute, we'll go back home. Five minutes is usually—"

Angel groaned. Her head lolled back and her right hand slipped from her lap and hung lifelessly at her side. The kitten looked right and left. Angel shuddered.

"You are the fisherman," she said in a preternaturally deep voice. "And you are the lake."

My neck prickled.

Mary Claire stepped away from the microphone and gave her daughter a concerned look. She might as well have been shooting at a rainbow; Angel wasn't there anymore.

"You float on the skin of your past," Angel said, her eyes wide and sightless, "suspended above the dark landscape below. There are hills there and valleys there. You created them but you've forgotten where they are."

Her mouth moved in time with the words, but it wasn't a little girl's voice. And yet it *was* her voice, there could be no doubt about it.

"You cast your line down into the waters and you bring up small pieces of yourself. They are bright, silvery, and quick. But how many more shimmer away, how many escape, every time your line splashes into the water?"

"Hot shit," Skippy whispered to himself.

"You must do more," the voice speaking through Angel said. "You must learn the map of that invisible landscape below. It is the map of your life."

"And a little child shall lead them," someone said behind me.

"Why should they escape, those silvery ones?" Angel said. Her body was limp and lifeless. Her spine sagged against the hard back of the chair. Only the jaw seemed to be animated. It moved as though it had a life of its own. The kitten had jumped from her lap and strolled offstage.

"They escape because you throw your nets, you cast your hooks, into the past. There is no past. You know that and you've always known it. A baby knows it.

"The eternal moment is now. Only by existing in now, now and only now, can you command the power you need to deal with a world that will break you, defraud you, destroy you, if you let it. There are things you must cast away.

"You have baggage with you. Cast it away; you can't fight with your hands full."

Skippy sighed beside me.

"You have memories with you," Angel droned on inexorably. "Cast them away; you can't float on the moment when you are anchored in the past. That is what the Listeners are for. To help you chart your explorations, to receive your memories.

"You have commitments with you. Cast them away; you can't diffuse your strength by fighting others' battles. You can only give them one thing, the gift of example, the example of someone who can survive in the world.

"You have your past with you. Cast it away. Become born in the eternal moment, the moment of now."

Except for the stretched, contorted voice, the hall was absolutely silent. No one coughed, no one shuffled his feet.

"There are devils in the world," Angel said. "They're not supernatural. They look like you and me. They *are* you and me." People cast sidelong looks at each other. "They're people who are stretched beyond their breaking point, people who are held together only by their skin, people who are trying to sustain the burden of their past, of all their pasts, in a world that exists only in the present.

"They are people who haven't learned to cast away the Four Last Things: possessions, memories, others, one's self— one's past self. Pity them."

Mary Claire had moved noiselessly across the stage to sit in the chair to her daughter's left. She looked worried.

"Your past is your enemy," Angel said. Her legs shivered, and suddenly she sat upright. Mary Claire put a hand on her shoulder but her daughter didn't feel it.

"You agonize," Angel said in a new and louder voice. Someone sobbed behind me. "You agonize because there are things in your past, things you've done, things you haven't done, things that were done to you.

"Release them.

"You feel inadequate. You feel inadequate because you are weighed down, chained down, with hopes, with fears, with old conceptions of your past. You're wrapped in a cocoon, the cocoon of your past.

"Break free from the cocoon.

"You are frightened."

Someone cried out, "I am."

"I can feel it," Angel said, "you *are* frightened. You are frightened because you can't look the moment in the eye. You can't look the moment in the eye because you're standing in a hole, the hole you've dug for yourself, the hole of your past, and you don't know how to step out of it.

"Step up, step out of it." Her arms lifted as though pulled upward by strings and crisscrossed in benediction.

"The moment is all," the voice said through her mouth. "The moment is harmonious. The moment is in perfect balance. The moment is a cross section of all that was, that is, and that will be. It is the pause between breathing out and breathing in. Without it there is no past, no present, no future. Everything is here. It is here now. Right now. You can learn to meet it. You are already in perfect balance with it. You just don't know it.

"Release yourself. Break free. Step up. Step up into the moment. Say good-bye to the Four Last Things and say hello to yourself. Say hello to the world as it really is. Say hello to power and fulfillment and satisfaction and perfect love.

"We can show you how.

"We can give you the key to the moment. It's so simple." She made a guttural sound that might have been a laugh.

"The key to the moment is the key to the world."

The little girl collapsed back into her chair and her eyes fluttered and then closed. Her mother placed a hand on her daughter's forehead and then got up and hurried to the microphone.

"That's all," she said. "I'm worried about Angel's stomach."

Two men in dark clothing came out and helped the little girl from her chair under Mary Claire's watchful eyes. Angel sagged between them as they guided her from the chair. Her head rolled back as though her neck were broken.

A murmur rolled through the auditorium. Skippy turned to me and placed a hand on my arm.

"Wow," he said reverently.

I looked around. People were watching the progress of the mother, the little girl, and the little girl's . . . the little girl's what? "Pallbearers" was the only word that came to mind. I turned back to Skippy.

"No shit," I said.

7

Absolutely everything was for sale. The room adjoining the auditorium was jammed full of tables, and each table was stacked with books, pamphlets, cassette tapes, and posters of Angel and Mary Claire. We'd been given a tote bag when we entered the room, and I stood next to Skippy, watching the church members drop the items into their bags like women at a hosiery sale. Nothing so vulgar as money changed hands; the people paid by waving their room keys.

Skippy seemed subdued. He'd acknowledged a few greetings from people he didn't seem to know very well, but other than that he'd said nothing since the Revealing ended.

"What is it?" I said.

"I wish you hadn't said that, about it being hard on her. Usually she doesn't seem to mind, but tonight I almost felt like she was fighting it." He looked around the room. A number of people had gathered around a table with a couple of industrial-size metal coffee urns on it. They were sipping from Styrofoam cups and chewing on pastries. "Most of the time she seems to enjoy it," he said. "She says she enjoys it."

"Skippy, how long have you been involved in the Church?"

"About five years."

"And she's how old, twelve?"

"I guess."

"So she's been doing this since she was seven at least?"

He looked bewildered for a moment. Then his face cleared. "No, no," he said. "I forgot, you don't know anything about it. She's the third Speaker. There were two before her," he added, helping me with my math.

"What happened to them?"

A heavyset woman with such round cheeks that she looked like she was carrying a week's supply of nuts in them came up to us and shyly asked Skippy for his autograph. Looking simultaneously pleased and distracted, he wrote his name on her tote bag. She blushed appreciatively and headed for the pastry table.

"What?" he said absently.

"What happened to the other two?"

"They stopped Speaking," he said. "It happens after a while. It'll happen to Angel in a year or two."

"And then what?"

"Some other little girl will start to Speak."

"They've all been girls?"

"Sure," he said a little impatiently. "Look it up, it's all in the books. The Speakers change but the Voice remains the same."

"And what's the Voice?"

"The Voice gives the Church direction. It's always the same Voice. It's a Spirit, Simeon," he said. "Its name is Aton, or Alon in the first Revealings. The first Speaker, poor little Anna, had a cleft palate, she couldn't say her T's, and all the early writings called it Alon. See, the writings come through the Speaker, and they're spoken onto tape and then written down, so the first writings got it wrong. But the Voice is the same, and it doesn't seem to care what you call it. I've heard two Speakers, and they sounded pretty much alike. If you don't believe me, all you have to do is listen to the cassettes. They're only nineteen-ninety-five. And the content, of course, the content is the same from Speaker to Speaker."

"Aton is Egyptian. The God of the Sun."

"The voice is American. It's told us that, it's said that it was an American last time around."

"Can we get some coffee?" I was beginning to feel like I weighed six hundred pounds. I hadn't slept much since Sally Oldfield was killed.

"I've got some whiskey in my pocket," Skippy said unexpectedly. "You want to step outside?"

Back out in the parking lot, Skippy shivered in the breeze as he pulled out a silver hip flask that could have dated from the twenties. "Glenfiddich," he said. "About a hundred years old and smoked over peat bogs or something." He handed it to me first.

I'm not a whiskey drinker, but the first sip converted me. It was warm and smoky and smoother than an Irish lie. I felt a red line of heat, like a thermometer in reverse, snake down from my throat to my belly button.

"I knew there was a reason for grain," I said, "other than roughage I mean." I handed it back. The world looked a lot better. The cypresses, black against the spangling of stars, achieved the spiral harmony Van Gogh had painted. Skippy gulped twice and then burped.

"This is a no-no," he said, wiping his mouth and giving the flask back. "No drinking during the retreat."

"I thought there weren't any rules."

"Normally there aren't. But this thing, this retreat, is like a fat farm for the consciousness. Just like you're not supposed to slip away to Winchell's for a doughnut while you're losing weight, you're not supposed to cloud your consciousness while you're here."

I took a much longer swig this time. The flask held more than I'd thought. "Sounds reasonable," I said, swallowing. "Are you sure this stuff is legal?"

I was positive that Skippy's answer made sense, but it was hard to make it out around the neck of the flask, which was lodged between his lips. I hadn't eaten in hours, and I felt suddenly light-headed. "Damnaroonies," I said. "Gimme that."

He did. This time I was the one who burped. I tried to hand the flask back, but Skippy was looking at his watch and I almost dropped it. "Any minute now, she should be coming in," he said.

"Who?"

"Angel. And Mary Claire. Don't you want to see them?"

Since I still had the flask, I took another swipe at it. "Sure, I want to see them. Let's go."

"Just a minute." Skippy turned the flask to a ninety-degree angle and drained it. "You know," he said confidingly, "as a great statesman and drinker once said, there is some shit up with which I will not put. That's Winston Churchill, when some twit tried to edit his prose. Why shouldn't a sentence end with a preposition?"

"Every sentence has to end somewhere," I said. "Unless you're Marcel Proust."

"Prowst. I always pronounced it Prowst."

"Well, he's dead anyway. Are we going in, or what?"

"In," Skippy said, shoving the flask back into his pocket. "About the shit I won't put up with, though. I mean, why shouldn't I drink? In moderation, of course."

"That goes without saying." I hiccuped. "Moderation is the important thing." Skippy laughed. Together we wove our way back into the hall.

It seemed brighter and noisier than when we'd left it. Also a lot more cheerful. The whiskey hummed a little Irish jig in my veins.

"So what happens to them?"

"Who?" Skippy said, squinting in the light. He was making a slightly erratic line for the pastries, with me trailing behind.

"The ones who stop Speaking."

"They grow up, I guess. Well, one of them, anyway. The first speaker, Anna Klein, she and her mother got killed a few years back. Automobile crash. They were on their way to one of the Church's cable broadcasts—did you know the Church has its own cable show?"

"No. How would I? I don't watch TV."

"Well, they were driving down from Yosemite, where they lived, she and her mother, I mean, and they blew a tire on the Grapevine. On the long downhill. Totaled. Terrible thing. You want a bear claw?"

"I'll take the whole bear." Skippy lurched around to hand me a pastry and succeeded in mashing it against my hand. "Oops," he said.

"Gee, you still remember your line. Were they alone in the car?"

"Yeah, I think so. Let me get you another one."

"That's okay. My stomach doesn't know what it's supposed to look like. Whose fault was it?"

Skippy's face was red enough to make Listener Dooley give him a hard look from across the table. Dooley's whiskey nose quivered like a divining rod.

"Whose fault was what? The bear claw?"

"No. The accident. The bear claw was John Barleycorn's fault." I gave Lister Dooley a winning smile. "Great pastries," I said. "My compliments to the chef."

Skippy said, "The accident was the tire's fault."

Dooley twitched audibly and Skippy followed my gaze. "'Evening, Listener," he said genially. "What, no coffee?"

Dooley's little raisin eyes were nuggets of suspicion. "Mr. Miller " he began grimly, "alcohol is not . . ." I put a hand on Skippy's arm to steer him elsewhere.

A celesta rang out. Everyone looked at the far end of the room.

The bells were struck again and the crowd parted to admit Angel and Mary Claire. Both of them had changed clothes, the mother into a simple dark dress, and Angel into a sky-blue middy blouse with matching skirt. Her dazzling blond hair was pulled back into a ponytail now, and she looked like any other beautiful little girl. She held on to her mother's arm as though the presence of all the adults made her feel shy. She'd left the kitten backstage. There were four men with them, dressed alike in vaguely naval white jackets and dark trousers. A shimmer of coral behind them drew my eye, and I saw Dr. Merryman following along in their wake.

"I guess her stomach's better," Skippy said. "See, Simeon, she doesn't look like she's been through anything terrible."

"Who are the Gilbert-and-Sullivan sailors?"

"Ushers. They're supposed to take care of Mary Claire and Angel. Just in case of crazies, you know?"

People were pressing in on them now, squeezing past the Ushers to greet Angel and thank her for the Revealing. A couple of them shook her hand. Mary Claire's hand fell protectively onto her daughter's shoulder, but Angel ignored it. She exchanged polite words with the adults, and when a girl her own age came up to her, a friend, apparently, she whispered something and giggled.

"I want to meet them," I said.

"Sure," Skippy said, "no problem." We started toward them.

"What do I call her?"

"What do you mean? You think she's the Queen Mother or something? When she's not Speaking she's just a little kid. Call her Angel."

We were about ten feet from them when something behind us fell with a loud crash. I turned quickly to see the heavyset woman who'd asked for Skippy's autograph, looking mortally embarrassed in front of an overturned table of books. She and two Listeners started to pick them up. When I looked back at Angel, she was surrounded by a white wall of Ushers, as alert as Secret Service men, standing shoulder to shoulder. Merryman had one hand on Mary Claire's shoulder and the other on Angel's. His face was set and hard.

"Come on," Skippy said. "The emergency's over."

Merryman caught sight of us as we approached and he relaxed into a pointy-toothed smile. "Ah, Skippy," he said, "I see you found Simeon."

"How's Angel?" Skippy asked.

"Fine. Too many french fries. She and her mother went into the McDonald's in Carmel this afternoon, and Angel, as they put it these days, pigged out. Have you enjoyed yourself, Simeon?"

"It's been very instructive, Dick." The electricity between us was so negative that if we'd been hanging from the ceiling on wires we'd have flown apart.

"You'll want to say hello to Angel," he said. "And Mary Claire, of course."

Mary Claire gave me a grave smile and a cool hand. Up close there was something coarse and worn about her. Her hair wasn't quite clean, and there was a slack looseness to her full lips. Angel was chatting animatedly with Skippy, asking him something about the young male lead on his show, but when Merryman touched her shoulder she looked up politely.

"Angel Ellspeth, this is Simeon Grist. This was Simeon's first Revealing, Angel."

"Pleased to meetcha," Angel said in a voice that was pure New York. "Didja like it?"

I couldn't have been more surprised if she'd sung the bass aria from *Aïda*. If I'd had my back turned I would have thought it was a joke, Skippy imitating the Dead End Kids in falsetto.

"Yes," was the best I could manage at first. Then I said, "Did *you* like it?"

"Sure," she said, pronouncing it "shooah." She looked puzzled at the question.

"What does it feel like when you Speak?"

"Great." She gave me a broad smile. "It's like I got a really good friend, you know?"

"Do you remember what you said?"

"Never," Merryman said. "It's ironic. Angel is the only person in the room who doesn't hear the Revealing."

We smiled at each other over how ironic it was.

"I listen later, onna tape," Angel said in the voice of a castrato Manhattan cabdriver. "I got a little Walkman, I play it on that." She looked up at her mother. "I don't get a lot of it, though."

"We learn about the Church through Revealings, of course," Merryman said, "but we learn about ourselves through Listening, and children don't begin Listening sessions until they're ten. Even though they're spoken through her, the Revealings are a little advanced for her." He threw me the smile again. I didn't throw it back.

"Hell," Skippy said, looking apprehensively from Merryman to me and back again. "They're advanced for me."

Angel tugged at her mother's arm. Mary Claire leaned down, and Angel whispered something in her ear. Merryman watched them closely.

Mary Claire raised a hand. People stopped talking at once. "Angel's tired now" she said. "I've got to put her to bed. Please stay and enjoy yourselves. Over on Table Ten, by the way, are tapes of the First Revealing, through poor little Anna. This is the first time they've been available in some time. Thank you all for coming."

The Ushers closed ranks around them, and Angel, Mary Claire, and Merryman went back the way they'd come. I found myself looking at the back of Angel's slender neck, bared by the upsweep of the pony tail. It was a neck made for the headsman's ax.

"Hey, the time," Skippy said. "Your plane is at when?"

"Ten," I said, watching them go. Angel had hold of her mother's hand.

"You'd better roll. Unless you'd like to stay here, I mean. I've got an extra bed in my cottage. I've also got some more Glenfiddich. You could sit up and chat with Dr. Merryman, you seem to like him so much."

"Thanks," I said. "I've got an early morning, and it'll be better if the clock goes off in L.A."

He walked me out to the rented car. As I sat there fiddling with the controls and trying to remember how the damn thing started, he cleared his throat meaningfully and I looked up at him.

"So," he said. "Do you think I'm crazy?"

"No." I gave the steering wheel a half-twist and turned the key again. This time the engine caught. "I think I am."

My plane left two hours late. At two-twenty that morning I coasted Alice to a stop in front of Sally Oldfield's house and watched the rain spatter the windshield.

There wasn't a lighted window on the block. I could have fired a load of grapeshot down the middle of the street and not hit anyone. Even the cats were inside waiting for the rain to let up. The clouds were low enough to reflect the lights of the city with a chill, chalky glow. It looked like the cats were going to have a long wait.

I wasn't dressed for this. By the time I'd pushed open the little gate at the side of Sally's house, I was soaked to the skin and colder than the glimmer of hope at the gates of hell. The low-hanging leaves of a ficus brushed at my face as I tracked along the side of the house. They felt almost warm by comparison. I rounded the corner into the tiny backyard and found myself looking at a perfectly maintained little vegetable garden. I was so cold that my thought processes had slowed; it took me maybe ten seconds to realize why I could see it.

There were lights on in the back of the house.

I ducked beneath a window and let the rain pelt me. I had visions of running into the boys in blue. Then I remembered that they didn't have Sally's name, and I had visions of running into something worse.

The time seemed ripe for a futile gesture, so I turned up the collar on my shirt and got exactly what I should have expected: an icy rivulet of water down my back. In the conventions of Japanese samurai literature, such moments usually bring the hero instantaneous enlightenment. What this one brought me was an overpowering desire to sneeze.

But I didn't. And then I didn't again. In all, I didn't sneeze about once every thirty seconds during the fifteen minutes or so I huddled there waiting for any kind of movement within the house. When the fifteen minutes were up I raised myself an inch at a time and looked in through the window. Another futile gesture. The blinds were drawn.

Well, either someone was in there or they weren't, and I couldn't squat in the lettuce any longer without running the risk of hypothermia. I went to the back door and opened it, failing to be surprised by the fact that it was unlocked, and shouted cheerily, "Hi, honey, I'm home." I felt like Ricky Ricardo. Lucy, Fred and Ethel, Little Ricky, or any combination thereof would have looked very good to me.

They weren't there, or if they were, they didn't answer. I was in a laundry room. The dryer was open and clothes were spilled out of it, a cascade of white onto the red clay tile floor. Sally Oldfield had looked like the kind of woman who sorted her whites. She hadn't looked like the kind of woman who emptied her dryer onto the floor.

Most laundry rooms open onto kitchens; it's cheaper for the contractors to keep all the plumbing in one place. Sally's house was no exception. I eased open the door at the end of the laundry room and stood there staring at chaos.

The drawers had all been pulled out and dumped upside down into the center of the room. Cooking implements were scattered everywhere. The top of the stove had been pulled off to reveal the gas pipes beneath. Pilot lights glowed a pale blue. The test of a great housekeeper is the area beneath the cooktop. Sally's was immaculate. I felt obscurely proud of her.

Whoever had taken the place apart had been uncommonly thorough. In the tiny dining room the table was upside down, as were the chairs, just in case something had been taped to their undersides. The sofa in the cozy little living room had been dismantled and the cushions and backs had been slit open. The oval hooked rug, probably a family hand me down, had been yanked to one side and turned over.

On the floor in a corner, near an uprooted potted palm, some rectangles caught my attention. I picked them up, shook the potting soil off them, and turned them over.

Pictures. Sally and a man who might have been Mr. Oldfield smiled into the camera, standing in front of someplace tropical, Hawaii maybe. Sally looked young and brave and full of conviction: this marriage was going to last forever. Their clothes, post-hippie loose and colorful, dated the pictures in the seventies.

The photographs had been torn from their frames. In two of them, a knife had made a savage X through Sally's face. The man who held the knife must have known he had all the time in the world, pausing for a meaningless act of spite. I felt murderous.

It was the same story everywhere. She had slept in a single bed, in a room that had once been almost Japanese in its austerity. The bed had been ravaged with the knife, one long jagged slash running from the head of the narrow mattress to the foot. Near an upended vanity table I picked up a hairbrush. It had a few of her hairs in it.

I sat on the box spring and pictured her getting up in the morning. She would have put on the pale blue robe that lay crumpled against the wall and gone into the bathroom for her shower. Then, probably even before she drank her coffee, she would have sat in the early sunlight streaming through the east-facing bedroom windows and brushed her hair. She'd had beautiful hair. She'd taken care of her hair, not out of vanity but out of self-respect.

"What was your secret, Sally?" I said out loud. "Why did

they do it?" This wasn't random, it wasn't a sex slaying that began and ended in some shithouse motel on Sunset. Sally Oldfield, as sweet as she had seemed to be, had gotten mixed up with pros.

In all, I sat there for an hour. Then I left, closing the front door on the odds and ends of Sally Oldfield's life and on her secret too.

8

Her name was Rhoda Gerwitz, and she'd just canceled her wedding.

"I mean, honest to God, the creep, he's got the emotional depth of a cold sore. All chin and no forehead," she said around a mouthful of hamburger. She'd briefly considered the chef's salad and then rejected it; after all, she could stop worrying about fitting into her wedding dress.

"Can you imagine?" She extricated a limp piece of onion from her mouth, looked at it critically, and put it on the edge of her plate. "Here's my best friend, my number-one bridesmaid, vanished from the face of the earth. I was going to heave the bouquet straight at her, and she's fallen over the edge somewhere. Well, how could I don the lace and orange blossoms and waltz down the aisle under such a cloud? Pass the catsup?"

I handed it to her and she upended it over her french fries. It made a gurgling sound. "If you're a girl," she continued, monitoring the catsup's flow, "men being what they are, odds are pretty good you're going to marry a jerk. No offense, I hope, present company excepted, and you seem like a nice-enough guy. But there's jerks and then there's jerks. If you're going to put up a sign that says NO JERKS, you're going to be an old maid." She giggled. "I always loved that expression," she said. " 'Old maid.' Like there's no way to have fun except getting married. If mama only knew. Still, like I said, there's jerks and jerks. A girl's gotta have standards."

"And his J.Q. was too high."

She stopped chewing and gave me a level gaze. "J.Q.?"

"Jerk Quotient."

She sputtered and grabbed a napkin. "Don't *do* that," she said. "Not when my mouth is full. Sally always says that the only problem with eating lunch with me is that she needs a raincoat." She stopped talking, looked at the burger, and put it down. "Aah, shit," she said, "Sally." She dabbed at a corner of her mouth with her napkin. It was the wrong corner. "How long have you known her for?"

I tried to remember what I'd told Rhoda on the phone, couldn't, and said, "A few months. Enough to want to try to find her." I'd spent most of two days finding out everything I could about Sally Oldfield, and I almost felt like I was telling the truth. Patrick Henry had used his L.A. *Times* clout to trace Rhoda Gerwitz's name from the license plate I gave him, in exchange for a renewed promise to speak to him and only him when and if there were anything worth telling. I'd called Rhoda at Monument Records and set up a lunch.

"The cops," Rhoda was saying. "If she's not dead, they don't want to know about it. It's enough to make you crazy. I've been to her house, knocked on the door, phoned her a dozen times. They didn't even know the color of her eyes. And then there's Herbert. Herbert—that's el jerkerino's name—says to me, 'You don't need a bridesmaid to get married, all you need is a groom.' Can you imagine? All I asked was to put it off until she turned up, or . . . well, you know. The sonofabitch. But listen, even if he's as dumb as a toadstool, you're not supposed to explain to a guy that's popped the question, so to speak, that a husband is a husband but a girlfriend is for life. This is not considered good strategy in the war between the sexes." The skin around her eyes crumpled up and she poked the hamburger with her index finger. It didn't poke back. "Do you think she's okay?" she asked the hamburger. "I don't think she's okay."

She blinked a couple of times, fast. "Can you return a wedding gown?" she said.

"I don't know. I've never bought one."

"Sally said . . ." She swallowed even though her mouth

was empty. "Sally said that the trouble with a wedding gown
was all those miles of fabric. If the bride had as much
mileage on her as the gown, she said, no man would ever
get married." She tried a smile but it didn't work out.
"Anyway, they had to let it out," she said. "After all those
salads. They're not going to take it back. And even if they
did, I think I'd keep it. As a reminder of all the jerks in the
world." She lifted her glass of beer.

"To Sally turning up safe," she said. "So you're a bachelor, huh?"

"I'm too old to be a bachelor. I'm an old maid."

"What're you anyway, thirty, thirty-one?"

"Thirty-four."

"Sally is thirty-two. Always worried about her birthday,
which, by the way, is coming up, always wrinkling her nose
like every birthday took her one step closer to looking like
Margo coming out of Shangri-La, you know that movie?
She's always checking her hair like she expects it to be four
feet long and gray." She swirled the beer in the glass. "Shit,"
she said, looking at it, "she'd better be okay."

The waiter appeared. It was Roberto. Everybody who
worked at Monument Records seemed to eat at Nickodell's,
and Rhoda had chosen it out of all the restaurants in Hollywood when I'd called to ask her to lunch. Roberto looked
more than professionally concerned. "Somethin' wrong with
the lady's hamburger?"

Rhoda summoned up a sweet smile. "No," she said, "the
hamburger's fine. Something's wrong with the lady."

"You wan' Pepto-Bismol?" Roberto asked. "We always
got a lot of Pepto-Bismol." He smiled sympathetically and
included me in it. "Pepto-Bismol is our insurance company."

"It's okay, Roberto." He started to leave. "Wait," I said.
"Last time I was in here, the guy I was with, you remember?"

"Terrible guy, bad-lookin' guy. Look like he wan' to eat
the Easter bunny raw. I remember."

"Did you ever see him before? Do you know his name?"

Roberto squinted at the wall as if he expected to see a
Technicolor film unspool on its surface. "Naw," he finally
said. "Somebody as mean as that, I remember." He shrugged.
"Sorry," he said, dismissing it. In a waiter's world there are
a lot of bad guys.

"No problem. Thanks anyway."

"So what was that about?" Rhoda said as Roberto vanished toward the kitchen.

"Nothing. Another shitty business lunch."

"Yeah. A business lunch is the shortest route between eating and the bathroom. Do not pass go. Do not taste. In fact, skip the esophagus entirely. It' supposed to punctuate the day, right? Sally said once that lunch was the only punctuation mark softer than a comma."

"You're good friends."

"She's a good friend. You think I'm easy to put up with? Until Herbert proposed I was five miles of barbed wire. Get married, everybody kept saying. Listen to your biological tock clicking." She picked up her beer and looked at it with one eye shut. " 'Tock clicking,' " she said. "Am I a cheap drunk, or what? So no wonder I was grouchy, the whole world waiting to watch me walk the plank to *Lohengrin*, all these damn women in Connecticut writing big fat books about the joys of late-life motherhood, and all I really want to do is go home to my dinky little apartment, feed the cat, and try to stay reasonably sober until it's time for David Letterman. Otherwise I don't get the jokes."

She drew a long breath. "Sally let me take it all out on her. When Herbert, may he catch a fatal case of athlete's foot and die slowly from his ankles up, when Herbert proposed and I didn't know what to do, Sally listened to me for weeks and weeks. Must have seemed like years to her. One day I was yes, one day I was no. Whichever way I felt, I'd ask for advice, which Sally would dutifully give, and I'd be back the next day with the same goddamned questions. And she'd listen again and give me advice again, and then we'd do it all over."

She picked up the beer and put it down again. "I'd like a real drink," she said. "A screwdriver, is that okay?"

I signaled for Roberto and ordered. "What advice did she give you? Did she want you to marry Herbert or not?"

Rhoda's laugh was short and dry. "She didn't give a shit either way. She just wanted me to do whatever would make me happy. It wouldn't have made any difference if Herbert was Bigfoot, as long as she was sure that he was what I wanted. Hell, if Bigfoot had been the boy of my dreams, she would have helped him rent a tuxedo."

"She was indifferent?"

She gave me a long look while she tried to figure out what to say. "No," she said finally. "She wasn't indifferent. She just wanted to make sure that I was doing what *I* really wanted. If I did, whatever that was, it was okay with her.

"She kept asking me questions. Sometimes they seemed dumb, like who was more important to me, my mother or me? Except, you see, that's not so dumb, because it's my mother who really wants me to get married. Or she'd ask me things about Herbert, like did he have a good time when he got drunk, and what didn't he want to talk about *ever*, and did he make love like it was fun or like he was trying to remember how he was supposed to do it, and did he seem to have a sense of humor about his underwear? Questions that made me look at him different. Wasted effort, the putz."

"Is Sally married?"

"Sally? Sally married?" She picked up the screwdriver and took a long pull. "Golly, do you know, I don't know." She looked stricken. "Gee, isn't that awful? That's the kind of question Sally used to ask, something that made you realize something about yourself. Oh, my God, I'm ashamed of myself. I was so busy talking to her that I hardly ever listened."

"In every relationship there's a talker and a listener. You're the talker, that's all," I said, trying to smooth her out. "Sally is the listener." Then I shut up so I could register the little click in my brain. I looked at a morose knot of disc jockeys at the bar; ratings must have been down. "Rhoda. What's Sally's religion?"

"Religion? *That* she does talk about, in the last year or so, anyway. She keeps trying to get me to go with her. I'm not much into religion, you know, I'm supposed to be a Jew but I might just as well be a Chevrolet for all the attention I pay to it. But one thing I've got less than zero interest in is trendy California cults."

"I'm sorry to do this," I said, standing up, "but I've got to go. Listen, the meal, anything you want, it's all on my credit card, and it's already signed. Have another drink,

have a burger, have whatever you like. Better still, call in
sick and go home, skip the rest of the day. Wash your hair.
Stop worrying about Sally. Maybe you did do all the talking,
but you're a terrific person and she was lucky to have you."

She looked up at me with her mouth open.

"And when Herbert calls," I said, "tell him to go fuck
himself."

Sally was a Listener. Listener Simpson's mania for clarity
had echoed Harker's insistence on understanding. That had
been the only part of my description of Harker that had
brought Skippy down from his plateau of bliss. I had to get
home and review my notes.

At the bottom of my unpaved driveway I caught a whiff
of something sharp, sweet, old, and slightly sickening. I
slowed down for a moment to check it out but didn't see
anything. Then, in a hurry, I slogged up through the mud at
a forty-degree angle, slipping and falling to my knees only
twice, not bad for a wet November afternoon on an unpaved driveway that asked nothing less from the world than
that it should be beamed up *Star Trek*-style and then let
down in Switzerland, where it could be pressed into service
as an Olympic ski ramp.

That would be all right if the house at the top of it were
worth getting to. It was slapped together in the twenties by
an embittered alcoholic hermit who wanted to flee the mad-
ding crowd. He kept himself relatively sober long enough to
build the thing—it couldn't have taken more than a couple
of months—and then went on a bourbon toot that ended a
year later when he saw workers paving Old Topanga Canyon about a half-mile below. He promptly tied a rope around
the living-room rafter and kicked a chair out from under
him.

He hung there, mummified by the dry summer heat, like
a big strip of bacon for a couple of years, sharing the house
with a pair of red-tailed hawks, until he was discovered by a
determined census taker. The house passed to the hermit's
sister, and then to her son, who went to the Balkans and
took himself a Balkan bride during World War II. He then
got himself killed in the war, and ownership of the house

devolved upon the Balkan bride, Mrs. Yount. The house was essentially a three-room wooden cabin, but it had the best view in Topanga, all the way from the massive red outcrop of Big Rock to the little settlement of Topanga on the way to the ocean. And there were acres of clean stars above it at night.

Of course, to get to all of that, you had to climb the driveway. Once I made it to the top and muscled open the swollen wooden door, I looked on top of the computer, the first place I always looked because it was where I put everything. And there they were. Before I looked at them, I got a fire burning in the potbellied stove.

With the wood crackling, steam rising from the damp carpet, and rain throwing handfuls of tacks against the roof, I surveyed my options. There were remarkably few of them.

I didn't have a client. I *did* have a grudge against Needle-nose. I'd liked Sally Oldfield. And I had some information. Whatever chain of events had culminated in the murder of Sally Oldfield had begun with the Church of the Eternal Moment.

The obvious thing to do was call the cops.

Generally, I'd prefer not to call the cops. If everybody called the cops, I wouldn't be in business, and I'd hate to start a trend. But nobody was paying for my time now that the ersatz Ambrose Harker had faded back into whatever woodwork he'd crawled out of, and somebody had to do something about Sally.

So I went over to the computer, got the folded printout of my notes on the case, smoothed them open, and read over them. Then I did what I didn't want to do. I called my pet cop.

Alvin Hammond, Sergeant, LAPD, didn't know he was my pet cop. Sergeant Hammond weighed a conservative two hundred and thirty-five pounds, ten pounds of which were bass voice and twenty-five pounds of which were potential whisker, and he wasn't given to terms of coy affection, however discreet. What Sergeant Hammond was given to was drinking lethal quantities of Scotch in cop bars, with the ultimate objective of being the last man in the room who could stand up. I'd begun risking life and liver in police bars

downtown when I first became an investigator. It had occurred to me that I might need to know one cop better than
you usually get to know the guy who's writing you a speed-
ing ticket. I'd remained relatively conscious longer than Al
Hammond on two or three nights, and that was the extent
of the bond between us.

"Records," said a young voice on the other end of the
phone. Al had been in Records for a year as punishment for
neglecting to read some well-connected alleged perp's rights
to him, and he wanted to get out about as badly as most
would-be transsexuals wanted to get to Denmark and the
right doctor.

"Is Al Hammond around?" You didn't call him Alvin, at
least not if you wanted to remain an operative biped.

"Sergeant Hammond is indisposed."

"What happened? They put a new stock of magazines in
the john?"

"Is that supposed to be funny, sir?" Great. A prissy cop.

"A thousand apologies for my lapse in taste. I thought I
was talking to the LAPD."

"Your name, sir?"

"Inspector Grist. What's yours, son?"

I could actually hear him sit up. "Um, Hinckley, sir. I
mean, Inspector."

"Um Hinckley? That's an unusual name. What is it,
Welsh?"

"Actually, sir, it's English."

"Well, Um Hinckley, why don't you trot along and see if
you can snap Sergeant Hammond out of his fleshy reverie
and get him to the phone. *Tout suite*, okay?"

"Yessir."

"And let's have a little snap to it."

"Yes, *sir*." The phone clattered to the desk.

I flipped through my notes, put the phone down to get a
pencil, and added Rhoda Gerwitz's name and phone number. When I came back to the phone, Hammond was already there.

"There's a patrol car on the way," he said.

"I'm in no danger."

"Yes, you are. It's against the law to impersonate an
officer. Poor Hinckley's shitting bricks."

"It's probably the first bowel movement he's had in months, then. If his ass were any tighter he could wear it on his forehead and no one would notice. Did you lend him your magazine?"

"The *Atlantic Monthly*," he said. "I never miss the book reviews."

"Where did Hinckley come from, anyway? Promoted directly from the Brownies?"

"Times being what they are, we're lucky to have him. You think he's bad"—he exhaled a lungful of smoke—"you should see Willis. It takes him ten minutes to get into his uniform and fifteen to do his eyes. What do you want, anyway?"

"Oh, you know. Catching up with an old friend. Taking notes on how a real man talks. Passing time until the videotape rewinds."

"I'm being paid by the city," he said with exaggerated patience. "These are your tax dollars at work, here."

"This will surprise you, but I don't want anything. I'm calling to give you something."

"Like what?"

"Like a Jane Doe. Recently deceased in the Sleepy Bear Motel on Sunset."

"That block, we call it Sinset."

"Clever."

"These are the jokes," he said. "You don't like them, go back to the VCR."

"I don't like them, I call the *Times*. They might be interested in an unsolved murder."

"I'm interested. If you were here you could see how my ears are standing up. You could see me reaching for a pencil and a clean sheet of paper. You could see me dreaming about getting out of here and making lieutenant."

"I don't want to talk on the phone," I said. "I've got some notes that I want to give you. When can I see you?"

"You know who she is? You know who bought her the big ticket?"

"The big ticket?" I said. "Al, are you on TV? Is there a *Sixty Minutes* crew in the room?"

"What have you got?" he asked impatiently.

"Some facts that might keep you awake."

"This is straight?"

"Straighter than Carrie Nation."

"Not here, then. I'd like to keep it to myself until I can pop it at the morning meeting. I get off at nine. How about the Red Dog?"

The Red Dog was one of Al's bars, all Scotch and sawdust on the floor. The male-hormone content at any given moment was higher than that of the East German women's Olympic track team.

"The Red Dog," I said. "Nine-thirty."

"What's her name?"

"And her address," I said. "But not till the Red Dog. You're buying."

"Wear a white carnation so I'll know you."

"In the Red Dog? We're talking about multiple fractures for dessert."

"Yeah," he said, hanging up.

I didn't have anything to do in the meantime, so I did it. After I hung up I tried to avoid the refrigerator, which was waving its handle at me to remind me of the three sixteen-ounce bottles of Singha Beer inside, resting innocently on their sides. I reviewed my notes and looked at my watch. After eleven minutes I stopped reviewing my notes, got up, and reviewed the refrigerator. It looked the same as ever on the outside, my shopping list scrawled on the door in erasable Magic Marker. It looked the same on the inside, too, until I closed the door. When I did, there were only two bottles of Singha inside.

Ten minutes later, and feeling considerably better, I was reopening the refrigerator door when the phone rang. "Balls," I said to the beer. I tracked across the living room and picked up the phone.

"Al?" I said.

"Who the hell is Al?" said a voice that I remembered only too well. "This is Ambrose Harker."

9

W ith my left hand I hit the RECORD button on the answering machine and vamped until the red light came on.

"I've seen many unexpected things on my journey through the world," I said, "but even to me it seems improbable that life is full of people named Ambrose Harker. And yet, apparently it is." The light blinked once and then glowed steadily. "Which Ambrose Harker is this?"

"I owe you money," he said.

The open refrigerator sent out a siren call that would have lured Ulysses onto the rocks even if he'd been tone deaf. "That's right," I said, "you do. Can you hold on for a second?"

"No." He hung up.

I looked at the receiver and then replaced it. "You'll be back," I said. I got up and opened a beer. I primed myself with several cold ounces and then primed the answering machine. By the time the phone shrilled at me, the tape was already running.

"It's your nickel," I said as I picked it up. I'd always wanted to say it to someone.

"It's a quarter," he said, literal as ever. "I need to talk to you."

"You need to talk to *me*? What a surprise. You hire me to watch someone, she gets killed, and then you vanish from the face of the earth, leaving me with nothing but a borrowed business card. How'd you know he was eating at Nickodell's anyway?"

"He always eats at Nickodell's. He's in the music business."

"And you're Dr. Livingstone, I presume."

"My name doesn't matter."

"Maybe it doesn't matter to you. To me, it matters. Sally Oldfield matters."

"Listen, that wasn't supposed to happen. Nobody was more surprised than I was."

"You were so surprised that you knew about it before I called to tell you. It must have been a terrific shock."

"I know you're not going to believe me now."

"Of course I'm going to believe you. You've got a phony name and phone number and you're involved in a murder, but that doesn't mean I'm not going to believe you. What about trust? What about the fellowship of man?"

"Honest to God. I didn't have anything to do with the murder."

"So who's the guy with the needle nose?"

There was a pause.

"Oh, come on," I said. "That question can't come as a complete surprise. What did you think I was going to ask you?"

"I can tell you," he said, lowering his voice. "I can tell you everything."

"You also said something about money."

"I owe you for two days," he said. "That's eight hundred dollars."

"I'll bet you've got a plan," I said, "about how you're going to pay me and explain everything to me and tell me your real name and then we'll both just sit back and have a good laugh over how complicated it all seemed."

"My name is Fauntleroy," he said unexpectedly. "Ellis Fauntleroy."

"This week."

"No, that's my real name."

"Well, why don't you come up here and show me your driver's license? Then we'll call each other by our right names for a while to get into practice and then you can tell me what you've got to say."

"I can't come there. What if they're watching you? I could get killed just for being in the same room with you."

"Who's they?"

Silence. Then he said, "You know."

"And you're telling me they're after you?"

He swallowed in his usual amplified manner. "I'm telling you that I'd be dead if they saw us together. You're going to have to come to me."

A gust of wind slapped the front of the house hard, and the rain rattled down. It was five-fifteen and dark. I didn't want to go anywhere until it was time to meet Hammond at the Red Dog.

"Same objection," I said. "If they're watching me, they're going to see us together, aren't they?"

"Not if you're careful. A detective as expensive as you, you should be able to spot a tail."

"How do I know I'm not walking into something?"

"You don't." No apologies and no attempt to persuade. That was reassuring in a backhanded kind of way.

"Why did you call me now?"

"Because I know too much. They made a mistake when they made me the one who hired you. I was the last person they should have chosen, and now they're worrying about it."

"Where do they think you are now?"

"They don't know. They haven't started to wonder yet."

I looked down at the cassette, its little hubs rotating slowly. "This is all very enlightening, but I could really use a name or two. Like exactly who hired you."

He made a noise that sounded suspiciously like a snicker. "First we talk," he said. "I need something out of you. If I get it, you'll get something out of me."

"You mean you really didn't call to pay me my money? Human nature is such a disappointment."

"The money's here. Are you going to come or not? I haven't got all night. I've got to get someplace where they can see me or they're going to start looking for me, and I'll be in even worse trouble."

I weighed it. There was no question in my mind that he was frightened. Harker, or Fauntleroy, was too unimaginative to be an actor. On the other hand, I could have been making an appointment to get my head blown off. I've grown fond of my head.

"You still there?" he said impatiently.

"How come it's always raining when I talk to you?"

"Ask the weatherman. I'm at the TraveLodge in Santa Monica, room three-eleven. You know where it is?"

Another motel. "Near Pico and the freeway."

"I'll be here for forty-five minutes." The line went dead.

I turned off the recorder in the answering machine and thought about it. A motel room with Ambrose Harker/Ellis Fauntleroy didn't sound like my idea of paradise, or even Florida. If I went, I might come back with part of me missing. If I didn't go, I'd probably never get back on the trail of the guy who'd murdered Sally Oldfield. Mentally I flipped a coin, giving Sally heads. Sally won. That's the trouble with flipping coins mentally.

I'd wasted seven minutes. No point in changing; I'd just get wet again. I grabbed the keys, slalomed down the driveway, and started Alice.

As I hit the bottom of the canyon and turned left onto Old Topanga Canyon Boulevard, the rain eased up enough to let me see that the creek had risen to the danger point. One more night of heavy rain and we'd all be listening to the radio to find out which roads had washed away and what the alternative routes were, if any. For the seventeen millionth time I wondered why I hadn't moved into town years ago.

At the intersection of New Topanga and Old Topanga, flares blossomed in the darkness. I slowed down to a near-stop, inching along behind a long line of other fools who didn't have enough sense to stay in out of the rain. An old white VW van lay on its flattened top at the side of the road. There were people in it. The cop with the flashlight told me to keep moving, as though I were about to leap from the car for a closer look. By the time I made the right onto New Topanga and started skidding down toward the sea, I'd lost more than twenty minutes.

Well, he'd either be there or he wouldn't. Either way, I decided to cancel my appointment with Al Hammond. Things were moving again, and as long as they continued to move I'd work for free. Instead of hurrying, I concentrated on observing the laws of physics that would keep me on the road.

The ocean was a mess, white-capped and choppy, and the rain guttered down again as I headed up the Pacific Coast Highway and made a right onto Ocean Boulevard. At least there'd been no more heavy traffic. The neon of Santa Monica scattered itself into broken reflections on the wet pavement, and the sidewalks were empty. Bad night for restaurants. I realized I was hungry and remembered that I'd left most of my lunch sitting on the table opposite Rhoda Gerwitz.

With three minutes to go I swung into the TraveLodge parking lot and ran for cover. This wasn't just rain; this was the kind of deluge that city idiots say will be good for the crops, and farmers swear at. Using my highly trained powers of deduction, I guessed that room 311 would be on the third floor and got into the world's slowest elevator. By the time the doors slid open again, I'd had plenty of opportunity to review my life in detail and to wrap the fingers of my right hand around the automatic I'd taken from Alice's glove compartment. Using my left, I rapped at the door to 311.

"It's open," Harker called from inside. "Come in."

"Sure," I said. "Right after you open it."

I stepped back, clutching the gun in my windbreaker pocket, and waited. After a moment the door swung open and Harker stood there.

"I was about to leave," he said.

"Might have been a good idea. Open the door all the way. Slam it against the wall."

He did. He was wearing dark trousers and a white shirt, his tie partly unknotted. He hadn't shaved in days. His left hand was in his pocket.

A double bed covered in an unappealing shade of pumpkin stood against the far wall. "Take your hand out of your pocket," I said, "and hold your other hand in it. Good. Now, back up slowly and sit on the bed."

He did as he was told. I pushed at the door and it banged against the wall again.

"Nobody here?" I said, stepping into the room.

"You think I'm crazy?"

"One question at a time. That the bathroom?" I gestured at a door to my right.

"No," he said nastily. "It's the sitting room. I always insist on a suite."

Through the open door behind me I heard the rain increase in volume to a dull roar. "Let's go take a look," I said. "You first."

"Oh, come on," he said. "I told you I was alone."

"But that's a lie," I said pleasantly. "I'm here too. How can I trust you when you can't even tell the truth about something as simple as that?" I took the gun from my pocket and gave it a little wave in the direction of the bathroom. "After you, darling."

He grumbled, but he did it. I made him stand in the bathtub with his back to me while I checked the dressing room and the closet. All empty.

"Well, golly, Ambrose," I said, following him back out into the living room, "I'm sorry about all this. But these days, you know, a girl can't be too careful."

"You want me to sit on the bed again?" he asked sullenly.

"Let's not pout. The bed looks very comfortable. Sit, sit."

He did, and I reached behind me to close the door. There was a blur of movement to my right and the man who had come in and positioned himself behind the door while we were in the bathroom caught me at the base of the skull with something hard and heavy. As I headed for the carpet I saw Harker start to stand up, and then there was nothing but darkness and the mermaids singing, each to each.

It was the smell that woke me up.

My skull was clanging "The Anvil Chorus" and there was a red film over my eyes, but the smell pushed its way through. It was a sharp smell, but not fresh. It was a smell I hated.

I'd been lying facedown on the polyester carpet, and the blood from the cut on the back of my head had run down over my face. I had to wipe it from my eyes before I could focus.

What I saw was a two-year-old's view of the world: carpet, table legs, and the bottom of a pumpkin-colored bedspread. Fighting the gravity of Jupiter, I lifted my head and saw a pair of black shoes dangling over the edge of the bed.

I laid my head back down on the carpet and said, "Shit." Sleep seemed like a good idea. I closed my eyes. Then whatever obscure corner of my brain was still up and about sounded the alarm to let me know that sleep was, all things considered, not really such a good idea. A fragment of Jack London pushed itself in front of me, something about people dozing off happily in the snow.

It took me maybe two minutes to get to my hands and knees and another minute, with some help from the table, to stand up. I had to wipe my face again before I could look around. Scalp wounds bleed ambitiously.

Ambrose Harker or Ellis Fauntleroy lay on the bed, clutching a pillow to his middle. He looked startled. The pillow had a couple of little black holes in it. The smell in the air was cordite, the stuff that makes guns go bang.

I held my head in one hand and picked up the pillow with the other. It was heavier than it should have been because it was saturated with blood. The pillow had functioned as a silencer and Harker's stomach had functioned as a target. Both had functioned flawlessly.

I let the pillow drop, and Harker made a rasping sound that trailed off into a gurgle. It was the last sound he ever made, and like all the others, it was louder than life.

My gun was gone. I should have known it would be gone. It didn't take an advanced degree in ballistics or an I.Q. much higher than room temperature to guess whose bullets had made such a travesty of Harker's viscera and whose prints were all over the gun.

After I washed the blood from my face I wiped everything I remembered touching and locked and closed the door behind me. A lot of good it would do. Somebody had the gun, and it wasn't anybody who wished me well.

On the drive home I had all I could do to turn four oncoming headlights into two and wonder where I'd put the iodine. By the time I'd scaled the driveway on all fours my head was slamming alarmingly and I was beginning to get mad.

The door to the house was open.

The message light on the answering machine blinked accusingly, but there was no way to know whether it had been Al Hammond or Mrs. Yount who'd called, because the cassette was gone.

II

Judgment

10

"If God doesn't want us to get drunk, why did He create alcohol? That's a good question," Dixie Cohen said, as though someone else had asked it. He was coasting into the final third of a sixteen-ounce bottle of Singha. I was lagging behind his pace while his ex-wife, Chantra, and my ex-girlfriend, Eleanor, sipped white wine together in the far corner of Eleanor's Venice apartment.

"Look at this group," I said. "The evening is rated double-ex."

"Dream on," Eleanor said without looking up. She and Chantra, who was an ex-Charlene, were looking over galley proofs of Eleanor's most recent book, *Two Fit*. Its literary aim was to help weight-conscious couples support each other in their fight against flab. Its publisher, an ultra-fit New Age vegetarian who, I'd been delighted to see, was losing his hair faster than most people lose cheap sunglasses, had proclaimed it an Important Book. Even more Important, he'd suggested in hushed tones, than her first, *Creative Stretching*, the third printing of which was selling briskly in better coed gyms and running stores from coast to coast. She'd already received an advance for her third work, *The Right-Brain Cookbook*, a new look at the old idea that some forms of nourishment qualified as brain food. I'd suggested it as an unpleasant joke and she'd taken it seriously enough to get a large number of dollars as encouragement from her publisher. Some joke. This was one of a number of social events designed to test what I sourly regarded as a completely spurious collation of creativity-enhancing recipes.

Dixie hefted his bottle and knocked back most of what remained. Chantra was going to be driving. "The first drunk," he intoned, warming to his subject as his blood alcohol rose, "after the Flood, of course, was Noah."

"The Flood," I said politely, picking for the thirtieth time that evening at the large bandage decorating the back of my head.

"Aha," Dixie said, eyeing my half-full bottle with more than a trace of envy. He rapped his own bottle with his signet ring and it made a hollow noise. "The Flood, indeed. Indeed, the Flood." From across the room Chantra said to Eleanor, "But what about complex carbohydrates?" I took Dixie's bottle away from him, poured three fingers of beer into it, and handed it back. "God had two chances to prevent the formation of Alcoholics Anonymous," Dixie said, drinking, "before and after the Flood. He blew it both times." He burped. "Good thing, too."

"Carbohydrates are in chapter thirteen," Eleanor said.

"Are you going to explain, Dixie, or do you want someone to ask you?" Chantra said. "Volunteers? Is there anyone in this room sufficiently immune to boredom to ask Dixie why God allowed alcohol to survive the Flood?"

"I think you just did," I said, getting up and going into the tiny overheated kitchen to grab a couple of fresh beers.

"Unless I'm deeply mistaken," Chantra said, "I've heard it before."

"According to Rabbi Eliezar—" Dixie began happily.

"No less," Chantra interjected.

"Woman, hold thy tongue. According to Rabbi Eliezar, no less, Noah took onto the ark a vine that had been cast with Adam out of Eden. Adam had his own problems with the grape, as you may recall. The oldest profession, actually, is probably that of wine-maker."

"No whores in Eden." I popped the bottle caps. "No money. *Nunc die gelt, ergo nunc die bimbos,*" I said in Latin and several other languages.

"Noah took the vine with him because he liked to eat grapes," Dixie continued as though no one had spoken. "Anyway, that's what he told everyone."

"He *could* tell everyone, too," Chantra said. "There were only twelve or thirteen people after the Flood."

"And that's just about the right number," I said, putting the bottles on the table. "Everything that's wrong with the world today comes from the fact that there are more than twelve people." My head hurt, and I rubbed the bandage again.

"Simeon," Chantra said, "what happened to the back of your head?" She'd been trying not to ask all evening.

"I cut myself shaving."

"When it came time to plant the grapevine," Dixie said doggedly, "Satan came along and offered to make sure there'd be a good crop. He suggested a sacrifice."

"Blame Satan," Eleanor said. "If he didn't exist, we'd have to invent him."

"These people were crazy about sacrifices," Dixie said. "They butchered a sheep every time they hiccuped. So Noah and Satan together, according to the rabbi, sacrificed a sheep, a lion, an ape, and a hog, using the blood as fertilizer."

"Blood is high in nitrogen," Eleanor said, sounding interested for the first time.

"Nitrogen, schmitrogen," Dixie said.

"He shaves the back of his head?" Chantra asked Eleanor.

"Only when he's going to meet someone behind him," Eleanor said.

"So Satan and Noah," Dixie plowed stubbornly along, "slaughtered all these poor stupid animals. And their blood fertilized the grapes. And that's why, after the first drink, one is as mild as a sheep, and after the second, one is courageous like a lion. After the third, one is stupid like an ape."

"One certainly is," said Chantra, who'd been keeping count.

"And after the fourth," Dixie said, glaring at her, "one wallows in mud, like a hog."

There was a silence that embraced the entire room. "That's the punch line?" I said.

"I don't know how to explain this to someone whose idea

of a theological authority is Don Rickles," Dixie said loftily, "but this is a sermon, not a joke."

"And I don't know how to explain this to a dinner guest," I said, "but most people in a small, convivial social gathering would prefer a joke to a sermon."

"California is so trivial," Dixie said.

"Boy," I said, "I bet their tongues would be hanging out in New York."

"Anyway, look what happened to poor Noah," Chantra said, coming to her ex-husband's rescue. "His own kid came in while Noah was sleeping it off and cut the poor old sot's balls off, or whatever he did."

"The most mysterious hundred and fifty words in the Bible." Dixie was warming up again.

Chantra emitted a ladylike groan. "I've made a *mistaaaake*," she wailed.

"So crime doesn't pay," said Eleanor, trying to put a conversational cap on it.

"I wouldn't go that far," Dixie said, taking a tremendous gulp from his bottle. "Look at the first murderer."

"A Bible class," Chantra said to the air. "Fifty-one years old and he has to take a Bible class."

"Fifty," Dixie said. "Fifty-one next week."

"What did happen to the first murderer?" I was interested in spite of myself.

"Say the magic word, win a hundred dollars," Eleanor said resignedly. She'd bandaged my head the evening before and she'd had enough of murderers for one week.

"Cain," Dixie said triumphantly. "Clobbered his insufferable schmuck of a brother in a field. Why? Because Abel's sacrifices—there we go again with the blood and guts—were accepted, and Cain's weren't."

I ran my personal mosaic of the Old Testament through my head and discovered that some pieces were missing. "Are you saying Cain got off?"

"Got *off*?" Dixie said. "He got the biblical version of overcharging on his Visa and having his credit extended infinitely. Cain was a dirt farmer. Abel was a shepherd, the earliest record of the kind of rivalry that was the basis of every western John Wayne ever made. The shepherd's sacrifices pleased God and the farmer's didn't."

"God's not a vegetarian?" Eleanor said. "Harold would hate this conversation." Harold was her rapidly balding publisher.

"Tofu hadn't been invented," I said. One of the things that most deeply divided Eleanor and me was tofu. "Anyway, why would anybody think God was a vegetarian? Look how many millions of years he spent jury-rigging evolution so it could produce incisors."

"Somehow," Dixie said, "I don't think the smoke from burning tofu would have brought Jehovah lickety-split to Cain's campfire. Anyway, who knows? Maybe Cain invented it. Never underestimate a Jew who needs a moment of God's time."

"Intriguing speculation aside," I said, "Cain got a slap on the wrist."

"A parking ticket in Beverly Hills would have given him a harder time, and this was his own brother that he killed. The Septuagint, the Greek Bible, which is more faithful to the original than the one King James cooked up, even suggests that Cain set Abel up, invited him to drop by some godforsaken field, you should pardon the expression, before he brained him. In a modern court of law we'd call that premeditation."

"A parking ticket in Beverly Hills," Eleanor said. "That's serious."

"So what was his punishment?" Dixie said rhetorically. "God told Cain he couldn't farm anymore, a blessing in disguise if there ever was one. No more scratching in the dirt to raise vegetables that he couldn't even sacrifice, much less gain a little weight on. So Cain threw away his hoe and cleaned up his boots or whatever they wore in those days, and founded a city, probably the first city in fact, a thriving little metropolis called Enoch. And he found a wife somewhere, we won't go into that, and had lots of kids and made it into the social register as one of Enoch's most important citizens, a regular pillar of society. Some punishment."

"What about the mark of Cain?" Eleanor said.

"On the whole," Dixie said complacently, "I'd prefer it to

the mark of Abel. A big F, for fertilizer or N for nitrogen, if you prefer."

I thought about Sally Oldfield. "Crime pays," I said.

"You weren't on the job," Dixie said to mollify me.

Eleanor sniffed twice and got up fast. "Oh, hell," she said, "something's burning." She hurried toward the kitchen.

"Let's hope it's the vegetables," Chantra said. "Otherwise you may have to set a place for Jehovah."

Over dinner, which we ate at a rickety card table that usually held the used Macintosh computer on which Eleanor did her writing, the conversation turned to the bandage on my head.

"I got in front of the wrong person," I said.

"If I'd known you were hurt, we would have canceled," Chantra said. Dixie, his fund of biblical insights exhausted for the moment, was chewing. Eleanor was banging pots together in the kitchen and casting resentful glances at me because I wasn't helping. "Simeon," Chantra continued, using a line that Eleanor could have written for her, "are you sure you're in the right line of work?"

"If I weren't an investigator, I wouldn't have met you," I said with shopworn gallantry.

"We were suspects," Dixie said reprovingly around a mouthful of potato. He had gravy on his wrists. Chantra, on the other hand, used her napkin more often than she used her fork.

"Mr. and Mrs. Jack Sprat," I said. "Sure, you were suspects. Everybody was a suspect in that one."

"No one in this room is sorrier about your head than I am," Eleanor said, putting an unrecognizable dessert on the table more loudly than was strictly necessary. "But I haven't done this much work alone since I was made blackboard monitor. And that was in fifth grade."

"I'll bet you were an angel in fifth grade," I said. "If there are Chinese angels."

"Why wouldn't there be? What do you think, there's a color line at St. Peter's gate?"

"Please," I said. "You'll get Dixie started again."

"Wrong Testament," Dixie said. "If I want fairy tales I'll

go to the Brothers Grimm." He inserted a fork experimentally into the dessert. "What is this?" he said.

"Pureed apples and cranberries," Eleanor said defiantly, "with creme fraîche, cinnamon, and raisins. Made without sugar or flour. Flour clogs the small intestine."

Dixie lost interest visibly. "Potatoes were great," he said.

"Lop sop," I said.

"Simeon," Eleanor said. "I speak Cantonese."

"You taught it to me."

"This is not junk."

"It's great," Chantra said with her mouth full. "I want the recipe."

"Nothing would have made me cancel tonight," I said to Chantra. "I need some information on things of the spirit." Things of the Spirit was the name of Chantra's store on Hollywood Boulevard, an emporium of New Age panaceas ranging from cabalistic texts and crystals to aromatherapy.

"The hidden agenda emerges," Dixie said, tasting the dessert. "Apple pie," he said, looking surprised.

"Information about what things?" Chantra asked.

"One thing, really. The Church of the Eternal Moment."

The silence that followed was punctuated only by the scraping of Dixie's fork. Like most skinny people, he could eat for hours. Eleanor sat down.

"Have I said something wrong?" I said.

"I know something about the Church of the Eternal Moment," Chantra said carefully. "Little girls and voices from beyond."

"See?" I said. "Ask an expert."

"It's not something I'd steer my customers to. People in my kind of business have to be careful to keep a distance from the frauds." Eleanor made a wordless noise of assent.

"I'm glad to hear it," I said. "Tell me what you know."

Chantra chewed the requisite twelve bites and I waited to see if her creativity was on the rise. "There are a lot of members," she finally said. "More than you'd think. Not just in L.A., but in Denver and Seattle and Chicago and New York. Anywhere, I'd guess, where there are large numbers of spiritually lost people with more money than sense."

"Some of it seems to make sense," I said, thinking about Skippy Miller and the Revealing.

"Sure it does. If it didn't, the people wouldn't keep forking over the money. I'm talking about priorities, not content. The content helps people, up to a point, at least. The priority, it seems to me, is keeping the cash flowing. If people get helped, fine; if they don't, well, keep the cash flowing anyway."

"And the cash does flow?" That was Eleanor, her chin on her hand. She never ate dessert, even when she'd made it. Her black blunt-cut hair framed the high bones of her face.

"It pours," Chantra said. "Do you know how much Listening costs?"

"What's Listening?" Eleanor said.

"How much?" I asked.

"About two hundred dollars an hour. And it takes fifteen, twenty hours to move up from USDA choice to USDA prime, or whatever the grades are. And when you get to prime, you find out there are about ten more grades."

"I asked a question," Eleanor said. "What's Listening? Is this something I could write about in the *Times*?"

"The *Times*?" I said.

"Didn't I tell you?" Eleanor said, watching with a satisfied air as Dixie ate.

I silently counted to ten. "Didn't you tell me what?"

"That I've been hired to write for the *Times*. The 'Style' section. On New Age phenomena. Every other week or so."

"No," I said, feeling affronted. "You didn't."

"Well, they called a couple of weeks ago," Eleanor said dismissively.

"Good for you," Chantra said around a mouthful of dessert.

"I guess it is. So what's Listening?"

"Nothing that would interest the *Times*, I think," I said, quoting from some of the literature that I'd charged to Skippy's room up in Big Sur. "A little Jung, a little Freud, a little high-tech nonsense." Chantra looked uncomfortable. "Get interrogated by a Listener a few dozen times, go into your past, find out what causes your knee-jerk reactions, and eliminate the Causes. That's what they're called, the

Causes. Sometimes they're experiences, sometimes they're preconceptions. Sometimes they're people. Once you're free of them, you can begin to function in the eternal moment."

"Which is now," I said.

"Which is now. Your past is your enemy, some rigmarole like that. You have to clear out your past before you can deal with the present."

"Your past is your enemy," Eleanor said. "What a perfect basis for fascism. It would give you a nice, comfortable moral high ground from which you could blow good-bye kisses to your ideals, your vows, your friends, even your family. So if the past is your enemy and the eternal moment is now, what about the future?"

"That comes later," Dixie said, emerging from dessert. "Yuck, yuck."

"Go back to sermons, Dixie," I said.

"It's like a sort of parody of confession," Eleanor suggested.

"Yes and no." Some of what I'd learned in my comparative-religions classes was coming back to me. I'd told my mother they'd be useful someday. "In confession the penitent accuses himself of sin in order to obtain absolution through the sacraments. But it's only necessary to confess the big ones—the mortal sins—although there's no harm in confessing venial sins. In Listening, as I understand it, the church member tells the Listener absolutely everything, from playing with matches to incest or murder, and the idea is to bring these hidden or forgotten—or repressed—experiences into the present, to deprive them of their power to shape your actions. Those are the Causes. Once you've illuminated them and the hidden landscape of your life, to paraphrase the only Revealing I've heard, you can deal with the present *in* the present, without dragging along harmful or irrelevant debris from your past."

"Whew," Dixie said. "I wish I'd said that."

"Also," Chantra said, "confession isn't humiliating. From what I've heard, a Listening session can be pretty humiliating."

"They could still have picked that up from the Catholics. In the early days of the Church, people sometimes confessed publicly," I said, "for the express purpose of self-humiliation. Remember, these were people who sometimes got dressed up in hair shirts and hit themselves with whips."

"Imagine your confessions being public," said Eleanor, who had less to confess than anyone I'd ever known.

"Well, in the Church of the Eternal Moment the whole point is secrecy," Chantra said. "Listening sessions are supposed to give you an absolutely confidential opportunity to work through your past mistakes."

"What about the little girls?" That was Eleanor.

"The Speakers?" Chantra said. "They're channels for Alon or Aton, however they're spelling it these days. They seem to be normal little girls when they're not Speaking. After a while they burn out or something, and go back to their movie magazines."

"Wait," Eleanor said. "You mean there's no permanent leader of the Church?"

"Actually, that's one of the reassuring things about it," Chantra said. "There's no one figure, like L. Ron Hubbard for Scientology or the Bhagwan Shree Rajneesh running around buying fleets of ships or Rolls-Royces with the proceeds of the church. There's just these little girls, Speaking as long as the spirit possesses them, and then moving on."

"Somebody's keeping the books," I said.

"Honey, somebody's making millions," Chantra said. "Somebody bought that big old hotel they use as their headquarters downtown and somebody built that television studio next door where they do their cable show. Somebody's franchising the new churches and moving all that money around. But whoever he or she is, he or she keeps a low profile. Like the Hunts. But as far as the faithful are concerned, it's a little girl, her mother, and whatever the hell Aton is."

"This is so cockamamie I can't believe it," Dixie said. "You mean people actually have faith in something that's run by a bunch of little girls and somebody who's dead?"

"There have been weirder faiths," I said. "Automatism, for example."

"There was never anything called automatism," Eleanor said hopefully.

"Automatism is a twentieth-century belief, like the Church

of the Eternal Moment. I'm sure this century isn't any weirder than any of the earlier ones, but we've forgotten a lot of the earlier aberrations. Automatists believe that man is a technological being, and that technological skill is what God gave man to set him apart from animals."

"I thought that was blushing," Dixie said.

"The automatists say that man will reach his height when he invents the machine that controls him. Or her," I added apologetically.

"Don't worry about sexist language in this context," Chantra said. "That's men talking."

"Computers?" Eleanor cast a hostile glance at her Macintosh, temporarily banished to the coffee table.

"Whatever. Faith is a peculiar thing."

"How would you define faith?" Chantra asked.

"I wouldn't even try. St. Paul, in the Epistle to the Hebrews, says that faith is 'the assurance of things hoped for, the conviction of things not seen.' In the Church of the Eternal Moment, I'd say that the things hoped for are wealth, power, and a sense of self. The things not seen are Aton."

"And the management of the Church," Eleanor said.

"Bingo," I said.

"Just be careful with the Church of the Eternal Moment," Chantra said. From what I've heard, people have a way of going in and not coming out."

"From what I've seen," I said, "they sometimes come out dead."

"Sounds like the *Times* to me," Eleanor said stubbornly.

I looked at her for so long that Dixie burped twice. "Maybe it is," I said.

11

"Are you sure this is the right place?" Eleanor said again.

The Congregation of the Present occupied a flyspecked one-story storefront wedged appropriately between the temporal parentheses of an open elementary school and a closed funeral parlor on a run-down block of Vermont Avenue. The flat-black asphalt and yellow swings of the school playground were slick with rain, and the funeral parlor's ragged hedges had snagged pounds of bright paper trash. I wondered how a funeral parlor could have gone out of business.

The Congregation squinted at the world through oily windows. Its derelict air was only partly relieved by a large and presumably symbolic sign that depicted an Egyptian pyramid incongruously balancing what seemed to be a stopwatch at its apex. The stopwatch, in orange neon, perpetually counted down the last fifteen seconds before eternity, and then, at eternity minus one, repositioned its second hand. The idea that eternity was negotiable provided the sole note of optimism.

There was no traffic at all. Even at four P.M. on a gray, rainwashed Sunday afternoon it seemed to me there should have been more.

Eleanor had asked her question the first time we circled the block, and now she peered through the window, furrows of worry lining her flawless forehead. "Why are they here? If religions make so much money, what are these people doing here?"

"Waiting for a bigger piece of the pie," I said, using an expression I knew she hated.

"Don't *say* that. It reduces the whole world to calories."

"Well, then, they're anticipating upward mobility," I said, looking for a parking space. "Demonstrating their faith. Think about the early Christians. Their sign was a drawing of a fish, carved in wood, not in neon. They met in dripping catacombs beneath the ground, in secret. If you'd been an early Roman real-estate agent, what odds would you have given that they'd eventually own the Vatican?"

"Anyway," Eleanor said, changing arguments as I maneuvered Alice into a microscopic slot between a Hyundai and a Hyundai, yet more evidence that the Koreans shall inherit the earth, "I think you've finally closed the door on whatever's left of your common sense. Impersonating a reporter? Don't you know that reporters are the only privileged class left in America?"

"Not quite," I said. "There are feminists."

"A laugh a line," she said.

"Besides, half the people who are real reporters are impersonating a reporter. Look at network anchors. You, at least, have a real press pass."

"I'm a writer, not a reporter," Eleanor said. "And this is Sunday. I should be correcting book galleys. Are you aware that this is Sunday?"

"Churches are open on Sunday, Eleanor. Remember?"

"I wasn't talking about the church. I was talking about you and me. Simeon, what the hell are we doing here?"

"We're going to ask these nice folks about the Church of the Eternal Moment. We're going to get a jaundiced view, to put it mildly. The Congregation of the Present, according to Chantra, is a grudge-carrying spin-off of the original Church, and they think they're talking to an L.A. *Times* reporter who just might nail the Church to the floor with a well-chosen adjective or two while making the Congregation look like the most reverent gathering since the Last Supper. Haven't we been over this before?"

"Judas was at the Last Supper."

"Every hostess makes a mistake once in a while."

"I'm not a detective," she said. "I've never wanted to be a detective. I didn't even want *you* to be a detective. Why did I let you talk me into this?"

"Why ask me? Do I know how your mind works? Have I *ever* known how your mind works?" I killed the engine, hoping I'd be able to bid it to rise again. "It's just this once, Eleanor. It won't kill you."

"Says you."

"Have you got your notebook?"

"If you ask me one more time whether I've got my notebook, I'm going to throw it out the window."

"Let's go, then." I reached across her and opened her door, less out of courtesy than from a conviction that she wouldn't get out at all if I didn't. She made a harrumphing sound and stepped out, directly into the path of the first moving automobile we'd seen in ten minutes. Its driver honked, swerved theatrically, and made a rude hand sign at us.

"Don't get killed yet," I said, getting out. "I'd just have to get a replacement, and I don't know where I could find anyone else dumb enough."

She stepped up onto the curb and straightened her skirt fussily. "You look very establishment," I said. "Just right for a card-carrying lackey of the imperialist running-dog press."

"Put a cork in the banter," Eleanor said shortly, "and let's get it over with."

The door to the Congregation of the Present swung open in front of us, revealing an empty waiting room. The congregation was evidently elsewhere. A bedraggled hanging arrangement of long neon tubes, trailing frayed-looking electrical wires, hummed at us and provided flat, cold light. The walls were a pale, sickly institutional green, bare except for two large and somewhat faded photographs of a woman and a little girl—not Angel and Mary Claire Ellspeth—and the floor was a hodgepodge of scuffed brown linoleum, warped and buckled in places. Here and there the linoleum had peeled away altogether, revealing the concrete slab beneath. A bucket in a near corner caught the slow drip of water that had collected on the roof.

"Very nice," Eleanor said. "We must spend more Sundays together. Your Los Angeles is so picturesque."

"Look intelligent," I said. "You're on *Candid Camera*.

Don't look around for it. It's in the far corner, up near the ceiling."

"Gee," she said, giving me a big mean smile. "I hope my seams are straight."

"Make a note. Glance around inquiringly and write something in your notebook. And don't overact."

Eleanor opened her spiral binder and uncapped her pen with her perfect white teeth. SIMEON IS A SCHMUCK, she wrote. As she snapped the pad shut, a door slid open beneath the television camera and an enormous woman came in.

"Good afternoon and welcome to our home," she said, looking dourly from Eleanor to me. "I'm Sister Zachary. May I help you?" Sister Zachary was as big as a split-level house and she had draped her bulk in something that looked like a dust cover for a couch. White and flowing, it swept the dirty floor as she approached us. It was the first time the floor had been swept in some time.

"This is Miss Chan, from the *Times*," I said. "She's here to see Dr. Wilburforce."

Sister Zachary had a small dark mustache above tight, disapproving lips. She regarded Eleanor over it for a moment, then nodded reluctant acknowledgment and turned to me. "And you are?"

"My associate," Eleanor interposed, "Mr Swinburne."

"That's an unusual name," Sister Zachary said grudgingly. "Are you related to the poet?"

"Very distantly. Not as distantly as I'd like, I'm afraid." Eleanor knew that I loathed Swinburne above all other poets, and that was saying quite a lot.

"Dr. Wilburforce is waiting for you, although I must say he was only expecting one." Her pursed little mouth turned down at the corners briefly and then she tugged it back up into a stiff, creaky smile of welcome. "Still, I suppose it'll be all right. Will you please follow me?" She swayed left as a preparation for turning, swayed back to the right to overcome inertia, and then launched herself back toward the door. Eleanor scrawled a note. YIKES, it said.

"Where's the congregation?" she asked Sister Zachary's back as the Sister slid the door open.

112 TIMOTHY HALLINAN

"We're between services," Sister Zachary said without turning around. "The next gathering is at six."

"How many gatherings each day?" Eleanor pushed imperiously in front of me to go through the door first. I followed like a good dachshund.

"There used to be four," Sister Zachary said. Her voice was a bit wistful. "Now there are only two."

"And why is that?"

"Faith is falling off, don't you know," the fat lady said over her shoulder. We were trailing in single file down a narrow hallway with pasteboard walls, an obvious architectural gerrymander that skirted the large room to our left, where the worshipers, or what was left of them, gathered for devotions. Sister Zachary's ample hips brushed the walls on either side. "It's not just the Congregation," she added defensively. "It's the national climate. Young people don't believe in anything anymore."

"Are you hurt by not having a Speaker?" I tugged sharply at Eleanor's hair to slow her down. Speakers were supposed to come later.

"Oh, no. Certainly not. You mustn't think that. We don't need show business"—she made the words sound so dirty that they should have been printed, Victorian-style, in asterisks—"to keep belief alive. What's true once is true for all time. Anna was speaker enough for us."

"But—" Eleanor said. I yanked her hair again, harder this time, and nearly got caught by Sister Zachary, who pivoted more rapidly than I would have believed possible. Eleanor rubbed the back of her head. I lowered my hand quickly, feeling like an elementary-school kid forced to palm an exceptionally large spitball. "This is Dr. Wilburforce's office," Sister Zachary said with tremendous dignity, knocking twice at a gray steel door. In my limited experience with religious leaders, it seemed that many of them preferred to work behind steel doors.

Something rumbled inside, and Sister Zachary pulled the heavy door open with no apparent effort. "I'll leave you here," she said. "Dr. Wilburforce will answer all your questions." The words were unequivocal but the tone was hopeful.

"Come," someone growled, British-fashion, through the open door. We went. The door remained ajar behind us.

THE FOUR LAST THINGS

The room, although largely empty, was bigger than I'd expected. So was Dr. Wilburforce. He rose from behind a scarred and notched wooden desk positioned strategically in front of a rainwashed window, laying down a thick book. We were obviously supposed to have interrupted his reading. Dr. Wilburforce had a generous expanse of stomach confined rebelliously inside a tweed vest, a none-too-clean shirt with curling collars, and an intriguing map of veins to guide the determined pilgrim from one of his wine-spotted cheeks to the other, across the Himalayas of the biggest, reddest nose I'd ever seen. He topped it all off with a high forehead, long, lank, straight brown hair, and disconcertingly wary black eyes.

"So you're the reporter from the *Times*," he said to Eleanor, summoning up a respiratory eruption that fell somewhere between a chuckle and catarrh. "I must say that I didn't know journalists were so pretty these days."

Eleanor waved an apologetic hand at me. "You should see him before he washes his hair," she said. "I'm Eleanor Chan, Dr. Wilburforce. This is my assistant, Algernon Swinburne. Have a seat, Algy."

Ignoring the demotion and the new first name, I sat. "Related to the poet?" Dr. Wilburforce said with leaden geniality.

"Intimately," Eleanor said.

"The song of springtide," Dr. Wilburforce said, smiling to expose a breathtakingly white set of false choppers. "Psalms of innocence and hope. They have so much to tell us, especially in this age."

"Don't they just?" Eleanor said. "Algy knows them by heart." She sat down next to me, dodging my kick without missing a beat. "It's so kind of you to find time for us."

Dr. Wilburforce gestured with vague regret at his book. "Ah, well," he said. "We can't scorn the media. It's the lubricant of a free society."

Eleanor flipped open her notebook and wrote SWILL. "May we quote you?" she asked.

"But of course, my dear. I know that nothing is off the record these days." He raised a hand to pluck at the hairs that joined his eyebrows over the bridge of his formidable nose. "At any rate, we have no secrets here."

"Really?" Eleanor said. "Most religions have their mysteries."

"Mysteries are the refuge of a weak belief," Dr. Wilburforce said with the air of one who'd just successfully steered the conversation to a long-planned punch line. He laced his fingers together over his vest, rose suddenly onto his toes, and then plopped down onto a corner of the desk. It groaned.

"No mumbo-jumbo?" Eleanor said.

He gave us the polyethylene smile again. "Whatever little bit of mumbo we may have here," he said playfully, "it isn't jumbo." He watched his bon mot float across the air toward us and then collected his features into an expression of High Seriousness. "You understand that I'm being completely frank with you. People like a little theater with their religion."

"Why is that?" I said, just to say something. I was beginning to feel like an extra chair.

"Ah, Mr. Swinburne. You, of all people, you, with the poet's blood flowing proudly through your veins, should understand. Religion itself is a mystery, an attempt to penetrate the veils of time and mortality and impose reason upon them. Do you, as we say, play the market?"

I was surprised in spite of myself. "Only on paper."

"Then you listen occasionally to the analysts. Stocks are up, they say, because we're headed for war. Stocks are down because people *think* we're headed for war. The analysts are wrong most of the time, but investors, or even would-be investors like you, listen to them because they provide the market with a mystique, one that you believe you eventually may learn to understand. Without them, you wouldn't dare to invest—I don't mean you personally, of course, since I hardly know you—because you'd have to face the fact that the market moves irrationally and at random, without any reference at all to human factors. Like the universe. The universe may or may not know we're here, but it certainly doesn't behave as though it cares."

"So you're in stocks?" I said. "What looks good?"

"If the Universe moves at random," Eleanor said, cutting off what I'd thought was an interesting line of inquiry, "then what possible good is religion?"

"It can prepare us to face the present," Dr. Wilburforce

said. "We're not talking about heaven or hell, purgatory or past lives in this Congregation." He twiddled his thumbs in a satisfied fashion. "That's part of what I mean about no mumbo-jumbo. One life is one more than most people can deal with. There's a Zen *koan* with a memorable payoff. You may already know it," he added charitably. "The supplicant asks his master what he should do to improve his life. 'Have you had your dinner?' the master asks. 'Yes,' says the supplicant. 'Then wash the dishes,' his master says." Dr. Wilburforce arched his eyebrows meaningfully. " 'Wash the dishes.' So simple. And yet many people can't even do that. But until you've finished washing the dishes, cleaning up the clutter you've left, you haven't dealt with your immediate past. And until you've dealt with your immediate past, you're no match for your more remote past, your Embedded Past, as we call it."

"Your past is your enemy," I said.

He unlaced his fingers in order to flop a dismissive hand around. "Dogma," he said. "Useful dogma, but dogma nonetheless. We've gone beyond that here."

"Beyond it to what?" Eleanor said.

"Oh, dear," Dr. Wilburforce said a trifle uncomfortably. "That's a very complicated question." His eyes wandered over the room and paused for a moment, fixed on a point over my head, and I suddenly knew that someone was standing in the corridor behind us, looking in through the partially closed door. I stifled a paranoid urge to turn around. Dr. Wilburforce picked up a large briar pipe and polished its bowl on the side of his nose.

"Very complicated indeed," he continued, backing off from his answer, "and I'm not sure it can be compressed to good effect in a short newspaper story. Do you mind if I smoke?"

"Without getting into the fine points of doctrine," Eleanor said, leaning forward, "can you explain the difference between the Congregation and the Church of the Eternal Moment? And, no, we don't."

Dr. Wilburforce lit up and blew plumes of bluish smoke through his nostrils. The pipe made a wet bubbling sound as he sucked at it, and his eyes once again flicked toward the door behind me "I could, of course," he said. "I could. Good heavens, of course I could. Who if not me, eh?" He gave a tense little chuckle, exhaling fumes that smelled of burning cherries. "Well, well. I hope you won't mind if I ask you: what is the general slant of your story?"

"We've heard rumors," Eleanor said, repeating word for word the line I'd given her, "of improprieties in the Church of the Eternal Moment."

"Improprieties." Wreathed in his fruity smoke, Dr. Wilburforce tasted the word like a sommelier trapped between a substandard wine and a smart customer. "Spiritual improprieties?" he said cautiously.

"Financial," Eleanor said.

Relaxation seeped through Dr. Wilburforce's outsize frame. His fingers groped toward each other and met again over his stomach like five overweight pairs of illicit lovers on safe ground at last. He actually sighed. "I'm not surprised," he said gravely around his pipe. "Not at all."

"But there *is* a relationship, isn't there, between your church and theirs?" Eleanor said.

"We make no secret of the fact. Man is descended, or rather ascended, as science tells us, from the apes. But science doesn't suggest that men are apes. We of the Congregation are ascended from the Church of the Eternal Moment in the same sense that Protestantism is ascended from the Romish church. Although," he added hastily, "I mean no disrespect to the Church of Rome, should either of you belong to it."

Eleanor, a Taoist to her toenails, surmounted the slur with a brave smile that put Wilburforce in her debt. "No offense," she said, "although I can't speak for Algy."

"I'm okay," I said. "I used to be a choir boy, but it finally cleared up."

"The Whore of Babylon," Dr. Wilburforce said loudly. Eleanor sat up, looking startled. "What is more important, I ask you, souls or profit? Yes, we share some points of doctrine with the Church of the Eternal Moment. Yes, we believe in the early Revealings and in the value of Listening. Yes, we believe that man's potential is infinite if he can clear away the clutter of his past. Or hers, of course," he amended mechanically for Eleanor's benefit. "We, too, concentrate our efforts on solving the problems of this world, this life, rather than wandering aimlessly around in the vast slough of time and space that we call the Cosmos." He pronounced the word with a pedantic pleasure, as though other people insisted on calling it something else. Satisfied with the sound of it, he drew vehemently on his pipe and coughed, his face turning a pulse-pounding shade of purple. "But do we speculate in real estate?" he said, blinking back tears. "We do not. Do we invest the donations of our faithful in pork-belly futures and other commodities and money-market funds? We do not. Do we go on television and mewl and puke of poverty for hours on end in order to bleed little old ladies of their food stamps? We most certainly do not. Do we put our tax-exempt dollars into an automobile dealership in Downey or a miniature-golf course in Reseda? Most emphatically we do not."

"A miniature-golf course?" I said. "Reseda?"

"Excuse me for asking, Dr. Wilburforce," Eleanor said pleasantly, "but how much of this is sour grapes?"

"My dear Miss Chan, what an extraordinary question. Ha, ha, ha," Wilburforce laughed, pronouncing each syllable separately and precisely, as though he were trying out a phrase in a language he didn't speak. "Sour grapes indeed. No, Hubert Wilburforce is not perfect. He too can succumb to temptation. Until he was cleansed by the process of Listening he grasped as greedily at the plums of the world as the next man. Like everyone else, he wanted a bigger piece of the pie." Eleanor winced. "Perhaps he's been fortunate that the temptations he's encountered recently have been relatively small ones, unlike those that are now, even now, distorting and perverting the Church of the Eternal Moment." He bit down hard enough on the stem of his pipe to crack it. Pulling it out quickly, he looked at it in dismay. Outside, the rain began to pour down in a serious fashion.

Eleanor glanced at me for a cue. "Let's start at the beginning," I said. "When and why did you break off from the Church?"

"When? Ten years ago." He drew experimentally at the pipe and looked over my head again. "And why?" I turned and saw Sister Zachary failing to duck out of sight in time. "Because the Church changed."

"Can you be a little more specific?" Eleanor said, writing something on her pad.

"It became a business," Wilburforce said distastefully. "When Alon stopped speaking through Anna, the Church was at a crossroad, so to speak. It was actually a moment of opportunity, had it been grasped. The leadership could have devoted itself to the study of the Revealings. It could have refined the Listening process, as we have, and worked to help its members to achieve their potential. That was all that Alon had ever wanted. Instead, the old leadership frittered and sputtered until a new leadership arose, spreading hysteria through the Church, demanding that a new Speaker stand forth. Suggestible little girls were examined for the ability to Speak, as though it were something physical, like acne."

"Or a cleft palate," I said.

"Anna did *not* have a cleft palate." Wilburforce puffed angrily on his damaged pipe. "She had a mild speech impediment, but there was no trouble distinguishing between her T's and her L's. What happened was that the second little girl got the name wrong and they had to stick with it. It became Aton. And it became nonsense."

"So the second Speaker was a fake?" Eleanor asked. "And the new one too?"

"Um," Dr. Wilburforce said, focusing over my head to meet the eyes of Sister Zachary, who'd evidently returned to the doorway. "I don't want this to degenerate into name-calling and finger-pointing. I'm sure the little girls are perfectly sincere. Many of the charismatic religions depend on spontaneous utterances to shape their doctrines. In the Salem witch trials, if you remember your history, there was no shortage of witnesses to condemn those poor harmless old ladies. Most of the witnesses were young girls. I'm sure they believed their testimony when they gave it. Young girls are particularly susceptible to that kind of hysterical reaction." He gave a hollow, slightly uneasy chuckle. "Remember the Beatles," he said.

"So the Church created Speakers?" Eleanor was writing busily in her pad as she asked the question.

"Intentionally, you mean?" Dr Wilburforce said, his discomfort increasing visibly. "No, no, no, no, you mustn't quote me as having said anything like that. The leadership of the Church probably believed that a new Speaker would arise. And they obviously believed they needed one. All I'm suggesting is that their, um, their very eagerness created a climate in which it was probably inevitable that one or more of the young faithful would begin to spout Revealings. Poor dear, it wasn't her fault that she got Alon's name wrong."

"Let me boil this down," Eleanor said. "You're saying that the leaders of the Church of the Eternal Moment created a climate, presumably twice, that would make little girls start to Speak, and that they then exploited those little girls to pull more revenue from the congregation, which they invested for sheer profit."

The door creaked open behind me and I turned to see Sister Zachary waddle into the room. "Don't put words in Dr. Wilburforce's mouth," she said sharply. "He said nothing of the kind." Dr. Wilburforce hastily retreated from the conversation and sucked at his pipe, focusing all his attention on its bowl. "You're the one who came in here talking about financial improprieties," Sister Zachary continued implacably. "Dr. Wilburforce has never alleged that the Church is involved in anything illegal. He's simply suggested that they are more interested in matters of funding than we are."

"There are libel laws," Dr. Wilburforce said weakly. "The Church is litigious in the extreme. As we've learned."

"Pipe down, you," Sister Zachary said. "I told you not to give this interview."

"Wait," I said. "Miss Chan and I are doing a piece on the Church of the Eternal Moment, not on your Congregation. We're not trying to cause trouble for you. Dr. Wilburforce can be completely candid with us without worrying about the consequences. If he wishes, if you wish, we'll treat this interview as deep background. We won't name him anywhere in the story."

"Tell me another one," Sister Zachary said knowingly. "We know what the press is like."

Eleanor opened her eyes so wide that Zsa Zsa Gabor's sunglasses wouldn't have covered them and ruffled the pages in her notebook. "I'll rip these out if you like," she said. "You can have them. We're not going to quote you. We just want to tell the truth about the Church." She actually tore one page out. It was blank.

Sister Zachary and Dr. Wilburforce exchanged a look. "How do we know that's true?" he asked.

"Remember Deep Throat?" I improvised. Dr Wilburforce coughed, and Sister Zachary's eyes began to roll. "I don't mean the porno movie," I added hastily. "I mean Woodward and Bernstein's source for *All the President's Men*. Everyone wanted to know who he was, but the two reporters never told anyone. Even now, now that it's all over, they haven't. We may not be Woodward and Bernstein, but if this story is as good as we think it is, we'll protect anyone who helps us."

There was a long silence. Wilburforce and Sister Zachary exchanged a glance. Sister Zachary shook her head. "Nope," she said. "I think it's time for you to leave."

We all sat there, if you didn't count Sister Zachary, who was standing.

"May I say something?" Eleanor asked in her sweetest and most submissive-Asian-female voice.

The tone seemed to lift Wilburforce's spirits. "Of course you may, my dear."

"I don't mean to sound pushy or anything," Eleanor said, smiling winningly, "but I've already got all these notes. Also, Algy's wired, which means that this whole interview is on tape. I mean, there's just no way you can deny what you've already said, and we've made no promises about keeping you out of the story so far." She looked from Wilburforce to Sister Zachary. "This is difficult for someone who's not used to confrontation," she said, "but you could probably get your asses sued to hell and gone if we just print what we have already." She shrugged apologetically, and I stifled the urge to kiss her. "If you see what I mean," she said.

"I told you," Sister Zachary said. "I told you you were asking for trouble." She subsided, tapping her foot angrily.

Wilburforce pumped several pounds of innocence into his dark eyes. "I'm a great admirer of the Church, actually," he said. "As you pointed out, we derived much of our doctrine from theirs, although we've, um, refined and purified it. It's absurd even to consider the possibility that anything I've said could be actionable." Distracted by the sheer ludicrousness of the possibility, he picked absently at his nose. "Still," he added, "you're the experts."

Sister Zachary snorted again, but other than that she held her peace.

Wilburforce dreamily examined his finger. "And since, as you say, your story is really about the Church rather than the Congregation, I suppose I should ask you how we can proceed. I think it was Jefferson who said he would prefer a free press with no government to a government with no press. A sentiment, I may say, that I certainly share."

"In other words," I said, "we can ask you some more questions?"

"More questions," Dr. Wilburforce said dully. He looked despairingly at Sister Zachary.

"In exchange, there will be no mention of any of this," Sister Zachary said after a couple of warm-up breaths. "Not me, not him, not the Congregation."

"Agreed," Eleanor said.

Dr. Wilburforce glanced at his weighty wristwatch. "We have your oath," he said. "The next gathering is due in a little more than an hour, and we have to prepare. You've got ten minutes." He lifted himself ponderously back onto the corner of his desk.

"What was your job in the Church?" I said. Sister Zachary pulled up a rickety-looking chair. I held my breath as she sat in it.

"He was Anna's personal physician," she said. The chair held.

"Why did she need a personal physician?"

"The Revealings," Wilburforce said from his perch. "No one understands the Revealings. Somebody had to monitor her vital signs, check her eyes, make sure that the Revealings weren't harming her."

"Tell me about the Revealings."

"She was a channel," Dr. Wilburforce said. "She had an amazing receptivity. Alon spoke through her whenever he wanted. At the beginning, it was random. Later, when he began to understand that it was more, um, productive to do it when the members of the Church were gathered, he popped up mainly during the formal Revealings. Other than the fact that she channeled Alon, she was a perfectly normal little girl."

"Is this on the level?" Eleanor asked.

Wilburforce looked affronted. "Absolutely," he said. "I'm a doctor. Do you think I'd participate in anything that wasn't aboveboard?"

We all let that pass.

"Does Angel, the new Speaker, have a personal physician?" I asked.

"A nonentity," Sister Zachary said. Her tone would have curdled cream.

"Does this nonentity have a name?" I asked, knowing the answer.

"Certainly," she said. "Richard Merryman."

"You don't like him," I said.

"That's neither here nor there," she said airily. "He's not Hubert Wilburforce."

He certainly wasn't. On the whole, I thought that Wilburforce, a good old-fashioned fraud if ever I'd seen one, was less dangerous than Merryman. "What percentage of your Congregation," I asked, "is made up of people who've left the Church?"

"Half," Sister Zachary said promptly. "The others are new seekers after truth."

"Among the people who've come to you from the Church," I said, "was there one named Sally Oldfield?"

"Yes," Dr. Wilburforce said.

"No," Sister Zachary said.

"We seem to have a difference of opinion," I observed.

"The answer is no," Sister Zachary said. "We never knew her."

"I was thinking of someone else," Dr. Wilburforce said apologetically. "Someone with a similar name. What was her name, dear?"

"Sarah Elder," Sister Zachary said promptly.

"And Sarah Elder is alive and well? I could talk to her if I wanted to?"

"If you could find her," Sister Zachary said. "She's no longer with the Congregation."

"No forwarding address?"

"I think she moved to Denver."

"Or maybe Boulder," I said.

"Maybe," Sister Zachary said. "Whichever, she's not here."

"What about Ambrose Harker?" This time their bewilderment rang true. "Or Ellis Fauntleroy?"

"What a dreadful name," Wilburforce said. "His parents must not have wanted children."

"He's never been here either," Sister Zachary said.

ZERO, Eleanor wrote in her notebook. Then she drew little candles around it. Eleanor always doodled candles. I dithered over whether they were phallic symbols or symbols of hope. Eleanor maintained that phallic symbols *were* symbols of hope.

"You said the Church had new leadership," I said. "Who are they? All the public sees are Angel Ellspeth and her mother." Wilburforce goggled helplessly at Sister Zachary. Sister Zachary shook her head tightly. Wilburforce began to search for a match.

Eleanor rose to an inspiration. "We know there are lawyers," she said. "You told us the Church was litigious. There are lawyers, aren't there?"

"Sweetheart," Sister Zachary said, "lawyers are the whole banana."

12

The lawyer's name was Meredith Brooks. Like Ambrose Harker, or Ellis Fauntleroy, for that matter, he had two last names. Unlike Ambrose Harker, he was who he said he was.

And then some.

Brooks, Martin, Soames, and Pearce occupied every square foot of a cloud-catching floor in Century City. In addition to the Waspiest name I'd ever seen on a lawyer's shingle, Brooks, Martin, Soames, and Pearce had the most medieval furniture.

"Good God," Eleanor said, shaking off the rain as the elevator doors whispered closed behind us, "where are the monks?"

A long, polished refectory table stretched down the middle of the waiting room, ornamented solely by a large brass urn that could have held the ashes of every saint whose name ended with a vowel, but which now was host to a spray of oversize, slightly carnivorous-looking flowers that had undoubtedly been picked only hours earlier from the slopes of some Pacific volcano. A warlike stained-glass window, bejeweled with flapping banners and knights in combat, gleamed at us. Wooden pews, ripped untimely from an English cathedral, lined the walls. I flipped up one of the seats and found a hand-carved wooden gargoyle goggling at me on its underside.

"Charming," Eleanor said. "And very popular in the Middle Ages. Let's hope it's not a metaphor: the beast beneath the brass and polish."

I let the seat fall. The brutish, leering face with its protruding tongue had unnerved me. "Beasts and lawyers in the same place?" I said. "You must be kidding."

A big brass-faced grandfather clock at the far end of the reception area began to chime ten.

"There's nobody here," Eleanor said, sounding only slightly less nervous than I felt. "Why isn't there anyone here?"

"Good morning," someone said behind us on the stroke of ten.

The occupants of the towers of Century City are almost uniformly white, and I hadn't expected her to be black. She was also beautiful and she had the self-possession you see only in the truly virtuous and in deeply corrupt politicians. She was wrapped seamlessly in a form-fitting neon-blue dress made of something that had to be silk.

"We're here to see Mr. Brooks," Eleanor said. She may have been apprehensive, but you'd never have guessed it.

"You're the ten-o'clock," the black woman said. "Miss Chan from the *Times* and Mr. Swinburne. Are you related to the poet, Mr. Swinburne?"

"He was my great-uncle," I said resignedly.

The woman smiled. "Into whipping, wasn't he?" she asked. "I read somewhere that the only thing he preferred to a rhymed couplet was a bare bottom and a nice flexible whip."

"It's not hereditary," I said. "I'll take a rhymed couplet any day."

"Over a bare bottom?" the woman said.

"I always recite a rhymed couplet over a bare bottom," I said grumpily. "Don't you, Miss Chan?"

"No," Eleanor said. "I'm usually the bare bottom."

"So was Swinburne," the black woman said. "Mr. Brooks is on the phone to New York at the moment. I'm Marcy, by the way. Would either of you like coffee?"

We both declined.

"It'll just be a moment," she said. "I'll let him know you're here." She turned to go. "By the way, Mr. Swinburne," she said, "what couplet do you usually recite?"

" 'What light through yonder window breaks?' " I improvised. " 'It is the east; and Juliet is the sun.' "

"That doesn't rhyme," she said accusingly.

"Bare bottoms distract me," I said. "They make it hard to tell what rhymes."

"I'll bet they make it hard, at any rate," she said with a sudden white grin. "I'll be back in a sec." Eleanor giggled.

A wide black patent-leather belt hung low on Marcy's slender hips. Dangling from it was a thin black rectangle of metal about the size of a television remote-control unit. She pushed one of the buttons on it with a tapering vermilion-tipped finger, and a door slid open in front of her. She shimmered through it, as iridescent as a hummingbird, and the door closed behind her.

"Pretty neat," Eleanor said, still giggling.

"A glorified garage-door opener," I said. "And don't push this Swinburne shit too far."

"Oh, Algy," she said. "You should be proud of your heritage."

"Fine," I said. "Next person we see, you can be Edna St. Vincent Millay's granddaughter, and we'll see how you like it."

The door at the end of the room opened again and the woman called Marcy came back in. "Mr. Brooks will see you now," she said. "If you'll just follow me?" We did.

The main counsel of the Church of the Eternal Moment was as shiny as a potato bug; he shaved so close it looked like he'd had electrolysis. Sitting behind a dark, massive desk, he looked up at us through lashless slate-gray eyes under pale little eyebrows. A bit further down he featured a nose that brought Richard Nixon's to mind, with a little cleft in its tip, a characteristic a friend of mine used to call a facial fanny. Below that were a fatty, pursed little mouth and three clean-shaven chins that suggested an escalator of fat running down to the knot in his bright red tie. He was the first balding man I'd ever seen who looked like his forehead was advancing rather than his hairline receding. He wore a dark, perfectly tailored suit with an almost imperceptible charcoal stripe. From the cuffs of the jacket protruded shiny little hands, the right ornamented by the discreet glow of a class ring. Unexpectedly, a fat gold-link bracelet was tucked sloppily into his left cuff, above a thirties-vintage gold Rolex on an alligator strap. Rain drizzled through the picture windows, wrapping the hills in gray. He didn't bother to get up when we entered.

"Yes, yes," he said, in answer to nothing. "Come in and take a seat. Time's short, I'm afraid." We sat, and he made an expansive gesture in the general direction of the beautiful black woman. "Marcy," he said peremptorily, "no calls. Give us fifteen minutes." She closed the door behind us and he crossed his hands on the desk and regarded us. Head-on, he looked much younger than his sixty years; he had the smooth, unlined face of the truly selfish, the face of a man who had never wasted a moment's serious thought on another human being.

"Ah, Miss Chan," he said. "I'm an admirer of your book."

Eleanor assumed vanity and preened. "I'm surprised you've read it. A man as busy as you are."

"Actually, I haven't," Brooks said pleasantly. "My people looked it up for me."

"Then how do you know you admire it?" I asked. I already didn't like him.

"I admire anything that gets America up off its ass to toughen up." He rubbed his chin lovingly with his left hand, the one with the gold bracelet tucked up its sleeve. "The America of our fathers, or make that our grandfathers, wasn't soft. If it had been, we wouldn't be here today. You must be Mr. Swinburne."

"I suppose so," I said.

"What an improbable name," he said. "It must have taken some getting used to."

"We can get used to anything, given time, Meredith. How long did it take you to get used to the fact that people expected you to be a girl?"

He wasn't about to get upset with a mere reporter. "Touché," he said with a studied chuckle. He was the first person I'd ever heard say it out loud. "When I was younger, people *did* expect me to be a girl. I suppose it's progress that now they expect me to be a woman. So," he added, getting down to business, "what is it?"

"I think you know what it is," Eleanor said. "It's a

newspaper article. Or, perhaps, a series of articles." She
managed to make the alternative sound faintly threatening.

"On the Church," he said in a matter-of-fact tone.

"Yes."

"How did you get my name?"

"It kept coming up," I said, "in the course of our
investigation."

"You *are* the Church's primary counsel, aren't you?"
Eleanor asked.

"That's no secret," Brooks said, with a reserve that suggested that he very much wished that it were. "But I'd like
to know who's advertising it."

"We can't disclose our sources," Eleanor said.

"How nice for you." Brooks's tone was a trifle acid.
"You pop up in my office at ten o'clock on a Monday
morning, with barely two hours' notice, and you won't tell
me what you already know or whom you've been talking
to."

"It's called privileged communication," Eleanor said. "Actually, I believe lawyers are its prime beneficiaries."

"And shrinks," Brooks added, rubbing his chin again.
"Although reporters don't really have the same protection
that doctors and lawyers do, even considering the First
Amendment."

"Do you have a problem with speaking with us?" Eleanor
said.

"My dear," he said, baring a row of uneven teeth, "if I
had a problem with speaking with you, you wouldn't be
here. Most people wait weeks to see me, and you've waited
barely a hundred and twenty minutes."

"Then let me rephrase the question," I said. "Why are
you afraid of us?"

Brooks's smile got a little broader. "Don't flatter yourself. I understand the media, that's all. I know that a good
story outweighs all ethical considerations, and I know that
ripping the living flesh off a religion is generally considered
to be a good story. It doesn't matter how many people are
being helped by the religion or how many will be devastated
by its destruction, the only point is that it sells papers.
Jackals," he said mildly. "Most members of the press are

jackals." He smiled disarmingly. "Present company excepted, of course."

"Who runs the Church?" Eleanor said bluntly.

"The Speaker, of course. And her mother, I suppose."

"No," Eleanor said. "They may be responsible for doctrine, but that's not what I mean. Who controls the finances?"

Brooks folded one hand placidly over the other. "I have no idea," he said.

"Who negotiated the purchase of that hotel downtown?" Eleanor said, playing one of the cards Chantra had given us.

"Hotel?" Brooks said, the picture of surprised innocence. "You know more about the Church's business than I do. I'm not a real-estate agent. Why ask me?"

"We're talking about millions of dollars. They must have had legal help."

"I'm sure they did," Brooks said prissily, "but it wasn't I. This is way outside my line."

"And the television studio?"

"Same answer. I don't do real estate. But even if I did, what's wrong with a religion purchasing property? What's wrong with a religion having a television studio? I hope you'll forgive my being presumptuous, but it seems to me that you've already drawn your conclusions and all you're looking for is confirmation. Well, I'll provide it. Yes, the Church makes money. You seem to feel that's wrong. Why shouldn't it? Do you think Americans are drawn to organizations that are financial failures? Would we help more, or fewer, people if we were to declare bankruptcy?

"You're out of touch," he continued. "What Americans want from a religion today isn't sanctuary for their souls through eternity. It's success in life, *this* life, that people want now. The afterlife was a powerful image three hundred years ago because life on earth was, for most people, brutish, grueling, and short. Well, that's not true anymore. For people today, the majority of white people at any rate, life is acceptable—but it could be better. It could be more materially successful. The Church of the Eternal Moment works because it *is* successful. If it didn't work, if it were a financial failure, it wouldn't have any followers. The more real estate the Church owns, the more hours on cable it can buy, the more the people who want success for themselves will believe in it. The more they *should* believe in it. The Church doesn't hide that. On the contrary, it flaunts the fact. Every win for the Church is a win for the worshipers. If the Church can't take care of itself, how can it take care of the faithful?" He gave his chin a triumphant massage.

"So it all comes down to bucks," I said.

"Mr. Swinburne," he said, "if that really is your name, which I find difficult to believe, please don't pretend a naiveté you don't really possess. What, in contemporary American society, doesn't come down to bucks? Money is the common denominator. Get rid of everything else, and what's left is a desire for material success. The Church of the Eternal Moment has never promised anything but success in this lifetime. We're not ashamed of it. We're proud that we have the key. If you printed this interview word for word tomorrow morning, we'd have five thousand new applicants by noon. And you know what? We'd satisfy them. They'd get what they came for." He stopped rubbing his chin and glanced at his watch.

"Seven minutes," I said. "How *many* dollars? What's the Church's annual income?"

"It supports itself. As a religion we don't have to give precise income figures to the IRS. I'm certainly not going to give them to the media." He rubbed his chin again. "Period."

There was a moment of silence.

"Money aside," Eleanor said, "you're saying that the Church provides no guidance on the eternal questions."

"And what are those?" Brooks asked.

"Life, death. Heaven, hell. Eternity. Anything that helps people relate their lives, whatever it is that they have to endure, to something more, um, permanent, something that helps them put life and death into some kind of perspective, something that suggests that people do more than just eat and excrete and procreate and die."

"Isn't that enough?" Brooks said. "Especially if you have a good time doing it?"

"No," Eleanor said. "It's not. For Dale Carnegie, maybe. As a self-help manual for the shortsighted. But it's not a religion, at least not as I understand the term."

He shrugged. "I don't really care how you understand the term."

"In what regard is the Church a religion, other than its tax-exempt status?" I asked.

Meredith Brooks tilted his head back daintily and laughed. It was a laugh Hubert Wilburforce could have learned from, a lilting, melodious, manicured little laugh, five light, tripping steps down the scale of mirth. I hadn't heard anything like it since *La Bohème*.

"Now let's hear you cough," I said. "This should be in the minor."

The laugh subsided into a complacent smirk. "Tax exemption for religions, as I'm sure you remember from school, is just a manifestation of the separation between church and state, which is absolute—to use the exact words of the California Supreme Court—'no matter how preposterous the belief.' It may relieve you, though, to know that we pay for our tax-exempt status. We have Internal Revenue camping on our doorstep eighteen hours a day. Even if we don't file returns."

"Poor you," I said. "The Church is a business."

"What's the L.A. *Times*?" Brooks said. "Amnesty International? Greenpeace? The League of Women Voters? The *Times*, like all newspapers, clings frantically to its First Amendment rights in the name of truth, justice, and the American way. And then they devote their hallowed pages to lingerie ads and half-baked exposés. Please. We're all adults here, even though Miss Chan's I.D. would probably be checked in any bar in town. The Church is completely candid about what it offers and what it delivers. You can pretend any kind of piety you like for your readers, but in this room it doesn't wash. If you'll excuse a lapse into the vernacular, give me a break." He shifted around in his chair and pressed something under the desk.

"*You're* not a religion," I said. "What are your annual fees from the Church?"

"We're not a publicly held corporation either," Brooks said winningly, "and our fees are none of your business."

The door opened.

"Sorry to interrupt," Marcy said.

"Don't be sorry," Brooks said, stroking his chin. "These lovely people were just going."

"Don't get up," I said. "I'd hate you to lose the shine on the soles of your shoes."

Brooks pulled the thick gold bracelet out from under his cuff and buffed it on his lapel. "Polish is everything," he said. "Nice to have met you."

"I hope you enjoy the story," Eleanor said, standing and stowing her notebook in her purse.

"I won't. I never read the *Times*. Marcy will show you out."

Marcy did, closing the door behind us firmly and leading us back toward the reception area.

"What a greaseball," Eleanor said disgustedly. Marcy made a reproving noise.

"What my colleague is suggesting," I amended, "is that Mr. Brooks is certainly smooth."

"Smooth?" Marcy chuckled. "Darling, the man makes Teflon look like stucco." She pushed her miniature garage door opener and we were in the lobby. "The elevator's waiting," she said. "Have a safe trip, now. It's a long way down."

13

"I'm not quitting, and that's all there is to it," she shouted over the music. "You may have gotten me into this, but *I'll* get me out of it, when and if I want to. You think I've got an On and Off switch that you can flick whenever you want?"

"Jesus," I said. "You mean there's an On switch too?"

"Of course there is," Eleanor said in as silken a tone as the volume level in the Red Dog would allow. "You used to know where it was, as I recall."

I hoisted my whiskey. "That seems like a very long time ago," I said. The whiskey burned its way down toward my stomach like a gunpowder fuse.

"Not to me, it doesn't. Time flies when you're enjoying yourself."

Off-duty cops and cop groupies boogied like white people in a little clear area in front of the jukebox. I'd never seen a cop who could dance. Under different circumstances I would have shared that insight with Eleanor.

As it was, we glared at each other over the dirty table. We'd been squabbling ever since we left Brooks's office. She picked up a handful of peanuts, started to eat one, changed her mind, and threw them angrily onto the sawdust-covered floor.

"Fooey," she said.

"What was that for?"

"The bunny rabbits," she said, curling her inverted upper lip. Normally, her upper lip was one of the prettiest things in an unreasonably pretty face. Now it looked like she was trying to imitate Ricky Nelson trying to imitate Elvis Presley.

"There aren't any rabbits here, and if there are, they eat red meat."

"Then I've been misinformed," she said, sipping at her fourth club soda. "I thought this was bunny rabbit central. It's so *cute.*"

Her fourth club soda, my third whiskey. Not anything as good as the stuff in Skippy's hip flask, just crappy old rotgut guaranteed to give you ulcers when you were sober enough to notice. I signaled for another, then reached over and picked up her glass. "Cheers," I said, pouring the club soda vengefully on the floor. "For the bunny rabbits."

"Okey-dokey," she said between her teeth, just as a weatherbeaten, miniskirted waitress threaded her way between dancing cops to reach the table, staring down at the splash of club soda in the sawdust. "I'll take a whiskey too."

"Oh, no, you won't," I said.

"Hey, bub," the waitress said in a well-smoked basso profundo, "the lady'll take anything she wants."

"Fine," I said. "You get her home."

"It'd be a pleasure," the waitress said, looking appreciatively at Eleanor. "Where do you live, honey?"

"Solvang," Eleanor lied.

"Stick with the club soda," the waitress said, picking up our glasses. "Unless you'd like to stay in Hollywood tonight, that is."

"I can't," Eleanor said sweetly. "Cats, you know."

"Let 'em eat mice," said the waitress, paraphrasing Marie Antoinette. "We could go to Duke's for breakfast in the morning."

"Two whiskeys," I said. "If I'm not intruding, that is."

The waitress looked longingly at Eleanor, who stared obliviously through the window onto Hollywood Boulevard. "Any special kind?"

"Bottled," I said.

"With a label," Eleanor added.

"I get it," the waitress said. "Well, you can't blame me for trying." She winked at Eleanor and sashayed toward the bar.

"You certainly can't," I said bitterly.

"You certainly can," she said with feminine illogic. "What if I'd accepted?"

"You'd have something to write about for the *Times*," I said.

"I already do. And I'm going to stick with it."

"Eleanor," I said. "Darling. This isn't Parcheesi. This is murder, and a couple of particularly unpleasant murders to boot. I saw the way they went through Sally's house. We're dealing with professionals here."

"What this isn't," she said, "is 'Style.' This is front-page stuff, and you're not going to cut me out at this late date. You may be passing yourself off as Algernon Swinburne," she added, apparently forgetting that she was the one who'd given me the name, "but I'm plain old Eleanor Chan, and all these professionally murderous individuals know it. I'm in the darned phone book, Simeon," she said, lapsing into what was, for her, profanity. "Anyone who's managed to memorize the alphabet and learned how to use Information can find me. And where can they find Algernon Swinburne? In Norton's *Anthology*, that's where. So who's more exposed, you or I?"

"So quit already."

"Too late. Anyway, I'm having fun. The cookbook, with all due thanks to you," she said, "is a drag. A cup of organic tofu, two tablespoons of grated kelp, a teaspoon of soy sauce, and don't let it boil." I shuddered at the thought of eating whatever it was. "This is something I can get my teeth into."

"We're talking about murder," I said as the waitress plunked down our drinks.

"These *shoes* are murder," the waitress said winningly to Eleanor. "Arch support is a doctor's delusion. I need a massage."

"So find a masseur," I said shortly.

"A woman's touch is what I had in mind."

"Find a woman, then," Eleanor said.

"Well, excuse me," the waitress said in an aggrieved voice. "I thought maybe I had. Enjoy your whiskey."

She retreated toward the bar. "I hate it when someone

tells me to enjoy something," Eleanor said. "Enjoy your dinner, enjoy your trip. Either I can enjoy it by myself or not at all."

We both drank. On the jukebox the Monkees, sounding even younger and more ragged than I remembered, shrilled the schedule for the last train to Clarksville, wherever that was. It was old cop's night at the Red Dog; they were too old to have the mustaches that seem to be issued with the uniforms to all cops under forty. I suddenly realized that Eleanor and I were probably the youngest people in the place. Even counting the cop groupies. A couple of them *did* have mustaches.

"Lovely establishment," Eleanor said. "So romantic."

"We're not here to bill and coo. This is a cops' bar and we're here to talk to a cop."

"Not I," she said. "I'm here to listen. And your cooer broke years ago."

"Yeah, but my bill's in great shape."

"I'll take your word. So where's this cop of yours?" She took a tough journalist's slug off the whiskey, real *Front Page* stuff, and gave me the pleasure of watching her choke slightly as it went down. "All of three years old," she said when she could talk.

A beefy, red-faced cop with white hair cut military-close and blue eyes so close together that he could have worked undercover as a flounder appeared at the table. "Wanna dance?" he said.

"I can't," I said. "Old war injury. It's sweet of you to ask, though."

"I'd love to," Eleanor said, getting up. "Nothing too fancy. I've got a pulled hamstring."

"You're going to break the waitress's heart," I said.

"So comfort her. She looks like she depends on the kindness of strangers."

"Have a nice twirl, Miss Dubois," I said to her back. "Try not to step on his feet."

I picked up my drink, thought better of it, and drank hers instead. It was decidedly better than what I'd been drinking, which tasted like something you'd use to start a barbecue. The hopeful waitress had upgraded Eleanor free of charge.

A heavy hand fell on my shoulder, startling me. "Yo, as that musclebound asshole always says in the movies," Al Hammond said. "One for me? Good planning."

He picked up my drink and downed it. His eyes started to water "Holy shit," he said. "You must have been mean to Peppi."

"Peppi?" I said, watching Eleanor sway in the arms of the beefy cop. An old Dionne Warwick song was on the jukebox. "Who the hell is Peppi?"

"The dike who served you this stuff." Hammond was a vehement homophobe. If he weren't, he wouldn't have been in Records. The alleged perp whose rights he'd neglected to recite before breaking his nose had been of the gay persuasion.

"How's Um Hinckley?" I said as he sat in Eleanor's chair.

"About as useful as a flat tire," he said, finishing the drink with a grimace. "Where are the men these days?"

"There's always Peppi," I said, waving for her attention. She looked past me, then saw Hammond and started toward us, jostling the cop who was dancing with Eleanor with unnecessary force.

"They're not joining the police," he said, pronouncing it, as all cops do, "pleece," "and that's for sure. 'The boys in blue' has taken on a new meaning."

"Al," Peppi said, looking down at the empty glass in front of him. "You didn't drink that, did you?"

"Peppi," Hammond said, "you should join the force. We need your kind of random malice."

"I can do more harm here."

"Well, don't do it to us. Give us a couple good ones, wouldya? Something that won't threaten my friend's private eyesight." He chuckled, emitting a sound that suggested gravel in a cement mixer. That was Hammond's idea of light banter.

"Two?" Peppi said. "Or three?"

"Three," I said. "Let her get home alone."

"Who's three?" Hammond said.

"Little Miss Chopsticks," Peppi said unpleasantly, "out there on the dance floor."

Hammond followed her gaze. "Cute," he said. "Why are you letting her dance with Monohan?"

"It's not a question of letting," I said.

"Lib," Hammond said. "I liked it better when it was short for libido. What're you, waiting for the bourbon to age?" he asked Peppi, who was looking moonstruck at Eleanor.

"Every minute counts," she said sulkily, heading for the bar.

"You want to watch her," Hammond said. "You want to watch Monohan too. He's old and fat and his eyes are on top of each other, but they go for him."

Monohan was younger and thinner than Hammond, but I let it pass. "So," Hammond said conversationally, "you're witholding information on a murder."

"This is witholding? Why are we here?"

"Why'd you stand me up the first time?"

"Oh, Al," I said, putting my hand on his. "I didn't know you cared."

He yanked his hand away and looked around to see if anyone were watching. "Some things I care about. Murder, for example. You may be a friend, Simeon, but you're still a civilian. Murder is a cop's landscape."

"Oh, good, the police are here," Eleanor said behind me. "Not another word, now, not until I come back. Where's the ladies' room, Monnie?"

"I don't think there is one," Hammond said. "Lady cops do it standing up."

"I'll show you," Monohan said gallantly.

"Monnie?" I said. "As in mononucleosis?"

Monohan's red face got a little redder and he opened his mouth. Then he looked at Hammond and shut it again.

"If there *is* a ladies' room, Monohan can show you to it," Hammond said with exaggerated politeness. "He uses it all the time. Don't you, Monnie?"

"How's Records, Hammond?" Monohan asked with a practiced sneer.

"If we had a ladies' room," Hammond said, "it'd be perfect for you."

"Come on, Eleanor," Monohan said in a dignified tone.

"The conversation will be better in the ladies'. Even if you're by yourself." He took her elbow and guided her away.

"God, I'm glad to know cops are as rude to each other as they are to everyone else," I said.

Hammond ignored me, watching them. "Ah, the mystery of the East," he said.

"Careful, Al. This is not just a squeeze."

"That's obvious. If your blood pressure were any higher you'd explode. Calm down, you look like a cop. What's her name?"

"Eleanor." She and Monohan disappeared down a corridor together.

"I already heard that, you twit. Monnie used it, remember? The girl who was killed. What was *her* name?"

"Sally, by which I mean Sarah, Oldfield. Is he going to go into the bathroom with her?"

"Not unless she lets him." Peppi showed up with three doubles. Hammond gave her a minimal smile in return. "Three more in five minutes," he said. "My friend's paying."

"I never would have guessed," she said.

"Put a sock in it," Hammond said. "And get us another chair."

"Get it yourself," Peppi said. "What do you think I am, a furniture mover?"

"There's a future in it. Nobody stays put these days."

"You couldn't prove it by me. Some people have already outstayed their welcome."

"Peppi," Hammond said, "this display of pique is not becoming."

"Yes, it is," I said. "It's becoming boring."

"Tell it to someone who cares," Peppi said. "This ain't TV. If you can't change channels, try changing bars."

"Three more," Hammond said. "Five minutes. Now, beat it."

Peppi beat it.

"Sugar and spice," I said.

"She's okay," Hammond said, displaying all his sensitivity in one fell swoop. "It's not easy to be a dike these days."

"It probably never was."

"Tell me about Sarah Oldfield."

"Tell us both about Sarah Oldfield," Eleanor said, seating herself on a chair that she'd pulled up herself and picking up her glass.

"That was quick," I said.

"It was awful," she said. "Too awful to use. Completely outside my frame of reference. Monnie's sweet, though."

"Well, I'm really glad to hear that," I said.

"I'm Al Hammond," Hammond said, putting out a paw. "And you're Eleanor. Simeon's told me so much about you," he added untruthfully.

She shook his hand and blushed. "He has?" She glanced at me.

"You're Topic A."

"Topic or toxic?"

Hammond laughed, a trifle uncertainly, and took refuge in business. "Sarah Oldfield," he said.

"This is not a gift," I said. "It's a trade."

"What do you want? And what are you giving?"

"To take it in reverse order, I'm giving you a name, an address, and some background. What you're giving me is in. I want in on everything you find out, and I want to know everything you can put together about three people. Make that four people."

"Have you got a client?"

"No. I've got a grudge. I don't think Sally Oldfield should be dead."

Hammond pulled out a tiny notebook, dwarfed in his hamlike hands. He felt around in his jacket pockets for a pen. "What's the background?"

"Have we got a deal?"

"How am I supposed to treat this information?"

"That's your problem. Pretend I'm an informant, someone on the street."

Hammond drank. Eleanor and I followed suit. "Is the information good?" he said.

"Better than anything you've got now."

He waved a hand for Peppi. "Deal," he said. "Shoot."

I told him about how I'd been hired, about the line of bull that had been fed to me about Sally. I described Needlenose, and he nodded. As I'd figured, he already had a description from the people who ran the motel. I shut up as Peppi served a new round, and then told him about the Church. He sat up and took notice. Hammond's pen was scratching away, but Eleanor hadn't yet taken a note. I told him about Rhoda Gerwitz and about Skippy Miller.

"They got your name from Skippy," Eleanor said.

"He said not."

"Simeon. He told his Listener."

I sat back and felt stupid. "You're good at this," Hammond said to her.

"I've been working at it all day," she said, looking pleased. "He's a good teacher. Simeon, what about the other murder?"

Hammond leaned forward. All the good feeling fled from his face. "What other murder?"

"I need to know we have a deal."

"My ass," he said.

"Good night." I got up to go.

"What do you want?" he said.

"I told you. I want in, and I want information on four people. Dr. Richard Merryman of the Church of the Eternal Moment, two folks from something that calls itself the Congregation of the Present, and one other."

"Names?"

"From the Congregation, Dr. Hubert Wilburforce and Sister Zachary." He wrote. "Number four is a man named Ellis Fauntleroy, or possibly not, deceased. I want everything you've got on any of them. Nothing held back, Al."

"Do I look like a man who'd hold something back?" Neither of us said anything, so he crossed himself. "You've got it," he said. "On my mother's grave."

"Your mother's alive," Eleanor said.

"How do you know?" Hammond said, looking surprised.

"You're not married," Eleanor said, "and you see your mother often. It's written all over your face."

"Well, I'll be damned," Hammond said.

"Where, specifically?" I asked, looking at Hammond's face.

"His forehead," Eleanor said.

"My mother notwithstanding," Hammond said, "you've got a deal. What's the other murder?"

"Friday night in Santa Monica," I said.

"Huh?"

"The guy I mentioned, Harker or Fauntleroy." Hammond still looked blank. "In Santa Monica," I said again.

Hammond said nothing.

"In the TraveLodge, for Christ's sake. How many murders *were* there in the Santa Monica TraveLodge on Friday night?"

Hammond laid down his notebook and spread two empty hands. "None," he said.

14

That was what I got for not reading the papers.

I'd been assuming all along that Harker's death had been reported, when obviously a clean-up squad had been waiting in the wings. For whatever reason, they'd waited until I'd cleared out and then sent in the housekeepers. And for whatever reason, I told myself again, they'd left me alive.

So, we were dealing with a number of people. At least three, I figured: one to kill Harker, probably one more to help him, as Hamlet said, to lug the guts into the neighbor room—bodies are heavy—and one to go to my house and slip the cassette out of my answering machine. One or more of them had obviously been listening in when Harker called me, and Harker had probably known it but it hadn't worried him. He'd thought he was part of the gang.

On the whole, that made me happy. The more people you have involved in a murder, the more likely it is that one of them will do something stupid.

Hollering over the music in the Red Dog, Hammond had made it clear that, as far as he was concerned, I was the stupid one. If I'd done what I was supposed to do, which is to say call the cops, they'd have a body. He'd used language that had turned Eleanor scarlet, and I'd had no choice but to listen. As we staggered out of the Red Dog and into the rain on Hollywood Boulevard, I'd asked whether our deal still stood.

Hammond didn't seem to notice the rain. He stood there,

solid and bulky, with water streaming down his face, and thought for a long wet moment.

"With a difference," he finally said. "The information is two-way. I get everything you get." He really wanted out of Records.

"Al," I said, "of course. I'd assumed that all along."

"Honey," Hammond said to Eleanor, who was shivering at my side, "go home with Peppi. She's a straighter guy than your buddy here."

"He's always been a liar," she said. So much for loyalty.

"All of it, Simeon," Hammond said to me. "And I mean it. Investigators' licenses are precarious things."

I got my legs to wobbling. "Look," I said, "you're making me weak in the knees."

Hammond took Eleanor's hand in both of his. "You're a beautiful little thing," he said, "and it's been a pleasure to meet you. Good-bye, jerk," he said to me. He turned abruptly and walked away into the rain. He hardly weaved at all.

"What a sweet man," Eleanor said. "His mother is a very lucky woman."

"Well, you beautiful little thing," I said, "where to now?"

"Home. We've got a lot to do tomorrow."

We hadn't even hit the Santa Monica freeway when the man on the radio said that there'd been a mudslide in Topanga, closing the boulevard from the Pacific Coast Highway to Old Canyon.

"Well, shit," I said. "That's an extra fifty miles."

"Stay at my place," she said absently.

"You're kidding," I said. Hope springs eternal.

"Why not? The couch is comfortable."

Hope, as Emily Dickinson once wrote, is a thing with feathers, and Eleanor had just twisted its neck. For lack of anything more interesting to do, I turned the windshield wipers onto high, and they responded by swinging back and forth at exactly the same rate as before. The silence in the car lengthened in an ominous fashion. I turned right from La Brea onto the long freeway on-ramp, heading west.

"Anyway," she finally said, "if you sleep on my couch

you won't be sleeping with that Roxy or whatever her name is." She rapped her fingernails sharply against the window.

I swallowed a couple of times and wondered how she knew about Roxanne Then I stopped wondering. The Women's Network, the world's most successful subversive society, had done its stuff. "Who am I supposed to sleep with?" I said, more defensively than I would have liked. "My teddy bear wore out years ago."

"Simeon," she said with elaborate unconcern, "I don't care who you sleep with, as long as you don't catch anything. I mean, I certainly hope you don't think I'm being possessive."

Childishly I sped up; Eleanor hated it when I drove fast. This time, though, she seemed determined to ignore it. She chewed distractedly on the ends of her hair and gazed out the window on her side.

"I want to interview the Speaker and her mother," she finally said, "and that Dr. Merryman you keep talking about."

"Great," I said. "And Happy Trails to you."

"Are you going to come along?"

"They know me."

"So what? They don't know you're a detective, do they?"

"No, but they know my name isn't Algernon Swinburne."

"Good thing. I was getting tired of that name anyway. I couldn't keep calling you Algy. It sounds like something that grows in a pool."

"This is dangerous, Eleanor," I said for perhaps the twelfth time. "These folks kill people."

"Why is it okay for you and not for me?" she asked with a sudden burst of energy. "Is murder something new, some passing fad? Do you think I like it when you swashbuckle around all night, like some Boy Scout fantasy, and come home with holes in your head? This is the first time since you started this stupid job that I've gotten a chance to see what it's all about. So it's dangerous. So is driving like a maniac when it's raining. Simeon, would you please slow *down*?"

"Then you're in this for keeps," I said.

"Oh, come on. Stop playing Lochinvar. I don't want to get rescued. There's a story here. It could make a big difference in my life. The New Age is getting old. Are you going to slow down or not?"

I eased my foot from the accelerator. "One of the Speakers is dead," I said. "Let's try to locate the one who isn't. She couldn't be more than seventeen by now."

"What's her name?"

I didn't know, and it made me feel dumb. "Get it from Chantra," I said. "If she doesn't have it, we'll go downtown to that hotel the Church owns and pick up some literature. And where is Mr. Ellspeth? The current Speaker must have a father, but the Church only books mother-daughter acts."

"Why is he important?"

"I don't know that he is. But maybe he's on the outside wishing he were in. If so, he could be resentful enough to talk to us."

"Like Wilburforce," she said.

"Like Wilburforce. Go into the morgue at the *Times*, if you can do it without having to explain what you're doing to too many people. Can you?"

"I don't know. I've never looked in the morgue before. I've only worked for them a little while. Morgue," she said. "What an awful word. What am I supposed to be looking for?"

"Anything you can find on the Church. Or on the Congregation. Look for stories on the death of a girl named Anna Klein."

"Why and when?"

"She was the Church's first Speaker. I don't know when, but it had to be within the last seven or eight years. The Church is only twelve years old."

"The one who died, right? Some kind of accident?"

"Maybe," I said. The wipers made another slow pass. "And then again, maybe not."

"Another one?"

"Could be."

"Holy smoke," Eleanor said. "She was just a little girl. Who'd want to kill a little girl? I know this sounds gruesome, Simeon, but there could be a mini-series here."

"Sooner or later," I said, "there could also be a man with

a gun in his hand. As your friend Peppi said, this isn't television."

"Why do you assume it's a man?"

"Good point," I said grudgingly. "The Church is riddled with women."

"That's a pleasant way to put it. But you're probably right. The bigwigs all seem to be men."

"It was ever thus."

A big-rig, a twelve-wheeler at least, howled past us on the left, throwing off sheets of water from its tires. The light in the cab was on, and I watched in fascination as the driver tossed back a couple of pills.

"Anything else?" she said.

"Yeah. Hold off on Merryman and Angel for the moment, if you don't mind. Let's talk to the people who don't know me first, okay? A straight line may be the shortest distance between two points, but it's also the place where you're most likely to walk into an ambush."

"You're so masculine," she said. It didn't sound like a compliment.

"Then why do I have to sleep on the couch?"

"Because it would complicate things. We've got days of talking to do before we sleep together again, if we ever do. Anyway, you've always got Roxy."

"Roxanne," I said. "You know her name, so why pretend to get it wrong?"

"Little heavier than you usually like them, isn't she?"

"It doesn't matter," I said offensively. "I'm usually on top."

"That must be novel," she said.

There was no way to win.

At her place, she waited for a moment for the rain to subside. When it didn't, she opened the passenger door anyway. "You're not coming in?"

"For what?"

"Okay," she said. "See you tomorrow." There was a moment of silence. Then she leaned over and kissed me on the cheek. "Don't be a lunk," she said. "Anyway, you've got a long drive." The instant she got out of the car, the rain stopped. It started again as she closed the front door behind her.

To get from Santa Monica to Topanga Canyon without going up the Pacific Coast Highway you have to track east, all the way into the San Fernando Valley, and then head north until you can pick up Topanga, turn left, and go most of the way west again. It's a meandering, basically U-shaped route, all freeways and blue-white light at night, a charmless drive under the best of circumstances. In a downpour, it always reminds me of Shelly Berman's famous definition of flying: hours of boredom relieved by moments of stark terror.

Between the yawns and the occasional red accident flares, I thought about Eleanor. We'd met at UCLA, where I was pursuing one of my long string of semiuseless degrees in lieu of doing anything better. She was the most wastefully beautiful human being I'd ever seen in my life, attractive way beyond the demands of natural selection. Two weeks after she moved in she had me kicking a two-pack-a-day cigarette habit that I'd thought was as permanent as a tattoo. A week later, to my infinite surprise, I was running along next to her on San Vicente Boulevard: wheezy, labored quarter-miles at first, then miles, then 10K's, finally marathons.

In spite of the fact that she couldn't get me to stop drinking beer, the pounds began to fall away. I'd been a shamefaced, sedentary 237 pounds when we met; six months later I weighed 175, and I was stopping to look for my reflection in store windows on Westwood Boulevard. It wasn't vanity; I just couldn't find myself. Until I learned to recognize my new silhouette, I'd had an eerie feeling that I was invisible on the street.

My blood pressure, which had been higher than the federal deficit, plummeted to textbook normal and stayed there. Several cups of nicotine-based goop gradually cleared from my lungs. I no longer woke up each morning to the sound of my respiratory system squeaking.

And then a cocaine-fried subhuman made a natural mistake, considering the state of his consciousness, and threw an inoffensive young woman named Jennie Chu off the top of one of the UCLA dormitories. Jennie Chu had been one of Eleanor's closest friends, a shy math student, gymnast, and part-time classical pianist from Taiwan who had never really mastered American English and who'd had the misfortune to wear eyeglasses that resembled those worn by the woman the coke freak had really intended to kill. The doctors said she had died instantly, but, as Eleanor said at the time, "What's instantly? It must have taken her a month to hit the ground."

A few days later I delivered the man who killed Jennie Chu to the LAPD with both his elbows broken, and I had found a career. I had learned that I enjoyed righting wrongs. I had also learned that, under the right circumstances, I enjoyed breaking someone's elbows. I'd been keeping tabs on the latter discovery in the two years since. I'd broken a couple of hands, hands that belonged to a man who'd come up with an interesting new use for pliers, but no elbows.

Topanga Canyon Boulevard stretched uphill in front of me, empty and wet. As empty, I thought, with several drams of self-pity, as the house I lived in, the house I'd shared with Eleanor until I'd fooled around one too many times and she'd stopped telling me it was okay and packed up and moved to Venice.

It's so easy to break things that it seems like it should be easier to put them back together. Once, when I was a kid, I was showing one of my mother's prize Irish crystal vases to a pretty classmate, feeding her wide-eyed awe by making up stories about the craftsmen who cut every facet by hand and died prematurely from inhaling glass. In my eagerness to get to the punch line, I dropped the vase. It broke into only three pieces, but I spent the entire afternoon sitting on the floor with a tube of glue, and the cracks were the first thing my mother saw when she got home that evening. The lesson didn't take. I'd broken a lot of things since.

Alice sputtered resentfully when I cut the engine at the bottom of the driveway. The rain drummed giant fingers on the thin Detroit tin of Alice's roof. It was like sitting in a big beer can.

Rain stopped for Eleanor, but I was too much of a realist to expect it to stop for me. I opened the door and hunched over, reducing the surface area vulnerable to the wet.

The smell hit me even before I got out of the car. It rolled at me out of the sagebrush, a concentration of corruption so vile that it should have been incandescent, like swamp gas. Its source, whatever it was, was dead beyond the resurrection dreams of even the most fervent born-again Christian. I forgot the rain altogether and clawed my way up the muddy driveway. At the top of the hill I realized that I'd been holding my breath and drew several shuddering breaths of clean, rainwashed air. Against my better judgment I raised my arm to my nose and sniffed my sleeve. The smell had impregnated the cloth.

Then I noticed that the kitchen light was on.

I hadn't left it on.

One of the design quirks of the shack I rent from Mrs. Yount is that there are absolutely no windows you can look through from the outside. They're all about eight feet above ground level. That's charming when you want privacy, which I usually did. Now, standing in the downpour, I considered the drawbacks. The one that immediately occurred to me was sudden death.

The house is heated by a wood-burning stove, and a wood-burning stove requires a woodpile. I went to the woodpile and selected a sodden piece of oak, about the length of my arm and just slender enough to wrap my hand around. The rain had become an ally: it muffled the sound of my approach. Even the sucking sounds I made as I pulled my shoes out of the mud were probably inaudible to anyone inside.

A foot at a time, I reached the door. I stood in front of it for what seemed like an hour. Just as I was about to convince myself that I *had* left the kitchen light on, I heard footsteps on the wooden floor inside. A shadow passed in front of the opaque glass in the door, heading for the kitchen.

I hefted the wood in my hand to make sure I had the balance right, and waited. Footsteps again. The shadow passed across the door again, and I threw myself against it and lurched across the threshhold, the piece of wood lifted high above my head.

Roxanne, wearing my heavy woolen bathrobe, whirled

and shrieked like the heroine in a forties horror flick. Then she registered who I was, lowered her hand from her mouth, and said, "Simeon, how nice. You've brought in some firewood."

Half an hour later, with wine warming our insides and wet wood sputtering in the stove, we fell asleep.

I woke up even more reluctantly than usual and stumbled to the bathroom. Roxanne, once again, was long gone, but the smell of coffee permeated the house. The rain had apparently stopped, and sun streamed improbably through the windows.

Since hot water in Topanga takes approximately the same time to arrive as the Ice Age did in Europe, I turned the shower on and snapped the door shut before I took a stance at the washbasin to scrape what tasted like several past lifetimes off my teeth. My toothbrush seemed too heavy to lift. When I looked at my face in the mirror, rabid foam dripped from my chin. I couldn't bear to look at myself, so I shaved from memory and stepped into the shower.

The water was exactly body temperature. Uncannily body temperature. Feeling vaguely uneasy, I began to scrub. I looked down and saw the streams running off my body turning a brownish-red rust color. Then the water stopped altogether and I looked up.

Blood gouted out through the shower head. Dark, thick, precisely body temperature, it poured forth, splashing off my shoulders and splattering the shower tiles in crimson Rorschach patterns. I leapt back, and it squished beneath my bare feet.

I heard my scream echo wildly. I tried to push the shower door open. It was stuck. I threw a shoulder, streaming with blood, against it. Nothing.

Someone was outside, holding it closed.

I hammered against it. It didn't give. The blood stopped flowing. Against all my better judgment I looked to see why. White worms, thin, pallid, not really white but a sickly pale gray, squeezed themselves through the holes in the shower head and began to dangle down toward me. I grabbed at the edge of the shower door and hurled myself into it. It opened an inch and then slammed shut again and I found myself looking down, staring transfixed at what had caught in the door.

Long blond hair.

Angel Ellspeth's hair.

The worms touched my shoulder.

The odor of death filled the shower.

The worms grasped me more tightly, their gaping mouths opening wide, gripping my shoulder, pulling me up, up toward the shower head.

"Simeon," they said in a girlish voice.

I tried to shake myself free. They hung fast. I closed my eyes.

"Simeon," they said. "Something stinks."

I opened my eyes, swallowed, and looked at Roxanne.

"It's really bad," she said, looking down at me. She was wrapped in my robe. "Are you awake, or what?"

"I'm awake," I said. I was also sweating. "What in God's name is it?"

"Well," she said in the gray light of a rainy morning, "I'm no expert, but my guess is that something's dead."

15

It took two toots from the truck's horn to tell me he'd arrived. I hoisted my steaming coffee mug, wrapped my leaky raincoat around my bare and unsteaming body, and headed down the driveway. Roxanne was gone but the rain was still with us.

About an hour before, at Roxanne's urging and jacked up by three cups of her coffee, I'd gone reluctantly down to check out the smell. If Roxanne hadn't been watching from the top of the driveway I'd have yielded to nausea and gone back up the hill to tell her a lie. She *was* watching, though, and I had a sacred masculine tradition of stupidity to uphold.

If the smell had been music it would have been Mahler. There was a rich, overripe majesty to it that actually made it difficult to tell whether it was getting stronger or weaker. Looking for its source was like trying to spot a candle after being blinded by a flashbulb. With every synapse in my nervous system screaming retreat in a hysterical falsetto, I forced myself into the bushes above the driveway.

And there it was, about five feet up the hill, a shapeless blob of blond fur: someone's beloved Fluffy the Cat. Around what once had been its neck was a pink collar that had been described to me in heartrending detail, making me surer than I wanted to be that it was, to be precise, Mrs. Yount's Fluffy the Cat. I didn't think she'd want her back. So I'd discreetly heaved the coffee and most of last night's hamburger onto the wet earth, feeling protected by the bushes from Roxanne's prying eyes. Then, bathed in chill sweat, I'd clambered back up the driveway with a ghastly semblance of jauntiness to figure out what to do.

Coyotes team up to take cats. One of them had probably chased poor old Fluffy into the underbrush and directly into a circle of teeth and claws. Cats must taste terrible, because they hadn't bothered to eat her. Fluffy had been deteriorating for about ten days while Mrs. Yount waited for me to turn something up, and I drove up and down the canyon tacking Xeroxes to phone poles. If I could have written them in coyote I might have gotten an answer. Or at least a long, echoing, moonlit horse-laugh.

Once I was safe inside the house, I'd called the city out of sheer desperation and been referred to the county. The county had given me another number to call, and someone at that number had given me another number. I was running out of space on my doodle pad by the time I found myself talking to the right person.

That person's job was to dispatch other people to pick up dead animals.

When the horn toots summoned me, I slogged back down in the drizzle to see a tall young black man in a yellow rubber slicker standing in front of a long white truck. His expression was as bright as a sunny day, cheerier than an orange Life-Saver in a packet full of limes. He balanced a shovel upright like an urban graffito based loosely on American Gothic.

"Say what," he said by way of salutation. "So where she be?"

I took a protective pull off my coffee cup and pointed vaguely toward the bushes, stifling a petticoat impulse to hold my nose. He nodded, slogged up the hill, and started in. First, though, he paused and looked back at me.

"No snakes in here, is they?" He sounded serious.

"None," I lied, without even thinking about it. "I've lived here five years and never seen one." I'd killed three with a hoe, right about there.

"I don't shine to snakes," he said. "Somethin' wrong when you can kill the front half and the back still lash around. Even when they all the way dead, I use the long shovel. The *way* long shovel. Sometimes, if they dead in the road and they ain't nobody watchin', I just run the truck over them four, five times to mash them into the asphalt. Then I jus' pretend they the dotted line and go home.''

"No problem. You're safe as milk," I said, wondering who at the county I could call to get him picked up if a rattler bit him. "Just follow your nose."

The brush closed behind him and I repressed a twinge of guilt and tried to think about something else. Anything else. "Wo," he said, unseen. "She be real ripe." I heard some scuffling in the brush and the handle of his shovel emerged once or twice. "Heeere, kitty, kitty," he said. I concentrated on feeling inadequate.

He came out backward with something blond and unrecognizable lolling off the end of the shovel. An explosion of odor rolled toward me. The black man extended the shovel to the left and faced all the way right, toward me. "I done developed this walk all by myse'f," he said. "Looks funny, but she works. Tell me if I gone hit a tree." Arms left, head right, he marched down the hill.

"You do this all day long?" I said after the cat was safely stowed in the bowels of the truck.

He wiped the shovel on some dead grass while he considered the question. "This ain't doodlysquat," he said at last. "Later, right before dinner, I got to unload the truck."

I looked for a tree to sag against. "No," I said. "Say it isn't so."

"Four dollar thirty-fi' an hour," he said, grinning. "And unloading them ain't the half of it."

"What in the world," I said, against my better judgment, "could you mean?"

"Well, they's a problem. See, sometime they get mixed up. Out come ol' Fluffy there and she got Fido's head. Then I got to sort them out. Like a jigsaw puzzle, you know? 'Cept in 3-D and Smellovision."

My pulse pounded forcefully in my ears a couple of times before sanity prevailed. "Wait a minute," I said. "Why do you have to sort them out?"

His smile widened. "For burial. We take 'em over to the Permanent Pet Playground, Inc., y' know? Fussy outfit. These fuzzy babies going to be frisking around for eternity, they got to have the right heads and tails. Otherwise they going to be fightin' with theyself. I mean, wo. What gone happen when that big bugle blow in the sky, huh? How all these good folk seized up by the Rapture gone recognize they pets when they pets look like they been put together by a committee?"

I looked at him for a long moment. His face was as innocent as a Girl Scout cookie. "I'm not sure," I said, "but I think you're full of shit." He gazed at me genially. "You want a cup of coffee?"

"Is the pope a polack?" He stashed the shovel carefully in the truck and followed me up the driveway.

I closed the door behind him and poured out the last of Roxanne's hour-old brew. He'd taken the slicker off to reveal an immaculate white uniform with the name DEXTER stitched into the pocket. It was hand-stitched, individual stitches leapfrogging each other over the pocket's surface. It looked like he'd stitched the pocket closed. He sat at what passed for a breakfast counter, sipped the coffee, and made a face.

"Wo, hot. But it taste good. Center slice from the loaf of life, y' know?" He blew on the chipped mug and surveyed the living room. "I know every man's home supposed to be his castle," he said, "but you pushing it, don't you think?"

"You don't like it?"

"Sure," he said, "it's real sweet. I was just trying to figure if I'd rather live in it or under it."

"That's because you haven't been under it."

"Ain't nothin' there I haven't picked up."

"How do you do it?" I drained the dregs in my cup. "And, while we're on it, why?"

He had a knack of making his eyes glimmer, and he glimmered them at me then. "You got a live boss?" he asked.

I thought. "Not at the moment."

"That's what I like," he said, "man who don't pick his words."

"Okay, sorry. I usually do."

"Me, I'll take a dead client anytime, huh? 'Stead of a live boss, I mean. Ol' Fluffy, y' know, she smell terrible, she done kiss the odor of sanctity good-bye for keeps, and she ain't no thicker'n a milkshake. But she ain't gone tell me what to do."

"You mean you do this of your own free will?" I asked disbelievingly.

"Free will?" he said. "That's quaint, y' know? I ain't heard no one say that since college."

"College," I said.

"Yeah. This philosphy professor. Must have weighed three hundred pounds on a good day, when he been skippin' potatoes, y' know? Man was *fat*. Always talkin' about determinism. Everything come from somethin' else, right? So if this clown know that, how come he's so fat? And, wo, could he smoke. If he know everything come from somethin' else, how come he don't know cancer comes from smokin' cigarettes? Enough to put you off education."

"Jerry Ryskind," I said.

"Wo," he said, sitting bolt upright. "Hey, the Bruins, huh? Fuck USC."

"In spades," I said, regretting the expression instantly. He saw my expression and laughed.

"Skip it," he said. "Fuck 'em in spades and hearts and diamonds too. So you a Bruin too. You know ol' Jerry."

"Philosophy 101," I said. "Many unfiltered cigarettes. Double-breasted suits."

"Triple-breasted. On the way to quadruple-breasted, last time I seen him. He gain five more pounds, they gone have to put a pleat in the room."

"I'm Simeon. Simeon Grist."

"Dexter," he said, pointing to the pocket. "Dexter Smif. S-m-i-f. This be a terrible house," he elaborated. "Shame you don't got none of the advantages."

"With your college education, how many negatives can you get into a sentence?"

"Five. Six, if I workin' at it. Hard thing is to stick with the odd numbers. If two negatives is a positive, then four is a double positive. Got to get past the last even number. 'I ain't got no idea,' well, you know and I know that that means I know something. 'I don't know nothing nohow,' right? That leaves some doubt in the mind, don't it?"

"It don't," I said. "Anybody can count to three."

He slurped at his coffee. "You wrong there. Somebody like you, got all the advantages despite this shit house, you can hit three without standing on tiptoe."

"So you took philosophy."

"Minor. It's a dead man's game. De hearse before Decartes."

"What was your major, urban English?"

"The degree's in poli sci." He gave me a slow grin. "You want me to talk different?"

"Well," I said, "if you'll forgive my saying so, it doesn't exactly add up. A political-science degree, and you spend your days scraping up dead mammals."

" 'Phibians too," he said. "Don't forget the 'phibians."

"You have a lot of invigorating political discussions with the dead 'phibians?"

"You forget the philosphy. This is a good job for a guy with philosphy flowin' through his veins."

"Thought you didn't like snakes."

"Don't be gettin' tricky, now. Any fool that can tell poop from pizza knows snakes ain't 'phibians. They riptahls."

"I'd love to hear you spell that."

"R-i-p-t-a-h-l-s." He smiled. "Easy." he said. "Almost as easy as 'Smif.' "

"No bosses," I said. "Lots of time to speculate on the implications of mortality."

"They only one implication I can think of. We all gone to end up in somebody's truck."

"The Chariot of the Gods."

He fished out a pack of cigarettes and lit one, crossed impossibly long legs, and leaned back. "So," he said, "we talkin' about my job. What career path brought you to this mansion on the hill?"

"I'm an investigator," I said. The word "detective" always made me uncomfortable.

"Can't be insurance. You don't look like you could get it, much less give it. Can't be a cop. Cops got to be macho, you know? Your average cop would have picked up ol' Fluffy out there with his teeth and then flossed with the tendons. You certainly ain't IRS. Got any more coffee?"

"I'll make some. It'll take a while. You don't have to go anywhere?"

"No bosses, remember? And Fluffy, she ain't no jug of perfume but she real patient. So I guess that means you in business for yourself."

I poured water into the top of the coffeemaker and put some beans in the grinder. "I guess it does."

"Wo, real gourmet. Beans and all. You got a ashtray?"

"Use the floor. The cleaning crew comes in today."

"They gone bring a wrecking ball?"

"A fire hose. You want it strong?"

"You like the job?"

I thought about it. "Some days."

"Explain the appeal." He stubbed out his cigarette in the saucer.

The coffeemaker gurgled three or four times as the water heated. "This is its idea of foreplay," I said. "In about an hour we'll have some coffee."

"Like I said, explain the appeal."

"Well, once in a while you get a chance to reduce the number of assholes in the world."

"That's a losin' battle. Ain't never gone to be no asshole shortage. We got oil shortages, grain shortages, coal shortages, every kind of fuckin' shortage you can think of, but there ain't no asshole shortage. Assholism is a dominant trait."

"It's still nice to take one out." I gave the coffeepot a useless whack to speed it up.

"You an idealist," he said. "Me, I'm a realist. You know the difference between an idealist and a realist?"

"No," I said, "but I have a feeling you're going to tell me."

"The idealist is holdin' the gun. The realist is on the other end."

"And where'd you pick up this bit of knowledge?"

"Nice little island name of Grenada. I was a member of the victorious invadin' force. We fought them on the beaches, we fought them in the streets."

"One of my favorite wars."

"Like the man say, democracy in action. 'Nother exercise in poli sci."

"So you went to college, went into the forces, and then put all that background to work picking up dead animals."

"Markin' time."

The phone rang. I went to pick it up, and Dexter went over to study the coffeemaker.

"It's Hammond," Hammond said.

"Damn," Dexter said to the coffeemaker, which still hadn't dripped a drop. "Come on, now."

"You were right about the Oldfield house," Hammond said. "They were pros. They even ripped the paper off the back of the mirror in the bedroom."

"Did they wipe the place?"

"Looks like it. Lots of smears around, hardly one good print, not even many of hers. Also, they left money. There was about three hundred in a flour canister. Canister was open but the money was still there."

"Be drippin'," Dexter said, rattling the pot and peering into it. "Move your ass."

"What did they take?"

"Well, that's hard to say," Hammond said with exaggerated politeness. "Because it wouldn't be there, would it? I mean, after they took it, we wouldn't find it, so we wouldn't know if they'd taken it, would we?"

"I knew there was a reason I hadn't joined the force," I said. "The difficulties you overcome in the line of duty. Was there a personal phone book?"

"No."

"Don't most women have a personal phone book?"

There was a silence. "Are you going to let me tell this my way, or are we going to play Twenty Questions?"

"Sorry," I said. "Just trying to gain insight into the police mentality."

"Police?" Dexter said. "Get a man out here to arrest this coffeepot. It gone on strike."

"Someone's there?" Hammond said.

"A man from the county," I said. "Animal Homicide."

"Ask a stupid question," Hammond said. "No phone book, no checkbook, no letters, no fingerprints. Not many photographs. They wanted to know who she'd been talking to, who she'd been writing to, who she really was."

"Who was she?"

"Sarah Theresa Oldfield. Married, divorced. Husband in Utica. That's in New York. No kids. In L.A. three years."

"Utica?"

"That's what it says. Sounds like something that hangs in the back of your throat. Booming little town. Saturday night, you ask your date if she'd like to go down to the beer factory and watch the gauges rise."

"How long in the Church?"

"That's coming. Ought to know this afternoon."

"You're not talking to the Church."

"Please," Hammond said. "We're going to check her bank records."

"I got a idea," Dexter said. He yanked the empty pot out from under the spout.

"You'll make a mess," I said warningly.

"Somethin' this contrary, a mess is what she want."

"Jesus," Hammond said, "it's nice to have your attention."

"Here she come," Dexter said with nicely modulated triumph. A stream of brown coffee splattered on the hot plate. Dexter slipped the pot back under the filter.

"I never thought of that," I said admiringly.

"There is much in heaven and earth, Horatio," Dexter said, "that is not in your philosphy."

"Maybe you'd like me to call back to tell you about Wilburforce," Hammond said. "Or maybe you'd like to call me when Animal Homicide has gone to that big kennel in the sky."

"Sorry. What about Wilburforce?"

"A real *shtarker*. An old-time con man named Jason Jenks, aka Jinks Jenks. Actually, I sort of remember Jinks. He was jugged about fifteen years ago for practicing medicine without a license."

"What's so memorable about that?"

"He was doing surgery."

"Ah."

"Pretty well, too. He cut them open and sewed them up again. Sometimes he even got what he was after. Apparently he had some medical school in a previous life. After that he was arrested for running a weight-loss clinic, pretending to be the doctor in charge. They put people on a diet and then fed them all sorts of bright little pills and injected them with water and B-12 every couple of days. Also, apparently, a little cat piss."

"Wilburforce running a weight-loss clinic?" I asked. "He's bigger than Luciano Pavarotti."

"He was svelte in those days," Hammond said. "Weighed a chic two-oh-five when he was booked. Called himself Dr. Pounzoff, with a Russian spelling. Place was called the Pounzoff Clinic. Cute, no? The fat lady is his wife, Clara. She was pretending to be a nurse then."

Dexter poured a cup of coffee and waved it questioningly at me. I nodded, and he went to the counter and got my cup.

"Why was he arrested?" I asked. "L.A. has more phony weight clinics than fire hydrants."

"Couple of customers got hepatitis and complained. This is in the early seventies, before AIDS. Even then, we dumb cops knew that meant that someone wasn't being really scrupulous about sterilizing needles. And then, of course, there was his surgery conviction. We couldn't have him getting delusions of grandeur and cutting honest citizens open again. Think how the doctors at Cedars would have felt."

"Since then?"

"After the Pounzoff dodge he dropped out of sight. Went somewhere and gained weight. Then he surfaced in the Church of the Eternal Moment."

"And you guys left him alone?"

Dexter handed me my cup. The coffee wasn't as good as Roxanne's, but it was better than nothing.

"Freedom of religion, remember?" Hammond said. "Anyway, he didn't seem to be bothering anybody."

"He was passing himself off as the little girl's personal physician."

"Well, we didn't know that. Unless somebody gets killed, we leave the religions alone."

"Somebody got killed," I said.

"Yeah, and you went all cute about it, didn't you? Our buddy Jenks was long gone by then anyhow. Set up his own shop, didn't he?"

I slurped my coffee. Dexter crossed his legs and examined the crease in his pants.

"So tell me about this year's Jenks. Dr. Richard Merryman."

"Nothing."

"By which you mean?"

"Nothing at all. Nothing illegal, nothing legal. He's a whaddya-call-it, a blank slate."

"Tabula rasa."

"You took the word out of my mouth. Or words, maybe. Not even a parking ticket. The lad is cleaner than a nun's conscience."

"Licensed for California?"

"Not so far as we can tell. He could have been licensed in the past six months or so. Sometimes they're a little slow up there in Sacramento."

"Can you get them to hurry?"

"Not without telling them why I'm interested. You want I should do that?"

"I'd rather you got leprosy."

"Wo," Dexter said. "That's cold."

"I agree with the man from Animal Homicide," Hammond said. "Anything happening on your end?"

"A dead cat," I said. "I'll call you when there's something more interesting."

"You'd better," Hammond said, meaning it. "Listen, one more thing about Sally Oldfield—you probably should know it although we're keeping it out of the papers."

"What's that?" I didn't like the edge in Hammond's voice.

"She was hurt."

I chewed the inside of my lip and remembered Sally's face, Sally's smile. "Hurt like how?"

"The man left with four of her fingernails in his pocket."

"The son of a bitch."

"She'd been gagged with her own panty hose, a big knot stuffed in her mouth. Kind of odd, don't you think?"

"To keep her quiet," I said, and then I said, "Oh. Right."

"Yeah," Hammond said. "Let's say in four cases out of

five the guy who takes the time to pull someone's nails out before he closes the door for good wants to learn something. And if the person whose nails he's removing wants to say something, he's not going to be able to understand her with a big knot of nylon in her mouth, is he?"

"He did it for fun."

"There was probably nothing on TV. But then he goes and tosses her house. So maybe there *was* something he wanted to learn."

"No," I said. "I think he did it for fun. I think he already knew whatever it was, or he wouldn't have killed her. I think he held off killing her until he was sure about what she knew."

"Then why take the house apart?"

"To find out if she'd told anyone else. Think about what they took, Al."

"Girl's hands were a mess," Hammond said. "You get any closer to the man, let me know. I'd like an introduction. He had such a good time that he jerked off on her before he left. Ten-four," he said, knowing I hated it. He hung up.

"Ten-four," I said automatically as my mind tried briefly to reject the last thing Hammond had told me. Thinking very hard about Needle-nose, I looked up into the eyes of Dexter Smif.

"Ol' Broderick Crawford always said that," Dexter said. "Ten-four. Like it mean something. How come the man can't say good-bye?"

"He couldn't get his upper lip down far enough for the B." I wanted to get up and out of the house, to work off a little unwholesome energy before focusing on the day.

"Lotta cops do that. Look like they tryin' to give they teeth a tan."

I pushed Needle-nose from my mind's eye and an image of Merryman floated in to take his place. "If you were a doctor," I said, "why would you go into religion?"

"This detective work?"

"No," I said. "It's the fevered questioning of a philosophical mind."

"Right, be nasty. Some lady been killed apparently, but be nasty. Take refuge in philosphy. Okay, me too. Nothin' comes from nothin', right? I'd say he's after a little less nothin'."

"Money."

"Why does anybody go into religion? I mean, unless they soul in peril. Most folks, they soul in peril, they the last one gone to know. Look at all those dildos in the three-piece suits and the dry-cleaned hair preachin' on the TV. All they worried about is the cost per thousand. It's the good folks worry about they soul."

"There's a sucker reborn every minute," I said.

"And they all got they dollar-fifty to send in every three days. From then on it's all multiplication. Be fruitful and multiply. 'Cept I don't think that's what it supposed to mean."

"So how do you trace a doctor?"

"Ask a doctor."

"Good idea." I picked up the phone and started to dial.

My friend Bernie picked up the phone on the third ring. Outside, the rain used the roof for a kettle drum. "Wo, listen to that," Dexter said. Have to go out through the valley."

"Bernie," I said. "How's Joyce?"

"Okay," Bernie said. "She's on call at the hospital."

"What are you doing?"

"Studying." Bernie was always studying. He was the only person I knew who had more degrees than I did, and he still couldn't bring himself to leave school.

"Can I buy you guys dinner?"

"Anybody can buy me dinner. But I don't know about Joyce. She thawed something before she went to work."

"Thawed something."

"I think it's lasagna. It's usually lasagna. Joyce cooks a boxcar full of lasagna and cuts the thing into one-foot squares and then freezes them. Our freezer flies the Italian flag."

"Well, then, how about I come over for dinner?"

"Listen to that," Dexter said. "Man invites himself."

"Like I said, I'll have to ask Joyce," Bernie said. "I don't know why there should be a problem. A square foot of lasagna is a lot of lasagna."

"It *sounds* like a lot of lasagna."

"It's good lasagna, though," Bernie said defensively. "Joyce makes a terrific lasagna."

"I'll bring the wine."

"Red," Bernie said. "I'm sick of Frascati."

Dexter picked up my doodle pad and wrote something on it. He waved languidly at me and headed for the door.

"I'm going to want to talk to Joyce," I said. "Will she mind?"

"Depends on what you want to talk about," Bernie said.

"See you," Dexter called. "Check the pad."

"Thanks for getting the cat," I said.

"Joyce likes cats," Bernie said. Then he said, "What have cats got to do with anything?"

"Nothing much. Seven o'clock fine?" Dexter pulled the door closed and went down the hill, whistling.

"Fine. Unless Joyce can't make it. Is this about cats?"

"No," I said. "It's about doctors. See you at seven."

I hung up and went to the kitchen to dump my cup in the sink. On the doodle pad Dexter had written DEXTER SMIF. 555-0091. CONSIDERIN ABOUT A CAREER CHANGE.

16

Mrs. Yount's pendulous lower lip trembled. So did the paper cup in her hand. The cup, courtesy of McDonald's, said FRESH COFFEE but the aroma was pure Jack Daniel's.

"I can't believe she's gone," Mrs. Yount said. "I always knew she'd come home. And now she won't."

Mrs. Yount's living room was in its usual state of chaos. Clothes were piled about eight inches thick on the carpet, if there was a carpet. An old, worn fur coat was spread out in front of the TV, which was tuned to a daytime show about the turbulent emotional lives of doctors and nurses. Two yolk-spattered plates, the refuse of Mrs. Yount's significant breakfast, littered the coat's shedding collar. Outside, a waist-high wall of empty whiskey bottles dripped water around Mrs. Yount's pathetic little garden. Mrs. Yount didn't like to throw her dead soldiers away. The trashmen might talk. Instead, she stacked them neatly inside the cinder-block wall that surrounded her scraggly patio.

"I should of felt something," she said. "Wouldn't you think I'd of felt something if she was dead?"

"I'm sorry," I said. "There couldn't have been any pain, the man said. She ran right under the truck, and it was over."

The lip trembled again. I was terrified that she'd begin to cry. "I guess that's something," she said. "He was a nice man?"

"Very nice. He felt terrible."

"What kind of truck?"

167

I wasn't ready for the question. "A beer truck. Making a delivery to the grocery."

"Fluffy liked beer. I gave her a little saucerful just before bed. She drank Anchor Steam."

"She had good taste," I said idiotically. "I drink it myself sometimes."

"Would you like one?"

"No," I said. "That's all right."

Mrs. Yount raised her paper cup to her lips and started to swallow, but then she made a sputtering noise and drops of whiskey spattered the crumpled clothes at her feet. A fat tear squeezed itself loose from her eye. "Oh, dear," she said. "Oh, dear . . . oh, dear."

"Please, Mrs. Yount," I said.

"What am I to do?" She looked at the television screen and the tears flowed down. "She was only three. What am I to do?"

"You'll be fine." I reached out and patted her arm.

She looked down at my hand and then heavily up at me, and there was a little click behind her eyes and the old Mrs. Yount was back. "A lot you know, mister," she said. "Go away. Send me a bill." She waved me away and picked up an empty Jack Daniel's bottle. Without turning back, she tottered toward the back door to add it to the wall of empties. "Just send me a bill, mister, that's all." The glass door to the patio slid open with a squeal that started a dog howling somewhere.

I left without saying anything about the leak in the roof.

In the high and palmy days of Hollywood glamour the place had called itself the Borzoi, and it had offered temporary and very expensive shelter to various Huntingtons, Hartfords, Sepulvedas, and Doheneys, not to mention a clutch of Barrymores. The Californians came there when the fires of autumn razed the elegant homes on the hillsides and when their wives were suing them for divorce, and the Barrymores when they were desperate enough for money to desert the adoring audiences of New York and hop the *Twentieth Century* for the three-day trip to Los Angeles. All day they'd labor in silence in the converted barns on Gower

and Sunset, letting their famous voices go to waste and
loathing themselves for pandering to a vulgar new medium,
and at night they'd return to the Borzoi in their long white
limousines to enjoy the fruits of their labors. They seldom
took much money back to New York.

What remained of the Borzoi's elegance was mostly in the
refined bones of the building, a sharp-elbowed piece of Art
Deco that laughed at gravity, and in the long-dark neon
portrait of two impossibly slim dogs that raced each other
over the spiky chrome doors leading into the lobby. There
were six pairs of doors in all, needing nothing more than a
little chrome polish and a few hours of work to be restored
to glory, but they hadn't been touched in years.

In fact, from where I stood, across the street, I couldn't
see that the Borzoi's current owners, the Church of the
Eternal Moment, had done much for the neighborhood.
The sign that for sixty years had said THE BORZOI in angular
letters had been replaced by a large, clunky hand-painted
affair announcing the new landlord's presence, but that was
about it. I'd arranged to meet Eleanor at one at the *Times*,
and since that meant going downtown it seemed like an
opportunity to take a look at Church headquarters. I don't
go downtown much, and every time I go I remember why.

The Borzoi faced west aross a sodden square that had
probably once been a pleasant little park. Dozens of homeless men and women had moved or been herded into the
square, using plastic trashbags and cardboard cartons to
shield themselves from the rain. It was about as effective as
it sounds. The sanitary facilities were as low-tech as the
housing, and the square smelled like an open sewer, which,
in effect, it was.

The extent of the Church's charity toward the dispos-
sessed on its doorstep was evident from across the street.
Ragged men and women sat, glazed and absent, in the
doorways on either side of the Borzoi, and lurched up and
down the sidewalk to the right and to the left. But no one
huddled for refuge in the Borzoi's doorways, and no one
strolled bedazedly in front of it. A waterlogged red carpet
ran from the six pairs of chrome doors to the very edge of
the curb. The carpet was flanked by thick black dripping

wire ropes that traveled down the steps on heavy metal stanchions and terminated exactly eighteen inches from the gutter. There was enough room for someone with minimal motor control to squeeze by on his way to or from the brown-bag store at the corner, but there was obviously no invitation to sit on the Borzoi's steps and rest a spell.

This message was further underlined by the presence of two beefy jokers wearing the nautical outfits I'd seen up in Carmel. They stood just inside the right- and left-hand doors and glared vigilantly out toward the street. They were obviously ready to protect that wet red carpet with their lives, if the need arose. The one on the right had the kind of face that suggested that he hoped the need would arise, and sooner rather than later: fat, downturned lips, a short thick pug nose, and two stupid little eyes lurking close together under a bony brow-ridge that I thought had been eliminated from the gene pool several million years ago. The other one just looked dumb.

As I crossed the street and set foot on the squishy red carpet, I decided on the dumb one. I didn't know whether I'd get a big smile, a salute, or a demand for a password, but whatever it was, I preferred not to get it from someone who was clearly upset that fate hadn't made him a Shi'ite Muslim with a lot of opportunities to die for something he believed in.

What I got from the dumb one was a burp, redolent of burger and onion, and a halfhearted attempt to open the left-hand door for me. I beat him to it without dislocating my shoulder, pushed it open myself, and went inside.

The sad old lobby arched dark and dirty above me. Spots of damp dotted the carpet and tainted the air. A few people came and went, looking businesslike. Above the long reception counter at the far end of the room hung a whopping color photo of Angel and Mary Claire Ellspeth. A pin spot dangling from the ceiling picked it out and made it dazzle. It was the only bright thing in the room.

When in doubt, as my mother always says, look like you know what you're doing. I nodded briskly to the two women at the counter and went to the elevator. The doors squealed open with a shrill plea for oil, and I pushed CLOSE DOOR and stood there for a moment, thinking.

There were six floors above me and one below. A sign on the elevator wall obligingly informed me that the second floor was the Listening Centre, quaint British spelling and all, and that the third and fourth were Church Offices. Five and six were labeled Residence Halls.

There was no label for the floor, presumably a basement, below me. There was no way to get there, either. One could go up simply by pushing a button. To go down, one needed a key.

That narrowed my options. They were further narrowed by the fact that I had no plausible business in the Church Offices and no interest in the Residence Halls. I pushed two and made a clanky ascent.

The doors opened on a narrow hallway illuminated by bare bulbs plunked into what once must have been elaborate sconces. A young man seated behind a desk that faced the elevator looked up at me incuriously. The sign in front of him said LISTENING CENTRE. The young man was pudgy and unhealthily white, with a dirty-looking fall of straight brown hair sloping across his forehead in a way that made him look like a latter-day member of the Hitler Youth.

"Room twelve," I said, hoping that there was one and that the number was high enough to place it around the corner and out of sight.

He pushed a register at me, tossed back the little fringe of hair on his forehead with a fat index finger, and held out a pen. "Down and to the left," he said. "Name and time, please."

ALGY SWINBURNE, I wrote. ELEVEN-FORTY.

He swiveled the register around again and crossed out the time. "Eleven-forty-four," he said with severe satisfaction, writing it above the scratch marks. "Your watch is slow."

"My gosh," I said, setting it ostentatiously, "it certainly is. Is Listener Simpson around?"

"She'd be in the studio now, wouldn't she?" He'd probably been a smartass since he was four.

"The studio?"

"The television studio," he explained with a hint of weariness. "She's working the noon broadcast."

"Of course, she is," I said. "Boy, there are days when I don't know my own name."

He looked down at the register. "How could you forget a name like Algy?"

"I can try," I said. "And thanks."

"For what?" he said, genuinely puzzled.

"Just an expression." I trundled off down the hall.

Most of the room doors were firmly closed. No ghosts of Doheneys or Barrymores, swathed in floor-length ermine trench coats, paced the hallway. For that matter, no one paced the hallway. The Listening Centre was obviously not the place where church members went to pace. I made it all the way to room eight without having to look businesslike.

The door to room eight was open.

I glanced back at the winning youth behind the desk. He had his back to me, probably gazing balefully through his forelock and trying to guess what kind of idiot the elevator would next deliver into his day. I went into room eight.

All remnants of the Borzoi's past glory had been resolutely swept away. The inevitable picture of Angel and Mary Claire hung in glorious color on one wall, but the furniture seemed to have been chosen for its drabness: a folding metal chair in front of a Formica card table, facing another folding metal chair. A sleek contraption that looked vaguely like an aluminum carton of cigarettes sat precisely in the middle of the table. It was bolted down. From the side of it facing the chair near the wall protruded a tangle of wires that terminated in a pair of thick cuffs. The cuffs sported electrodes, round and black, about the size of eye patches. The side of the contraption facing away from the cuffs and the electrodes featured an on-off switch, something that suggested a volume control, and a couple of dials. It could have been one thing and one thing only: a lie detector. Crude, but probably effective.

A door at the end of the room led to a bathroom. The entire place smelled of cigarettes and sweat. The cigarettes were just cigarettes; the sweat was probably fear. For that matter, the cigarettes were probably fear too. The little machine didn't look very forgiving, and it wasn't hard to imagine the anxiety of being hooked up to it and asked questions about the most intimate aspects of your life. I'd once been scared half to death by a psychiatrist, and at least I could lie to her.

I sat on the metal chair nearest the wall, where I figured the person who was being Listened to would sit. I picked up the cuffs: Velcro snaps clasped them together. I put one idly around my left wrist and sat there thinking about Sally Oldfield sitting in a room like this one, pouring her heart out to someone she'd never met, someone who nodded and smiled encouragingly and watched the dials. Sally Oldfield, fresh out of Utica, New York, and lost in the city, looking for the key to her life in the eyes of a stranger. Telling that stranger something very dangerous.

Peeling off the cuff, I looked at my recently reset watch. Twelve noon. I didn't think I wanted to see much more of the Listening Centre. Unless I was very wrong, it was just more of the same.

As I got up, my attention was caught by a sudden pop and whine from the television set sitting on a little table behind the Listener's seat, right where the—the what? the Talker? the Listenee?—would have been forced to look at it. Cartoons? The soaps? *News of the World?* Alistair Cooke? None of them sounded very likely. And none of them, so far as I knew, had the power to turn on sets automatically, although I was sure that somewhere some producer was working on it. I sat back down as the screen came to life.

I was watching something called "Celebrity Corner," if the large sparkly sign hanging on the back wall of the set was to be believed. On chairs that looked much more comfortable than anything to be found in room eight, three familiar-looking people sat smiling into the camera. One of them was Skippy Miller, one was an actress whose name I couldn't remember, and the third was an anemic-looking young man with shoulder-length hair. The other two chairs were occupied by Angel and Mary Claire Ellspeth.

". . . sharing gains," Mary Claire was saying. "Not all of them, of course," she added with a smile. "We've only got an hour."

The three celebrities beamed. Angel looked slightly fuddled, as if she wondered why she wasn't in school. "Clive," Mary Claire said to the anemic-looking young man, "why don't we begin with you?"

"Wul," he said delightedly in an accent that was pure Midlands English, "why don't we, then?"

"Now, you're an extremely successful young man," Mary Claire said. Clive gestured in a self-deprecatory fashion. "Gold records, fans all over the world, a promising movie career." She consulted a small card in her hand. "Homes in Los Angeles, London, and the Bahamas. What kind of gains could the Church deliver to someone like you?"

"Meself," Clive said promptly. "And that's the important thing, in't it?"

Depends, I thought.

"Of course it is," Mary Claire said coaxingly. Clive nodded. Mary Claire smiled. Clive smiled back. "Um," Mary Claire said. She wasn't very good at this. "You told me, just before we went on the air, a very interesting story about how you found the Church. Would you share it with our viewers?"

"I was in the limo after a show," Clive said with uncommon nasal resonance. His adenoids must have been bigger than Univac. "You know, everybody thinks that rock stars must feel great after a show, but for me that was always the lowest time. It was like my whole life was over, like I didn't have any more reason for being alive. The better the show was, the lower I felt. You know what I mean?"

"Of course," Mary Claire said, rapt. There was really something very unattractive in the looseness of her mouth. "With a triumph in the past, what can the present hold?"

"Yeah," Clive said. "That's it. I was low. So I told the driver to turn on the radio."

"This was in New York," Mary Claire said, "so that meant you were listening to our affiliate there, WHOP-FM. Good gain, WHOP." She pronounced it "W-HOPE" rather than "WHOP" She clasped her hands over her head in praise of WHOP.

"I guess so," Clive said a bit impatiently. He was a lot more interested in himself than he was in the good folks at WHOP. "And I heard this little angel's voice."

"Our little Angel," Mary Claire said. She stroked her daughter's hair, and Angel pulled away slightly. Her eyes wandered away beyond the cameras. I found myself wondering again about the two little girls who had Spoken before her. Had they gotten bored? Had they suddenly become problems?

Then I heard voices in the hall, a man and a woman.

I stood up and waited. The voices became louder, and I opted for discretion and went quickly into the bathroom. Leaving the door open, I stepped into the bathtub and drew the shower curtain.

The man and the woman came into the other room.

". . . should be closed," the man said.

"He probably went over to the studio to watch the broadcast," the woman said. "You know how the new ones are."

"That doesn't make it right. Put him down for discipline. Doors are supposed to be closed when the rooms aren't in use."

"He just wanted to see Angel in person."

"Well, it'll be a while before he sees her again," the man said. "Basement him."

The man's voice grew nearer.

"You can't basement him," the woman said. "He hasn't been here long enough. You'll lose him."

"Then we lose him," the man said. He was at the bathroom door. "We can handle him if he gets smart. There's no room for carelessness." He flicked on the bathroom light.

On the TV, Clive droned on. I bent my knees into a half-crouch and brought my hands up, ready to go for the eyes if the man opened the curtain.

"Let's go," the woman said. "I want to see the show."

"See it on tape. We've got the rest of the floor to check."

"Only because you were late," the woman said. "We should be done by now. Sometimes I wonder about you. Sometimes I wonder why you're in the Church."

"What's that supposed to mean?"

"None of it seems to mean anything to you. Not even Angel."

"Don't be silly," he said, but there was an edge of wariness in his tone. "Of course she means something to me."

"Well, it doesn't seem like she does," the woman said calmly.

"What do I have to do, drop to my knees?"

"Then let's go watch her. Come on, it's the only show of the day."

The man drew his breath in and let it out. Then he

snapped off the light. "Okay," he said, "but if they ask you, we checked the whole floor, right?"

"Sure, sure," she said. "Come *on*." After a moment the outer door closed behind them.

I stayed in the bathtub for a full three minutes, watching the second hand on my wristwatch. Only when the third minute was up did I step out and cross the room. I shut the door silently behind me and headed for the elevator.

There was no one in sight. It seemed likely that most of the faithful were glued to the tube, watching the testimonies of the rich and famous. Even the lad at the desk had deserted his post, although the rock star could be seen on the screen of a set hung above the elevators.

I reached the elevator and pushed the Down button before I saw the fire stairs. There they were, right where they were supposed to be, with the customary warning that they, rather than the elevator, were to be used in case of fire.

Everything had been labeled but the basement. The man and woman had used the word "basement" as a verb and had argued about it. The elevator wouldn't take you to the basement if you didn't have a key. On the whole, it seemed to me, I rather wanted to have a look at the basement.

So I took the stairs.

They were grimy, even for the Borzoi, and ill-lit. More important, though, they didn't stop at the lobby. There was a rickety waist-high grate closing them off, the kind of thing people in two-story houses buy when they have a baby, with a sign across it that said NO ACCESS. I accessed by stepping over it and continued down.

The stairs ended in a heavy metal fire door. I turned the knob slowly and inched it open just far enough to peek through. Nothing that I could see. I opened it quickly and stepped through.

The smell of damp was stronger down here than it had been in the lobby: the place smelled like it hadn't been dry in years. A forty-watt economy bulb hung from a wire above my head. The wire, an electrician's nightmare, was actually stripped bare in places. The Church obviously saved the high-wattage light bulbs for Revealings.

I was at the end of a concrete-walled corridor. By the

time I'd realized I was in a cul-de-sac, the door had closed behind me with a soft, steely sound. Experimentally I tried the knob. From this side, the door was locked. I was going to need another exit.

Something dripped, and I looked down. The floor was covered evenly with a quarter of an inch of black water. Another drop plopped into it, sending out dull concentric ripples that pushed bits of suspect debris before them. Water had seeped through, or condensed on, the ceiling, and it dripped more or less continuously into the fluid on the floor. This was not the kind of place tourists bought maps to find.

Well, I couldn't just stand there. Sooner or later someone was going to come through the door behind me or round the corner at the other end to check out my little hallway, and I didn't think they'd be happy to see me. If they didn't want to see me, I certainly didn't want to see them.

So I sloshed through the water toward the open end of the corridor. Something entirely too large for my liking scuttled past me in the other direction: a rat. It was wet and black and sleek and it looked mean enough to eat snakes. I accelerated away from it and found myself standing in a wider corridor that crossed mine like the longer stroke of a T. My heart was going like a bass drum.

Neither left nor right was particularly appealing, but I had to go one way or the other, and the right seemed to be more brightly lighted. Figuring that the people were likely to be where the light was, I headed left.

I'd covered more than twenty yards before I found a door. It opened into a small service closet, even wetter and darker than the hallway, with nothing in it but a couple of buckets and some old rags. I closed it and went on, feeling like Jean Valjean in the sewers of Paris. At least he'd known that his enemies were behind him. I had no idea where mine were.

A second cul-de-sac, this one jutting off to the left, led to an enormous and apparently new air-conditioning system, probably installed right where the old gravity furnace had been. It roared along at full output, making me doubt my senses. Who could want air conditioning on a day like this one, fifty-five degrees and raining? And then I remembered the television studio and all those bright lights. Couldn't have beads of sweat on little Angel's upper lip.

Big ducts, almost three feet square, branched off from the business end of the air conditioner like the legs of a spider, except that most of them seemed to lead in one direction: toward what would have been the left side of the hotel if I'd been outside and facing it from the street, which I very much wished I were.

A square opening had been cut into one of the ducts with a blowtorch, and then the piece of metal had been removed, hinged, and replaced, perhaps for maintenance access. I thought about the man who would willingly crawl through those ducts in this rat's nest and asked myself whether even Dexter Smif would do it. Probably not the career change he had in mind. I opened the little door and looked up the duct. It was blacker than the back door to hell and probably narrower.

The main corridor now swung to the right, and I paused at the corner to make sure I had my bearings straight. It wasn't much fun being down there under the best of circumstances, but it would be a lot less fun if I were lost. I'd been counting not only turns but hanging light bulbs as well. When I was certain I could get back, I went on.

I found, first, a changing room, with hooks spaced on the wall at regular intervals for uniforms or street clothes, and then a bathroom with the most ungodly brown water I'd ever seen brimming over in the toilets. On the doors to the toilet stalls hung signs that said DIPPING POOL. Each dipping pool was numbered. I wondered what got dipped in them.

I left the dipping pools behind and entered a large empty tiled room with no features at all. Every room has features, I thought, studying the walls by the light of what seemed to be a ten-watt bulb. I spotted something dark and round in the center of the floor and went over to it. A drain. When I looked up, I saw the shower heads.

The details of the morning's nightmare came back to me more vividly than I liked. I had to force myself not to look up for the gray worms as I very slowly left the room, and I tried not to acknowledge the relief I felt when the door opened in front of me.

Two empty closets and one backtrack later, I found the kitchen of the Borzoi.

It was vast and cavernous and empty. What seemed like acres of filthy wet counter stretched in every direction, lighted by the standard-issue hanging bulbs. The old gas ranges were cold and rusty, their oven doors hanging open. I didn't much think I wanted to look in the ovens.

In addition to the one I had entered through, there were four doors in the kitchen. Two opened into dish closets, still stacked high with authentic dinnerware of the twenties that Eleanor would have killed for. The third was as wide as it was high, and as heavy as it was wide. I had to use both hands to pull it open.

When I did, a wave of cold air broke over me. I had obviously found the refrigerator that had once served the kitchen, keeping the Barrymores' caviar chilled. I was holding the door open with one hand and feeling around on the inside wall for a light switch with the other, when something in there moved. Then it moved again. Then it scuttled toward me. It had at least four legs.

The largest rat in the world swam into my imagination, and I yanked my arm out and backed away so fast that I cracked my hip on the edge of a counter. The refrigerator door slowly swung shut. Whatever it was, it was going to stay inside.

The fourth door was worse.

It was narrow but tall, and it opened to reveal a dumb-waiter that in the old days had carried hot food up into the chandeliered dining room. When I tugged it open, I saw nothing but a bundle of rags that had been wadded up and thrown inside. I reached in to test the ropes, wondering if I could somehow haul myself up to ground level, and the bundle of rags stirred. A bunch of darker rags slowly lifted itself and became hair, and I was looking into the face of a woman.

A girl really; she couldn't have been more than twenty. Her face was pasty and hollow. Her eyes were black and flat, as empty and lifeless as windows into a dark room. She looked first at my face and then down at my clothes. Then she sighed and started to lower her head again.

"Honey," I said. "For Christ's sake, let's get out of here."
I put my hand on her shoulder, but she didn't even shrug.
She was barely breathing. I shook her and got no response.
I left the door open and backed away, and she reached out a
slender white arm and slowly pulled the door closed again.

Getting out had become an urgent priority. I left the
kitchen and backtracked the way I had come. At the cul-de-
sac leading to the fire stairs I paused. Then I went into the
small hallway and, avoiding the lethal bare patches on the
wire in an effort not to be electrocuted, reached up and
unscrewed the light bulb. I needed time to think. Mentally
bidding Mr. Rat to keep his distance, I leaned against the
door and listened to the water drip.

At least I'd learned what people meant when they used
"basement" as a verb. Now what I needed was to unbasement
myself as quickly as possible.

In the class-conscious twenties, a hotel like the Borzoi
wouldn't have subjected its guests' sensibilities to the sight
of the help, people largely lacking in real style, coming and
going. That meant there had to be a service entrance or two
at street level, and also, since so many of the poor souls had
slaved in the basement, there had to be a service elevator.
And since I'd pretty much exhausted the territory to the
left, it had to be to the right. Where the lights were.

I'd moved only a few steps when I heard voices. I was
learning to back up very quickly, and I did it now, heading
for what had become the friendly, rat-filled darkness of my
cul-de-sac.

Huddled against the fire door, I watched three people
pass from right to left. The first was a short, fat man dressed
in drab, loose clothes. The other two were in quasi-military
uniforms, faintly Italian in their spit-and-polish, and calf-
high boots. As they passed, the man in the lead stared
hopelessly at the floor but the man in the middle looked
back, away from me, said something, and laughed. It wasn't
a contagious laugh. Virulent, maybe, but not contagious.

The third man laughed too. He was carrying a bucket.

Judging from the woebegoe demeanor of the man in the
lead, they were probably heading for the kitchen to pop
another simp on the barbie. What the hell, I figured, and
followed.

But they weren't going to the kitchen. They turned left at the short corridor leading to the air conditioner. I edged along the far wall until I could see the cooling unit and the three figures in front of it.

The man who had laughed pulled open the hinged door in the duct and made an extravagant after-you-Alphonse bow. The fat little man bowed his head submissively, and the one with the bucket lifted it and poured its contents over the bowing man. Then the bowing man got onto his hands and knees and crawled into the duct.

"A little cooling-off period," said the one who had laughed. It seemed like a well-worn joke, but the wind-chill factor in that duct must have been something for even a dry man to reckon with.

"Thank you," said the one in the duct. He sounded like he meant it. There are more ways of being crazy than there are of being sane.

The joker closed the door, and I made a beeline for the first closet and counted to a hundred very slowly. Water dripped regularly onto my head. When I shifted my position it dripped onto my shoulder *and* my head. I shifted back.

I didn't hear anything outside. I eased open the door and sloshed quietly back to my cul-de-sac. The place had probably become too familiar, too safe by contrast to the rest of the labyrinth. I was backing into it when I felt something move behind me. An arm went quickly around my throat, cutting into my windpipe, and the light went on.

The guy behind me had to be the one with the bucket. And the one with the laugh, the one in front of me, was my old friend Needle-nose.

17

"Well, gee," I said through my constricted throat. "Hi."

He didn't seem to recognize me. The guy behind me tightened his chokehold to keep his interest up.

"I'm lost," I said in a voice that sounded like Daffy Duck.

Needle-nose smiled, not a pretty sight, and lowered his hand from the light bulb. "You certainly are," he said. His eyes were a pale gray, flecked with brown. They weren't smiling. They flicked to meet the eyes of the one behind me, and the forearm relaxed a little. "Perhaps there's something we could help you find." His voice was very soft, almost girlish. The gray eyes were extravagantly fringed with sable lashes.

"I don't know," I said. "A Burger King?"

"A Burger King." He considered the answer very seriously.

"I'd kill for a Whopper," I said.

He gazed at me in the gloom. The light bulb above us swung back and forth in a tiny arc. Then the sharp tip of his nose quivered and his eyes narrowed slightly. I lowered my head as far as I could against the restraining arm, throwing my face into shadow, and hoped he'd come closer for a better look.

When he did, I kneed him in the balls.

Surfing a tidal wave of pure adrenaline, I snapped my head back against the face of the man behind me. I heard a crack as the back of my head struck his nose, and the arm around my neck loosened. I grabbed the arm and shoved it straight up, up toward the frayed electrical wire with the bulb hanging from it.

He must have realized what I was going to do, because he didn't choke me with his free hand or try to dig a finger into my eye. Instead, he grabbed at his own arm and tried to yank it down. He didn't make it.

I felt a numbing jolt as I leapt back. The man's whole body convulsed and jerked. Sparks flew from the wire. Then the man collapsed, taking the wire with him. Luckily for the rest of us, since we were all standing on the same wet floor, the wire snapped. The corridor went dark.

I heard a damp slap as the man's body hit the floor, and a small flat explosion as the bulb broke. Something scrambled behind me. Needle-nose. I stood absolutely still.

The lights were obviously wired in series, 1920's-style, because the bulbs in the main passageway had gone out too. It couldn't have been any darker in the belly of the whale.

My heart was hammering, and I was soaking wet. I tried to unfocus my eyes and let a form emerge, but there was nothing. Then there was a ragged intake of breath, and I heaved myself toward it.

I would have gotten him on the first pass if I hadn't tripped over the body of the man on the floor. As it was, I grasped a handful of jacket, and then a hand clawed over my face, searching for the base of my nose. The hand snapped up, trying to shove cartilage into the brain, and hit my cheekbone instead. I struck under it and drove three stiff fingers into an armpit.

Needle-nose went "Ooooof." I scrabbled over the body and wrapped an arm around his neck. He pulled in the opposite direction, and instead of yanking back, I pushed with all my strength. Between the two of us, we hammered his head into the concrete wall. It sounded like a breaking egg.

He sagged in a satisfying fashion. I let go of his neck and stood up, a little more shakily than I would have liked. Then I remembered that he might have Sally Oldfield's fingernails in his pocket. Who knew? Maybe he kept souvenirs. I went back, located his head, and lifted him by the hair. Twining my arm around his neck again, I slammed his face into the concrete floor. Then I did it again. He didn't even sigh. There was just a faint slobbering sound as he breathed into the wet. I left him facedown and edged toward the main corridor, wishing the water was a couple of inches deeper.

Unless I wanted to run into these guys' teammates, I could think of only one way out. It was only slightly better than staying.

I felt my way to the end of the cul-de-sac and turned left. Light glimmered in the distance, and I headed toward it.

The air-conditioning unit was right where I'd left it, and the little metal door was shut tight. I opened it, and the fat man inside looked up in surprise. It wasn't time yet.

"Excuse me," I said. I had so little support for my voice that I had to say it again. "Excuse me. Duct patrol."

He looked bewildered. "Duck patrol?" he said. It was something new.

"Duct," I said. "Duct, goddammit. You'll have to get out for a minute."

He thought about it for a second. Then he shook his head.

"You can get right back in," I said. He shook his head again. I heard a rapid tapping and turned to look behind me before I figured out that it was the sole of my shoe. My left leg was shaking uncontrollably. "Listen, it's a rule. All the ducts have to be patrolled every twenty-four hours."

Agonizingly slowly, he shook his head again.

"Get out," I said savagely, "or I'll take you to the dipping pool."

That did it. He squeezed out and squatted next to the opening. He was trembling, and no wonder. He was probably freezing.

"When I'm gone," I said, "you get back in here and close the door tight, understand? No fooling around."

"No," he said. "I'll get in."

I crawled into the duct. It was just big enough to allow me to progress on my elbows if I kept my rear end down, and the air was cold against my sweat-slick skin. I'd made three or four yards when I heard the little metal door slam shut. Was he in or out? I really didn't want him wandering around asking questions about the duct patrol.

He answered my question for me. "Thank you," he said from behind me.

I couldn't bring myself to tell him he was welcome, so I just grunted and kept pulling myself along.

With him wedged in behind me, the force of the cold air wasn't quite as great. And I could smell him as I crawled, a fat little man who hadn't bathed in a while. Maybe he hadn't been allowed to bathe.

It might have been a hundred yards altogether; actually, it was probably less, although it felt like a lot more. The first really difficult stretch began when the duct angled upward at about twenty-five degrees for fifteen or twenty feet. The floor of the duct was smooth and slippery, and for every foot upward I slid six inches back. I was concentrating on the positive by congratulating myself on having quit smoking when I hit my head on the end of the duct.

"Oh, no," I said out loud. "No, no, no." The words echoed around me, and I shut up. Why would an air shaft go nowhere?

It didn't, of course. The air, and the fat man's body odor, continued to flow past me. I touched the wall to my right and the one to my left. Each time, I half-expected rats' teeth to close on my fingers. Instead, I slammed them into duct wall. Solid. That left only one direction, so I reached up. More cold air, no rats.

Swell. Up. Ninety degrees up. But for how far? I was pretty sure that the duct was too narrow for me to climb it like a rock chimney. Anyway, rock chimneys have always scared the hell out of me.

I rolled over onto my back and looked up. I needn't have bothered; there was nothing to see. But at least lying on my back I could bend ninety degrees. Only Eleanor could bend ninety degrees on her stomach. And I'd told her that yoga was useless.

I sat up and then worked myself to a standing position. I was facing in the wrong direction, back the way I'd come.

My cheekbone was beginning to throb where Needle-nose
had hit it. I hadn't felt it until then. I'd been too busy. I
dismissed it and made a half-turn and brought my hands up
in front of me, which was trickier than it sounds. The duct
was almost too narrow for my elbows.

The wall of the shaft felt smooth and slick and slightly
greasy as I slid my palms upward. Despite the chill air, I was
still sweating. When I'd signed up for duct patrol, they
hadn't said anything about having to go backwards.

The edge was about six inches above my head. There the
duct angled off again, going in the same general direction.
Taking the long twenty-five-degree incline into consider-
ation, that would put me just about at street level. If I could
get there.

Praying to the patron saint of private detectives, whoever
that might be, I curled my fingers over the edge and tried to
pull myself up. I got all the way to tiptoe before my fingers
slipped and I landed on my heels again. The duct above me
slanted up—not much, but enough to deny me the friction I
needed.

Now I was smelling my own sweat. This was no place to
spend the rest of my life.

The fat little man behind me coughed. It was nice to
know he was where he was supposed to be, but he sounded
discouragingly near. How far had I really gone?

I tried to drag myself up again, with the same result.
Okay, try something else.

I used my right foot to worry at my left running shoe until
it came off. Then I repeated the action with my left, until
both shoes lay at my feet. Unfortunately, there was no way
to bend down and pick them up.

I turned around again and sat down, the shoes lumpy
beneath me. Pushing them aside, I wiggled into a semiprone
position, with the duct yawning above me, and slipped my
hands into the shoes. I hadn't worn socks because the rain
would have soaked them, so I was barefoot. The air was
cold on the soles of my feet.

With the shoes wedged onto my hands, I stood up again
and turned around. I was half an inch shorter now, something I didn't really need. I realized that some obscure part

of my mind was rattling off the Lord's Prayer. Bidding it to shut up, I tried to get my hands above my head, but the added thickness of the running shoes made it impossible. My forearms were too long.

I slumped against the wall and closed my eyes, which made it no darker than it already was. Other than the cough, I hadn't heard anything behind me: no boots echoing down the hallways, no shouts of "Look in the duct." My cheekbone hurt. Without thinking, I reached up to rub it and hit it with my shoe. That was a surprise in more ways than one. The duct was rectangular; I'd been assuming it was square. Maybe it was an answer to the Lord's Prayer.

By crossing my arms in front of me I was able to get my hands, shoes and all, above my head. I slipped them as far into the new air shaft as I could, planted the soles firmly on the floor of the duct, stood on tiptoe, put my bare left foot against the wall behind me, and pulled.

The shoes gave out a rubbery squeal, but they held. My right foot was off the ground. I braced it against the wall, advanced one hand an inch or two, and pulled again. Right hand, left foot, left hand, right foot, hoping the traction would hold, I inched upward.

Just as I got my underarms over the edge, I slipped and fell. The corner of the duct slammed my chin, and my knees banged against the wall in front of me, but the shoes didn't fall off my hands. I was very grateful for that. I wasn't sure I had the strength to go back down and get them.

It took me three more tries before I was lying on my stomach in the new duct. I heard a something that sounded like an asthmatic's cough and realized that I was sobbing. I wiped my face on my shirtsleeves and breathed slowly until it passed. Now I could hear noises, but they weren't pursuing me. They were in front of me.

After another ten or fifteen yards at a slight upward grade the duct angled left and leveled off. Light poured through the far end. Using the shoes on my hands, I pulled myself along at record speed. New Olympic event, I thought. The duct-crawl. I focused all my attention on the light as I dragged myself toward it. After what seemed like a decade it grew brighter. Then it was so bright that I had to stop and close my eyes for a moment. When I opened them I was looking at a grate.

Well, of course. They don't leave ducts open. They put grates over them. Otherwise, you might get rats.

It was a perfectly ordinary-looking grate, perhaps a little sturdier than was absolutely necessary. Beyond it I could see a wooden floor. Heavy electrical cables lay on the floor, and a murmur of voices burbled through the grate. Voices could pass through it, but I couldn't, at least not unless I could cut myself into long inch-square strips like a julienned potato. I'd never seen a julienned potato put itself back together again.

I shrugged the shoes off my hands and pulled at the grate. It didn't give an inch. I pulled again, and then again. Zero. Then I had a brilliant idea. I pushed, and the grate gave way with ridiculous ease and slammed to the floor. I shoved my head and shoulders through, and a bearded man with his hair pulled back in a rubber-banded ponytail leaned down and said "Ssshh."

He was dressed in faded jeans and a T-shirt that read HUSSONG'S CANTINA, MEXICO. He carried a clipboard. "Ssshh," he said again, jerking a thumb over his shoulder. Behind him, in a blaze of light, I saw the flower-bedecked set of "Celebrity Corner." It was apparently Skippy's turn, because he was talking earnestly. The rock star, Clive, whom I remembered from a century ago, looked like he'd nodded off.

"Boy," I whispered to the man with the ponytail. "Have *you* got problems." I wiggled the rest of the way out of the duct and started to put on my shoes.

"I have?" he said anxiously, squatting down.

"Filtration system's shot to shit. And this grate is loose."

He looked relieved. "Tell it to the Air guys," he said. "I'm Lights."

"Yeah," I said. "Well, the lighting down there is pretty terrible too."

"Hey," he said. "I just do the show. Talk to the Church."

I finished tying my shoes and stood up. "You're not Church?"

"Puhleeze," he said. "I'm a lighting engineer, not an asparagus. No offense, I hope."

"Are you kidding? I'm with the city."

He gestured for me to keep my voice down and glanced around the studio. "What a bunch of spaniels," he said, "although the little girl is cute." He looked at me and edged away. I looked down at myself. I was so filthy I would have edged away too. "Boy," he said, "the things you guys will do for a buck. I wouldn't go down there even if I was straight."

"This is nothing," I said. "I used to pick up dead animals."

"I bet you got some stories," he said, taking another step. "I lit Art Linkletter once."

"We'll sit around and horrify each other someday," I said. "Well, I guess I better get this grate down to Defect Control."

He nodded like he was glad to be rid of me, and I picked up the grate and circumnavigated the stage. People rarely look twice at someone who's carrying something, and nobody focused on me now. There was absolutely no way of knowing how much time I had. I had no idea whether the man who'd grasped the wire was dead, and I didn't really care if Needle-nose was. Even if they were both alive, I didn't think it was likely that either of them would file a complaint soon. When I looked at my watch, it was only twelve-fifty.

"Thank you, Skippy," Mary Claire said over the public-address system. "That was very enlightening. Angel, would you like to say something?"

"Thank you, Mr. Miller," Angel said in her best Brooklynese. The kitten had fallen asleep in her lap. "And thank you, Miss deWinters. I can't wait to see your new picture." She turned to Clive and said, "Would you gimme your autograph?"

"If you'll give me yours," Clive said, reviving briefly. People laughed, and I could see that beyond the lights lay a darkened auditorium that seated about three hundred. It was full of the hopeful, people still wearing their raincoats, leaning forward into the splash of light to catch every word. People who didn't know about the basement yet. I doubted that Angel knew about the basement. But who could tell what Angel knew?

"We're going to close with a special treat," Mary Claire said. "Some music of the moment from our very own group, the Time Signatures. I know you're going to enjoy this."

Lights came up to reveal the sextet who had tormented the audience at the Revealing. A blond woman whose hair looked about as flexible as the fossil record leaned toward a microphone and sang, "This is the moment . . ."

After all I'd been through, it didn't seem fair that I'd have to listen to "The Hawaiian Wedding Song" too. I was contemplating joining the more discerning members of the audience, who were already shuffling toward the exit, when the lights on the main set went down and everybody stood up and started congratulating each other. Angel and Mary Claire shook hands all around and headed stage left, where they were joined by a slender man in beautifully tailored white linen slacks and an aqua shirt. I had to take a couple of steps closer, my grate firmly in hand, before I could be certain that it was everybody's favorite internist, Dr. Richard Merryman.

Merryman took Mary Claire's arm and put his free hand firmly on the back of Angel's neck, parting her long blond curls to get at it. He steered them quickly away from the set. I followed.

Merryman was talking hard and fast, obviously displeased about something and not caring who saw it. Mary Claire gazed up at him unassertively, but Angel's back was stiff and straight. At one point her steps lagged behind his, and he yanked her forward. The little girl stumbled and dropped the kitten. Merryman leaned down and picked it up roughly by the scruff of its neck. It writhed and twisted in his hand. He passed it to Mary Claire, took hold of Angel's neck again, and jerked her along in his wake. They vanished through a door at the back of the stage. The door had a little sparkly star on it, and the name ANGEL ELLSPETH. I lagged behind, scuffing my foot professionally at some imaginary irregularity in the stage floor. After a moment, Mary Claire came out alone and the door closed behind her. She looked unhappy.

Well, I wasn't very happy either. I went down a series of steps at the edge of the stage and joined the throngs who were fleeing the implacable music. Out on the sidewalk I put my grate down in the rain and went around the corner to Alice. I drove around the block once, checking out the building that housed the TV studio and traversing the alleyway behind the hotel to locate the Borzoi's service entrances. Then, nursing my bruised cheek, I drove off to pick up Eleanor. I knew I was coming back.

III

Heaven

18

Eleanor was fuming.

"You look like Jett Rink after he hit his gusher," she said. "You've got a bad bruise on your cheek that someone should take a look at, one of your knees has bled through your pants, and your clothes are filthy."

I drove west on Olympic Boulevard without saying anything.

"And your hands smell like your feet," she said. "Simeon, are you going to tell me what's going *on*?"

"How'd you find him?"

"Just forget it." She folded her hands primly and stared through the windshield at the rain.

"It's the middle of the day. How do you know he'll be home? Doesn't he work?"

She sniffed. We seemed always to be fighting in cars lately. "You could get killed," she said to the air, "and no one would know for days."

"So could you. That's what I've been trying to tell you. These people do not give to UNICEF."

"Stop treating me like Miss World Porcelain of 1988. At the risk of being tedious, let me remind you of a few things. I'm the one they can look up in the phone book, I've been more than a little helpful so far, and I'm the one who found him. I'm also planning to write this whole story, and I think you owe me. I want to know what's happening."

"I think maybe you should move."

"Don't be dramatic. In fact, don't be anything. Just shut up and drive."

I drove.

"Anyway," she said in an acid tone, "you're supposed to be good at your job. Surely it's not anything we can't figure out."

"We already know *who*," I said. "What we want to know is who else, and why. It's whether we can figure them out before they figure us out. And I doubt it."

"I don't. I'm an optimist."

"Are you ever."

"Optimism, as Larry McMurtry said, is a form of courage."

"It can also be a form of stupidity."

"Oh, Simeon. You're always so eager to stomp on anything that's growing. Except your stupid roots."

I didn't feel like someone who was ready to stomp on anything that was growing. But Eleanor usually knew me better than I did.

"So what happened to your cheek?" she asked a few miles later.

"I hurt it killing somebody."

"Am I supposed to believe that?"

"Up to you."

"Today?"

"Of course, today. Was I walking around with this cheek last night?"

"Jiminy Christmas, don't you think I ought to know about it? Who do you think you are, Clint Eastwood? I don't believe this. I don't believe you could kill anybody, and if you did, I don't believe you wouldn't tell me." She glanced discreetly at the speedometer and tightened her seat belt. Then she sighed. "I don't know, maybe I do believe you could kill somebody."

I didn't say anything.

"Oh, stuff it," she said violently. For Eleanor that was real profanity. "I don't feel like I really know you at all anymore. I'm not even sure I want to."

"I'm not sure that you should," I said.

For the next few minutes I concentrated on driving while Eleanor cracked her knuckles very deliberately, one by one. That was always a bad sign. When she started on the second joints I knew we were in for trouble.

"Turn right on Fourth," she said very quietly. "And pull over."

I made the turn and parked Alice under a big deciduous tree that still had a few leaves clinging hopelessly to its branches. Rain strummed flamenco on the roof of the car.

"Here?" I said.

"Here is fine. I've got something to say to you, and I want you to listen. I'm not going to rake over the past, and I'm not going to do character analysis on how you got to be the way you are. You weren't like this when I met you. You were a sweet guy who didn't know where he was going, but you were good at enjoying yourself. Now you're not so sweet anymore, and you don't seem to enjoy yourself very much either. Sometimes I look at you and it's like seeing a stranger through the window of a train. But other times, you're still Simeon."

I flicked off the windshield wipers.

"Maybe it's because we've never really stopped seeing each other," she said, "maybe if we had I'd notice a big change in you. As it is, it's been sort of day-to-day and more-or-less, like getting older. But instead of just getting older, you've been getting different." She fiddled with the buckle of her seat belt, making a metallic snapping sound. "But you don't seem to notice that I've changed too. I've been taking care of myself for three years, Simeon. I've published two books, okay? I've got a good job, if I decide to keep it. I've been through some men, nothing as serious as you were, but they've been there when I decided I needed them. When *I* needed *them*. Are you listening to me?"

I nodded.

"I want you to stop acting like I'm the person you met all those years ago. I am *involved* in this. Maybe I'm in danger. If I am, I want to be able to defend myself, and you have to stop pretending that you're wearing forty pounds of armor and biceps, and I'm the fair lady who needs protection. I'm not helpless. I'm not a little girl. I don't scream when I see a mouse or faint at the sight of blood. You have no right to keep anything from me because you think it might make me safer, and I don't believe for a minute that knowing less is going to reduce my vulnerability. And if you've really killed somebody, then I want to know about it not only for me, but for you too. Simeon, I want you to *talk* to me." She reached over and put her hand on top of mine.

"Okay," I said. "Here?"

"Right here. Right now. If you don't, I'm going to get out of this car. You can go find him alone."

I told her all of it. When I'd finished she sat quietly, chewing on the ends of her hair.

"Are you going to tell this to Hammond?" she finally said.

"Eventually. When I have to."

"Why not now?"

"I want to work it out, Eleanor. I want to get the bastard who killed her."

"It sounds like you already did. But of course, he's not the one you want."

"No," I said. "I want the one who told him to do it."

"He really pulled her fingernails out," she said, as though she was trying to digest a fact that contradicted everything she'd ever been taught.

"Is there someplace else you can stay?"

"I'll think about it. I suppose I could move in with Chantra for a week or so."

"That ought to do it. If I'm not finished by then I'll give it all to Hammond."

She directed a clear gaze at me. "Is that a promise?"

"Promise." I gave her my hand, and we shook. Then she pressed my hand to her cheek, folded her other hand over it, and lowered it to her lap.

She leaned back against the seat of the car and let out a slow breath. "I'll tell you how I found him," she said.

She'd called the *Times* bureau in Sacramento and asked a woman there to check the Church's board of directors. "It's a California corporation, right?" she asked rhetorically. "That's what that sleazy Brooks man said. That means their corporate articles and their board of directors have to be on file with the Secretary of State. It's a big board, and one of its members is a Mrs. Caleb Ellspeth. Mary Claire, in other words."

"Well, well. Did you get the whole list?"

"Of course."

"Have you got it?"

"In my purse."

"And Caleb Ellspeth was in the phone book."

"No," she said, sounding pleased in spite of herself. "He wasn't. He was on the *Times* subscription list. I went into the computer, and there he was, Caleb Ellspeth, right in Venice, only about a mile from me. I was so *excited*, Simeon. I mean, how many Caleb Ellspeths can there be in L.A.?"

"Give me the list of directors." She pulled it from her purse and handed it to me. I put it in my pocket. "Now tell me why you think he'll be home."

"The phone listed was his work phone. His supervisor or somebody told me he had special dispensation to spend afternoons at home and to work mornings and evenings. A sick kid, he said."

"What company?"

"Miska Aerospace."

"What's he do?"

"Some kind of engineer."

"Fine. Better than fine. Listen, I don't know how he's going to react. My guess is that he's been told not to talk to anybody. It could get a little rough, so keep a brake on the humanitarian impulses, okay?"

"Oh, lighten up. You make me sound like Dear Abby. Golly, Simeon, what have we just been talking about?"

"Golly," I said mockingly. "I'm sorry about that. Just getting the ground rules straight." I leaned over and kissed her hair.

"Will wonders never cease," she said, blushing slightly. "A sporting metaphor."

I started the car. As I pulled out into traffic, she said, "Those men would have killed you."

"Yes," I said. "I think they would have."

Thirteen-twelve Ashland was a peeling one-story house with a glassed-in porch built in the thirties by a refugee from the East who didn't believe, and rightly so, that the California winters would be as mild as advertised. When he'd built the house it had had a view of the Pacific. Now three-story stucco apartment houses, the architectural litter of the fifties, made the block seem landlocked. The ocean could have been twenty miles away.

Naturally, the porch leaked. I tried to remember the last time I'd been dry. I was giving up when Caleb Ellspeth opened the door.

He didn't open it very far. A four-inch chain held it in place. His eyes were just about level with the chain. "Yeah?" he said, looking at the grease on my clothes. Then he saw Eleanor. "Can I help you?"

"We're from the *Times*," she said.

He started to close the door. I got a hand against it and shoved back. He wasn't very strong.

"Give me a break," he said. "No one else has in years." He had a wrinkled, oddly transparent face: pale skin like crumpled cellophane over prominent cheekbones, a hawk nose, muddy brown eyes, a skinny neck that vanished down into a white shirt that seemed several sizes too large. His hair looked like a hat. He wore it in a style that had last seen the light of day on a member of Richie Valens' backup band, a black Reddi-Wip wave at the top and heavy graying sideburns that disappeared into the collar of his shirt and, for all I knew, ended at his knees.

"We only want to ask a few questions," Eleanor said.

"I'm out of answers," he said. "I was just going to run down to the store, pick up a few. You want to tell your mechanic here to let go of the door?"

Eleanor laughed. "He does look like a mechanic, doesn't he?"

"He doesn't look like a reporter."

"And I'm not," I said. "I'm a detective." Eleanor looked startled.

"Better and better," he said. "You two ought to talk it over. Ring the bell again when you decide who you are. If I'm anywhere near the door, I'll answer." He tried to push the door closed again, but I shouldered it back. The chain snapped tight and held.

"What we are," I said, "is a double-whammy. A reporter *and* a detective. We're everything you don't want camped on your doorstep."

"Leave me alone," he said desperately.

"How would you like to be in *People* magazine? 'Church Prophet's Father Living in Poverty.' Then, of course, there'd be the *National Enquirer*. How would you like to be called as a witness in a murder trial?"

"This isn't poverty," he said. "And I don't know anything about any murder. And also, don't talk to me about the fucking Church. Beg your pardon," he said to Eleanor.

"I'm used to it," she said.

"You have a security clearance out there at Miska, don't you?" I said. "What are you cleared to? Secret? Top Secret? Eyes Only? How wide is your need-to-know scoop?"

"Hey," he said. "What do you got in your head, bugs? You can't stand out there and shout that kind of stuff."

"Then let us in."

"What do you got to talk about my security clearance for?"

"How long do you think you'd keep it after you got famous?"

"You wouldn't do that."

"I wouldn't even have a hard time sleeping."

"You must be some guy."

"A very nice lady has been killed. The Church is in the middle of it—not Angel and probably not Mary Claire, but the Church. I'll do anything I have to do to figure out why. Now, are you going to let us in, or do you want to practice your signature so you can sign autographs in supermarkets?"

He tilted his head back, toward the rear of the house, like a man listening for something. Then he said, "And if I let you in?"

"We ask some questions about the Church and then we go away and leave you alone."

"You'll never see us again," Eleanor said.

His mouth twisted. "You come in," he said, "you gotta be quiet."

"We'll be quiet," Eleanor said.

"Okay. You want to move your big fat hand so's I can get the chain off?"

"If you lock it," I said, "I'll kick it in."

"Breathe a little more fire," he said. "It's a cold day." He pushed the door closed and the latch rattled. Then the door opened again and he stood there, a small wiry man whose clothes were too big for him. "Come in and wait here," he said. "I got to check on something." He turned and shuffled off down the hall. He wore battered leather slippers.

We went in. The house was dark and smelled of food and an elusive chemical taint. Sickness. On a little table next to the door was a pile of unopened junk mail, computer-generated trash addressed to three or four misspellings of his name.

"This is awful," Eleanor whispered. "Half his mail is from Ed McMahon. It doesn't even feel like a house. It's just, I don't know, indoors."

"It's not going to get any better," I said. "Don't turn into the Problem Lady."

Caleb Ellspeth appeared at the end of the hallway and beckoned to us. "In here," he said, "in the living room."

The living room was a cramped little cubicle with so much furniture that it looked like a couch convention. The furniture had seen too much wear. Magazines written by, and for, engineers and machinists were scattered across the two coffee tables. *Reader's Digest* book condensations marched in uniform across a small bookshelf. *War and Peace* democratically shared a volume with *A Tree Grows in Brooklyn.*

"So what do you want?" he said. "Wait a minute. If we're going to do this, we might as well do it. Coffee? All I got is instant, but I could use a cup."

"Sure," I said. "Black."

"How about you, miss?" he said with an unexpected sweetness that made Eleanor's eyes widen. "Some tea? A Coke, maybe?"

"Coffee," she said. "That'd be fine. Black, like his."

"Okey-doke," he said, shuffling off in his slippers.

"Gee," Eleanor said, blinking.

"You softy."

"You're really *not* as nice as you used to be," she said. "I don't know, with everybody else, I have the feeling that the plumbing fixtures are going to stay put. How come with you I feel like they're always pulling away from the wall? Why do I always feel like you're poking around under the plumbing?"

"Because that's where the bugs are."

We spent several moments in silence. The room was cluttered and threadbare but as clean as Sally Oldfield's front seat. A picture of a woman in a beehive hairdo turned out, on closer examination, to be Mary Claire, squinting into the California sunshine as if its dazzle obscured her future. Finally Caleb Ellspeth came in carrying an invalid's tray. On it were three cups that were even worse-matched than the ones I used at home, a sugar bowl, and a creamer. He looked too frail to carry the tray, and Eleanor started to get up to help. I had to grab her wrist to keep her down.

"Just in case anyone changes his mind," he said, putting the tray down in front of us. "Me, I can't drink this stuff without a little help." He began to spoon sugar into his cup. "Okay," he said, "let's get it over with."

"I want to know about the beginning," I said. "How you got into the Church. How Angel became the Speaker. What happened to you and Mary Claire."

He snorted. "Me and Mary Claire," he said.

"Anything," I continued, "about how the Church works inside."

He stirred his coffee. "Is this going to be in the papers?"

"Not with your name in it," Eleanor promised.

"If you tell me," he said to her, "I'll believe it."

Eleanor took out her pad. "When did you join?"

He shrugged. "Mary Claire joined first. About eight years ago. This was in New York, where Angel and Ansel were born."

"Ansel?" Eleanor said.

"My son. Anyway, she liked the Church pretty much, gave her something to do when Ansel got her down, which was most of the time." He put down his spoon and studied the surface of the invalid's tray. "Ansel's brain-damaged," he said flatly.

"I'm sorry," Eleanor said.

"Me too. Where was I?"

"In New York," she prompted.

"Yeah. So she joined and she kept at me to join, and I wasn't that hot for it but Ansel got *me* down sometimes too, more than I could tell her, so finally I went with her and wound up hooking into a Listener."

"Did it help?" I asked.

He looked at me reflectively. "Didn't hurt," he said. "Nah, that's not right. Sure, it helped. I couldn't talk to Mary Claire because she always wanted to believe that it'd all be hunky-dory in the end and that I was the one who could make it happen. Anyway, it wasn't as hard on me as it was on her. I was in the Navy and I was gone a lot, you know? And she was always home, always having problems with the kid." He took a sip of coffee. "Ansel, I mean," he added. "Ansel was pretty rough on her. It's not easy when you're a woman, knowing that something came out of your body that probably ought to be dead. Anyway, that was how we felt at the time. So, yeah, it helped. It gave me someone to talk to."

"And when did you come to California?"

"Not long after that. Mary Claire wanted to come, she was crazy about little Anna, who was the Speaker then, right? And I managed to get a transfer, and we came. The four of us," he said. He swallowed once. "You're not drinking your coffee, miss."

"Sorry," Eleanor said, taking a brave pull at it. "Just listening."

"Listening," he said with an unamused smile. "Let's hear it for Listening."

"So you came to L.A.," I said. "Then what?"

"Things were better at first. We got a Mexican dame to hang around with Ansel, and Mary Claire started spending more and more time at the Church. There was a new Speaker then. It was okay with me if it made her happy, even when the bills started to add up and I figured that the Church cost more than everything else in our lives put together. So I was working at the naval station in Long Beach and she was passing out stuff at the Church, and so what? Like I say, it made her feel better."

He tilted his head again in the same listening attitude we'd seen at the door. I hadn't heard anything at all. "Excuse me a minute," he said, standing up.

"May I come with you?" Eleanor said unexpectedly.

He shifted his weight uncertainly. "Sure," he said at last. "I mean, I guess so. You're pretty. He might like to look at you."

We followed him out of the living room and through the kitchen, a fussy, bleak, single man's kitchen with an old chipped gas range. The door at the end of the kitchen was ajar.

"These were the maid's quarters," he said. "I guess everybody had a maid then. Got its own bedroom, bathroom, everything. All I had to do was put in heat. California people don't think maids need heat." He pushed the door the rest of the way open and said, "Quiet, now." Eleanor nodded soberly and we all went through the door.

I stopped in my tracks so suddenly that Eleanor bumped into my back. "Gee," she said.

It was like Dorothy stepping out of the house and into Oz. Here, everything was color. Two walls were painted bright yellow and a third was peach. The fourth, the one that held the door we'd come through, was covered with a kind of middle-earth fairyland, complete with mountains, castles, hobbits, and elves.

The entire ceiling was plastered with pictures. It must have taken Ellspeth days to paste them all up there. Illustrations cut from nineteenth-century children's books were interspersed with pictures of Disney characters, rainbows, waterfalls, an autographed picture of the Roadrunner and the Coyote signed by the genius who created them, Chuck Jones. There must have been two hundred of them.

In the center of the room was a hospital bed cranked halfway up. The chemical smell was strongest here. In the middle of the bed, lying on his back and connected to a gleaming chromium respirator, was a little boy.

He had Angel's golden hair, but his body was contorted and misshapen. His fingers clawed anxiously at the air. The respirator covered the lower half of his face. Ellspeth smiled, and years fell away from his face.

"Hello, darling," he said. "Look, I've brought you some new friends. See the pretty lady?"

"Hi, Ansel," Eleanor whispered. "What beautiful hair you have."

Ansel's fingers extended and two of them pointed toward Eleanor. Some kind of a sound came out of the mask.

"Well, well," Caleb Ellspeth said. "Well, well." Eleanor went past him and took the crooked hand in hers.

"Aren't you the lucky boy?" she said. "Your own room and your own window. I never had my own room when I was little."

It was true. Eleanor had grown up in the back room of a Harlem grocery. She'd slept in a double bunk bed with her two brothers until she was twelve.

Ellspeth picked up a glass and held it in front of Ansel's face. "Lemonade," he said. "I'll make you some lemonade in a few minutes and give it to you." He looked at Eleanor, who was stroking the yellow hair. "Maybe the pretty lady will bring it if you're good."

Ansel's fingers had curled around Eleanor's palm. She looked back at me.

"Sure, I will," Eleanor said. "In fact, why don't I stay here? You finish talking and I'll keep Ansel company. Would you like that, Ansel?" The boy blinked.

"I couldn't ask you," Ellspeth said.

"You don't have to," Eleanor said. "But if you don't think Ansel would like it . . ."

"He'll like it," Ellspeth said. "Won't you, Ansel?" Ansel held on to Eleanor's hand.

Ellspeth backed slowly away from the bed. "Call if he's any trouble," he said.

"He won't be any trouble," Eleanor said. She was beaming. "I've just thought of a Chinese fairy tale that I'll bet Ansel has never heard. I'll bet you don't know any Chinese fairy tales, do you, Ansel? Is there a chair I could sit on?" she asked Ellspeth.

"Sure, sure," Ellspeth said, as if embarrassed. He pushed a fragile-looking chair over from the wall and Eleanor sat down without letting go of Ansel's hand.

"That's better, isn't it, Ansel?" Eleanor said. "Now we can be closer together. Now, listen, do you know where China is? No? Well, it's a long way away, farther even than New York, where you were born. Things in China take a long time to happen, and this is a long, long story, so if you go to sleep while I'm telling it to you, you won't hurt my feelings. But, boy, this is a *good* story."

Ellspeth tugged my sleeve. As I followed him into the kitchen, Eleanor said, "Do you see how black my hair is, Ansel? In China everybody's hair is black, just like mine. But this story is about a very special little boy, a little boy with bright gold hair, exactly like yours, but not so pretty. . . ."

Ellspeth went to a roll of paper towels hanging on the kitchen wall, tore one off, and blew his nose on it. "The kid needs a woman," he said fiercely.

"How much does he understand?"

"The words? Not much. But he can feel her. He can tell a good person better than I can."

"She's a pretty good person," I said.

"Marry her," he said, "if you're in a position to do it. You're a dope if you don't."

"Well," I said lamely, "we were talking about you."

"Right." He opened a cabinet under the sink and tossed the towel into it. "The big marriage expert. Let's go back into the living room."

In the living room he reseated himself and looked down into his coffee cup. "The Ballad of Caleb and Mary Claire. Like I told you, I was in the Navy," he said after a gulp of cold coffee. "This is about four or five years after we got to L.A., and Mary Claire and I were getting along pretty good, I thought, I mean we were both in the Church and she wasn't picking at me about Ansel anymore. She seemed better, you know? Anyway, when they wanted me to travel I said okay and relinquished my hardship deferment. They sent me to the Philippines, Subic Bay. All these randy, cute little girls, all these guys going ashore, coming back with drip, syph, God knows what. I was the only guy didn't invest that ten bucks in cab fare, the only guy came home with a dry wick. I'd been writing her regular, getting not as many answers back as I wrote letters, but I figure, she's got the kids to worry about all day, and the Church, and what am I doing? Lying around reading *Playboy* and keeping the machine clean, so I plan this big surprise. I get home three days early, right off the boat I buy a dozen roses, a bottle of champagne, make reservations at Perino's, where I've never even been before—I mean I am ready to party Mary Claire out of her skin. Rent a limousine, get home about eight, P.M., choke off the impulse to call out 'Surprise,' and stand in the front door listening to her moving furniture around upstairs. She was like that, you know? Ever since Ansel was born, too much nervous energy. Wake up at four A.M., start shoving the couch around. So I go up the stairs wondering where the bed's going to be this time, and open the door, and the bed's right where I left it, only it's fuller. She's on it with two guys. Two guys from the Church. I mean one of them was my Listener. I told everything to this guy, and here he is trying it all out on my wife with one of his buddies.

"Well, where I come from, Michigan, you don't hit women. So I took it out on the guys. I threw one of them through the window without bothering to open it, we were in a two-story apartment at the time, and the second guy, the Listener, had it easier because, first, the window was already busted, and second, he had the other guy to land on. Then I turn around to her and she's yelling, 'Don't hit me, don't hit me! I just changed the sheets.'

" 'Mary Claire,' I say, 'I wouldn't hit you with somebody else's fist.' And I shake up the bottle of champagne and pop the cork in her direction, and she's sitting there all wet, holding the sheet up above her tits, and I say, 'Welcome home,' and throw the flowers at her. 'Yeek,' she says, like I hit her with a baseball bat, and then I'm out of there. I don't even stop to see Angel or Ansel, not even Ansel. It's like I'm mad at them too, for some reason. The car's still waiting outside, although the driver's pretty gaga at these two naked guys who just sailed out the window and are now crawling for the shrubbery, and it's time for Perino's. So I go. But first I go back onto the lawn and give my Listener a good kick or two. Then I go to Perino's and drink my dinner to the point where it takes three waiters to get me back into the car, and I tell the driver to take me back to the ship. Two days later I sail for Christ knows where, and I still haven't talked to my kids."

Behind him, Eleanor came into the room. "Asleep," she said, seating herself next to me.

Ellspeth nodded to her, tilted his head back for a second

in the listening postion, and continued. "I *have* talked to my lawyer, though, some jerk from the Church—I didn't know who else to ask, I'd spent all my time in L.A. with my kids and my wife and the people in the Church—and the lawyer tells me not to worry.

"So, like the world's ultimate end-of-the-line asshole, pardon me, miss—I don't worry. And then, I think I'm in Tokyo at the time, I learn that she's run up my credit cards to nine thousand bucks, which is as high as they'll go without dissolving in the hand, and she's got the apartment and four-fifty a month for her plus another five each for Angel and Ansel, and my pay is attached because I owe on the credit cards. So the light dawns in the east that maybe she's been porking my lawyer too."

"Sounds like a logical assumption," I said.

"Yeah, and so forth and so on. Except it turns out that maybe it's wrong, because a couple of months later, who's the Church's new Speaker? My little girl, Angel, who's never said anything more complicated than she wants a glass of water. I mean this was a kid who didn't learn to read until everybody else in the class was doing square roots or something. Slow, Mary Claire used to say, the kid's slow. She's going to wind up scouring some clown's pots and pans, Mary Claire used to say, like there was something wrong with that, like Angel was supposed to be a nuclear physicist or translate the Bible into Farsi. And all of a sudden she's the Speaker, spouting stuff . . . Well, you've heard it—sounds like the Gettysburg Address in drag."

"What did you do?"

"Went down there, naturally. What would you have done?"

"And what happened?"

"They wouldn't let me see her. Like she's the Queen of England. First I get these two weight lifters at the door, guys that look like they bench-press the Arco Tower on Saturday morning, and they ripple their muscles at me like their tailors got nothing to do but fix the tears in their cute little uniforms. So I make some noise and they take me inside after they figure I'm not going to shut up, and they put me in a room. And who comes in? My shithead lawyer."

"Meredith Brooks," I said.

"Meredith Fucking Brooks. Only guy in the world who polishes his face. Eight million bucks' worth of clothes and he still looks like twenty pounds of cat shit. So what's the first thing he says to me?"

"I give up."

"He says, 'Jesus, I wish you'd been here. The judge figured you'd run off, that's why he gave her everything.'

" 'I had a lawyer,' I said. 'I thought maybe a lawyer, all that college, could manage to explain that I was in the Navy. I thought maybe "He's on a boat" was something a well-trained lawyer could manage to say. And by the way,' I said, 'she fucks pretty good, huh?' Sorry again, miss.

"Well, he got all grave-looking. You know how he rubs his chin?"

I said I knew.

"Guy loves to rub his chin. I figure when work is over he goes home, fixes dinner for his chin, and then the two of them sit around and watch TV. After Johnny Carson they go to bed and he rubs it different. Well, he rubs his chin and says I shouldn't talk that way about Mary Claire. She's the Speaker's mother, you know? So I get up to murder him and the two weight lifters pick me up and smear me across a wall and hold me there with my feet off the ground. And I'm kicking and swearing a blue streak and Meredith Brooks gives me the world's oiliest smile and tells me that I'd better be careful because all my Listenings are on tape."

"What had you told them?" Eleanor asked unwillingly.

He leveled his brown eyes at her and blinked twice. "I might as well say it right out," he said. "At least then I won't have to worry about it anymore."

"What was it?"

"That once, right after he was born, I'd tried to kill Ansel."

19

I had about four hours to kill before I was due to turn up at Bernie's, bottle in hand, so I killed them by driving Eleanor back downtown. She was silent for the first twenty minutes or so, and when she spoke, all she said was, "That woman should be in jail."

"When she goes," I said, "she's going to have a lot of company."

Before dropping Eleanor at the *Times*, I parked around the corner from the Borzoi while she ran into the lobby to buy some of the books and tapes I'd seen on sale there. If anyplace in the Borzoi was safe, it was the lobby.

Nevertheless it seemed like a hell of a lot longer than ten minutes before she opened Alice's door and slid onto the front seat, clutching one of those flimsy plastic shopping bags that the cheap supermarkets now give you, the ones that manage somehow both to break easily and to remain in the environment forever. It had a picture of Angel and Mary Claire on it. It was a new picture: Angel was holding her kitten.

"The collected works of Angel Ellspeth," Eleanor said, "and one tape by the little girl called Anna. Eighty-one dollars and forty cents, if you can believe it. Who's paying for this?"

"That's a good question. For the moment, I guess you are."

"I'd better get a story out of this. I can't put all this wisdom on my expense account if I don't write something."

"Poor you," I said. "I haven't even got a client."

"Sure, you do. Truth, justice, and the American way."
Eleanor spoke in series commas.

When she opened the door to get out at the *Times* she
kissed her index finger and touched it lightly to the tip of my
nose. "I'll call Chantra," she said. "It's only for a week,
right?"

"At the most."

She gave me a long look. "So now who's the optimist?"
she said, sliding out. She crossed the crowded sidewalk and
hurried into the building without glancing back, and I headed
Alice around the block and back toward the Borzoi.

I found what I needed only about a block away from it:
the Russell Arms. The Russell Arms had never been as
fancy as the Borzoi, and it might never be home to a hot
new religion, but the rooms were not dirty enough to be
terrifying, the place was almost empty, and the desk clerk
was willing to take cash. I booked myself in for the night,
ignored the unspoken question about my luggage, grabbed
the change of clothes I kept in Alice's trunk, and went up to
the room.

The stream of water from the shower was lukewarm and
irresolute, and it took all the soap the Russell Arms was
willing to provide before I stopped looking like a particularly slovenly anthracite miner. I pulled back the shower
curtain and looked out twice before I finished. Nobody
there but a cockroach. There was no singing in the shower.

Leaving the ring around the tub for the maid to swear at,
I took the stairs down to the street and checked out the
service entrances to the Borzoi again before popping Angel
into Alice's cassette player and hitting the thickening traffic
for Westwood.

As I drove west on Wilshire, Angel creepy-crawled her
way over various hidden landscapes, offering the listener the
use of a spiritual flashlight. No question about it: you had to
be there. In a room full of believers she had seemed almost
frighteningly potent. On tape she just sounded like an ex-
traordinarily bright, highly articulate, and spiritually bent
little girl.

But not quite. There was an odd, halting inflection in her

voice, a kind of verbal limp, that I couldn't identify. It wasn't the hesitancy of someone trying to remember a long speech. Angel's trance had seemed real enough, and at the Revealing I'd attended with Skippy she'd stemmed the tide twice to respond to the audience. Her spiel wasn't memorized. The words were flowing through her in real time, and she could be spontaneous. Wilburforce had said that the first little girl was a channel. I didn't think I believed in channels.

Out of curiosity, I ejected Angel in mid-phrase and fished around in the plastic bag for the tape of poor little Anna. Jesus, even I was calling her poor little Anna. I slipped it in and turned up the volume.

Her voice was lower, more resonant, with a husky, dark edge of urgency to it and a natural, sinuous strength. Like Angel, Anna had been taped at a Revealing, in front of a large audience, and her listeners responded to her much more vocally than Angel's had. Compared to Angel she was a real spellbinder, a girl with revival-tent potential.

A phrase floated into my mind: the Burned-Over District. Something to do with revival. I put it on hold and refocused on Anna.

The front of the cassette box pictured an ordinary-looking little girl with long, straight brown hair. It would have been uncharitable, but true, to call her plain. She had the wishful, plaintive smile of someone who hopes that this is the picture that will finally turn out.

But there was nothing plaintive about her voice. It was as different from Angel's as a bassoon is from a flute. And much more persuasive.

I played parts of Anna's tape again and then parts of Angel's. Then, with Angel droning in my ears, I drove west, wondering what the hell the Burned-Over District was.

"The Burned-Over District?" Bernie said. "You've got to be kidding. You mean to tell me you don't remember the counties of the Burned-Over District?"

"No, Bernie," I said wearily. "What were they?" I inwardly gritted my teeth and groaned, hoping Bernie wouldn't use the question as a cue for one of his famous lists.

"Let's see, Chautauqua, Genesee, Wyoming," Bernie began. I settled in for a long winter's night. Once, in a liquor store, I made the mistake of asking Bernie why he was buying a bottle of vodka. Then I stood there, eyes glazing over and my life passing me by, while Bernie listed at least thirty drinks that boasted vodka as their *elixir vitae*. Lists are a weakness of graduate students.

"And the cities too," Bernie continued happily, holding up five more fingers and picking up steam. "Utica, Rochester—"

"Utica," I interrupted. "New York." Something was coming back to me.

"And New York, of course. Not at first, though."

"I mean, these are all in New York."

"New York *State*," Bernie corrected me. Like all born New Yorkers, Bernie only used "New York" to refer to the city. Everything else was a featureless landscape, fit only for pity and not too much of that.

"Bear with me, Bernie," I said. "It's been a long day. Why was it called the Burned-Over District?"

"The fires of revival," he said dramatically, tugging a hand through his coils of Brillo-like hair and taking some of it with him. "They burned there more or less nonstop in the early nineteenth century. Shame on you, with a degree in comparative religions. That's where it all started. Haven't you read Whitney Cross's book?"

"What's it called?"

"The Burned-Over District," Bernie said with a hint of disappointment. "You could have guessed that, you know. I think maybe you ought to come back to school." Bernie's school career had spanned almost two decades and five degrees, and he still hadn't found his major in life.

"Later," I said. "Eighteen-twenties, right? Early revivalists. A reaction against European Calvinism. Predestination."

"Predestination was a terrible idea," Bernie said. "Only a few will be saved. The rest will roast in hell through eternity, shriveling on the spit. It doesn't make any difference how you live your life, how many alms you give or prayers you pray. If you're gonna fry, you're gonna fry." Bernie manipulated his large hands as though marionettes dangled from them, and made a sizzling noise. "Not much of a religion for a country where all men and women were supposed to be created equal. Also, not much of a religion for capitalists." Bernie was ensconced happily several notches to the left of Chairman Mao.

"Why not for capitalists?"

"Nineteenth-century capitalists were highly result-driven. They hadn't been introduced to Japanese principles of management yet. They needed a religion that allowed them to get results. So anyway, as you probably remember, the American Methodists and Baptists junked predestination in favor of free will doctrines, the New Light doctrines, that let people have a say in whether they were going to burn or not. You could just accept Christ as your savior, and, bang, you were born again. It didn't matter if you'd been predetermined for hell the first time around; when you were reborn, you started over. The spiritual equivalent of coming to the New World. A brilliant, simple concept. Perfect for an age of revolution."

"And the preachers of the Burned-Over District took the New Light doctrines and began cranking out new religions."

"Dozens of them," Bernie said with relish, holding up his fingers again. "It must have been something in the water. Lots of Arminian doctrines, Joseph Smith and the Mormons, Millerites and, later, Seventh-Day Adventists, Shakers, the Oneida Colony—real communists, by the way—"

"Yeah, and look where it got them. Making silverware."

"What, communists are supposed to eat with their fingers? They practiced free love, too, and controlled conception at the same time. Somehow. You want some wine?"

"I thought you'd never ask."

"I thought we might wait for Joyce."

"You wait for Joyce. Where is she, anyway?"

"Still at the hospital." He got up to go to the kitchen. "I can't tell you how nice it is to need a corkscrew for a change," he said. "Nothing worth drinking comes with a screw-off cap."

Bernie and Joyce were living in a standard student apartment on the fringes of Westwood, walking distance from

UCLA, where she worked and he pursued his sixth degree, in a field seemingly completely unrelated to his previous five. The smell of baking lasagna floated in from the kitchen. I canvassed the books on the bulging rattan bookshelves from Pier One while Bernie fished noisily around in drawers and finally popped the cork. "Bernie," I called, "it wasn't all completely kosher Christian, was it? I seem to remember some fishier stuff."

"Mainly Christian," he yelled, clinking some glasses together promisingly. "There were some Swedenborgians rattling around, practicing mesmerism and phrenology on anyone who was willing to sit still, but they certainly thought of themselves as Christians. Lots of mediums, spiritualists popping up all over the place. They would have been horrified if you'd suggested they weren't Christian. Just because it's Christian doesn't mean it's not fishy, Simeon." He came in with a full glass in each hand and the bottle tucked under his right arm, and sat very carefully on the floor without being able to use his hands or to move his right arm from his side. Only then did he put the glasses on the table. Eighteen years of college, and he was still helpless. "What is it with you and the Burned-Over District?"

"Little girls," I said, sipping the wine. It could have used a few minutes to breathe but it wasn't going to get them. "Something about little girls and voices from beyond."

Bernie looked at me in a shrewd fashion and then turned to survey the bookshelves, one hand clutching a white-stockinged foot. Bernie had always worn white socks. "Little girls," he said, drinking deeply out of the glass in his other hand. "Two little girls. Knox or Fox or Pox or something, maybe Fitzgerald." He scooted over on his rear and reached up for a book with the hand that had clutched the foot. Bernie wasn't one to put down a glass.

"Knox or Fox or Fitzgerald?"

"Frances Fitzgerald. *Cities on a Hill.* Got a terrific summary of the Burned-Over District." He flipped through the end of the book. "Fox," he said triumphantly. Margaret and Katie Fox. About twelve and fifteen, I don't know which was which, farmer's daughters, famous for their ability to communicate with the spirit world through the ghost of a dead man who haunted their family's house."

"Now I remember," I said. "They had double-jointed toes."

"They had toes like tympani," Bernie said. "If they'd been born in this century they would have played them in a band. They popped their toes like mad under the table and interpreted the noises as rappings from their friendly ghost. They were very big in Rochester."

"I'll bet they were a hit in Utica too. Who was running the show?"

"Must have been their parents. Raking it in, too. I think the little girls came up with the trick themselves. Mommy and daddy just handled the receipts."

"I don't think my little girl came up with her trick herself."

"And which little girl is this?" Bernie poured some more wine. His glass was already empty.

I told him about the Revealing.

"I've seen posters," he said promptly. "Big color shots of mother and daughter. Mostly ripping off Raphael for composition. You know, those circular Madonnas and Child. How did the Revealing work?"

"That's sort of a new twist."

" 'The only thing older than the old story is the new twist.' That's F. Scott Fitzgerald. What is it?"

"She's supposed to be a channel."

"Spare me," Bernie said. "There are enough dull people in the world without millions of equally dull disembodied spirits popping up and putting in their two cents' worth every time some actress closes her eyes. What are the criteria for becoming a disembodied spirit, anyway? Do they get degrees? Does some panel certify them? How do we know we don't get the worst of the bunch? How do we know they haven't been disembodied because they were bores and liars? Being disembodied doesn't sound to me like something you get for good behavior. And if they're so terrific, how come they're hanging around waiting to get a chance to talk to *us*? It sounds sort of like spending eternity at a pay phone, waiting for some change to drop out so you can dial a number at random. And only knowing one area code, and not a very good area code at that."

"Bernie," I said, "I'm only giving you the party line."

"Campus is full of these jerks," he said. "It used to be you could go over to Kerckhoff, get your synapses jangled on coffee, and talk about Kierkegaard or something. Now it's all these bananas with clear eyes and turbans listening to New Age music on nonanimal headphones and humming along."

"It's been a while since I've seen any animal headphones. What are they? Little imitation dog ears?"

"You know what I mean. Not even any real rubber, it's like those little faucets hurt the trees or something. And the way they dress, Simeon. Remember how hard we used to work to look a little sloppy? These kids dress like actuarial tables. Put a bunch of them together and they look like a graph illustrating the contents of the typical middle-class airhead's closet." Bernie had somehow managed to convince himself that he wasn't middle-class.

"Well, so what?" I said more quarrelsomely than I had intended. "We wore blue jeans as a uniform of nonconformity and learned to meditate. I remember saying a one-syllable word over and over until I fell asleep, and when I woke up, trying to convince myself that I'd had a mystical experience. It was the religion of the month, and the smart ones wore it out in three weeks. Now we've got channels and fire-walking and Shirley MacLaine. I'm not sure there was a new religion every fifteen minutes in the fifties, but there have been a couple of thousand since."

"You know the theories," Bernie said. "New religions tend to arise in times of transition, when old values are being challenged or are wearing out. That leaves out the fifties. Christianity was first a Jewish response to the oppression of Rome, and then, centuries later, a Roman adaptation to the decline of the empire. Luther arose as the political systems of Europe began to fall apart. Et cetera. It's all too neat for me. I take a messier view of history."

"And the Burned-Over District?"

"Society in transition with a vengeance. The Revolution

only fifty years old, immigrants streaming in from Europe, people still worried about violence in the streets every time a president's party lost the election, and the country beginning to fall apart at the seams over slavery. People talk about two hundred years of American stability, the peaceful transference of power and all that, as though it actually happened. This country wasn't even a hundred years old when it self-destructed. It wasn't until Lincoln appropriated what he called War Powers and turned the presidency into a functioning kingship, and then sent Grant to crush the South, that things settled down."

"Bernie," I said, "you can't sympathize with freedom and the pre-Civil War South at the same time. Don't get sidetracked. You're being very helpful."

He sat back, a little surprised. "I am?"

"So where do all the new religions go? And don't say heaven."

It was the kind of question he loved. He drank a full glass of wine for lubrication while he gathered his thoughts. I poured for us both.

"As we said, they tend to arise in times of social change, when people have begun to doubt that the world will automatically continue to obey the million or so rules that keep them safe in their dinky little houses. Cults usually either fervently embrace the values that are being threatened—like, say, the Muslim and Christian fundamentalists do these days—or fervently challenge them, as did the original Christians and the Oneida Colony, to choose a couple of examples.

"Most religions are founded by a single charismatic individual. He or she, as Anthony F. C. Wallace says, has an experience, a hallucination, a moment of divine inspiration, an encounter with a greater force. Moses and the burning bush, Muhammad and the voice, Joseph Smith and the book of gold. The leader is changed by the experience and communicates it. Some of his listeners become converts." He picked up the book and flipped back a couple of pages to an underlined passage: "Listen, here's Fitzgerald paraphrasing Wallace: 'Some of these converts experience an ecstatic vision such as their master had, while others are convinced by rational arguments, and still others by reasons of expediency.' Boy, I'll say. 'The converts organize and then, almost inevitably, encounter some form of opposition.' In fact, they need the opposition. It solidifies their internal discipline and gives them a them-against-us attitude. We're so terrific we frighten them and they have to oppress us, but, oh boy, one of these days. . . . Look at the Old Testament for the best example. It's one long wail of oppression, the longest protest song on record." He put Fitzgerald on the shelf, spilling wine as he did it.

"And then what happens?"

"Simeon, you know all this stuff already."

"What do you want me to do, Bernie, talk to myself? What's the problem, is it time to rotate the lasagna?"

"Then one of three things can happen. Either the religion adapts to a more mainstream position, or the society changes to embrace the religion's position, or both. Usually both, actually. Or the religion disappears. It's not that much different from any social movement. The Mormons moved west and dropped polygamy. The Millerites somehow survived the day in 1841 that Christ was supposed to show up, although their leader got canned and they changed their name to Adventists after they came down from the mountain, which must have been a pretty embarrassing trip. Imagine telling your neighbors that the world was about to end and then having to go home and mow the lawn."

"So most religions that aren't fundamentalist start out radical and then move to the right."

"Sure. They have to be radical at the beginning to attract a core of converts. Then, when they want to attract a much larger number of converts—when they start looking for a real power base—they have to settle down a little bit. It's like a presidential campaign working its way through the primaries. They start out all sharp edges and ringing challenges and then get worn smooth as they approach the convention. Those that don't, or can't because their primary appeal is to a noncentrist minority, drop out."

"The Burned-Over District produced some social movements too. In addition to the religions, I mean."

"Practically every important American movement of the nineteenth century. Abolition, temperance, educational reform, feminism—"

"What about feminism?" said a woman's voice from the kitchen. "Bernie, are you being boring?"

"I don't know," Bernie said. "I wasn't listening. You'd have to ask Simeon."

I got up and toted the other bottle of wine to the kitchen door. Bernie had finished the first. "On the contrary," I said to the woman standing at the oven. "He's been a veritable display of fireworks."

"He's all over the sky," she admitted. "What he needs is some direction." She closed the oven and held out a hand. I'm Joyce," she said, "and you're Simeon."

"What a domestic entrance," Bernie said from behind me. "I didn't even know the back door worked."

"It's still raining," she said. "I parked in the garage and ran for it." She was about thirty-six, maybe a year older than Bernie, with a pleasant, no-nonsense face, faded blue eyes, and a thin, high-bridged nose. She wore a white coat. "Sorry I'm late," she said. "I've wanted to meet you for a long time. You didn't get him onto agrarianism, did you?"

"Not yet."

"Good. If I hear one word about the Green Revolution and more productive strains of rice, I'm going out for pizza."

"It's important," Bernie said mildly. "We either increase the productivity of the land or you'll have to ship them lasagna."

"I think I'd prefer cooking to listening. What have we here?" She indicated the bottle in my hand.

"Merlot."

"Ducky. Looks like Bernie's already gargled with some. There must be another bottle somewhere."

"Hidden under the couch," Bernie said.

"Well, Simeon, why don't you open that one, and Bernie can set the table, such as it is, and I'll do the salad."

"Joyce is organized," Bernie said, sorting silverware. "When we pack for a trip she pins my socks together."

"Bernie's idea of packing is to empty his drawers onto the

floor and then push the suitcase in front of him, wide open, until it's full. When we get there he never has any sunglasses or toothpaste, but his books are packed alphabetically by author."

"Good," I said, worrying at the cork with the world's flimsiest corkscrew. "I was afraid he was still trying to figure out the Dewey Decimal System. Bernie and I lived together once. Whole libraries vanished into the void."

"Gang up on me," Bernie said from the other room. "I like the attention."

"He does," she said. "He's worse than my patients."

"You're a gerontologist."

"Ask her about the graying of America," Bernie called. "Then, when she gets going, I can talk about the Green Revolution and she'll never notice."

"This is a two-issue relationship," Joyce said. "Gerontology and whatever Bernie's talking about at the time."

I poured her some wine. "Sounds interesting."

"I love it. I was way too focused before I met him. You have to learn to listen to him, though. It took me about six months before I learned I could change channels just by mentioning some other buzzword. That's the wonderful thing about Bernie. He's got more channels than a cable TV box."

"He's on twenty-four hours a day, too."

She grinned at me and gave me the appraising glance a woman saves for her lover's oldest friends. "And you've got as many degrees as Bernie and you're using them to be a detective," she said. "Where have we gone wrong, the mothers of America?"

"We'll talk about that over dinner, okay?"

"Fine," she said. "Anything but the Green Revolution."

"So," I said later as the lasagna steamed on the plates. "How do you track a doctor?"

"Track a doctor?" Joyce said in a suspicious tone, instantly joining the Physicians' United Front Against Everybody Else. "How do you mean?"

"Let's just say I wanted to make sure that someone who says he's a doctor really is one. Can I call the American Medical Association or something?"

"Used to be you could," she said, "but it's unconstitutional now. Has been for some time."

"The AMA is unconstitutional?" Bernie said with his mouth full, getting up to go to the kitchen.

"No, of course not. The AMA is as constitutional as the Supreme Court, and about half as lively. It's requiring doctors to join that's unconstitutional. Used to be every doctor had to be a member. Now it's only about half."

"So you mean there's no central data bank for doctors?"

"Well," she said, "what's a doctor?"

"What do you mean, what's a doctor?" Bernie put a fresh glass of wine down in front of me. We were working through it pretty fast. "A doctor is somebody who wears a white coat and cures people. A doctor is somebody who's not a nurse and works in a hospital."

"There are doctors who do nothing but research. There are doctors who go straight into admin and never see a patient. Christ, there are chiropractors, glorified masseuses who call themselves doctors and crack spines for a living. Even worse, there are people who take M.D.'s only to go on and become lawyers so they can specialize in making doctors look bad in court, the scumbags. Is there a central data bank that includes all those people? No."

"Swell," I said. "That's just what I didn't want to hear."

I must have looked dejected. "It's made more difficult," she added, thawing slightly, "by the fact that doctors are certified to practice on the state level. There's no comprehensive central registry that contains all the state certifications."

Bernie bustled nervously, a specialty of his, before sitting in the chair opposite me and lifting his glass. "Suppose you're working in a hospital," he said helpfully, "and someone applies to practice there. How do you check him or her out?" He drank.

"You start with the school," Joyce said. "He or she had to take an M.D. But of course, you have to know what school it was." She raised her glass to her lips and then sputtered, spraying wine onto the table. "Wait," she said, wiping her chin. "I tell a lie. There *is* a central data bank for everyone who graduates with an M.D. It's run by the AMA, and it's in Chicago. It doesn't tell you whether people ever practiced or not, just whether they graduated. I mean, they may not ever be certified or hang out shingles, such a quaint term, but they've got the right letters after their names."

"Could you check that for me?"

"I guess so. What name?"

"Richard Merryman. An internist, or supposed to be. Living in California but not licensed here."

"What's he do, then?"

"He's the private physician to a little girl."

Bernie raised an eyebrow and looked interested. "That little girl?"

"That's not legal, not if he's not licensed," Joyce said in a tone of righteous outrage.

"I don't think this guy cares very much what's legal."

"Does he dispense drugs?"

"I don't know."

"If he does, he's got to be registered with the DEA in Washington. Oops, there's another list. Harder to check, though."

"Could you do it through the hospital?" Bernie asked.

"This is a bad guy?" Joyce demanded.

"If I'm right, he's about as bad a guy as I've ever met," I said.

Joyce toyed with her lasagna. "I'll give it a shot," she said. "All they can say is no."

An hour later, at the door, I kissed Joyce good-bye and gave Bernie a hug. It had turned into that kind of an evening. We'd gone through both the bottles I had brought and one with a screw-top that held some kind of white plonk from Argentina or someplace. Bernie had finally gotten to talk about the Green Revolution.

I talked my way past the cop at the entrance to Topanga Canyon by showing him my driver's license with the Topanga Skyline address on it. Bad mudslides, he said. No one but residents allowed in. He implied that the roads could be closed completely in the morning if the rain kept up. The rain was supposed to keep up.

The wine and the good fellowship had dissolved the knot of unease in my stomach, and the Russell Arms didn't exert much appeal. I needed to pack some stuff, and when I got out of the car I was toying with the idea of sleeping at home and finding my way out over the fire roads in the morning, if necessary.

No odor at the bottom of the driveway; I silently thanked Dexter, wherever he might be. Halfway up the drive I saw that the lights were on again and did my best to accelerate, anticipating Roxanne. I tried to remember whether there was any beer in the refrigerator.

The door was open. Roxanne didn't like the cold. She wouldn't have left the door open.

I went back down to Alice and got a gun out of the dash compartment, then climbed quietly back up and went into the house. It had been thoroughly and ambitiously tossed.

20

The first thing I did was call Eleanor. I was swearing by the time she answered on the fifth ring, sounding serene and unconcerned.

"Get out of there," I said. "Go to the place we were talking about earlier. Don't take anything, just go. I'll come back with you tomorrow to help you pack."

She didn't get rattled, just said she'd be out of the house in five minutes. I hung up and looked at the answering machine. It was on Play, so they'd listened to it, but they'd left the cassette this time.

I rewound it and picked around in the rubble trying to figure out what to take while I listened to the messages.

Mrs. Yount sobbed into the phone that she *knew* Fluffy was alive, she could feel it in her heart, and I wasn't off the case. I should phone her at once. Al Hammond had called, sounding gruff and upset. There didn't seem to be any Ambrose Harker in the whole world except the one who was alive and well and working at Monument Records, and certainly no Ellis Fauntleroy. To the best of Hammond's knowledge, no one had been killed in the Santa Monica TraveLodge, although someone had stolen a bedspread and a couple of pillows from room 311, and when could he expect to hear from me, anyway?

I wasn't really crazy about the fact that they'd heard that last message. Well, at least Hammond hadn't identified himself as being with the police.

Then I learned why they'd left the cassette.

It was a man's voice, very hushed. "Get out of it," he

said. "No one will tell you again. Get out of it and stay out. If we have to come again, we'll do it when you're home." He hung up. It was a thin, chilly little voice. It sounded sincere.

I didn't know who it was, but I knew that it meant Needle-nose was alive. He was the only one who'd seen me at the Borzoi who could link me to Sally Oldfield's death. I didn't think it was Needle-nose's voice, although it sounded vaguely familiar. There was no mistaking the next voice.

"Wo," it said, "this be Dexter Smif in your car. I took the liberty of writin' down your number off the top of your phone. Good, huh? Think I got a future? Call me if you be needin' a man of talent."

I could use one, I thought as I pulled some stuff together. They couldn't have been any more thorough if they'd passed everything through a sieve. Twice now they'd walked right into my house and right back out again. They'd killed two people under my nose. A lesser man might have had an identity crisis.

Everything fit into one small bag. I made a desultory effort at straightening up, but the sound of the drip from the leak in the living-room roof sapped me of any excess energy I might have devoted to cosmetic efforts. There was too much to do without worrying about little things like whether the couch was right-side-up.

I unplugged the phone and the answering machine and removed the cassette, replacing it with a new one. Tugging a few tacks loose, I pulled back a corner of the carpet. With a hand drill that I'd bought during a short-lived attempt to learn carpentry, I made a neat little hole in the floorboards and fed three or four feet of phone cord through it. The floor of my living room hangs right out over the hillside where the hill slopes down to meet the retaining wall onto which a bunch of hazy freaks who occupied the house before me had built the leaky little room under the sun deck.

Then, clutching the answering machine in one hand and a flashlight in the other, I went outside and around to the side of the house. The rain had let up, but the creek churned loudly through its course at the bottom of the canyon.

After using the flashlight to locate the phone cord and to

check for any scorpions, snakes, or tarantulas that might be
thoughtful enough to be hanging around in plain sight, I
screwed my courage to its rather low sticking point and
crawled in. I seemed to be doing a lot of crawling lately.
The farther I crawled, the better Dexter's offer sounded.

I hooked up the answering machine to the phone jack and
then swore at myself briefly and vigorously. I slithered back
out, tracked mud into the kitchen, and poked through the
debris that had been dumped on the floor until I found a
long extension cord and a black plastic trashbag. I plugged
the extension cord into a living-room socket, lowered the
female end through the hole in the floor, and recovered it
with the carpet. Then I went outside and back under the
house.

When I was finished, the answering machine was on and
functional, wrapped in the trashbag against mud and water,
and, I sincerely hoped, hard to find. It could be activated to
give me my messages from any touch-tone phone. You
never knew when Hollywood might call, and I didn't think I
was going to be home for a while.

In a final bid for confidence, I took the knife I'd borrowed from the pimp and put it into my pocket, along with
the cassette from the answering machine. Then I hefted my
suitcase and slid back down the hill.

The San Fernando Valley glittered hard and bright as
Alice creaked her way down toward the fragment of
Mulholland that intersects Old Canyon Boulevard and de-
posits you at a Kentucky Fried Chicken restaurant on Ventura. The cops hadn't blocked Old Canyon, so I had an
uninterrupted ride.

The freeway was black and slick and largely empty. It's
been obsolete since the day it was opened, and it was almost
exhilarating to coast along at the speed limit for a change. It
would have been even more exhilarating if I'd had any good
idea where I was going.

Woodland Hills, Tarzana, Encino, and Sherman Oaks
whizzed wetly by. I turned on the radio, got a DJ, and
turned it off again. I tried listening to Angel and then Anna,
but I wasn't in the mood for spiritual guidance. While I was

mulling girls' names that began with A, it occurred to me
that Alice was a highly conspicuous vehicle, and it might be
a good idea to rent something a little less electric-looking
for the next few days. Especially if I was going anywhere
near Eleanor.

The cassette from the answering machine pushed the handle of the pimp's knife uncomfortably against my thigh. I
pulled Anna out of the cassette player and inserted the tape
from the machine.

Mrs. Yount blubbered, poor soul, and Hammond growled.
Then the thin voice came on again. I listened to it three
times, trying to pin down its familiarity.

Brooks? I didn't think so. I hadn't really heard enough of
Merryman to judge. Needle-nose? Once again, I'd only
heard a few words. I knew this voice better, somehow.

"Yo," Dexter said through the speakers. He made his
offer again and I was reaching out to eject the tape when I
heard another click. I hadn't played it all the way through.

"Hello?" a woman's voice said. "Is this the right number?
I mean, I know it's somebody's number, but is it the number I dialed? That message could be anybody. Anyway, this
is Rhoda Gerwitz and I've thought of something that might
be something. Something important, I mean. Oh, and have
you found Sally yet? If this is the right number, call me.
I'll be up until Letterman's over. Unless it's a rerun. If it is,
call me in the morning. Good-bye, I guess."

Just off Highland I found a phone booth that, miracu-
lously, still had a directory in it. Gerwitz, R., lived on
Yucca, at the foot of the Hollywood hills.

She answered the door in a surprisingly short and fluffy
nightie. "Whoosh," she said, peering out at me, "I thought
you were going to call."

"I was in the neighborhood."

"Well, hold on until I slip into something a little less
comfortable, could you? I mean, I can't let you in like this.
Well, I suppose I could. You're not going to eat me. You
know, you asked me about poor Sally's religion and then
you ran away. Not even an exit line, and there I was alone
with all those disc jockeys."

"You said something about letting me in."

"Boy, did I get swacked," she said, opening the door. "And then I did like you said, I went home and washed my hair, just like Nellie Forbush in *South Pacific*, except with me it worked. I washed what's-his-name right out of my system, mixed metaphor, and then I called Mom. She wasn't too happy, but then she didn't know him, the lox. Him, I mean, not Mom. Jesus, I'm talking about *anything* just to avoid talking about Sally. Listen, you go into the living room and sit down and I'll be right back."

The living room was a comfortable, messy little nest dominated by a big color television from which David Letterman grinned in a gap-toothed fashion. The couch was a litter of magazines, curlers, and wadded paper tissues. The magazines were largely back issues of *People* and *Us*. The tissues had makeup on them.

"I had a good cry tonight," she said in an explanatory fashion, coming back in. "And then I laughed till I cried again." She'd put on a caftan. "You know stupid pet tricks? They had them tonight, one dog like a Labrador or something, he sat at the dinner table and drank beer. Looked just like Herbert. There, I've said his name and I didn't even blink. And to think I was considering changing shampoos. Do you believe in Shampoo Buildup?"

I said I really didn't have much of an opinion one way or the other.

"You're probably part of that eight percent that's always in the polls. Do you think nuclear war would be good or bad for the world? Sixty percent bad, thirty-two percent good, and *they're* probably dupes of the military-industrial complex, and eight percent undecided. On the other hand, if I had hair like yours I could probably wash it in Cascade and it wouldn't make any difference. I mean, it would still look good," she added hurriedly. "Should I turn this down?" She extended her chin reluctantly in the direction of the television set.

"If you don't mind."

She came back from the set and plopped herself down on the couch, scattering the magazines. "Geez, what a mess," she said. "But who knew? Do you want a drink?

"No, thanks. Tell me about Sally."

"Sally." She reached up and rubbed the bridge of her nose. "I'll have a little one. A greyhound. Sure you won't join me? Well, never mind. The road to hell is probably paved with greyhounds. Or paced by them, anyway." She poured a little grapefruit juice into a glass from a bottle on the table and added about a pint of vodka. "See?" she said, hoisting it. "Vitamin C and everything."

"Especially everything."

"Oh, well. Girls just want to have fun. So ask."

"You said you'd remembered something about Sally."

"Boy, did I. But you left just when we started talking about religion."

"And this had to do with her religion." I felt like a painless dentist faced with a difficult extraction.

"If you want to call it that. Still, I guess it was the only one she had. Although why anybody would need one is beyond me."

"Cultural uncertainties," I said pontifically, with Bernie's voice in my ears. "Seeking after values."

"If you say so," she said politely. "Or just being scared of everything."

"Was Sally scared?"

"Well, you know, out here from some plotzy little town in upstate New York or somewhere. Trying to make it in, you should excuse the expression, the big city. Anyway, yeah, she seemed scared at the end."

"At the end."

"About a week before she . . . she disappeared. Before that prick, whoever he was, killed her," she added bitterly. "Maybe not scared exactly, but upset and confused. Scratch all that. She acted scared."

"What did she say?"

"This was one day at lunch. I was going on about the Herbert Question as usual, like it was the only thing in the world, and she all of a sudden broke in and said she was glad I hadn't gone to a church meeting with her, she had found out that the people who ran it were a bunch of phonies. Crooks, that was what she said. And I said, well, that's religion for you, look at all those awful popes, always claiming the Alps for their kids, and they weren't even supposed to have kids. At least I don't think they were."

"What did she find out?"

"That one of them was a big crook. I said, what, only one?"

"Did she say who?"

"I don't think I gave her a chance," she said reflectively. "I talk a lot."

"Did she tell you what she was going to do?"

"That was the trouble. See, she still believed in the religion. She said it had really helped her. With her problems and everything. I guess Sally had more problems than she let on. Than I *let* her let on." She picked up a wad of Kleenex and snagged at it with long, manicured nails. "Why can't I ever shut up?" she asked David Letterman.

"Don't worry about it. It can't help Sally."

"No, but I could have. Maybe." She swallowed half of her drink and shuddered. "I've been drinking more since the day she vanished," she said with an air of self-discovery. "I thought it was Herbert."

"Well, that won't help her either. Rhoda, what was she going to do?"

"She said she'd heard of this other man," she said, rolling the shredded Kleenex into a tight little ball. "He had left the church or something and he had his own setup but he still believed in the same junk. Only it wasn't a church, exactly."

"It was a congregation," I said.

"Yeah," she said. "That's it. A congregation."

21

"Go away," Sister Zachary said at the door.

In the bright morning light her fat face was bumpy and pitted, as though there were loose gravel beneath the skin. The tentlike dress was crumpled and dirty.

"Mrs. Jenks," I said, "it's either me or Homicide. You and Jinks may have even fewer choices in the immediate future."

"Homicide?" she said, not even noticing the use of her name. "What's Homicide got to do with it?"

"They haven't traced Sally Oldfield here yet. They'll be real curious when they do."

"Why shouldn't she come here?" she said defiantly.

"Even more interesting, why should you two lie about it?"

She caught the name this time. Her face stiffened. Her features were all squeezed tightly into its center, making her look like the end of a cigar that's been crimped and bitten off.

"What do you know about Jinks?"

"Not as much as I'll know in fifteen minutes."

"We told you she didn't come."

"And I know differently. Now, are we all going to sit down for a chat, or am I going to come back with the cops?"

"You're going to get us into trouble," she said childishly.

"I certainly hope so."

"I don't mean the cops. We're used to cops."

She wavered irresolutely while the morning traffic on

Vermont puttered north and south behind me. "I'm not going anywhere," I said. "I'm not the kind of problem that disappears if you don't think about it. Come on, let's go talk to Jinks."

She decided. She tipped her two hundred pounds left, swayed, and then lurched to the right, hauling the door open as she went. I followed her, closed the door behind me, and snapped the lock.

Wilburforce was right where we'd left him, sitting on the edge of his desk. He had an accountant's ledger on his lap and he looked up, startled, as Sister Zachary waddled swiftly into the room with me in panting pursuit.

"Counting souls?" I said, sitting down in the same uncomfortable chair.

"What? What?" he said a little wildly. He sounded like an outboard motor. "Oh, *souls*, I see. Souls, indeed. A little newspaperman's joke." He summoned up a rheumatic chuckle from the lower depths.

"Newspaperman, my ass," Sister Zachary said. "He just threatened me with the cops."

"You're not a newspaper reporter?" Affronted innocence flooded his eyes.

"So we all lied a little," I said. "You didn't tell me about Sally Oldfield, and I didn't tell you I was a detective."

His eyes got very small and he looked over at Sister Zachary, who was sulking in the corner. "Show me your buzzer," he said.

"I don't have a buzzer, Jinks," I said, reaching for the book. He was quicker than I was. He slammed the ledger shut and placed it carefully on the desk behind him.

"That was a former life," he said with an air of great dignity. "That person no longer exists. And if you haven't got a buzzer you're not a detective, are you?"

"I'm a private detective."

"Well," he exhaled, giving me the false choppers from ear to ear, "then I don't have to talk to you. You might as well be a Campfire Girl."

"Wrong. You're withholding evidence in a murder investigation. I'm involved in that investigation in a semiofficial capacity."

"Semi," he said, with a blinding grin. "A miss, as they say, is as good as a mile."

"And the Homicide cops," I said, smiling back at him, "are as near as your phone."

"He knows she was here," Sister Zachary said. "Stop farting around, Jinks. He knows she was here."

"My dear," Jinks said reprovingly. "Language, language. Remember what Malagrida said. 'Language was given to man to conceal his thoughts.'"

"Who was Malagrida?" I asked in spite of myself.

"I don't have the faintest idea. Stendhal quotes it in a chapter heading for *The Red and the Black*."

"That must be a useful book in your profession."

"We can all learn from Julien," he said sententiously. "It's a young man's education in the ways of the world, really. It's not Julien's fault that the world's machinery is oiled with religious hypocrisy. There's a lesson in it for all of us."

"This is fascinating," I said. "If we had the rest of the morning we could probably get through *The Charterhouse of Parma* too. But we don't. I know Sally Oldfield was here, and I know that you—both of you—went to some lengths to convince me that she wasn't. I want to know why you lied and I want to know what happened here."

"I don't mean to be thick," he said, "but could you explain again why we shouldn't just throw you out?"

"No. Mrs. Jenks here just indicated that the cops were no worry compared to—what?—the Church?"

"You didn't," Jenks said, stricken. Sister Zachary gave him a sullen shrug.

"As far as I'm concerned, you can have them both," I said. "Talk to me, and I'll try to see that you only get the cops."

"Un embarras de richesses," Jenks said bitterly in second-year French. "We have a nice little life here. We're not breaking any laws, we're not hurting anyone. I haven't performed surgery in years, not even an appendectomy. The nearest hypodermic is probably down on the sidewalk. Why should you come along all of a sudden and ruin everything?"

"Ask Sally Oldfield."

"She's dead," Jenks said promptly.

"Precisely."

"Oh," he said. Then, after a minute he said, "She was just a girl."

"She found out something about the Church. She came to you. What did she say?"

Husband and wife exchanged a long, fraudulent look. "Who told you she came here?" Sister Zachary said at last.

"Forget it. I want to know what happened."

"It doesn't seem fair," he said.

I got up, and both their heads snapped up to follow me. Their chins and sub-chins quivered.

"Listen," I said. "As Mrs. Jenks said, stop farting around. Who was it? Who'd she find out something about?"

"Merryman," Mrs. Jenks said. She pronounced the name very quickly, as though it were something she had to get out of her mouth before she tasted it. "It was Merryman." Jenks looked at her as though she were Benedict Arnold.

"My dear," he said.

"Oh, shut up," she snapped venomously. "Which do you want, the cops or the Church? It was that crap doctor."

"What did she find out?"

"We didn't ask," Jenks said. "We didn't want to know."

"They'd known each other somewhere," Mrs. Jenks plowed stubbornly on. "Or she'd known him, anyway. She recognized him from somewhere, and she was dismayed. She was crying."

I looked around the office, picturing Jenks, or Wilburforce, sitting fatly behind his desk and Sally crying. She'd run here. Of all the places in Los Angeles, of all the places in the world, she'd run here.

"You didn't ask what she'd learned?"

"As I said," Jenks repeated, "we didn't want to know. We've had our little experience with Dr. Merryman, thank you. He's nobody you want to fool around with, unless you're a snake charmer. And even then, you'd have to be careful. We wanted no part of it. Did we, dear?" he asked Sister Zachary.

"Not an iota," she said.

"So tell me about Merryman."

Jenks looked, if possible, even less comfortable. "He's Angel's physician," he said. "Although my guess is that he's not really an internist at all."

"Why?"

"My good man," Jenks said with a hint of his old manner. "I know more about the thorax than he does. What Merryman doesn't know about internal medicine would fill a library."

"So what is he?"

"My personal guess is that he's a classic sociopath. But who am I? I haven't practiced psychiatry yet. He could be a hat salesman for all I know."

"But he takes care of Angel," I said.

"She's a healthy little girl. They've all been healthy little girls. Most of what a doctor does, you know, is waiting for fatal signs to develop."

"And then what?"

"He sends the patient to a specialist."

"And where did you send Sally?"

"Good Lord," Jenks said. "Do I really have to tell you that?"

"First tell me what Merryman's real position is in the Church."

"Well, he's sort of in charge, isn't he?" Jenks said, looking at his wife for support. "He and Brooks, I mean."

"Meredith Brooks."

"Who else? Not that they like each other. Doctors and lawyers, you know."

"Sssssss," Sister Zachary hissed.

"Well, my dear," Jenks said placatingly, "he's going to find out anyway."

"Is there a feud?"

"That's one way of putting it."

"Serious?"

He pursed his lips retentively. "Perhaps. There is the potential there, let us say, for killing the goose that lays the golden eggs." He seemed very happy with the phrase.

"How long has he been with the Church?"

"Seven or eight years. He came about a year before we . . . withdrew."

"He threw you out."

"Yes," Sister Zachary said.

"No," Jenks said, over her. "We've explained all this. We left after Anna was killed, and they—by which I mean Brooks—started trying to draft a new Speaker. And then, when they found, or rather created, little Jessica, Merryman came with her, more or less. He was involved with Doris Fram, that tramp. Jessica's mother. Then, of course, he was involved with dear Mary Claire. Dr. Merryman is a man who likes to be involved. I always thought Angel was as dull as dirt," he added irrelevantly.

"Where's Jessica now?"

Jenks swallowed. "Jessica? What do you want with her?"

"That's not important. Just tell me where she is."

He looked at Sister Zachary. Sister Zachary gave a minuscule nod. "You're going to keep us out of it?" Jenks said.

"If I can."

He hesitated, then lifted himself off the desk and trudged around behind it. His pants were shiny in the seat. He opened a drawer in the back of the desk and pulled out a slender address book. He riffled through its pages and then looked back up at me.

"You promise," he said.

"If I can do it, I will."

"That's not much."

"It's all you're going to get."

"Give it to him," Sister Zachary said fatalistically. "What else can you do?"

He wrote something on a card and then bustled back around the desk and handed it to me. He looked very nervous.

"Tell me how the Revealings work."

"I really don't know," he said. "Anna was a bona fide channel. I've always assumed that the other two were suggestible enough, and wanted approval badly enough, to hear voices of their own."

I looked at him skeptically. "If he knew how to do it," Sister Zachary said with a bite in her voice, "don't you think we'd have a Speaker too?"

The two of them glared at each other.

"So," I said, pocketing the card, "who'd you sell Sally to?"

Jenks looked surprised that I'd had to ask.

"To Brooks, of course," he said piously. "Merryman would have killed her."

Out on Vermont I squinted into the sunshine and plotted my day. The sky was almost clear for the first time in a week, and the pavement was already drying. Heaven seemed near at hand. It was the kind of day when you could drive forever, which was probably what I was going to do.

I ticked off the possible stops on my itinerary. Get a different car, take Eleanor back home to help her pack, talk to Speaker Number Two—Jessica Fram—and nail Brooks's ears to the nearest wall. The order sounded about right. I wanted to get Brooks at home, not at the office. I didn't think the formidable Marcy would let me back in.

Wrent-a-Wreck on Hawthorne had just opened for business as I pulled in. The manager was a potbellied little man in a tight white T-shirt. The T-shirt said nothing. It was a real, honest-to-God undershirt.

"I didn't think they made them anymore," I said.

"They're not easy to get, let me tell you," he said. "Try to find something white at a white sale. But if somebody wants to write on my chest, let 'em pay me rent, that's what I always say." He gave Alice an appraising eye.

"Low-rider special, huh? Haven't seen one of these since JFK. What's 'Sweet lice' mean?"

"It used to be Alice," I said defensively. " 'Sweet Alice.' The A came off."

"You want to sell her? I could probably do some business with a heap like this. Penetrate the Cholo market. Big Hispanic bucks in L.A. now."

"What I want," I said, "is to leave her here for a couple of days and drive away in one of yours. Some nice, dull, anonymous, average, medium-size car with no pizzazz and no writing on it and very small license plates."

"Bank job, huh?" He gave a short barking laugh.

"No," I said. "I'm only going to drive it to church."

*   *   *

Getting Eleanor moved was harder. For one thing, she didn't want to leave the office at that point.

"I just got here," she said. "How can I turn around and walk back out?"

"How about I call in a bomb threat and when they evacuate the building you can just get into my car?"

"You remember Jackie Vinh?"

"Sure. She was with your ex-idiot at that Halloween party. What has she got to do with anything?"

"I talked to her this morning. That's why I'm late. She's a nursing student. She said she'd call Mr. Ellspeth today and see if she can help out with Ansel. She's a nice girl."

"You're not so bad yourself. Let's go."

"I can't. You'll have to come back."

"Eleanor, I have a day in front of me that does not make it possible for me to waffle hither and yon. I can manage hither maybe once if the traffic lights aren't against me. Why don't you make out a list of what you need and then give me your key, and I'll drop the stuff by right after lunch."

"Do you really think this is necessary?"

"After last night, I certainly do."

"Well," she said grumpily, "I think it's melodramatic. And you'll never find everything I need."

Nevertheless, she gave me the key and a relatively brief list and I headed out toward the beach.

Jenks and Mrs. Jenks had made it pretty clear that there was a major split in the Church and that the main splittees were Brooks and Merryman. If my reading was right, Brooks controlled the dollars and Merryman controlled the Speaker. They needed each other. And they hated each other.

When Sally recognized Merryman for whatever or whoever he really was, she'd run to kindly old Hubert Wilburforce, who had promptly sold her to Brooks for $100,000 and the dismissal of a suit the Church had pending against the Congregation. Brooks, I would have thought, would have put her in a safe-deposit box as a piece of highly negotiable currency if she really knew something heinous about the good doctor. Instead, she'd been killed.

I was very anxious to have another talk with Brooks.

Eleanor's place seemed secure. The door was locked, none of the windows had been broken, and when I got inside, things were in their usual obsessive state of Eleanor neatness. It took me maybe forty-five minutes to pack everything she'd listed. I threw in a few things she'd forgotten, too. Shoes, for example. Eleanor belonged to the Bernie school of packing.

When I left, it was barely noon. Jessica Fram lived in the Valley, so I took the Santa Monica freeway to the 405 and pointed my awful, rattling little Camaro due north. It was a depressing shade of battleship gray that laughed at dirt. That's probably why they paint battleships that color. All that swabbing for nothing.

Jessica's house was in Reseda. It sat in the center of a flat little tract block that managed to stay brown even after all that rain. What lawns there were seemed to be made largely of mud. Dogs of indeterminate breed sprouted from it.

The only difference between the Fram house and the ones flanking it was an eight-foot-high chain-link fence with an extra foot of barbed wire on top. One of those boxes with a button and a microphone sat perched on a pole next to the driveway, looking like a forlorn transplant from Bel Air.

For about fifteen minutes I sat in the Camaro at the end of the block and studied the house. Nothing moved. The curtains were drawn against the day's new sunlight, and two cars, washed by the rain, sparkled in the driveway on the other side of the fence. They were the only sign that anyone was home.

At twenty minutes to one the front door of the house opened and a middle-aged woman with short steel-gray hair came briskly out. The gate slid open. The woman gave the neighborhood a practiced once-over, pausing only for an instant at my car, and then hopped into a butch black Land Rover and backed out into the street. She ignored me completely as she passed. Maybe there *was* something to be said for the Camaro's color.

I pulled the Camaro up to the black speaker box and pressed the button. After what seemed like weeks a woman's voice bellowed, "Hermia?"

"No, it's not Hermia," I said. "I'm here to see Jessica."

There was a pause you could have driven a motor home through.

"For what?" the woman said. "She's in bed."

I looked at my watch again. Twelve-forty-five. Jessica certainly led a difficult life. I mentally flipped another coin.

"Dick sent me," I said.

After a long moment the gate rolled crankily open. I drove in.

22

Her hair was long and straight and bleached and deader than the Dead Sea Scrolls. She lay on the living-room couch under a handmade quilt with her arms stretched out on top of it, palms up, like an ascetic nun waiting to receive the stigmata. She couldn't have been more than seventeen.

A vague, frayed lady who had to be Mrs. Fram had ushered me into a tiny Formica dining room and asked me to wait. Unwatered house plants languished despondently in a window box. Mrs. Fram was either the most laid-back woman I'd ever met or the most heavily sedated.

"Sit," she'd said blearily. "There's four chairs." There were six. On the wall was an absolutely enormous color photograph of her and Jessica. It might have been taken before World War I for all the resemblance it bore to Mrs. Fram.

"Pretty picture," I said conversationally.

"Uh," she said, looking at it as though she'd never seen it before.

"Spontaneous generation," I suggested. "Pictures are always appearing on my walls too."

She watched my mouth as I talked, looking like a lip-reader trying to follow a silent movie. Then she took a woozy look at the picture.

"Me and Baby," she said. "Sit. You just missed Hermia. She'll be back."

Since I was already sitting, there wasn't much for me to do. "I'm not here to see Hermia," I reminded her.

"Dick sent you," she said with an effort. She might have been pretty once—the picture certainly suggested that she had—but now the flesh hung slack and heavy on her face, and deep circles had worn themselves darkly and permanently into the pouchy area beneath her eyes. The creases around her eyes and mouth, even the creases in her forehead, all pulled downward. It was a face created by erosion. "Dick," she said again in a harsh tone. "He was here. Just a couple days, I think."

"Well," I said brightly, "he's sent me this time. I think you said Jessica was in bed." I wiggled my eyebrows encouragingly. It was like talking to someone a hundred yards away; I found myself using body language to get the point across.

And a lot of good it did, too. She looked at me as I talked, and then, when I finished, she went on looking at me. I had a feeling she'd forgotten what I'd said. Then she said, "Tuesday. It was Tuesday." Satisfied with her feat of memory, she scratched her forearm absently for a moment. Then she told me to sit down again, pivoted uncertainly, and left the room. She dragged her feet when she walked, and her shoes slapped against the floor. "Baby?" I heard her call. "Baby. Time to get up."

I spent the next ten minutes or so watering plants and snooping through the mail on the dining-room table. Quite a lot of it was from the Church: invitations to Revealings, an announcement of a retreat to be held up in Ojai, a strong suggestion that members consider establishing a system of annual tithing, a sort of pre-Christmas sale on certain advanced levels of Listening. Most of it was bulk stuff; ex-Speaker or not, Jessica didn't seem to be on any special mailing list.

At the bottom of the pile was a color photo of Angel and Mary Claire, the new one with the kitten in it. At first glance it looked like the kind of thing a junior-high-school kid might do—blacking out front teeth or drawing in a mustache. But it was more spiteful than that.

Holes had been poked through Mary Claire's eyes. A bullet-entrance wound had been painstakingly drawn into the center of her forehead, and vivid red ink poured from it. Her bosom had been slashed raggedly with a razor blade.

Nothing had been done to Angel.

The picture was an unsettling combination of immature malice and adult hatred. It looked like the kind of thing the cops found hanging in David Berkowitz's bedroom when they finally nailed him as the Son of Sam. The person who'd done it wasn't all there, but she had her hatred down cold. And, of course, it had to be Mrs. Fram.

I heard her shoes slapping against the hallway floor and shoved the picture back under the pile of mail. She pushed the door leading to the hallway closed from the other side before she passed by it. Apparently I wasn't to see Baby until Baby was ready. "There, Baby," she said from the living room. "Right there. Right there."

There was some muffled moving around. "Cover up, now," Mrs. Fram said in her slurred, mannish voice. " 'Tsa man, you know. A man from Dick."

"Dick," said a small voice. "Dick's not coming?"

"I don't know," Mrs. Fram said curtly. "Scoot up a little."

"But I need him to come. He has to come." The voice was thin and querulous, like that of a young actress trying to play an old woman.

"Hush. You hush. How do we know why this man's here?"

I stepped back from the door just as Mrs. Fram came through it. "Okay now," she said, concentrating her gaze in my general direction. "Baby's in there." She waved a hand behind her, in toward the living room. She went to the table, pulled out a chair, and sat heavily. She looked without interest at the pile of mail. I went into the living room.

"Hello, Jessica," I said.

She'd been rouged and lipsticked crudely for the occasion, but the patches of color only heightened the pallor of her skin. The dead hair had been brushed straight down and then lifted and held in place with a black bow. She looked like a teenage Miss Havisham.

"Is Dick coming?" she asked.

"Not right now," I said. "Maybe later, though."

She clenched both her thin fists and tightened her mouth childishly. "He likes to make me wait," she said. "He enjoys it."

"Wait for what?"

"The little yellow ones."

Mrs. Fram coughed in a tubercular fashion in the next room while I evaluated this. "Don't you have enough left for today?"

"Of course I do," she said impatiently. "Enough for tomorrow too. But he knows I get nervous when I get low. He likes it. I know he does."

"No, he doesn't," I said. "He just doesn't want you to have too many of them. He's just being careful."

"That's what *he* says. That's what Aunt Hermia says too."

"Well, and they both care about you, don't they?"

"I guess so," she said reluctantly.

"What does your mother say about it?"

"Her," Jessica said. "What does she know?"

"Is Aunt Hermia really your aunt?"

"No." Jessica gave a spiteful little smile. "She's the dragon at the door," she said, "and I'm the fair maiden. We should have a house with a tower so I could sleep in the very top room, and we could chain Aunt Hermia to an iron post next to the front door."

"And where would your mother sleep?"

"On the floor if she wanted to. She does about half the time anyway. Sometimes she sleeps standing up, like horses are supposed to."

"Jessica," I said, "you never Speak anymore, do you?"

"No," she said, looking directly at me for the first time. "That's finished. It ended when I got sick."

"And what's wrong with you?"

"I've got a Wasting Disease," she said with a certain amount of pleasure. "I can't pronounce it, but Dick says it's getting better."

"Have you tried to Speak?"

"You can't try. Don't you know anything? It's either there or it isn't."

"What is?"

"The Voice, silly. What else?"

"And where does the Voice come from?"

"I don't know. I don't remember hearing it. I just know that I heard the tapes later, and it was my voice saying all those things, except not my voice exactly."

"When was the first time you Spoke?"

"I was twelve."

"Where were you?"

"In Dick's office. His office then, not his office now."

"And what happened?"

"He was examining me."

"For what?"

"To see if I could be the Speaker," she said, as if it were the most obvious thing in the world. "Anna was dead."

"Was he examining other little girls too?"

"Sure. Lots. He even examined Angel, and she was only seven then." She smirked unpleasantly. "Imagine a seven-year-old Speaker."

"What kind of an examination was it?"

"Dick and Mr. Brooks were looking for a Speaker," she said as though that explained everything. "Everybody wanted to be the Speaker. Every little girl in the Church. You got to wear all those pretty clothes and have your picture taken and be famous. Who wouldn't want it?"

"I'm sure they all wanted it. But you were the one who got it, weren't you?"

A glow of pride suffused her face. "I was the only one who heard the Voice," she said. "I was the only one it wanted to talk to."

"And how did Dick examine you?"

She started to say something, glanced up at me, and then closed her mouth. After a moment she rearranged the quilt and crossed her hands demurely on top of it. "If Dick sent you," she said, looking at the top of the quilt, "how come you have to ask all these questions?"

"We're going to write a book," I lied. "Dick and I. A book about you."

"What are you going to call it?"

"Jessica Speaks."

"Will it have my picture in it?" There was real pleasure in her face. It almost made her look young.

"On the cover."

"One of my good pictures, one of my then pictures. It'll be one of those, won't it?"

"The prettiest we can find."

She took a sidelong peek at the dining-room door. "Not her," she said softly.

"No. Just you."

"Fine," she said.

"So you see, I need to get as much information as I can in your own words."

She nodded gravely and regarded her hands. "Okay."

"Tell me about the examination."

"Just a regular exam. You know, my pulse and my blood pressure. My eyes and ears and stuff."

There was no way to avoid the question. "Did you have to get undressed?"

Real color appeared beneath the rouge. "Sure," she said.

"And was your mother in the room?"

"Not then," she said. "She came in while I was Speaking. She says she saw me sitting on the table and Speaking. She was real happy about it. She liked Dick then. I don't remember her until after."

"After what?"

"After I'd finished Speaking."

"Your mother liked Dick then?"

"Oh, sure. She was crazy about him."

"And later?"

She looked me straight in the eye. "Dick didn't tell you to ask me that," she said. "He'd have never told you to ask me anything about that."

It was the kind of moment that always made me wish I still smoked. It would have been very nice to have something to do for a few seconds.

"You're right," I said. "He didn't. We won't talk about any of that. Tell me, what did it feel like to Speak?"

She tilted her chin up and gave me an evaluative gaze. Her eyes were long, widely spaced, and slate gray.

"Like I said," she began, "I don't remember the Voice. I

just remember that it always felt like someone was holding me in his arms. Somebody a lot bigger than I was. Somebody warm, who loved me."

"And then what happened?"

"When?"

"After the first time you Spoke."

She looked as though she didn't understand the question. "We went home," she said.

"When did you Speak again?"

"For Mr. Brooks. It was a few days later. It was the same, except longer. Then the third time was a Revealing."

"And then you did it how often?"

"Every week, usually. Sometimes the Voice didn't come, though."

"How often did that happen?"

"Once in a while. I just sat there with everybody looking at me. It was terrible."

"When the voice did come, what happened?"

"We went out onto the stage, you know, after the welcome and the music, and maybe sometimes there was a guest star who got up and talked about what Listening had done for him. Then she"—she indicated the door to the dining room—"and I went onto the stage and sat down. I always sat on the right, because *she* was supposed to say something into the microphone before anything happened. Usually, while she was talking I would hear a kind of whisper in my ear. It would say my name a few times. Then it was like I was being filled slowly with warm water, and I would go away. When I came back, it was over."

I needed a moment to think, and I got up and pulled open the curtains covering the living-room window. Sunlight poured into the room. Jessica squinted and stretched a hand out in front of her to block the light. "Don't," she said. "It hurts my eyes." I pulled the curtains closed again, and she settled back onto the couch.

"Did you understand the things you said when you were Speaking? Afterward, I mean, when you heard the tapes."

"No. Not most of it."

"And did Dick go on examining you?"

The color returned to her cheeks and she looked away.

"Sure, always. That's what the Speaker's doctor is for." She sounded defensive. "Before Dick it was that fat man. He was Anna's doctor."

"Jessica. Did either Dick or Mr. Brooks give you anything to read? Did they ask you to learn anything?"

"Like what?" she said blankly.

"Yeah, like what?" said a deep voice behind me.

I turned to see the steely-haired lady who'd left in the Land Rover. She was clutching three bags that said TACO TIKI, and she was regarding me very narrowly indeed. "And how'd you get in here?"

"You're Hermia," I said happily. "I just missed you."

"What's going on?" she said. Mrs. Fram lurched into the dining-room doorway and stood there with her jaw slack. She looked at Hermia's bags. "Taco Tiki," she said.

"I can't leave for a minute," Hermia said. "What are you, some kind of spy?"

"Dick sent him," Jessica said. "They're going to write a book about me and make me famous again. And there's nothing you can do about it."

"Is that so?" Hermia said softly, looking at me. "A book. All about little Jessica. Now, isn't that interesting?"

"We have high hopes for it," I said, wondering if Hermia were armed.

"You and Dick," she said.

It sounded thin even to my ears. "His name goes first," I said.

"Merryman and what?"

"Aren't you going to put those bags down? Your food will get cold."

"Doris," Hermia commanded, holding out the bags. Doris tottered over to get them. "Get out of here," Hermia said. "Put them in the other room. Stay there." Mrs. Fram trudged through the door, looking like the Night of the Living Dead if the Living Dead had come back for junk food.

"You're going to ruin things," Jessica said accusingly to Hermia.

"You bet your cute little hairbow, I am," Hermia said. "Now, you, what's your name?"

I stood up. She was almost as tall as I was. "Hermia," I said, "there's a lot going on that you don't know about."

She blinked. "Like what?"

"Changes. In Century City."

It didn't exactly stun her; she didn't stagger backward or clutch at her throat, but she was listening. "Which direction?" she said after a moment.

"The wrong one, dear," I said. "If you're not careful."

"I'm doing my job."

"Then how'd I get in here?"

"I had to get food. Who else is going to go out?"

"What were your instructions?"

"They wanted tacos," she said, trying for a tone of calm reason. "They can't live on pizza, and Taco Bell doesn't deliver."

"They wanted tacos," I said pityingly. "Do you know what she told me? What she would have told anyone who walked in while you were doing *what*? Going out for tacos?"

Nobody said anything. Then Jessica said, "I *like* tacos."

Hermia shot her a glance and she subsided. "How long since you were basemented?" I asked.

Hermia licked her lips. "Never," she said.

"What an experience you have in store," I said. "If you call the wrong person."

"Which one?" Hermia said.

I licked my index finger and held it up. "Check the wind," I said.

23

_____

"Try the American Dental Association," I said to Joyce. I was standing in a pay phone on Ventura Boulevard. Across the street, furtive-looking men stole in and out of an adult bookstore.

"I don't have to," she said. "That's what he is, a dentist. He's listed in the ADA data base. How'd you know?"

"Just a guess. Have you talked to the DEA?"

"Yeah, that's what's odd. He graduated in 1972 but he only registered with the DEA seven years ago."

"That's about right," I said. "Where'd he practice?"

"I don't know. He graduated from a college in New York."

"Good work. Just to make sure, can you check with New York to see if he was certified there? He probably practiced in or near a town called Utica."

There was a pause. "It's after five o'clock there," she said. "They'll probably be closed."

"Tomorrow morning is fine."

I figured Brooks worked until five-thirty or six, so I had a few hours. I dialed my own number and entered a two-digit code when I heard my recorded voice say hello.

"Number of messages," the machine announced, "four." I hated its smug tone of voice, and also the fact that the damn thing couldn't count.

"One," it said.

"Simeon? Roxanne." Music was very loud in the background. She must have been calling from McGinty's of Malibu, the bar where she worked. "I've been cold the last

252

couple of nights. I drove by last night, but no Alice, and I didn't feel like getting threatened with another piece of firewood. Give me a call if you feel like sharing your warm feet." There was a pause. "Everybody here is very drunk," she said.

"One," the machine said again.

"I am Mrs. Yount," Mrs. Yount said. "That house is a mess, mister. I was just there. There's no excuse for it. Now, normally I'd just tell you to move out. But if you find Fluffy I'll forget all about it. I know she's alive. I could feel it in the inside of my bosom if she wasn't. I want to hear from you, young man." She hung up decisively.

"One," the machine said implacably.

"This is Al Hammond, goddamm it." I pushed the six button on the pay phone and the machine skipped to the next message. "One," The machine said.

"May you roast in hell," I said.

The next caller had hung up. I started to do the same.

"One," said the machine.

"You said four," I told it.

"Wo," Dexter Smif said. "Mus' be you busy. Man can't return his calls mus' be on the go mostly all the time. Just lettin' you know they a man of talent available. I ain't gonna give you my number again. If you done lost it I don't want to work with you anyways."

Dexter hung up. This time I waited. "Last message," the machine said. "Thank you for—" I was already heading for the car.

Brooks wasn't in the directory. The list of the Church board of directors, to which he belonged, didn't bother with addresses. So at five-fifteen, having dropped Eleanor's suitcase at the *Times*, I was parked in my invisible gray Camaro across the street from the exit to an underground parking structure in Century City. I'd circled the structure twice, dismayed at finding two exits. For a moment I'd actually thought of calling Dexter. But then what would we have done? Talked to each other on our two-way wrist radios?

I finally calmed down. One of the exits led south and the other led north. South was Culver City, Palms, Mar Vista— perfectly nice places for secretaries and support staff to live.

North was Westwood, Bel Air, Beverly Hills, and several other perfectly nicer places. I had Brooks pegged as a Westwood man. Quiet and substantial.

At five-forty on the dot he came out. He'd made it easy for me by putting down the top on his cream-colored Mercedes. The streetlights flickered and then hummed above us as I followed him down the Avenue of the Stars to Santa Monica Boulevard.

At the stoplight, he checked himself out in the rearview mirror. He smoothed his hair, examined his teeth briefly, and then rubbed his chin. He seemed pretty happy with what he saw. Of course, he'd had a lot of time to get used to it.

He turned left onto Santa Monica and then right onto a cute, crooked little street that edges along the golf course of a country club. I've never known which club it is. I stayed about thirty yards behind him, just close enough to squeak through a yellow light if one got frisky with me.

Together we crossed Wilshire. He drove fast and economically, downshifting when he wanted to slow. I don't think he hit his brakes once except for the stoplights. He hit them again in the middle of the very expensive part of Beverly Glen that stretches for about half a mile south of Sunset. Then he turned right, into the yard of a big traditional colonial house with white shutters.

There was a paved parking area to the right of the house with a detached carport at the end of it. By the time he had the car in the carport, I had passed the house, parked the Camaro under a tow-away sign, and was crossing the yard. Jingling something in his pocket, he strode across the paving stones to the front door. He had no inkling of my presence behind him until he put the key in the lock and turned it and I pulled out the nasty little gun and touched it lightly to the back of his neck.

He froze in a well-bred fashion. Then he slowly turned his head to look at me. When he saw my face, his muscles relaxed slightly.

"Mr. Swinburne," he said. "How tiresome."

"It'll get more interesting," I said. "And you know my real name. You're the one who had me hired in the first place."

"And why would I do that?"

"Because you weren't sure you could trust the people you gave Sally to. And you were right. You couldn't."

"Sally who?" he said without conviction. It sounded as though it was purely for form's sake.

I gave the back of his neck a little jab with the gun. "Open the door," I said. "We'll talk inside."

"You won't use that," he said.

"After what I've seen today, I wouldn't think about it twice."

"Today?"

"I talked to Wilburforce. And I paid a visit to Jessica. She's certainly on the road to recovery, isn't she? What is it besides Valium addiction?"

"Oral insulin," he said after a beat. "It keeps her blood sugar abnormally low. She's not in any danger."

"She's a junkie," I said. "You've turned a child into an addict. Two other people are dead. Maybe three. I wouldn't any more worry about shooting you than I would about stepping on a slug."

He pursed his mouth. "Then I guess we'd better go in," he said. He turned the key and the door swung open.

"Just a minute," I said. With my free hand I patted his jacket pockets. "Put your hands in your pockets," I said, "and keep them there. I'll get the key."

He did as he was told, and we stepped into a big entrance hall furnished in what looked like genuine Early American. A pine dry-sink filled with an autumnal arrangement of bare branches, grasses, and pine cones stood at its far end.

"Have you got a study?"

"Of course." He sounded affronted.

"Which way?"

"To the left."

"Let's go."

I lowered the gun to his middle back and followed him into an enormous cathedral-beamed living room. Lamps burned here and there. As we entered, a pleasant-looking gray-haired lady in a blue silk dress stood up from the couch, laying down an embroidery hoop as she rose.

"Why, Merry," she said with obvious delight. "You're early."

"I got to missing you," he said. "Dear, this is Mr. Grist. Simeon Grist. Mr. Grist, my wife, Adelaide."

"I'm so pleased to meet you," she said, crossing the room with her hand extended. "You've brought Merry home early."

I dropped the gun into my pocket and shook her very slender hand. "It was his idea," I said. "We could have done this anywhere."

"Well, aren't you sweet. Merry's usually business, business, business. I just know you had a hand in this, and I'm grateful. I don't get enough time with this husband of mine."

"No rest for the wicked," I said. Adelaide Brooks laughed.

"For the *weary*, you mean." She looked from one of us to the other. "May I get you men a little something to drink?"

"No thank you, Addy," Brooks said. "Mr. Grist won't be staying very long."

"Oh, that's too bad. Should I go into the other room, or will you be using the study?"

"The study will be fine," I said. Brooks nodded curtly.

"It's such a lovely room," Adelaide Brooks said. "So masculine. Merry calls it his Think Room." Brooks colored slightly. "All right, then. You men run along and figure out a way to make lots and lots of money. Call me if you change your mind about a drink, Mr. Grist."

I said I would, and Brooks and I marched in silence down a short hallway and into a room that could have belonged only to a lawyer. The furniture brooded there in heavy conspiracy: a massive wooden desk, red leather chairs, mahogany end tables, and books of exactly the same size and color ponderously lining three of the dark walnut walls. Brooks started to sit behind the desk, but I shook my head and gestured him toward one of the armchairs. He sat sullenly and I closed the door.

For a long time I just stood there looking at him. "Well," I finally said. "Domestic bliss. The little lady. Embroidery. And Merry, no less." His blush deepened. "So," I said, "here we are in the Think Room, Merry. What do you think about it all?"

"She doesn't know anything," he said.

"No, I don't imagine she does. She probably thinks you're a real lawyer."

"I am a real lawyer. May I take my hands out of my pockets now?"

"It's *your* Think Room. Do what you like. No, you're not a real lawyer. You're a fungus with a wardrobe. You're running a gigantic blackmail racket, sucking blood out of people who need help. Poor, frightened, lost little people who don't know where to turn, so they come to you. And you squeeze them dry, don't you? You move them up the levels of Listening, pulping more money out of them every week. You tape everything they say and you file it for future use. You pervert little girls to turn them into ventriloquist's dummies because it's good show business. And you kill people."

"I guide the Church in its investments," he said stubbornly, slouching deeper into his chair. "I provide legal advice. I serve on the board of directors. I serve on many boards of directors."

"Come on," I said. "You run the money and Merryman runs the Speakers. You help out with the Speakers sometimes too, don't you?"

"No," he said tightly.

"Caleb Ellspeth wouldn't agree with you."

Brooks sat up suddenly at the sound of Ellspeth's name. His eyes wandered nervously over the rows of law books.

"Looking for a precedent?" I said. "There isn't one. This is about as shitty as it gets."

"I haven't killed anybody."

"No. You wouldn't have the guts. That's a fine point anyway. You've profited from their deaths. I imagine you'd qualify as an accessory."

He gripped the arms of his chair tightly and made an enormous effort to stand up. "I have nothing to say," he said.

I leaned over, put my fingertips on his chest, and pushed gently. He fell back into the seat. "Fine," I said. "Let's call Adelaide in and we can continue our discussion."

His mouth opened and closed several times. He looked like a fish snapping at something. "You can't," he said at last.

"What did you think? Did you think you could swim

through the scum all day and then come home and shower it off? Did you think nothing would ever come in through the front door with you? You've been tracking it across the rug for years, Merry. You're covered in it. That's why your face shines."

He rubbed his chin. "It's Merryman," he said.

"That's what everybody tells me. It's always Merryman. The really awful thing is that you might actually have gotten away with it if the two of you hadn't gotten even more greedy. Merry and Merryman, the Gold Dust Twins. Except that both of you wanted to run the whole show, didn't you? Like a couple of big blue horseflies dive-bombing each other over a pile of shit. And Sally Oldfield got caught in the middle."

Brooks slowly closed his eyes. He kept them closed while I counted to fourteen. Then he opened them again and looked at me.

"What's your deal?" he said.

"Who says I have a deal? Maybe I'm just God's flyswatter. I liked Sally Oldfield. I never talked to her, but I liked her. She should be in the living room right now, chatting with Adelaide. Adelaide would have liked her too."

"Keep Adelaide out of it."

"No way in the world." I shrugged sympathetically. "Poor Adelaide," I said.

"If you didn't want a deal you wouldn't be here," he said. "If you know all you seem to know, why not take it to the police? Why talk to me?"

"I wanted to get a chance to see you up close. People like you don't come along all that often."

He turned his attention back to the books. He rubbed his chin in an abstracted fashion. "Who's your client?" he finally asked.

It had taken him long enough. "Haven't got one," I said. "I thought maybe you were."

He looked a little more self-assured. He rubbed his hands over his thighs and then straightened the crease in his pants. "What's your fee?" he said.

I cocked my head and looked at him appraisingly. He returned the gaze.

"One million dollars," I said.

He didn't blink. "For what?"

"For keeping you out of it. For going away. What do you think it's for?"

"For going away," he repeated. "For closing down completely."

"In cash," I said.

"Tomorrow," he said.

"Small bills."

"Tomorrow," he said again. "Nothing bigger than a twenty."

"Fine," I said. I put out my hand, and after a moment, he shook it.

"I'll need some insurance," he said.

"For example."

"I imagine you have a license." The Brooks I'd first met was back. He got up and began to pace. "I need to know what you've got and how you got it. Then I'll need a signed statement that makes it clear that you've violated a number of laws in obtaining your information and keeping it from the police. We may have to add a few things to it to give it weight, but you'll sign it anyway, for a million dollars. You'll have me, I'll have you. I go to jail, you go to jail."

"Fair enough. But one thing at a time. I tell you what I know tonight. We can draft the statement tonight. But you don't get a signature until you hand me the million and I've counted it."

He gave me a small, malicious smile. "Counting it will take quite some time," he said.

I returned his smile. "I figure it'll come out to about ten thousand an hour."

He went to the desk and took out a yellow legal pad and an automatic pencil. "Begin," he said peremptorily. "I'll take notes and we can draft the statement from them." He clicked the pencil twice and looked critically at the point. "Wait a minute," he said. "Do you want that drink?"

"Sure," I said. "Bring it in a bucket."

"Scotch?" He was mein host to his fingertips.

"Unblended."

"Of course," he said. He went to the door, opened it, and left with a whisper of woolen slacks.

I passed a few minutes looking at the spines of the law books. There it was, the law in all its indifferent, magisterial glory, referenced and cross-referenced, a legacy of protection for the individual that marched in a straight line from Athens and the Roman Codification through the Magna Carta, the Age of Enlightenment, the Revolution, and more than two hundred years of earnest attempts to right injustice. Human rights, citizens' rights, government's rights, property rights, equal rights, civil rights, women's rights, even animal rights. All of it printed and proofread, handsomely bound and numbered to fill the shelves of men and women who could defend it or destroy it. The books didn't care who used them. They were as indifferent as the law.

Brooks came back in carrying a rattan tray with two large perspiring cut-glass tumblers on it. "Here we are," he said, laying it carefully down on the desk to avoid scratching the surface. He picked up his drink. "Tally-ho," he said, clinking it against mine.

I couldn't bring myself to say tally-ho, so I just nodded and drank.

Brooks put his glass down and picked up the pencil. "Let's start," he said.

I moved aimlessly around the room as I talked, picking up pipes, paperweights, awards, mementos, and the other flotsam and jetsam that bobs to the surface of a man's den. Other than my voice, the only sound in the study was Brooks's pencil gouging into the pad and an occasional muted expletive when the point broke.

"Eight or nine years ago, you must have had it all pretty much your way," I said. "However Anna did it, whether she really was a channel, or a schizophrenic or whatever, it was easy to manage. She pretty much did it on cue, and there was only Wilburforce to contend with. And we both know that Wilburforce was no match for you. He's all pressure points. He is that rarest of creatures, a total fraud. There's not a real thing about him.

"But then Anna died, or Merryman killed her. That's one murder, if it was a murder, that I know you had nothing to do with. It put you into a real quandary, didn't it? The Church was up and running, cranking out money day and night, and you had no Speaker. Where was all the doctrine supposed to come from? What was the authority for Listening? Where was the glamour? *Did* Merryman kill her?"

He shook his head. "I have no idea," he said. "This is your story."

"So it is. So there you are, with the best idea for making money since the invention of the printing press, and it looks like it's time to shut down. But a savior comes along in a bright-colored polo shirt. Dr. Richard Merryman—an internist, he says—proposes that he can create a new Speaker for you. His cut is half, or thereabouts."

"Not half," Brooks said automatically. "Not until later."

"A substantial bite nonetheless," I said. "Enough to wear a callus in your wallet. I would imagine that Merryman didn't tell even you how he made Jessica Speak. Or Angel later, when Jessica got too old to appeal to him."

Brooks looked up at me quickly. "Oh, that too," I said. "This is going to make some story if it ever comes out. There's hardly a single disgusting aspect of human behavior that it doesn't contain. It'll fascinate Adelaide."

"She'll never hear it," Brooks said serenely.

"I think a million is a little cheap."

"We have a deal," he said.

"But the story is just getting good. I'm not sure I want to tell the rest of it for only a million."

"If I understand you," Brooks said, "you're the only one who knows all of it."

"That's more or less true."

"You haven't bought yourself an insurance policy by sharing this with the police, because they'd act on it and you wouldn't collect your million. Other people, that little Chinese girl, for example, may know bits and pieces, but you're the only one who's got the big picture."

"The big picture. Admirably said. Yes, you could put it that way and not stray over the line into falsehood."

"Then consider," he said, "two alternatives. One is that you get a million dollars. Two is that something happens to you, something from which you would not recover. Either way, as you yourself put it, you go away. Both alternatives pose risks for the Church. You might not stay bought. You would certainly stay dead, but someone might connect it with us. We, or at least I, would prefer simply to buy you. Which would you prefer?"

"This is so civilized. Here we are, sitting in a book-lined study discussing my death as though it were a matter in which we were both only mildly interested. This is what I always wanted to do when I grew up."

"I asked you a question."

"Well, I'd prefer the million, obviously. Who wouldn't? The question was whether I could up it a little."

"You can't."

"Don't get huffy. I just wanted to clear it up. The free-enterprise system doesn't keep moving unless people push it. Where would you be if you'd settled for less?" I took a long swallow off my drink. "Gee, look at this swell house, and Adelaide and everything."

"You needn't mention her again. Go on with the story. I have to change for dinner."

"Okay. So Merryman gets Jessica up and yakking, and it's even better. You're not just selling a little girl who likes to talk, you're selling a spirit who speaks through a series of little girls. Things really take off. Membership grows and you begin to sell franchises, just like McDonald's, and everything is, as you might say, tally-ho. And Merryman gets tired of Jessica after her breasts begin to develop and he auditions new Speakers and comes up with Angel, who's just perfect. Great-looking, wonderful name, and she functions like clockwork.

"Of course, there's a flaw in the ointment, as a friend of mine used to say, because it's not your show anymore. You literally can't do it without Merryman. Still, you guys are making millions of dollars every year between Listening fees, franchises, merchandising, and blackmail, and there should be plenty to go around. Except that there isn't. One of you, and let's concede for the sake of tact that it's Merryman, is a real pig. Plus he's a doctor, doesn't like lawyers anyway, and he figures that you are a very expensive piece of superfluous manpower. How are we doing so far?"

He nodded. "Close enough," he said.

"You've got Merryman by the short hairs for the time being. You know where the money is. He can figure it all out eventually, but it could take years. Nevertheless, you're getting nervous. Years aren't really that long, not where millions of dollars are concerned. The problem is that Merryman can run the Church without you, but you can't run it without him. What you need is leverage. You need to be able to control him and keep him quiet somehow, running the little girls for the TV cameras while you sit back and work on your bank balance.

"And, lo! the Lord in his infinite wisdom and mercy delivers unto you a very nice young lady named Sally Oldfield. Sally's just the kind of poor sap the Church was created to milk. She's got low self-esteem, she's lonely, she's got some disposable income. All the qualifications for enlightenment. She sees Angel and she's entranced. She goes through Listening and she actually finds out some things about herself. Happiness and fulfillment are dangled in front of her, and she goes after them. Paying for the privilege, of course."

I rattled the ice cubes in my glass. Brooks stopped writing and watched me, his tongue wadded into one side of his mouth.

"And then she sees Dick, and it all falls apart. She knows who he is. She knows he's a dentist from Utica, New York, the home of religions based on the wisdom of little girls, and that he uses hypnotism as an anesthetic. And she sees his proximity to the Royal Family, and she knows all at once how it works. He wires her, doesn't he?"

Brooks said nothing, but he'd stopped writing.

"Her hair is always down when she's onstage and up when she's not. I'll bet that she's wearing a cute little Dan Rather button in her ear. He must have examined a lot of little girls, not that that would have been a trial for him, to find two who are as susceptible as Jessica and Angel. As their doctor he examines them in their dressing room before and after every Revealing. He probably puts them under while he's checking their pupils and installs the wire. Then she goes out onstage and he watches the TV set until it's time for the magic. He says her name five or six times into a headset, and off she goes. She repeats everything he says from then on, until it's over. Angel mimics him so perfectly she even loses her accent. Then he examines her again and takes out the wire. After that, he fools around with her for a few minutes, tells her to forget everything, brings her out of it, and everybody goes into the next room for the party. Of course, Merryman's already had his party."

Brooks still hadn't written anything.

"No notes?" I said.

"I'm not putting this on paper."

"That's probably a good idea. Sally knew Merryman but Merryman didn't know her. That means he must have been famous in some way back in Utica, some way that was vivid enough to make her remember him all those years later. My guess, knowing his habits, is that he was charged with child molestation.

"So Sally goes running. She believes in the Listening, even if she doesn't believe in Angel anymore. She goes to Wilburforce, who promptly turns her over to you in exchange for cash in hand and the promise to drop a lawsuit that was going to put him out of business. He tells her you're an honorable man and that Merryman is a disease you're trying to cure. What I don't understand is why you turned her over to Fauntleroy and that other creep."

He didn't say anything.

"Or maybe I do. She wouldn't talk to anyone but a Listener."

His eyes flickered, and he looked down at the pad in front of him.

"So you gave her to Fauntleroy and Fauntleroy gave her to Needle-nose—a Listener—whose name I'd really like to know. I don't suppose you'd like to tell me what it is, would you?"

Brooks shook his head. His face shone in the lamplight.

"You didn't want to lose sight of her and you didn't want anything to happen to her, so you had Fauntleroy hire me to follow her while she was having her Listening sessions at the Sleepy Bear Motel."

"No," he said. "That was Ellis's idea."

"Anyway, the problem is that the Listener, who shall for the moment be called Needle-nose, is either already working for Merryman or else he gets the idea when he hears what Sally says that he could be on the way to becoming a very rich man. One way or the other, he cuts you and Fauntleroy out of the information Sally's giving him and passes it on to Merryman instead. When he's sure he's got it all and that no one else knows what it is, he kills her. On Merryman's orders, of course. Then he defects openly to the other side. Starts hanging out at the Borzoi, scrubbing the faces of the faithful with steel wool whenever they backslide a little. Is any of this new to you?"

"Some of it."

"Is it worth a million dollars?"

"What happened to Ellis?"

"They killed him. More or less in front of me, to scare me off. They didn't think I knew much of anything. Hell, I didn't know much of anything. Then, I mean."

"Well," he said, "you've certainly caught up."

"You didn't know what Sally had on Merryman."

"No. As you say, they cut me out."

"You know now. Think it gives you the lever you need?"

"If it doesn't, I've wasted a lot of legal training."

"So is it worth a million?"

He stood up and ripped the pages neatly from his pad. Then he ripped out the four or five blank pages beneath and tore them into tiny pieces. He made a little heap of pieces on the desk and looked back down at his notes. He smiled at me.

"I should say it is," he said.

24

We agreed to meet at five the next evening to exchange the statement for the money, and I left. Adelaide saw me to the door.

"Please come back," she said. "Sometime when you can stay for dinner."

"After the holidays," I said, thinking that Merry was going to have a very long holiday indeed. Adelaide leaned forward and kissed me on the cheek.

Well, dismiss it. Too bad for Adelaide. All the dead and violated crowded into the Camaro with me as I drove: Sally, Anna and her mother, Ellis Fauntleroy, Jessica and Mrs. Fram, Angel. Mary Claire? I didn't know about Mary Claire. They all sat there in reproachful silence as I drove downtown.

What was needed was something decisive, and very, very public.

It was well after seven when I got to the Russell Arms. I parked the Camaro on the street and walked over to the Borzoi.

I began to spiral in on it from two blocks away, noting the names of the streets, counting paces, looking for pedestrian tunnels, manholes, anything that suggested the possibility of passage. When I finally angled into the square the Borzoi dominated, I was on the opposite side from the hotel.

The homeless, temporarily liberated by the end of the rain from their cardboard and plastic, milled about aimlessly, talking to each other, talking to the sky, talking to themselves. Bottles were passed from hand to hand, no less carefully than Brooks had placed the tray on the polished desk. People wore anything—large coats, small trousers, pieces of rope, boots, bedroom slippers—as though their clothes had attacked them and fastened themselves to their bodies for life, like Spanish moss or mistletoe trailing from trees. The smell of humanity, concentrated and distilled, rose in eddies of conduction and roiled across the street toward me. The people in the square probably bathed more frequently than Louis XIV and his court. I closed my eyes and breathed it in, imagining the scent of Versailles.

The front of the Borzoi was as brilliantly lighted as the Winter Palace of the czar. So was the studio adjacent to it. Glaring white light, enough to make me wince when I looked directly at it, poured across the sign that said CHURCH OF THE ETERNAL MOMENT. The reflected light scattered itself carelessly over the people in the square, bringing a face into sharp relief here and there, glinting off bottles, zippers, buttons, buckles, the occasional gold tooth. The light of sanctity was only loaned to them; when the Church was finished with its business, it would leave them once again in the dark.

Well, the more people there were in the square, the better I liked it. I sat down on the curb and began to sketch the Borzoi and the studio on a pad I'd stolen from the Russell Arms. It said HOLIDAY INN at the bottom, which dulled the edge of my guilt.

I drew the buildings high up on the pad, allowing everything but the three lowest floors of the Borzoi to run off the top of the page. Then, in dotted lines, I started to draw the basement as I remembered it.

"Very nice," said the man who had sat down next to me. He was wearing mismatched running shoes of different sizes and colors, and loose trousers that looked like they stayed up mainly because they were so sticky. The ensemble was topped off by what seemed to be a very good, if amazingly dirty, Giorgio Armani jacket.

"Thanks," I said.

"God didn't make buildings," the man said, holding out a half-pint bottle of Johnnie Walker Red. I took a nip and handed it back.

"He didn't?" I said, trying to orient the area of the

basement that contained the kitchen. The man's hand fell on the pad, and I was forced to look up.

"No," he said slyly, "but he made the men who made the buildings."

I edged his hand off the pad. "I guess that's true."

"He pulls their spirits upward with invisible strings," the man said, "and they build skeletons of steel so they can follow him toward heaven. The truest seeker after God in this century was the man who invented the elevator."

"Huh," I said, feeling like Mrs. Fram. I wasn't at all sure of my scale, and I needed to be.

"Even at sea, men put tall masts on ships so they can climb upward toward the Lord."

"I thought they were to hold the sails," I said.

"That's what they tell people," he said. He gave an abrupt laugh. "Sails," he said in vast amusement. He laughed some more.

"Busy over there," I said, sketching.

"Always on Friday," he said, subsiding into mere chuckles.

"And tomorrow?"

"Tomorrow's the big day. The little chiclet."

"Have you been inside?"

"No," he said, drinking. "They don't let real people in." He held the bottle out again and I declined. He looked at the pad again. "Why are you drawing basements?" he said.

I stood up. "I want to get as far away from God as possible," I said.

I walked out of the square and then down a side street. Taking a right, I angled back to the alley that ran behind the Borzoi.

It was empty and almost dark except for a couple of bare bulbs wearing tin hats that created cheerless cones of light that flickered down the rear wall of the building. I found the service entrances again and also a couple of casement windows that opened into the basement. I hadn't noticed any windows when I'd been down there, and now I knew why. They'd been painted a thick, sooty black on the outside. That way, no one inside could scratch a line of light into them.

The locks were junk, in line with the Church's policy of

spending only on what was directly in the line of sight. One peculiar touch was that both doors had chains on them like the one that Caleb Ellspeth had been so reluctant to undo. The chains were on the outside. And why not? Who would want to get *into* the basement?

I checked for wires, leads, connections, electrical tape— any sign of an alarm system—and found none. The man they had put in the duct had said "thank you." The woman in the dumbwaiter had closed the door on herself after I'd opened it. They didn't need alarms. They'd implanted the alarms in the people.

At the far left of the building I found the intake for the air conditioner and heating system. It was a big, heavily screened area about four feet square. The screen was fastened with new screws but they'd been screwed into an old wall. I didn't think they'd be much trouble.

The TV studio was a bigger problem. There were entrances and exits on three sides, one of them a big loading dock with an airplane door. People were working there, toting television equipment from a long green semi into the studio. Among them was my friend in the Hussong's T-shirt. I watched from a doorway as long as I felt was safe, and then walked back to the Russell Arms.

In my room, I transferred the sketch to a larger piece of paper, added the doors and windows to it, and then used a red pen to trace the path I thought the ducts took. When I'd finished that, I drew the whole thing over from above. Then, for practice, I reversed my first drawing and tried to sketch the entire basement complex as it would appear from the alley behind the Borzoi. I taped all three sketches to the wall and sat on the bed to study them.

Of course, more of the area than I would have liked was purely hypothetical. I'd never been to the right of the cul-de-dac at the bottom of the fire stairs, the direction that led toward the light. The fire stairs, though, ran down the inside of the wall that the Borzoi shared with the TV studio. The corridors to the right could only lead to the studio.

The question was: who was between the Borzoi and the studio? Whoever they were, they were in for a rotten time.

But I couldn't do it all by myself. I needed some help. I needed a man of talent. I needed Dexter Smif.

25

"Have you got a gun?" I asked into the phone.

"Does Archie got zits?" he said. "What caliber you want? Twenty-two? Thirty-eight? Automatic? Revolver? Belly-gun? Smith & Wesson? Uzi?"

"You've got an Uzi?"

"Nah. I lied about the Uzi."

"Can you get your uniform?"

"I don't need no uniform."

"Why not?"

"White reflects light, don't you know that? Black absorbs it. Black skin is the cloak of invisibility, least as far as white people are concerned."

"I'd still rather you wore the uniform."

He let out an exasperated breath. "Man don't trust the power of metaphor," he said.

"What about the truck? Can you get it?"

"Why not? Who else gone want it?"

"Can you get them tonight?"

There was a pause. "Thass a problem," he said. "The yard's closed for the night."

"What time do they open?"

"'Bout five-thirty in the ayem."

"Fine. We won't begin until noon or so. You can pick them up at ten." I sat there thinking.

"You gone tell me what we doin'?" he said into the silence.

"I'll explain it when you get here. How long will it take?"

"Well, that depend on where you are, don't it?"

270

I told him where I was.

"They got room service there?"

"Hell," I said. "They've barely got rooms."

"Order us up a pizza. You'll see me before you see it. One thing."

"What?"

"No anchovy on that pizza, or I'm gone."

He beat the pizza by about two minutes, lugging a six-pack of Mickey's Big Mouth, and sauntered around the room looking both amused and pleased with himself. "My, my," he said, "you do live in style, don't you? One fine domicile after another. Ain't you afraid of gettin' soft, pampering youself like this?" In the cramped confincs of the Russell Arms he looked even taller than he had at my house. He had to duck his head to pass under the lighting fixture that hung from the center of the ceiling.

"I got a couple of questions," he said, popping the top from a Mickey's and handing it to me. "This gone to be dangerous?"

"No more dangerous than Grenada."

"Good. I slep' through that. Next question. We the good guys or the bad guys?"

I put my hand over my heart. "Dexter," I said, "you wound me. Look at this face."

He grinned. "Thass the pizza," he said. I hadn't heard anything. A moment later, someone knocked.

"Jus' in case," he said, stepping behind the door.

It was the pizza. The delivery boy, a bent and befuddled octogenarian, was terrified when I closed the door behind him to reveal Dexter looming two feet above his head.

"This hinge is terrible," Dexter said to himself, examining it. He looked down at the delivery boy. "Oh, *hello*," he said in a British accent. "I'm the doorman. This door needs help. You wouldn't have any WD-40, would you?"

The delivery boy shook his head helplessly and wobbled backward out of the room. He forgot to give me my change. Dexter opened the box and folded himself somehow so that he could sit on the edge of one of the beds. His knees jutted out at acute angles, reaching almost to his chin. He took a bite of pizza.

"Okay," he said. "Let's hear what you proposin'."

I gave him five or six minutes of background. When I got to Sally he stopped chewing, and when I told him about Merryman and the little girls he put the pizza down. "Riptahls," he said. "Snakes and 'phibians." I told him the rest of it. He shook his head, not looking like anyone I really wanted to know.

"This all got somethin' to do with those pieces of paper on the wall?"

"Well, yes," I said with more than a little reluctance. I took down the overhead view and told him what I thought we might do. He listened in absolute silence, except for one brief cackle of laughter. When I'd finished he sat quietly for longer than I would have thought possible, following the floorplan with his eyes. Then he grunted and looked up at me.

"From a purely determinist viewpoint," he said, "we might not get killed. I ain't sure I always agreed with ol' Jerry about determinism, though."

"Have you got a better idea?" I said. It hadn't sounded exactly watertight to me either.

"Maybe one or two little improvements," he said.

It took him two minutes to fix things to the point where I could almost believe the plan would work.

An hour later he was stretched out on top of the other bed, sound asleep. His head was touching the headboard and his bare feet dangled over the end. He hadn't bothered with the blankets. Other than the boots, he hadn't undressed. Neither had I. I turned off the light and lay for what seemed like hours, looking up at the ceiling and listening to Dexter breathe. When I eased myself off the bed to go to the bathroom, a hand grasped my wrist. I looked down at Dexter. I hadn't even heard him move.

"All right," he said, gazing up at me. When I came back a minute later he was asleep again. A few minutes later, so was I.

The phone rang from very far off, at the end of a long, narrow, dark corridor. I had to navigate the corridor to get to it, but it kept receding in front of me like the shimmer of a mirage. When I finally caught it and picked it up, the handset turned into a snake. I woke up.

The phone was ringing, and Dexter was lying on his side with his eyes wide open. "Hard man to wake up," he said.

"Nobody knows this number," I said. "Nobody but Eleanor." I picked it up and said hello.

It wasn't Eleanor.

"Simeon," a familiar voice said. "How nice to know you're in the neighborhood."

"Who is this?"

"Please. You disappoint me. Simeon, it's Dick."

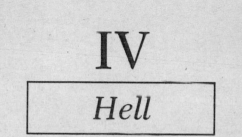

IV

Hell

26

I signaled to Dexter, but he'd already gotten up without looking at me and started to pull on his socks.

"Hi, Dick," I said, fighting a wave of blind terror. "What's up?"

"Well, I've been having the most fascinating chat with your Miss Chan," he said. "She has a genuinely amusing idea. She wants to make a mini-series based on the Church. Think of it, Simeon. We'll all be famous."

Dexter was tucking in his shirt. He hadn't made a sound.

"How'd you get her?" I said.

"We just bumped into her last night in the parking lot of the *Times*. Coincidence of the sheerest sort. Well, I hadn't actually had the pleasure of meeting her, although all sorts of other people had, so naturally we brought her over here."

"Last night." I felt like I'd been kicked in the stomach.

"Oh, we've had hours. It's been very entertaining. I must say, though, it took some persuasion to get her to tell us your new phone number. You move around so. Still, I suppose if people can walk in and out of your house with ease, it's a good idea to take up temporary residence elsewhere. And, of course, it's given me an opportunity to get to know Miss Chan."

"She's a little old for you, isn't she, Dick?" I said. Dexter had pulled on one boot.

"Now," he said, "that's no attitude to take. I find her delightful. Even attractive in an exotic sort of way. Her skin is so much smoother than you'd expect in a woman her age. Perhaps I should have discovered Oriental women earlier."

"If you've hurt her I'll kill you," I said.

"I don't think you'll get the chance," he said lightly. "Listen, Simeon, it really is convenient, your being in the neighborhood. This mini-series idea is intriguing, but there are a few details I'd like to discuss with you before we give you exclusive rights."

With both his boots on and laced, Dexter was straightening the bed and gathering up everything he'd brought. He hadn't met my eyes since I picked up the phone.

"What I'd like you to do," Merryman said, "is come straight over here, on foot, alone, without calling anybody first. And to make sure you don't, I've sent someone to walk with you. In fact, he's there already."

I looked helplessly up at Dexter. He picked up the automatic he'd brought and glanced down at me carelessly. It was the first time he'd looked at me. Then he examined the room to make sure he hadn't forgotten anything.

"At the sound of the tone," Merryman said, "it will be eight o'clock."

Someone knocked on the door.

Dexter ripped the floor plans off the wall and stepped into the closet, closing the door after him. I didn't know whether to laugh or cry.

I went to the door and opened it, and found myself looking at Needle-nose.

"Hi, I'm Barry," he said in a toneless voice. "I'll be your flight attendant this morning. Dick told me to say that. Would you like to get your shoes?" He looked incuriously around the room. "What a shithole," he said.

I put my shoes on while he went over and picked up the phone. "I've got him," he said. He listened for a second and then hung up. "Aren't we going to have fun?" he said.

I pulled on my jacket.

"Turn around," Barry said, "and put your hands against the wall. Higher." He patted me down professionally and removed the automatic from the jacket pocket. "Naughty, naughty," he said reprovingly. "Anything else?"

"No," I said. He'd missed the pimp's knife, which I'd shoved into the jacket lining just behind the base of the zipper. It banged against my stomach as we walked toward the door. He opened it and motioned me through. "Say good-bye," he said.

"Good-bye," I said obediently. "This certainly messes up my timing." I hoped Dexter could hear me through the closet door.

"It doesn't matter," Barry said, closing the door. "It doesn't matter at all."

We went down in the elevator in silence.

"Now, you're not going to give me any trouble," he said as we stepped into the bright, warm morning, "because of your pretty little Chink girl. I don't have to hold a gun on you or nothing. Just think about her and walk a nice straight line. You know where the hotel is."

"Attention to detail is essential to success," I said as we shouldered our way into the foot traffic on the sidewalk.

"Say again?" he said.

"One of my mother's maxims," I said. "She's a fool for detail."

"Isn't she going to be sorry to hear about you?" he said.

I supposed she probably would be. Anyway, it wasn't the kind of remark that invites a rejoinder.

"My friend's in the hospital," Barry said from behind me. "He's got bad burns. I wonder how you're going to like bad burns."

"I don't think it's something one looks forward to," I said. "What slum of the spirit did they find you in?"

"I found them," he said. "Just like I found you."

We crossed the square. Most of the homeless were still asleep beneath their washing-machine boxes. I hadn't known so many washing machines were sold in Los Angeles. The people on the sidewalks all looked normal and safe, on their way to enviably boring jobs. No one caught my eye. I guessed I didn't look like someone who was on his way to die.

The Borzoi lobby yawned dingy and empty. We went straight to the elevator and up to the floor marked EXECUTIVE OFFICES. Barry stood very close behind me, using the privacy to indulge himself in the luxury of poking a gun, probably my gun, into my back. That was the second gun I'd had taken from me.

"God, I'd love to puncture your kidneys," he said as the doors opened. "Second door on the right."

The door said DR. MERRYMAN. I pushed it open.

"Simeon," Merryman said, "nice of you to come. I know it's early." He was wearing a turquoise shirt this time, and pale yellow slacks. "And look," he said, smiling. "Here's a friend of yours."

I turned, looking for Eleanor, and saw Meredith Brooks.

27

Brooks looked like he hadn't slept in days. He had on the same clothes he'd worn the night before, and his hair was rumpled and his mouth drawn into a line of disgust as though he suspected his tongue was contagious. For what was probably the first time in forty years, he hadn't shaved. He seemed to regard Merryman with almost superstitious dread.

"Where is she?" I said.

"Where she'll keep," Merryman said. "Don't worry, Simeon, you'll see her soon enough." He glanced at Needlenose and said, "Shut the door, Barry," in the tone of a man who had given a lot of orders in his life. Barry shut the door. "You've met, I believe," he said to me.

"Only recently," I said. "But I've admired his work for some time."

"Barry has his uses," Merryman said as though he and I were alone in the room. "He's a genuine textbook sadist, rarer than you'd think. It's always a pleasure to work with someone who enjoys what he does."

"There's nothing like cheap labor."

Merryman flashed his teeth at me. "Won't you sit down?"

"I thought you'd never ask."

I sat down in a heavy metal chair. Merryman seated himself behind his desk, every inch the professional man despite the vivid color of his shirt. Brooks and Barry remained standing. On Merryman's desk were the congealed remains of a dinner and two breakfasts. The meeting had clearly been going on for some time, but Merryman looked like he'd had twelve hours' sleep, followed by two sets of tennis and a sauna. He gave me an anticipatory smile and then glanced over my shoulder.

"For Christ's sake, Meredith, stop hovering like that," he said sharply. "Sit down and don't fidget. Brooks has been having pangs of conscience," he said to me.

"That must be a new experience," I said.

"Yes. He's quite unprepared for it. It's sweeping through him as measles did with the Indians. After a life of more or less perpetual professional betrayal during which he never developed so much as a night sweat, his immune system has suddenly sprung to life, and the result is the shivering, shambling wreck you see sitting there. Of course," he added confidingly, "he'd never really made plans to betray *me* before."

I didn't say anything.

"Although we must remember that we haven't firmly established that he did. This isn't a court of law, and if it were, Meredith would be more at home in it than any of us, wouldn't he?" He smiled again.

"Do you want an answer?" I said.

"I have a number of grievances with you, Simeon," Merryman said, letting the smile slip a notch or two, "not the least of which is that you tried to divide Meredith and me. We've had our little problems, I won't deny that. We're not naturally congenial with one another, any more than you and I are, although heaven knows I've been pleasant enough to you. But Meredith and I, in spite of the occasional friction between us, complement each other. We built this operation together. He's a brilliant man of business. I'm a brilliant stage manager. Together we give the people what they want and persuade the people to give us what we want. And we take what they've given us and together we build with it. What's wrong with that?"

"I wouldn't know where to start."

"Don't bother." He winked brightly at Barry. "You'll be talking soon enough."

"He offered me a million dollars," I said.

Merryman's eyes flicked to Brooks. "He did? That's not quite the way he tells it."

"This man came to my house—" Brooks began.

"He called me," I interrupted. "Told me he didn't want to see me at the office. Said he knew I'd been working on Sally's death and he wanted to know if I'd found out what she had on you."

Brooks sputtered. "Dick," he said, "this is—"

Merryman held up a hand. "Go on, Simeon," he said.

"Well, I *had* been working on it. I kept working on it even after you phoned to warn me off. I knew there was money in it but I didn't know how to use what I'd learned. I was going to come to you to see what it was worth, but then Brooks called and offered me a million on a platter. He invited me over, introduced me to Adelaide—nice lady, by the way . . ."

"Is she," Merryman said equably, resting his chin on his hand. "I haven't had the pleasure."

"And he asked me what I had. I asked him what it was worth, and he said it was worth a million, cash, if it was something that would allow him to control you absolutely, keep you working for him, but deprive you of whatever power you had in the Church. I said that what I had would do all of that and more, and told him what it was, and we arranged to meet at five this evening for the payoff."

"Isn't that interesting?" Merryman said conversationally. "We hadn't learned that it had gone quite that far."

"It hadn't," Brooks said. His face was filmed with sweat. "He barged in with some cock-and-bull story about dentists and Utica—"

Merryman's gaze flattened and grew opaque. He looked straight at Brooks. "That's enough, Meredith," he said. "It's certainly provocative, isn't it, that you didn't call us after your visit with Simeon last night. If we hadn't had the courtesy to call *you* to tell you our news about Miss Chan, we probably still wouldn't know all that Simeon knows about dentists and Utica, would we?" He arched his eyebrows and smiled inquiringly. "And it's such fascinating information."

"The Fox sisters," I said. "When you first fell into the Church it must have felt like old home week."

"Meredith doesn't know anything about the Fox sisters," Merryman said. "I'm amazed you do."

Brooks slumped further down in his chair, studying one of his cuff buttons.

"Of course, Simeon," Merryman continued in the same chatty tone, "I realize, and I'm sure that Meredith here does too, that you're just continuing in your effort to divide us. I certainly have no intention of taking seriously anything you've just said. For one thing, I'm positive that Brooks doesn't have a million dollars anywhere that he could have given to you without my knowing it. Do you, Meredith? That isn't the way our bookkeeping works, is it?"

"Of course not," Brooks said faintly.

"You see, Simeon?" Merryman said, shrugging his shoulders. "With a discrepancy like that, how could I take you seriously? The idea that Meredith keeps two sets of books is too absurd to contemplate. Good Lord. I've known the man for eight years."

"Would you miss a hundred thousand?" I said. Brooks shifted nervously in his chair. Merryman put one hand on top of the other, very much the listening doctor.

"You have my attention," he said.

"I'm sure it's all there, of course, right out on the books where it should be. One hundred thousand dollars for delivery of Sally Oldfield."

Merryman looked at Brooks but directed the question to me. "Paid to whom?"

"Hubert Wilburforce." I tried to sound surprised. "You mean you didn't know how Brooks got hold of Sally?"

"No," Merryman said. "I'm embarrassed to say that I didn't. A hundred thousand dollars, Meredith. How much is that per pound? She didn't look like a very big girl. And paid to good old Hubert, too. I must call Hubert one of these days."

He regarded Brooks for a long moment and then sighed. "Well," he said, "it seems my partner hasn't been completely candid this morning. Especially where the books are concerned. We'll have to look into that. Not for a moment, of course, do I believe that Brooks is really a threat to me," he went on almost dreamily. "He's got ink in his veins, foolscap for skin. He's a paper man. Aren't you, Meredith?"

Brooks made a little dry noise that might have been assent.

"But since he hasn't been completely candid, and since I need to know everything you know, Simeon, I'm going to have to ask you a few questions. Then you can go join Miss Chan while we debate the matter of your reward. Stand up."

I looked around me. Barry was standing directly behind my chair. Brooks was still seated, staring fixedly at the floor. He looked old.

"Have you searched him, Barry?"

"I found a gun," Barry said, displaying it.

"Listen to my question, Barry," Merryman said, as though he were speaking to a child. "Have you searched him? Pocket by pocket?"

Barry hesitated.

"No, he didn't," I said.

Merryman smiled up at me, all white teeth and dark skin. "I appreciate the impulse to get Barry into trouble, Simeon, but you'll learn it's counterproductive in the long run. What you want is for Barry to like you, to have a teeny smattering of regret that he has to practice his craft on you."

"I think it's a little late for that," I said.

"You're probably right." Merryman suddenly sounded impatient. "Search him."

Barry patted me down again, then went through one pocket after another. He pulled out everything I'd stashed away the night before: my money, my car keys, my address book, my wallet, a comb, a little travel bottle of after-shave, and two handkerchiefs. I'm not in the habit of carrying a comb, but I thought it would make the after-shave look a little less odd, just in case someone should get a chance to look in my pockets. Barry lined the items up on Merryman's desk. Merryman examined them in turn, pausing to flip through the address book, then picked up the handkerchiefs.

"Is our nose running?" he asked in the first-person plural of medical people all over the world.

"I don't know about yours," I said, "but mine is." I picked up the handkerchiefs and put them back in my pocket.

"We'll keep these for the moment," he said, pocketing the keys, "and I'll want a closer look at this." The address book followed the keys. He opened the after-shave, sniffed it, and handed it back to me. "A bit heavy for my taste," he said. "I prefer real lime."

"So do I," I said, "but who can afford it?"

"Now, Simeon," Merryman said as though I hadn't spoken. "I need to know absolutely everything you've found out, figured out, intuited, guessed, whatever. The complete dossier, anything that might help us to evaluate how much your silence is worth to us. You can think of it as a Listening session if you like, except that we haven't got the time to do it absolutely properly, so we're going to have to accelerate the process. Sit down again."

I sat. Barry passed a belt around my lap, threaded it through the rungs of the chair, and pulled it tight. Then he took my left hand, pulled one of the handkerchiefs from my pocket, and twisted it around my wrist. He knotted the handkerchief through the belt.

"Didn't bring your tools?" I asked. My voice wasn't very steady.

"He doesn't need tools," Merryman said comfortably. "He's very ingenious."

Barry took hold of my right hand and turned it palm down. He held it in a surprisingly strong grasp while he reached over to the nearer of the two breakfast plates and picked up a fork. Then he slipped one of the tines of the fork under the nail on my index finger and shoved it in.

I screamed for what seemed like a very long time. I kicked the chair backward and scuttled like a crab until I cracked its back against the wall. Then I kept scuttling, going nowhere but away from Barry, screaming until my throat felt like rags. Barry leaned against Merryman's desk and watched me with total absorption, turning the fork over and over in his hand. His mouth was open.

When I'd finished screaming and was leaning forward in the chair, fighting down an urge to retch, Merryman held up both of his beautifully shaped hands, fingers spread wide. "Ten," he said. He curled his right index finger. "You've got nine to go. Then, if you want to experience really exquisite pain, Barry can go back to the one he just did. You have absolutely no idea what it feels like a second time." He turned to Barry with an indulgent expression.

"Would you like to do another one?" he asked.

Barry nodded and got up. I was screaming before he took a step, twisting against the bonds of the chair. Merryman leaned forward and placed a restraining hand on Barry's arm.

"Later," he said. "I think Simeon's ready to talk to me now. Is that right, Simeon?"

I managed a nod.

"Nothing to be ashamed of," he said. "All those stories about people resisting torture are nonsense. No one can stand up to the prospect of real pain once they've felt it. That's why we started the conversation with a little attention-getter. So I wouldn't have to waste time asking you the same question twice.

"Wait outside," he said to Barry. "I'll call you if I need you." He turned to Brooks, who was looking ashen. "I think I'd like you outside too, Meredith. Just to create an atmosphere of perfect candor. Do you mind?" He might have been offering him a ride home. Brooks waved off the question with one heavy hand and stood up, with some difficulty, to follow Barry out of the room.

"I should be afraid of *him*?" Merryman said to me as the door closed. It had been loud enough for Brooks to hear. "Hardly. He has the narrowest comfort zone of any human being I've ever met, including other lawyers. The slightest change in the status quo turns him to milk. That's one reason he's good in business. Very conservative, very steady. With all the cash we have to deal with, an impulsive man would be disaster. Still, I'll have to look into those books." He crossed his arms across his chest and regarded me in a friendly fashion from across the room. "All right, Simeon, tell me. If anything strikes me as false or incomplete, or if you fail to answer any of my questions in a forthright manner, I'll call Barry back in. Once he's in the room, I won't stop him no matter what you say, so don't make me call him. Have I made myself clear?"

"Yes."

He reached up and smoothed his hair. "Start at the beginning, if you don't mind."

I did. I told him about Harker, about the assignment to

tail Sally, about Sally's murder and the fact that I'd seen Barry on the scene. I explained about the real Ambrose Harker and about Skippy Miller being my only link to the man who'd hired me.

"Why didn't you just wash your hands of it and go to the police?" he asked. He hadn't taken his eyes off me since I'd started talking. "A girl is murdered virtually under your nose and you don't go to the police?"

"What for? What were the cops going to give me? I didn't even have a client. All I wanted at first was to get a little money out of it. Then, as I learned more and more, I realized that there was more than a little money floating around and that I could probably catch as much of it as I could hold in two hands."

He gave me a long, absolutely level gaze. Most people look you first in one eye and then in the other. Merryman had the knack of looking directly into both eyes at once. After perhaps a full minute he said, "So you went to Big Sur to see Mr. Miller. Driven by the profit motive."

I ran through all of it. I told him about my first interviews with Brooks and Wilburforce, explaining that I'd used Eleanor only for her connection with the *Times* and emphasizing that she knew only what had been said on those occasions. I didn't mention Hammond or the Red Dog.

"We know what Eleanor knows," he said. "She was very cooperative last night. She was more cooperative, in fact, than you're being. She told us, for example, that you asked her to look into the death of poor little Anna, which she didn't, and to locate Caleb Ellspeth, which she did. I'd say Eleanor knows quite a bit more than you're telling me. I wonder whether we shouldn't call Barry in here?"

"No," I said, very quickly.

"You've just gotten your only break," he said. "If Barry comes back in, I'm going to let him do a double. He'll enjoy that much more than you will. Was your talk with Mr. Ellspeth productive?"

"He told me more about Meredith than he did about you."

"Of course. He barely knows me. The man was away from home practically all the time. Do you think he's a danger to me?"

"No. He's frightened. I had the impression that you had something on him."

Merryman was watching me very intently. "He didn't tell you what it was?"

Praying that Eleanor hadn't told them, I said, "No." If I didn't get out of there, I didn't want them going after Ellspeth and Ansel.

After a moment, he dropped his eyes and studied the nails of his left hand. "Good," he said. "Then that's under control, isn't it? Still, I think we'll have Barry drop by and remind him that we'd really rather he didn't talk to strangers."

"Why tell me?" The confidence didn't make me feel comfortable.

"Why not? I feel as though you know everything already. I have to congratulate you, Simeon, you've done very thorough work. There are a few details wrong here and there in the account you gave Meredith, a few wild guesses, but by and large it's been very instructive. There are any number of loose cannon rattling about, it would seem. You've done us a service, actually. You've been profoundly irritating, but you've identified quite a few points of entry that should be shored up immediately."

"Glad I could help," I said.

"The first ten or fifteen years, before you get to be institutional, are always the most vulnerable in a business like this," he said. He sounded like he was talking to a trainee. "Everybody, when faced with something new, wants to take a crack at it. Politicians, the media, the competition. We know that. We've invited it by making the Church as vivid as possible. Beautiful little girls, a billion-year-old spirit, rather nice sermons, if I do say so myself." He waited for a compliment.

"The one I heard was very impressive."

"Thank you. I had no idea I could write until I actually had to sit down and do it. And even then, it wasn't until we printed little Jessica's first twelve Revealings and I saw them on the page that I knew how good they really were."

"You can't delegate that?" I said, just to make conversation and to keep Barry out of the room.

"Oh, no." He gave a manicured little laugh. "Very few

people know how the Revealings work. Not even Mary Claire. Just you and I. And Brooks, of course. And Miss Chan."

"She doesn't know," I said.

"She certainly didn't seem to," he said absently. "She would have told us if she did. She would have told us anything. Barry rarely gets a chance to work on a woman. There was Miss Oldfield, of course, but that was over almost before it began. From Barry's point of view, I mean. I imagine it seemed longer to Miss Oldfield." He gave me the smile again.

"At any rate, we made the Church colorful on purpose. We wanted to be good copy. We wanted a certain amount of challenge. A religion can't survive without opposition. It knits the membership closer together, builds loyalty and so forth. The bunker mentality. And then, there's all that publicity. So, as I say, we invite a certain amount of adversity."

"Very wise," I said. My right hand felt bigger than the Goodyear blimp.

He leveled a finger at me. "But you're something quite new. I suppose we should be thankful that both you and Miss Chan had good reason to keep quiet about what you were doing. You wanted your money and Miss Chan wanted her story. That keeps the circle small. Manageable, in a manner of speaking. If you hadn't, I suppose I'd be packing now."

"Instead of sitting here talking to me."

"I almost wish we'd met under different circumstances." He sounded wistful. "You're smart and thorough and greedy. We could have used someone like you."

"You still can."

"No, I'm afraid not. You know too much to justify the level at which you'd be employed. It would make me uncomfortable, Simeon, and I can't work when I'm uncomfortable." He looked at his gold Rolex. "Barry," he called. I flinched.

Merryman laughed as the door opened and Barry came in. "Don't worry," he said. "Not yet, anyway. Meredith? Could you come in too, please?"

Brooks came through the door like a man walking into a forty-knot wind. He didn't look at any of us.

"Look at him," Merryman said cheerfully. "What you're seeing is the mummy when it's unwrapped. After centuries of miraculous preservation, he's about to turn to dust. You've been a bad boy, Meredith. We're going to have to evaluate our deal. In the meantime, I'm sure you'll be glad to know that this little forest fire is confined almost entirely to Simeon and Miss Chan—Eleanor, I mean." The name came out of his mouth coated with oil.

"When do I get paid?" I asked with a bravado I didn't feel.

"Well," Merryman said expansively, "I'm afraid you don't. If it had been just you, I might have bargained you down a few hundred thousand and let you go on your way. Even though you've irritated me. But there's Eleanor too. I could believe in your greed, but what am I going to do about Eleanor? She seems to be a pure spirit. Anyway, I've already promised you to Barry."

Barry grinned like a hound in a steakhouse. Brooks sagged against a wall.

"Don't like it, do you, Meredith?" Merryman laced his fingers behind his head and leaned back in his chair. "You'd rather be behind your big clean desk in Century City, adding up zeros while I take care of the loose ends. Well, you're in the middle of this one, my friend, and you're going to get very dirty. And then we'll sit down for a little heart-to-heart and see who has what on whom. Who knows? Maybe I'll even get to meet the fair Adelaide."

Brooks swallowed audibly. "Sure, Dick," he said. "Just an oversight."

"Maybe we'll all do lunch," Merryman said in a gleeful parody of a Hollywood agent. "Just you and me and Adelaide. I think we should all be a lot closer, don't you?"

Brooks managed a nod that looked like it fractured all his cervical vertebrae. He opened his mouth, but nothing came out but air.

"Fine," Merryman said. "All settled, then." He gestured dismissively at me. "You can have him, Barry. You can have both of them. But for Christ's sake find somewhere to put them this time. Not like poor Ellis."

Barry took two steps toward me.

"Wait," I said. "There's a kicker."

"Kicker?" Merryman said politely. His voice was almost indolent, but the muscles in his shoulders tensed and bunched. "And what would that be?"

"There's a cop involved," I said.

"Too late," Merryman said, relaxing. "You and Miss Chan have been very persuasive on that point."

I forced myself to shrug, although my shoulders weighed a hundred pounds apiece. "What can I say? We lied."

Merryman looked at Brooks, and Brooks found his voice. "This is nonsense," he protested. "You were after a million dollars. Why would you talk to the police?"

"Merry," I said, "I don't know how to tell you this, but I wasn't really planning to collect the money."

Everybody looked at everybody else.

"Then why are you doing this?" Brooks finally said.

"Oh, who knows?" I said. "Adventure. Diversion. You know, Merry. Tally-ho."

There was a long pause. Then Merryman said, "Barry. Do something to him."

Barry did something to me and then he did something else, and a cloud of red came down behind my eyes and I heard my voice torn to tatters in my ears. When it was over and I was whimpering, Merryman said, "Are you finished, Simeon?"

"Al Hammond," I said in a whisper. Then, louder, I said, "Al Hammond." I think I said it three times.

"Hammond," Merryman said tonelessly.

"Hammond comma Al," I said. "You heard the messages on my answering machine," I said to Barry. "You know that Al Hammond called me."

"Barry?" Merryman said in a voice that would have frozen vodka. The charm-boy was long gone now, vanished to sunnier climes.

"There was an Al Hammond," Barry said. "He didn't say he was a cop."

"Is he a cop," Merryman asked, "or are you playing games?"

"He's a cop. Call the LAPD. Ask for Records and then

ask for Al Hammond. Sergeant." I said. "Sergeant. Alvin. Hammond." I couldn't talk anymore.

Merryman pointed at the phone. We all sat there while Barry dialed and asked for Al. Then he hung up very slowly. "He's there," Barry said.

Merryman gnawed at the inside of his cheek. "I knew it was too easy," he said to no one in particular. "There are far too many loose mouths in this organization. Time to clean house." He seemed suddenly childish, anxious to fix blame.

"But this is awful," Brooks abruptly said. "The police? This is terrible."

"Shut up, Meredith," Merryman said. "You act like it's the end of the world."

"It is," Brooks said. Then he swallowed again.

"Not by a long fucking shot it isn't," Merryman said, gaining strength. "Go home to Adelaide. Borrow one of her dresses. When you've got it all out of your system, come back and we'll talk business." He looked at me. "This *is* a business, you fuckhead, a good business, and you're not going to disrupt it. Barry," he said, "put him on ice."

Barry came around behind me and I tensed, but all he did was undo the belt. He prodded me to stand up. When I did, he untied the handkerchief around my wrist and stuffed it into the pocket of my shirt. "There," he said. "You're beautiful again." He gave me a yellow grin and took my arm.

"One minute," Merryman said, assembling his poise piece by piece like a knight tying on his armor. "I want you to know something, Simeon, because you're going to wind up in Barry's hands sooner or later. It's inevitable. This is just a delay. Anyway, I want you to have something to think about in the meantime. His name isn't really Barry. We chose it for him because it's a name rich in the annals of sadism. Have you ever heard of the Doll?"

I shook my head.

"He was a guard, a very handsome guard, at a concentration camp. Some of the women in the camp developed extremely complicated attitudes toward him. He was that handsome, you see."

"His real name was Barry?" I said.

"No." Merryman gave me the full fifty-kilowatt smile. "His dog's name was Barry. A big German shepherd, passionately devoted to his master. Actually, an ordinary enough dog by all accounts. Except that he had a trick. Would you like to know what the trick was?"

"Not really."

"Well, darling, too bad for you. It was only one trick, but it was a good one. He was trained to chew off the genitals of male prisoners. He got very fat." He paused to see the effect of his story. I didn't speak. Merryman shrugged. "So," he said, "that was Barry."

"And you," I said, "haven't got any genitals. You piss sitting down. Out of choice. And when you're finished you dry that teensy little thing in the breeze and go bother some twelve-year-old because anything else would be too loose for you. You haven't got a cock. You've got a hypodermic."

Merryman looked very ugly all of a sudden. "You shouldn't have said that," he said. "And if you did say it, you shouldn't have said it in front of anyone else. Barry is going to take special care of you, aren't you, Barry?" Barry nodded fervently. "But first, in front of you, Barry is going to take special care of sweet little Eleanor."

"Zip your trousers," I said. "Your mole is showing."

Merryman's face filled with blood. "Put him on ice," he said to Barry.

Barry grabbed me under the arm and hoisted me up in a lopsided fashion. "Walking time," he said.

We went out the door and down the hall to the elevator. In the elevator, Barry produced a small silvery key and inserted it into the slot marked BASEMENT. We started down. I leaned against him adoringly.

"Lover," I said, "what a surprise. You're taking me where we met."

He pushed me away roughly. "Later," he said. "We'll have our laughs later."

"What do you eat for breakfast?" I asked. "Babies?"

"Tomorrow, I'll have liver. Yours."

"I'll bet you say that to all your dates," I said.

"Keep it up," he said. "You don't know what a long time is yet."

The elevator doors opened and he pushed me out into a dark hallway. It was still wet from the rain. It was probably always wet.

"Have you been to Venice?" I asked as he steered me along. "You'd feel right at home. Water, rats, the whole schmear. You could probably get work chewing barnacles off the bottoms of gondolas. Or else you could eviscerate chickens in the marketplace. *Somebody* has to do it. Italians love chicken." Three of my fingers felt like water balloons that had been filled with blood. "Listen," I said, "why don't we go out to dinner? I'll buy. Italian, Mexican, Thai, you name it. I love the way you handle a fork. I'd love to see you try it on food."

"You're going to see a lot more of it," he said. We were heading toward the kitchen. "You'll see it on your girlfriend."

"You're going to fork my girlfriend?" We passed the air-conditioning unit, humming busily away. "That's not very polite. Where I come from, a gentleman doesn't say that to another gentleman."

He grunted.

"So much for snappy patter," I said as he propelled me into the kitchen. "Oh, I see. Put me on ice. It's that sweet little refrigerator, isn't it? Good. I have a theory. All shivering is caused by the attempt to reduce the amount of body surface exposed to the cold. Open up, I always say. Open up and let the cold in. Then you won't shiver. What do you think?"

"I think," he said, opening the refrigerator door, "that you're going to want to be cold in a few hours."

"Jesus," I said. "You sound like a Friars' roast for one of Bob Hope's writers."

"Bundle up," he said, pushing me in and closing the door.

Somebody inside sighed.

"Well," Eleanor said, "what took you so long?"

28

The darkness was absolute. The rods and cones of my retina worked overtime to impose squirmy little red and green paramecia on the air, but when I looked down I literally could not see my body.

"He hurt my fingers," she said.

"It's his hobby," I said. "Some men collect stamps or guns or varieties of begonia. He collects fingernails." I was babbling. I'd been talking compulsively ever since I'd unloaded on Merryman. It was as though that action, childish as it had been, had pulled the cork on all the emotions I'd been choking down since Merryman's call woke me up. I bit down on my tongue until it hurt and counted to twenty. Then I leaned over and tried to kiss her on the cheek. I felt her lips beneath mine, and then her arms went around me. She'd been looking at me in the total darkness, the way a lover will. Her hands on my neck were icy. I put my arm around her waist. The slenderness of her was familiar and sweet.

"How long have you been in here?"

"Forever. I can't tell. What time is it now?"

"A little after nine."

"Four or five hours, then. Simeon, there are rats in here. One of them touched my hand, and then it ran over my feet. I screamed. I felt so stupid, screaming in a refrigerator when obviously no one is going to come and help me. I mean, why do you scream? For help, right? But this was just screaming. The way I screamed when that man hurt me."

"We're going to kill him," I said, wishing I believed it.

"Oh, be real. We're locked in this thing and there's no way in the world to get out. That door is six inches thick and they've pulled off the handle on this side. There's nothing there but some greasy-feeling rollers. I threw myself against the door so hard that I've got a bone bruise on my shoulder, but it's closed tight. Even if we get out, we're in this awful basement and we're surrounded by zombies."

"Listen," I said, laughing at the cliché in spite of myself, "I have a plan."

"Well," she said, "I'd love to know what it is."

I felt around in my windbreaker and located the bottom of the zipper. I peeled back the lining and pulled out the pimp's knife, then took her hand and dropped the knife into it.

"What's this?"

"It's a pimp's knife," I said.

"What are we going to do, commit double suicide? Boy, wouldn't that burn them up?"

"The door closes through a system of rollers, the ones you got your hands all greasy touching. We're going to use the knife as a lever to manipulate the rollers. Then we're going to push the door open and walk out."

"Into the arms of the zombies."

"One thing at a time."

"Okay," she said, "I'm game. Anything's better than sitting here feeling like the Thanksgiving turkey. What do you think the temperature is, anyway?"

"Low forties. Cold enough for hypothermia."

She handed the knife back to me.

"What do you want me to do?"

"Wait for a while."

"What for?"

"The Revealing. It's on television from the studio next door. Everybody goes to watch. It will cause a sudden drop in the zombie population. Also, we're waiting for a man."

"Who?"

"I don't really know how to tell you. If he shows up, I'll introduce you."

"If he shows up?"

I gave it a moment's thought and then shrugged. "I didn't have time to put him under contract," I said. "You came as a bit of a surprise."

"They were waiting for me in the parking lot. I'd just said good-bye to Jeannie Seaver, she's in Features, and I opened the car door and got in, and this man got in next to me and pushed me into the passenger seat. It was the one called Barry, the one who did that thing to my fingers. Then he unlocked the back door and another man got in, and they drove me here."

"Where you met Dr. Merryman."

"Is he that ghastly handsome man? Oh, Simeon, he oozes poison like a toad. Barry's awful, he's sick and revolting and vile, but the other one's worse. He smiles at you and even flirts with you, and there's nothing in there but cold. When the other man, the old man, I mean, Brooks, arrived, Merryman peeled him alive in front of everybody. This was about midnight. He just poured abuse on him for an hour or so and then got up in the middle of a sentence and left the room. When he came back he'd changed his shirt, and he picked up exactly where he'd left off."

"He's my favorite too," I said.

"They wanted to know all about Mr. Ellspeth. I thought at one point they were going to go right out and kill him. I told them he was scared of his own shadow, that he only talked to us in the first place because we threatened to publish his name and address if he didn't, and how would they have liked that, I asked them. Every reporter in America making a campfire to cook wienies on his doorstep. Merryman gave me that veneer of a smile and said they wouldn't like it at all. Then he said to Barry, 'Play a little tick-tack-toe on her.' "

"You didn't tell them. You're something."

"That pig," she said. She settled against me. "How come you're always warm? I've wondered about that for years."

"The banked fires of genius."

"We're going to need them."

"Fortunately, they didn't think of throwing water on me."

She stiffened. "Oh, no. Did they hurt you too? Jesus," she said uncharacteristically, "I didn't even ask."

"Not much," I said, feeling brave.

"That's just like you. Eagle Scout to the toes. Did they?"

"I'll be a few short on my five-finger exercises for a while."

"Oh, my gosh. Do you think you'll lose the nails?"

I laughed again. "I certainly hope so. That would take weeks."

"We're going to get out," she said. "We're going to get out and then we're going to glue those two together with Krazy Glue and give them to Al Hammond. Merryman's front to Barry's back. No, reverse that. I think Merryman would enjoy it."

"I think they'd both enjoy it. Why don't we just glue their lips and nostrils closed and watch them try to breathe through their ears."

"Poor old Brooks," she said. After a moment she said, "On the other hand, fuck him." I'd never heard her use the word before. "Let's just worry about us."

"The problem," I said, "is how to measure time. Getting out of here early would be almost as bad as not getting out of here at all."

"That's easy," she said. "We'll just wait until we think it's time and then we'll wait a lot longer." She shivered. "How long do you think it might be?"

"Two hours, maybe three."

"That's a long time. What do you want to do in the meanwhile?"

"We could neck."

"We could keep warm if we made love," she said, startling me, "if it weren't for the rats, that is."

I wrapped both arms around her, feeling an absurd surge of desire. "To be perfectly frank, though," she said, "I've made love with rats before. We'll have to keep most of our clothes on, obviously."

"No problem," I said.

For the next hour or so, in pitch-darkness, we rediscovered each other. All the sweet familiarities flooded back, all

the half-forgotten textures, smells, hills, mounds, the secret
valleys, the most intimate landscapes. I twined her hair
around my fingers and inhaled the yeasty scent of her skin.
She licked the side of my neck in long, languorous cat-laps.
It had always driven me crazy, and I was obscurely touched
that she'd remembered.

"You need a shave," she whispered.

"Do it with your teeth," I said.

The clothes got in the way, and it didn't matter. When the
cooler came on I noted the noise but didn't feel the drop in
temperature. We achieved release together, just as we almost always had. Then Eleanor laughed.

"I hope you understand," she said, "that I don't usually
do it in refrigerators."

"Plead special circumstances," I said.

"Oh," she said, "I do. I do." She blew warm breath into
my mouth. "Another first," she said.

"I do my best."

"You do better than anyone. Gee. Suppose someone had
come in."

"This bunch, they'd have enjoyed it."

"Not as much as I did."

Then she was silent. I heard her fingers scrabbling over
elastic and buttons.

"What are you wearing?" I said.

"Oh, Simeon. You always used to ask me that on the
phone. Remember?"

"And you used to answer me." The basic, horrible fact of
our situation reasserted itself.

"A pink blouse. And those black pants you bought me
in Santa Monica, the ones with the big zippered pockets.
Flats."

"Good. A skirt would have gotten in the way later."

"When has a skirt ever gotten in your way?" She was
teasing on the square. This was the Eleanor I'd grown
accustomed to over the past few years, and it had been my
fault.

"Did you explore?" I said to change the subject.

"Only the door," she said. "After that I sat down and the

rat touched my hand. Then I didn't want to go anyplace. I just sat there, and after a while I think I went to sleep."

"You slept?" Eleanor could sleep anywhere. She invariably fell asleep in planes before they took off, while I was coiled in my seat clutching a drink and repeating a secret mantra that went "Oh, my Lord, preserve the lives of those on board." And I didn't even believe in God.

"I was up all night," she said. "And what that man did to me wore me out."

"Of course it did," I said, getting up.

"Where are you going?"

"Out for a little air."

"Very funny. I think I should get straight answers at this point."

"I'm going to fool with the door."

"It's not time yet. It can't be more than ten-thirty."

"I want to know what I'm up against."

"What *we're* up against," she said a trifle acidly.

I felt around the edges of the door. The walls were all tile, about four inches by four inches, separated by narrow grouting. Moisture had condensed on the tiles. The door itself felt different: cold, metallic, and slightly rough to the touch. Zinc, maybe. The rollers were on the left side of the door, about hip-high. They felt rubbery. As she said, the handle had been removed. I felt around the rollers, closing my eyes even in the darkness to envision them.

"Piece of cake," I said.

"My hero," Eleanor crooned.

I pulled out the knife and pushed the button. It snicked open with a lethal little click.

"What's that?" she said.

"The knife," I said. "I'm going to fool around a little."

"Don't cut yourself," she said automatically, and then she was laughing and I was laughing with her. Still laughing, I located the largest of the rollers with my fingers and slipped the knife into the crack between it and its neighbor. I worried it back and forth a little bit, feeling a reassuring give in the rollers. "God," I said, "this thing is ancient." I pushed the knife farther to the right.

The knife snapped.

"What was that?" she said.

I stood there, looking down through the darkness to the place where the broken knife blade would be. "Goddamn cheap fucking pimp," I said. "Stingy, skinny-nosed, cocaine-sniffing son of a bitch."

"What is it?" she said.

"What kind of asshole economizes on his knife? If you're dumb enough to carry one, you should be smart enough to carry a good one. Cheap piece of Taiwan shit."

"It broke," she said.

"Of course it broke. I should have known it would break. Gold wire wheels. Of course it broke."

"So what are we going to do?"

"We're going to wait for them to come for us," I said, sitting back down next to her. "Then we're going to rip them to pieces. What else can we do?"

"That was your plan?" she said. "The knife?"

"That was the beginning."

She leaned against me with a long sigh. "I wish I hadn't asked," she said.

About two hours later she said, "There must be a light."

I'd been dozing in a sort of fitful free-association, and when she spoke I started. "What?" I said.

"A light," she repeated. "People worked in here with the door closed to keep it cold. There was a handle on this side originally. Why wouldn't there be a light switch?"

"Why would there be a bulb?" I asked a little nastily. "So we can see our breath?"

"How do you know there isn't?"

"Because these people don't work that way. They want us to be in the dark. They didn't bother to give us blankets, did they?"

"Don't be insufferable. Have you got anything better to do with your time than look for the light switch?"

"No," I admitted.

"Well," she said, "if it's here, it must be near the door."

I let out an exasperated sigh, just to be doing something,

and got up. I found the door and ran my hands around its perimeter. Then I put my palms flat against the tile wall and slid them upward along the right side of the door. Then I tried the left. There it was.

"Well, what do you know?" I said, and flipped it up.

Dim, chalky light filled the room. Eleanor, looking beyond me, squinted once and then screamed.

I turned around and screamed myself.

Standing in the corner, looking me straight in the eye, big as life and twice as dead, was Ellis Fauntleroy. He had a sign hung around his neck.

The sign said SURPRISE.

29

"Relax," I said to Eleanor. "He's dead."

"That's very reassuring," she said, chewing on the side of her hand.

I went over to poor old Ellis. His shirt had turned a dreadful brown color and it was full of sharp creases where the blood had stiffened it. His jaw hung slackly, making me think of the scene in Dickens in which Marley's ghost unbinds the wrappings beneath his chin and his jaw drops to his chest. It had convinced Scrooge.

"Who is he?" she said.

"He was one of them," I said. "He was on Brooks's side. I guess it was the wrong side."

"How can he be standing?" She'd gotten the better of her fright, which put her half a move in front of me, and she was determined to be analytical.

"Good question," I said, making the supreme effort to put my hand on his shoulder. He turned quite easily. "Meat hook," I said. "They stuck it through his jacket." The entire wall was lined with meat hooks. Fauntleroy dangled there like a parody of the carcasses, the slit pigs and sides of beef, that had hung from them for the delectation of the gourmets upstairs in the dining room of the Borzoi.

I backed away and looked at my watch. After twelve. The Revealing was due to start in less than twenty minutes. And where, I wondered, was Dexter?

"This is a horrible place," Eleanor observed with an attempt at objectivity.

I looked at dead old Ambrose, or rather Ellis, and suddenly I remembered Nickodell's. "Holy shit," I said. "His fingernails."

"They don't keep growing," Eleanor said. "That's a myth."

"This was a man who was crazy for clean fingernails." I started to rifle his pockets.

"Yeah, and look where it got him."

"Swiss precision," I said. "It's got to be here. Why would you take a dead man's knife? Bingo." It hung, red and heavy and shiny, from my fingers. "Nine million blades," I said. "More blades than an army of ninjas. Even a screwdriver. It's got everything we need except a bazooka."

"Let's go, then. He gives me the creeps."

"He wasn't much better when he was alive," I said. "Let's give it ten minutes. You sit there and read your palms or something and I'll make sure I've got this door figured out."

"The hell with that," she said. "I'm going to do some breathing. We both need to be calm and centered." She closed her eyes, folded her hands in her lap, and breathed rhythmically.

"Anyone in the world, transported magically through time and space into the center of this refrigerator," I said, fooling with the cylinders, "would know immediately that he was in Los Angeles. I should be forcing this lock with a crystal. Then we could make a slow, slushy escape while New Age music shimmers on the soundtrack." Eleanor just breathed.

The screwdriver was the thing that did it. It was short, so there wasn't much leverage, but it was very thick. I knew in a minute and a half that I'd be able to force the lock. Leaving the screwdriver wedged in the cylinders, I sat down next to Eleanor and breathed for eight minutes.

I tapped her wrist. She was up and ready instantly, her eyes clear. Feeling intent and slightly light-headed, I went to the door and worked the knife back and forth.

"Turn off the light," I said. I was using both hands.

She reached past my shoulder and snapped it off, and I pushed the cylinder all the way to the right and put my shoulder to the door. It opened slowly, and the two of us stumbled out into the kitchen.

"Oh, my God," Eleanor said, paling. "What in the world could that be?"

"Hold your breath for a minute," I said. "It's called Eau de Fluffy, and it's on our side. That means Dexter's here." I pulled out the two handkerchiefs and poured the after-shave over them. I gave one to Eleanor, who promptly clamped it over her nose and mouth, and I breathed through the other. The smell of dead animal was so intense that it cut through the cheap scent. Dexter must have dumped half of the contents of the truck into the intake for the air conditioning.

We moved quickly across the kitchen and out into the corridor. I paused for a moment to check my orientation and then headed for the air-conditioning unit, my first landmark. Two or three people passed us, people who had been basemented apparently, but no one gave us a second glance; they had their own problems. Each of them had something wadded up and clutched over his face. We looked just like everybody else.

The big air-conditioning unit was pumping its evil-smelling lungs out. It was set at MEDIUM. I unscrewed the face plate of the control panel with the screwdriver on the Swiss Army knife and then turned the selector to HIGH. Then I slipped the flimsiest of the blades under the rotor switch and angled it so it touched all the contacts, forging a permanent connection between the selector and the HIGH contact. I snapped the blade off and left it there and then replaced the face plate. Short of crawling under it and disconnecting it, that thing was going to be murder to turn off.

"Someone's coming," Eleanor said.

Another person fled down the hallway, coming from the direction we'd come in, and made a beeline for the TV studio. I recognized Listener Simpson, she of the Nordic blue eyes, pinching her nose closed and walking very fast. I wondered whether she'd been basemented, and if not, what she was doing down there. I debated backtracking her to see what I'd missed, and then looked at my watch again.

It was time for the Revealing.

We navigated the corridors, me checking my mental map at every turn and Eleanor holding her handkerchief screwed up to her face. We moved deliberately; now was not the time to get lost. Another person blundered past us in high gear, fleeing the stench. He bumped heavily against Eleanor.

"The manners these people have," she mumbled into her handkerchief.

With the man in front of us, we could accelerate. He led us past my familiar little cul-de-sac and down the broad corridor toward the light. It opened onto a room that flickered under the bluish glow of fluorescent tubes. Four chairs were gathered around a desk. They were empty. Playing cards winked up from the surface of the desk. A cigarette burned in an ashtray next to a pair of spectacles.

"It's like after the neutron bomb," Eleanor said.

A door at the far end of the room opened onto a flight of steps that led upward to street level. A metal door at the top of the steps had a single small square window at face level. Above it, a red sign said ON THE AIR.

The smell was much less pronounced here. When we opened the door and stepped into the TV studio, the air was relatively fresh. Not for long, though. The banks of lights were burning, the air conditioner was pumping away, and the stench from the effluvia Dexter had dumped into the air conditioning vent was beginning to breeze through. Already people were casting sidelong glances at each other and wrinkling their noses, shrugging their shoulders. One man lifted his foot and checked the sole of his shoe.

A tiny knot of people had gathered at the opposite end of the stage from the set, the people who had bolted from the basement. They were having a heated discussion. Guys wearing headphones turned and shushed them. They subsided guiltily.

I didn't see Merryman, which made sense, or Brooks or Barry either. On the set, Mary Claire was standing at the podium talking and Angel was seated, petting her kitten and waiting for fate to whisper in her ear. There were the usual masses of flowers.

The auditorium was packed. Not a seat was empty. A camera had been set up in the middle of the audience area to catch every nuance of the ecstasy of the ardent. This was live, to almost half a million people, according to Skippy. If things worked out, they were going to get quite a show.

Eleanor and I leaned against a wall, more or less out of the light. Mary Claire rambled on, throwing an occasional look at Angel. The smell was growing more pronounced.

"What now?" Eleanor said. "We can't just stand here."

"For the moment we can. Everybody's busy."

On her chair, Angel let her head loll forward. Now even Mary Claire smelled it. Knowing the camera was on her daughter, she looked past the lights with a questioning expression. Angel was past smelling anything.

"You inhabit a burned-out building," she said, looking sightlessly forward. "You see out through scorched and rippled windows. You built the building, and you burned it. You built it day by day and room by room, and then you closed the doors to those rooms and built new ones. And behind you, the fire crept in and made everything black and twisted."

"Not a bad beginning," I said to Eleanor.

"I don't know what she's talking about," Eleanor said peevishly. "Where is everybody? Those creeps, I mean."

"Don't worry. They're going to come to us."

"Well, goody. And how are we going to make them do that?"

She put the handkerchief to her face and breathed. It was really beginning to stink. People in the audience were fanning their faces with their souvenir programs. Angel's and Mary Claire's faces, printed in four colors, flapped back and forth across the room.

"Just wait," I said.

A spasm struck Angel. She started to stand up. I held my breath. Then she slumped back into her chair and a broad smile crossed her face.

"Wo," Angel Ellspeth said, "don't we all be lookin' *fine* tonight?"

30

All over the studio, people stood like statues. The lighting man with the Hussong's T-shirt dropped his clipboard.

"I a new spirit," Angel said. "Name of Darnell." Mary Claire stared at her daughter, her jaw loose.

"Aton been given eternity off," Angel said happily. "He been jerkin' you people around pretty good. Wo, what a lotta catgut. Burn down the buildin' indeed. We say to him, Aton, for Chrissakes, cheer *up*. Spirit don't listen. He that kind of spirit. Been stubborn for a billion years."

A fat man in a San Diego State sweatshirt was frantically slicing his throat with his forefinger. No one looked at him. They were transfixed by Angel.

"Come on," I said to Eleanor, moving quickly away from the wall. I took the man by the sleeve of his shirt and tugged hard. He looked up at me unseeingly. I pinched the skin of his forearm, and he focused.

"Knock it off," I said. "You're a hired hand. Don't you know when your footage is going to make the NBC News?" He sawed reflexively at his throat a couple of times and then something clicked behind his eyes. He looked at me with fresh attention.

"You know what they'll pay for this?" I asked.

The man licked his lips.

"Keep the tape rolling," I said. I winked at him. He closed both eyes back at me. He was one of those guys who can't wink. "Practice," I said, opening my right eye horribly wide with my fingers and closing my left. "Works wonders in a singles bar." I tapped his shoulder for emphasis. "Keep the tape rolling," I told him again.

By now the reek in the studio had climbed to the treble clef. Some members of the audience had gotten up, frantically fanning their faces, and were heading for the exit. They were probably the same faint hearts who had left during the music. Even a few of the stagehands were deserting in the direction of the loading dock. One of the cameras was unmanned, peering dolefully at the floor. The people who remained in the audience seats, though, were watching Angel as if their lives, or the life of someone interesting, were flashing before their eyes.

So, I was sure, were the people at home. They couldn't smell it.

"Here they come," Eleanor said.

There was a sudden explosion of activity at one of the exits. A sort of roiling force propelled itself in ripples through the people streaming out through the door, and Brooks came in, shoving his way frantically through them and dragging Barry in his wake. Brooks had had a rebirth of energy; he threw people aside like a mother trying to get to a drowning child. Which, in a sense, he was. He pulled Barry behind him like a carry-on bag on wheels.

"We follow them," I said.

"I knew you were going to say that," Eleanor said.

Angel had begun to clap her hands. Dexter was improvising. "Every clap," Angel said, "gone open your eyes a little more." *Clap*. "No more bullshit about the past." There goes NBC News, I thought. *Clap*. "No more sendin' in money to these folks. They just spendin' it on dope and loose women." *Clap*. "No more watchin' TV. How come you not readin' somethin right now?" *Clap*.

Brooks and Barry had fought their way to the stage. The stairs were clogged with departing technicians, but Brooks vaulted to the stage like a fourteen-year-old gymnast and yanked Barry up after him. The two of them sprinted past a bewildered Mary Claire and right in front of the remaining functional camera, manned by a dutiful gent who was holding his nose. I looked up at a monitor and saw them speed across it.

"Great," I said, "they're on tape. Let's go."

Brooks was hammering on the door of the dressing room, which was locked. "Allow me," I said, tapping him on the shoulder. He nodded blindly, without even looking at me. I lifted a foot and kicked the door in. It jolted me all the way to my teeth.

Dexter looked up from his headset and gestured at all of us with the automatic in his right hand.

"Damn," he said. "I thought you'd never come. I runnin' out of bullshit." On the P.A. system, I heard Angel say in the same singsong voice, "I runnin' out of bullshit."

Barry took a quick step back. I put the tip of Fauntleroy's Swiss Army knife against his throat and said, "Please try to get away." He rolled his eyes at me and froze, as still as a Civil War photo.

Merryman was facedown on the floor, his hands tied behind his back with one of the handkerchiefs I'd given Dexter. With the door open, the stench was beginning to pour into the room. I pushed Barry forward, and Eleanor took Brooks's arm.

"I think you should go inside, Mr. Brooks," she said politely.

Brooks was in shock. "Thank you, my dear," he said in a courtly manner. "I believe I will." He looked older than J. Paul Getty.

All of us filed in. I closed the door against the smell. Dexter, the automatic trained squarely on Barry, said into the headset, "Th-th-that's all, folks," and took it off. Then he gave me the broadest smile I'd ever seen.

"That's all," Brooks repeated lifelessly.

"Any trouble getting in?" I asked Dexter.

"Trouble?" Dexter said. "I tell the man I come for the dead animal and he almost pick me up and carry me in." He beamed.

"Five million dollars," Merryman said from the floor.

Dexter gave me a quick glance. "Say what?" he said.

"Five million. Cash. Today," Merryman said. He gave up looking at me and looked at Dexter. "Seven million. In an hour, if necessary."

"Dick," I said, "your little girl just did a spiritual minstrel show. It's going to be on TV for some time to come."

"I can fix it." Merryman stopped craning his neck and rolled onto his back. "I'll think of something."

"Man don't let go," Dexter said admiringly.

"We can do business," Merryman said. "Seven million dollars."

"Must be makin' a pile of money."

"Oh, he likes the money, all right," I said, "but what he loves is the little girls."

Dexter stared at Merryman and made his eyes glimmer. Merryman, after a moment, looked away. "I ain't forgettin' that," Dexter said softly. "You gone be a big hit in the joint," he said to Merryman. "All them teeth. Man, they gone to be linin' up for you. You a two-cartons-of-Marlboro man any day. In about two weeks, you gone to have a rear end you can slip your head into. Probably you be pretty flexible by then, too."

He got up and crossed the room to Merryman, towering over him. "So I gone do you a favor," he said, "slow them boys down a week or two. Give you a little time to get acclimated. You'll thank me later." Then he lifted his foot and put his shoe on Merryman's face. It was a very big shoe, black and highly polished. He ground it around for a while over Merryman's mouth and nose as though he were putting out a cigarette.

"What about Angel?" Eleanor said, watching with a kind of clinical interest.

"Thank you, Eleanor," I said. "Go out and get her and Mary Claire, would you? Mary Claire may take a little persuasion."

She left the room and I turned to Dexter. "May I borrow one of your guns?" I said.

"Wif pleasure." He reversed it and handed it to me with a flourish, butt-first. "You," I said to Barry. "Down on your knees."

He looked from me to Dexter. Merryman was trying very quietly to spit out the taste of Dexter's shoe. His nose was bleeding nicely. Brooks was staring at a wall, looking like a man trying to do long division in his head. Barry went down on one knee and gave me a great sacrificial gaze.

"You're doing great," I said. "Keep going." He closed his eyes and knelt.

"Now turn around. Face the wall." I held out a hand to Dexter, and Dexter materialized his other pistol from the waistband of his uniform trousers. He handed it to me.

I pressed the barrel of the automatic against the base of Barry's well-barbered skull. An involuntary muscular ripple ran down his back. "You enjoyed yourself with Sally Oldfield," I said, "and with Eleanor. You enjoyed yourself so much with Sally that you left a little souvenir on her face, didn't you? After you pulled out her fingernails. If you hadn't done that, Barry," I said, "if you hadn't masturbated on her, I think I probably would have given you to the police. As it is, I won't."

"No," he said. "Please. You can't."

"I sure can," I said. Dexter was watching me with one eyebrow elevated. I even had Merryman's attention.

"Good-bye, Barry," I said. I pushed the gun against his head sharply and pulled the trigger of the other one.

Barry swayed once and collapsed. He lay on the floor like something swatted.

Eleanor came in with Angel. She was carrying Angel's kitten. She looked from Barry to me with wide eyes. I held up the other gun, the one I'd fired into the floor.

"He fainted," I said. "Let's call Hammond."

Hammond brought five men with him, one of them the redoubtable Um Hinckley. They stood there clutching handkerchiefs to their faces and looking bewildered at the two men on the floor, the vacant lawyer, and the little girl.

"Welcome," I said, "to the Burned-Over District."

Hammond ranted at me while I told him what had happened. He ranted at me while his men put cuffs on Merryman, Brooks, and Barry and hauled them out to patrol cars. He continued to rant while his men brought in Mary Claire, who'd been hiding behind the podium. He stopped ranting when I took him down into the basement and showed him Ellis Fauntleroy hanging from his meat hook with his sign around his neck. When he saw Fauntleroy, he had a photographer start taking pictures.

"The Santa Monica TraveLodge," I said. "Room three-eleven."

"Tell me the whole thing again," he growled. "I wasn't listening."

I told it again while I led him on a tour of the basement. "Macaroons," he said, "this'll make the news. Hell, it'll make *Time*."

"You're out of Records," I said. "It's all yours."

"You mean that?" he said suspiciously.

"You figure out how to keep me to a minimum," I said. "This is the work of Alvin Hammond, grade-A cop."

In a drawer in Merryman's office we found stacks of small bills, almost thirty thousand dollars' worth. I flipped through it, counting, while Hammond watched.

"Mad money?" Hammond asked.

"He was pretty mad," I said. "But we didn't find this," I added, pocketing it. Hammond looked at me, the picture of innocence.

"Find what?" he said.

The only time he went stubborn was when we had to decide what to do with Angel. Merryman had brought her out of her trance as we all watched, and she had watched the proceedings in silence ever since, shrugging off Eleanor's attempts to comfort her.

"She goes to the Hall," Hammond said doggedly. "Her mother's in the can."

"Her father isn't," I said. "She hasn't done anything wrong." We were back in the dressing room.

"She's a material witness."

"She's a little girl."

"They got a place for little girls at the Hall." Hammond's mouth was as straight and implacable as the center line in a game of tug-of-war. Angel looked up at us indifferently. She might have been sleepwalking.

"Al," I said curtly, "she's going home."

"Little girl belongs at home," Dexter said. It was the first time he'd spoken since the police arrived.

"Thank you for your opinion," Hammond said with the charm he reserves for black people.

"Tell your cops to go outside," I said to Hammond.

He gave me a hard, stubborn stare, then motioned them out of the room. I took the money from Merryman's desk out of my pocket and gave roughly half of it to Dexter. Hammond scratched the back of his neck in disbelief.

"Without this man," I said to Hammond, "you'd still be watching Um Hinckley pick his nose."

"How you doin'," Dexter said to Hammond with the aloofness of a subatomic particle that can pass through a cubic foot of solid lead without hitting anything. He put the money into his pocket.

"This is the Spirit Darnell," I said to Hammond. "Also known as Dexter Smith."

"Smif," Dexter said.

"Smif," I amended. "He has the makings of a first-rate cop."

"No, thanks," Dexter said, buttoning his pocket. "I don't shine no more to cops than I do to riptahls."

Hammond turned dark red.

"You're going to want Dexter to keep his mouth shut," I said. Dexter zipped his lips closed. "And neither Dexter nor I will keep our mouths shut if you don't let Angel go home to Daddy."

Hammond wavered.

"I don't want Daddy," Angel said in her New York cabdriver's accent. "I want Dick."

"You shut up," I said to her.

Angel, Eleanor, and I were driving toward Venice. A police medic had bandaged our fingers and let us go. It was nine o'clock, and the rain was back with us. A patrol car, Hammond's compromise, was following at a demure distance.

"There has to be a cop," Hammond had said. "There has to be a report, Simeon. No discussion." I'd let him win the point.

Eleanor had maintained a remote silence all the way. It was as though the interlude in the refrigerator had never happened. I reached over and took her bandaged hand. She withdrew it.

"I have to think," she said. I put my hand back on the wheel. The kitten on her lap mewed twice.

"This is your kitty-cat, Angel," Eleanor said to the little girl huddled in the back seat.

"Toldya I didn't want him," Angel said spitefully. "He's got fleas. He was *her* idea." Angel, like Jessica, referred to her mother as "her." Another of Merryman's legacies.

"Just leave him in the car," I said as I pulled to the curb in front of Caleb Ellspeth's house.

"You don't like cats," Eleanor protested.

"I love cats," I said, thinking about the way she'd pulled her hand away. "I live for cats. I'm leaving all my money to a home for stray cats."

"All your money," Eleanor said pointedly. She'd seen me give a wad of it to Dexter.

"You've got your story," I said. "Come on, Angel, we're home."

"Home?" Angel said, looking at the house. "This junk heap?"

"Home is where the heart is," I said, yanking her hand a little harder than I had to. She followed me sullenly up the walkway, with Eleanor one step back and two bewildered cops trailing behind us.

The porch light was on. When the door opened Ellspeth looked at me glacially and then stared at the cops. "Look down," I said.

He did, and saw Angel.

"Hello, darling," he said. Angel said nothing. She was staring at her feet as though the answer to a riddle were written on her Alice in Wonderland shoes.

Ellspeth darted a questioning glance at me.

"All over," I said.

He dropped to his knees in front of Angel. She looked past him. He took her hand between both of his and said, "Angel." One of the cops behind me shuffled his feet.

Eleanor put a slender hand between Angel's shoulder blades and patted her.

Angel drew a deep breath. Without looking at her father she said, "Is Ansel here?"

31

I t was after ten by the time I got to Mrs. Yount's.

With the kitten purring comfortably into my jacket, I trudged through the mud and climbed to the top of the wall that surrounded her awful little garden. I'd dropped Eleanor at home in a kind of monolithic silence.

All the lights inside were turned off, but the television screen was glowing. Mrs. Yount sat silhouetted on the floor on her old fur coat, her back to me, eating something out of a tall box. Crackers, maybe. She was looking at a woman named Linda Evans who was coming down an impossibly long stairway wearing a new fur coat.

"You're home, baby," I whispered to the kitten. The kitten didn't say anything. I gathered my muscles and jumped.

I'd forgotten about the Great Wall of Bottles. I landed on top of it with a deafening, shattering tumult of breaking glass. I scrabbled to keep my balance as bottles rolled back and forth under my feet, and then I fell decisively on my backside. Broken glass bit my rear end through my trousers. To add insult to injury, the kitten began to claw at my stomach.

Inside, Mrs. Yount leapt up from the old fur coat and streaked toward the front of the apartment. She was screaming in some Balkan language. She pulled open a closet door and turned around, holding what looked in the half-light very much like a forty-five.

I cleared the wall in a single bound with the kitten still scrabbling at my viscera with its claws, and landed on my hands and knees in the mud. Behind me, there was a boom, and the sliding glass door was annihilated in a silvery cascade of glass.

Something right in front of my nose turned its body into a startled arc and spit at me. It was Fluffy, pink collar and all.

Fluffy hurtled off toward the front of the building and I heard the glass door sliding unnecessarily open. There couldn't have been much glass left. Mrs. Yount fired at the stars while I sprinted for the gray Camaro, bent over and keeping close to the ground.

I tossed the kitten roughly onto the front seat and then slid behind the wheel and tried to catch my breath. The kitten sat down calmly, licked one of its forepaws, and began to clean its face. I started to laugh. Mrs. Yount had always said she'd know in her bosom if Fluffy were dead. Two more shots boomed heavenward.

When I'd finished laughing, I drove home with my cat.

Timothy Hallinan's second Simeon Grist Suspense Novel is *Everything But the Squeal*, which was published as an NAL Books hardcover in April, 1990. Below is the first chapter of this exciting new novel from the author whom *The Washington Post Book World* praised for his "genuine ability to write effective prose, engaging repartee, sharp and witty characterization . . . verve, guts, inventiveness and sense of humor."

"Hey! No, no, no, no, no. How many times I gotta tell you, huh? You gitouta here. Git*ou*ta here." The Mountain's wooden *geta* sandals clattered over the concrete as he grabbed the Guitar Player by the frayed strap of the unstrung, bogus Stratocaster guitar he toted up and down Santa Monica Boulevard day and night. The Guitar Player's eyes, which had been closed in temporary bliss, opened as wide as they could, which is to say halfway, as the Mountain—three hundred quivering pounds of food-stained plaid shirt, scrubby beard, and yellow fangs—yanked him to his feet and launched him toward the sidewalk. The neck of the guitar knocked to the floor the dingy plastic tray containing the Guitar Player's cardinal sin: a package of store-bought sliced ham that he'd been surreptitiously dipping into somebody else's side order of the special teriyaki sauce, the one that Tommy, the Mountain's Okinawan boss, used only for teriyaki tacos.

There was no house rule against leaving leftovers for others—not much ever made it back into the kitchen—but bringing in food from outside was tantamount to *kamikaze*.

The eighty-six, which was part of the nightly floor show at the Oki-Burger, caught people's attention as though it were something new. At the other end of the Guitar Player's picnic-type table, the Toothless Man—two missing in front, top and bottom, nodded his head. "Maximum force," he aspirated approvingly to the Young Old

Woman, fourteen years old from behind and fifty from in front. The Young Old Woman, the only one who could understand him most of the time, cackled. She translated his conversation for the others and made his alibis to the cops. His speaking-tongue dog was what the others called her. When she wasn't being his speaking-tongue dog she worked the darker doorways with her back to the street, giving unpleasant surprises to fools on the prowl for pubescence.

One of the *genuine* teenage girls, seated at a table strategically near the sidewalk where a glimpse of her might make a straight hit the brakes, paused in a heroin nod-out long enough to giggle as the Mountain dispassionately lobbed the Guitar Player across the sidewalk and onto the back of a concrete bus bench. At the last possible instant, as he did almost every night, the Guitar Player managed to twist his body so that his ribs, rather than the imitation Stratocaster, cracked against the edge of the bench. "Wuff," he said. He straightened up, wrapped himself in a tenuous shred of affronted dignity, and set off down the street toward the sheltering hedges of Plummer Park. The kids did a lot of business in Plummer Park.

The nodding girl continued to exceed the limits of her body's chemical tolerance long enough to giggle again and say something to an equally loaded friend through what sounded like a mouthful of highly glutinous mush. Me, I just took a sip on my very old Diet Coke and a sniff at my even older purple T-shirt and wondered how long it would be before everybody stopped thinking I was a cop.

It was three A.M. at Tommy's Oki-Burger, and all was as well as it was going to get. A little earlier the clatter of silverware two bright orange tables away had announced the fact that a skin-head in black leather had hit the bottom of the curve on downers. He'd bounced twice on the cement floor, and the Mountain had hauled him into the men's room to be treated to a refreshing dip in the toilet. A girl had broken out in bugs that no one else could see, and the Mountain had sprayed her with an imaginary can of Raid to calm her down. It worked. The LAPD cruised slowly by every fifteen minutes or so, one of them checking out the girls and trying to keep his tongue from hanging out the window while the other one drove. They switched seats and tongues on alternate passes.

"To protect and to serve," the Mountain read off the side of the squad car, mopping down the table with a malodorous rag that might have been a recycled mummy wrapping. "Who they protecting, you think?"

"Each other," I said. To my great relief, my Diet Coke had finally dried up. I pushed the empty cup away as though it had contained uranium.

"And who they serving?" The Mountain picked up the empty cup and rattled it and then snapped the rag at a fly guilty of being out after curfew. A vaguely cheesy and thoroughly unwholesome smell spread its leprous wings beneath my nose.

"They're not serving Diet Coke," I said, fanning the vapor away. "And you're not either, not if you've got any pity in your soul. God, there must be something else to drink in this dump."

The Mountain lowered his voice. "Don't spread it around," he said, narrowing his eyes conspiratorially, "but I could offer you Diet Pepsi. And anyway, what do plainclothes cops care?"

On the whole, I liked the Mountain. He eighty-sixed people with style and he rarely held a grudge. I'd been hanging around the Oki-Burger four days and I'd told him at least twelve times that I wasn't a cop. I told him again now, scratching at my chin. My carefully cultivated four-day beard itched.

The Mountain gave me a knowing look and wiped his face with the damp mummy-wrap, making my skin crawl. "Nobody as grungy as you isn't a cop," he said. "Whyn't you go to Jack's? They're not as sharp there. You might pass for a human."

I knew good advice when I heard it. I hauled my backside off the hardest wooden bench this side of bankruptcy court and headed for Jack's.

Jack's Triple-Burgers is on Hollywood, near La Brea, and Tommy's Oki-Burger is on Fountain, near Fairfax. It's easy to map the physical geography—they're about a mile and a half apart, and Jack's is farther north and east than Tommy's—but the emotional geography is more subtle. It had taken me a couple of days to figure out that Tommy's got the new runaways and Jack's got the Old Hands. The drugs of choice in Tommy's are downers, mainly codeine and other painkillers, but at Jack's nobody screws around with anything you don't enjoy at the sharp point of a needle. The occasional exceptions in both places are freebasers, folks whose idea of a day at the beach is a waterpipe filled with a brain-jolting mixture of cocaine and ether and, occasionally, PCP. The freebasers are rare in both establishments, though. Cocaine makes you alert and jumpy. By and large, both Tommy's and Jack's cater to a crowd that puts a high value on anesthesia.

The other difference is that the boys and girls at Tommy's sometimes say no to a straight. He has to be pretty repulsive and not very prosperous-looking, and he's probably asking for something that would stun the Marquis de Sade, but the kids will say no. The boys and girls at Jack's don't. At Jack's, "Just say no" is a punch line.

To get to Jack's, I took the streets no one knows are there. Between Santa Monica and Hollywood boulevards there runs a network of narrow, pinched little avenues, paved when cars were smaller, and lined on either side by small houses, mostly stucco, built in the thirties. They were dark now, most of them, tucked away behind weedy lawns, climbing roses, and chained dogs. Here and there light spilled through a window, and at one point I heard the sad strains of Brahms' Double Concerto. There were few families. Most of the children in these neighborhoods come and go with the night, passing back and forth between the boulevards where the money is, looking at the houses from the wrong side of the chain-link fences.

I'd parked Sweet Alice, my car, on Cherokee, about halfway between Tommy's and Jack's. I won her in a game of chance that had begun in Malibu, not far from

where I live, and ended in Pacoima. Her flamboyantly
mustachioed owner, one Jaime, had painted her an indel-
ible shade of iridescent horsefly blue, lowered her so far
in front that she would have bounced going over a pack
of Luckies, and hung a surrealistically large pair of furry
dice from her rearview mirror. I'd removed the dice by
way of expressing my individuality. Other than that I'd
kept her, as they say in the used-car trade, as is. I patted
her on the fender as I passed her and headed on up to
Jack's. The sodium lights of Hollywood Boulevard gleamed
luridly against the low-hanging April clouds. Jack's and
the Boulevard were up the street, and Easter was around
the corner.

Jack's squats on what L.A. realtors call a corner lot.
Hollywood Boulevard runs vaguely east-west, and Gardner, the north-south street, culminates to the north in
what the same L.A. realtors call a cul-de-sac. In English,
that's a dead end. Normally, a cul-de-sac is regarded as
an especially safe configuration by couples with young
children. There weren't many couples on that little stretch
of Gardner, but for the children who patronized the
place, it was a terrific place to shoot up.

A heaviness in the air told me that it was about to
drizzle. The week's weather had been all over the map.
Normally in L.A., the weather is as orderly, and about as
interesting, as a family tree: warm blue day breeds warm
blue day. But this April, counting down toward Easter,
was made up of days that arrived like runaways from
other climates. The week had begun as clear and cold as
North Dakota and then turned warm as a mass of tropical air wheeled up from Baja. Wednesday was marked by
a chilly rain that had obviously made a wrong turn on its
way to San Francisco and then decided it liked L.A. long
enough to hang around through Thursday.

The drizzle started as I hit the Boulevard. At this hour,
probably eighty percent of the people in Hollywood were
holding, loaded, on illegal errands, or all three. There
was the usual complement of parked bikers sneering on
their black-and-chrome hogs, surrounded by the usual
flock of biker girls. They were there day and night.

"So?" said Muhammad, the counterman. Unlike Tommy's, where there is a Tommy, there's no Jack at Jack's. The place was bought by Koreans several years ago, and the help is all either Hispanic or generically Middle Eastern. Muhammad was a generic Iranian.

"Coffee," I said, sitting down. My back hurt. I was getting old for this stuff.

"How many sugars?" Muhammad said. Junkies eat a lot of sugar.

"Four," I said, trying to turn my wince into a smile.

"You want fudge, say so," Muhammad said. It was his standard rejoinder. I was too frayed for standard rejoinders, so I leaned across the counter and took his skinny black tie in my hand as he turned away. He jerked his head back to me, looking alarmed.

"If I want fudge," I said, "I'll mug the Good Humor man. Give me a coffee with four sugars, and clamp the stirrer between your teeth until I leave."

"Jesus," Muhammad said, tugging at his tie, "what's with you tonight?"

"Lip," I said, giving the tie a little yank. "There's too much lip on Hollywood Boulevard."

"So call the Lip Squad," he said. He wrapped the tie around his fist and pulled it free. Against my will, I laughed, and he gave me a bleak smile. "I'm tired too," he said. "If I rub my face one more time tonight I think I'll hit bone."

"Sorry," I said. "Make it a large coffee. And hold the sugar."

The smile went wise. "Knew you were a cop," he said.

I gave up and drank it. Five years ago, no one would have taken me for a cop. I was obviously getting older. Behind me a fifteen-year-old girl fought fuzzily with her pimp. "I left them in the jar by the bed," she said. "You didn't have to take them all."

"Girl," the pimp said, "there wasn't enough for both of us. You should be happy they made *me* happy."

"You're a pig," she said.

I heard a gagging, snuffling noise and turned to see the pimp push the girl's dish of soft ice cream into her face.

He clamped the back of her head with one hand and held the dish over her nose and mouth with the other while she choked and kicked her feet under the table. "You want a extra mouth," he said, "open the one you already got one more time." He sat back and regarded her. Ice cream ran down her chin and neck, onto the lavender cloth of her cheap blouse. She began to cry.

I leaned forward onto the counter, rested my head on my arms, and listened to my heart beat in my ears. It almost drowned out the sound of the girl's sobbing. Once I might have wrapped the pimp's chair around his neck. That was a long time ago, four full days. After four days spending time with kids who had an average life expectancy of only three more years, all I wanted to do was drink my coffee and go home.

The girl kept on crying while the pimp finished her ice cream. I rubbed my chin-bristle and felt sorry for myself. Four numbing days and nights, and not a glimpse or a whisper of Aimee Sorrell.

MYSTERY PARLOR

☐ **THE CAT'S MEOW by Robert Campbell.** Someone has killed poor old Father Mulrooney of St. Pat's Church and Democratic Precinct Captain Jimmy Flannery suspects the motive lies at the bottom of land deals, buried secrets, and sudden death. "A captivating read."—*Kirkus Reviews* (164318—$4.50)

☐ **THE FOUR LAST THINGS—A Simeon Grist suspense novel by Timothy Hallinan.** Shadowing a young Los Angeles woman suspected of embezzlement, Simeon Grist finds her suddenly dead and himself smack inthe center of a million-dollar religious scam. Now he's next on the hist list. "Imaginative ... brilliant.... A great new detective series!"—*Pasadena Star-News*
(166000—$4.95)

☐ **THE 600 POUND GORILLA by Robert Campbell.** When the boiler in the local zoo goes kaput, Chicago's favorite gorilla, Baby, gets transferred to a local hot spot. But things heat up when two customers are found beaten to death and everyone thinks Baby went bananas. But precinct captain Jimmy Flannery is about to risk his life to prove it's murder ...   (153901—$3.50)

☐ **FADEAWAY by Richard Rosen.** From the Edgar Award-winning author of *Strike Three You're Dead.* A few months ago Harvey Blissberg was a major league outfielder. Now he's a private investigator trying to find out if there's life after baseball. There is. It's called basketball. "Blends sports and crime in a novel full of snap, crackle, and grace."—Robert Parker, author of "Spenser" novels.   (401484—$3.95)

Buy them at your local

bookstore or use coupon

on next page for ordering.

Ⓞ SIGNET (0451)

MORE DEADLY DEALINGS

☐ **TRIGGER MAN by Arthur Rosenfeld.** He's the best in his business—and his business is death ... until he awakens one morning to discover his identity stripped away. Still, he's been offered a job too tempting to turn down. It's easy. He knows the man he is supposed to kill. His target is himself. Now he must learn a few more things: Who he *really* is? Who wants him dead? And how he can stop a killer on a desperate trail—where hunter becomes the hunted at every turn ... ? (160460—$3.95)

☐ **WHEN THE BOUGH BREAKS by Jonathan Kellerman.** Obsessed with a case that endangers both his career and his life, child psychologist Alex Delaware must plumb the depths of a seven-year-old girl's mind to find the secret that will shatter a grisly web of evil that stretches from the barrio of L.A. to an elite island community... coming closer and closer to a forty-year-old secret that makes even murder look clean....

(158741—$4.95)

☐ **OVER THE EDGE by Jonathan Kellerman.** The death of a former patient leads Alex Delaware through a labyrinth of sick sex and savage greed, penetrating to the inner sanctums of the rich and powerful and the lowest depths of the down and out. Alex's discovery of the secret life of one of California's leading families sets off an explosion of shattering revelations. "Mesmerizing!"—*Booklist.* (152190—$4.95)

☐ **THE DRUG WARRIORS: NARCS II by Robert Coram.** Their battlefield is wherever drugs are smuggled and sold. And now their enemy is the biggest importer in the business, the Doctor, who covers America with a blizzard of snow. "Coram is to the drug war what Tom Clancy is to submarine war."—Stuart Woods (160568—$4.50)

Prices slightly higher in Canada
